# THE SPACE SAMARITAN

Cindy and Mindy both appeared on my comm screen, wearing less than Samoan nudists at the springtime fertility rites. If my eyeballs hadn't weighed a little more than three times normal they would've popped right out of their sockets.

"We truly appreciate what you're doing for us, Sam," they said in unison, as if they'd rehearsed it. "And we want you to know that we'll be *especially* appreciative when you come back to us."

"Extremely appreciative," breathed Cindy. Mindy?"

"Extraordinarily appreciative," the other one added, batting her long lashes at me.

I was ready to jump off my couch and fly to them like Superman. Except that the damned g load kept me pinned flat.

All of me.

# BEN BOVA

# SAM GUNN FOREVER

AVON · EOS

"Acts of God" © 1995 by Sovereign Media. First published in the May 1995 *Science Fiction Age*.

"Sam's War" © 1994 by Bantam, Doubleday, Dell Magazines. First published in the July 1994 *Analog*.

"Nursery Sam" © 1995 by Bantam, Doubleday, Dell Magazines. First published in the January 1996 *Analog*.

"Tourist Sam" © 1997 by Ben Bova.

"Sam and the Prudent Jurist" © 1997 by Sovereign Media. First published in the January 1997 *Science Fiction Age*.


AVON BOOKS, INC.
1350 Avenue of the Americas
New York, New York 10019

Copyright © 1998 by Ben Bova
Published by arrangement with the author
Inside back cover author photograph by Eric Strachan
Visit our website at **www.AvonBooks.com/Eos**
Library of Congress Catalog Card Number: 98-92628
ISBN: 0-380-79726-7

First Avon Eos Printing: December 1998

AVON EOS TRADEMARK REG. U.S. PAT. OFF. AND IN OTHER COUNTRIES, MARCA REGISTRADA, HECHO EN U.S.A.

Printed in the U.S.A.

WCD  10  9  8  7  6  5  4  3  2  1

*To Janet and Chris, with boundless thanks for a
wonderful visit to Oz, from both of us.*

# Contents

**INTRODUCTION: ABOARD TORCH SHIP *HERMES***

NOW THAT SAM GUNN IS APPARENTLY ON HIS WAY BACK TO the solar system after having allegedly fallen into a black hole somewhere beyond the orbit of Pluto, I have been asked to produce a coherent record of his past activities.

This is far from an easy task, inasmuch as Sam Gunn's past activities have been extremely diverse, and the man himself—for all his self-promotion and heavy media publicity—has actually been quite secretive about his operations, his plans, and especially his past life.

Therefore, I have had to trek across the length and breadth of the solar system, from Mercury to this nuclear torch ship accelerating out beyond Pluto's orbit, to track down the people who could give me firsthand accounts of Sam Gunn's past life.

As you will see from the following interviews, his checkered career is filled with contradictions. It seems highly unlikely that any one man could have done all the things that have been attributed to the aforesaid Mr. Sam Gunn.

Yet the interviewees all swear they have told me the truth, as they themselves experienced it.

## Statement of the Rt. Hon. Jill Mcd. Meyers (Recorded aboard torch ship *Hermes*)

As the one and only woman who ever married Sam Gunn, I certainly can tell you more about him than just about anybody. After all, I knew Sam back in the days when we were both astronauts working for the old NASA.

His age? Well, Sam must be just about my own age. Never mind what that is. Suffice it to say we've both been around a long time. And neither of us is anywhere near finished yet. I never did believe that he died out at that mini–black hole beyond Pluto's orbit. Not Sam.

That's why I'm riding out there. We're still legally married, even though I haven't seen the little sonofagun in almost twenty years.

What're you doing with your keyboard? Trying to calculate his age? Or my age? If you want me to tell you about Sam, you'd better pay attention and stop the figuring. All right, Sam must be nearly a hundred, maybe more. It's hard to tell. He acts like he's twelve or thirteen, most of the time. I'm younger, of course.

Yes, he's a womanizer. And yes, he's made and lost more fortunes than I've got freckles on my nose. So what? He's Sam Gunn, the one and only.

Let me tell you about the time he tried to sue the Vatican . . .

And stop trying to calculate my age!

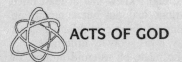 **ACTS OF GOD**

WHO ELSE BUT SAM GUNN WOULD SUE THE POPE?

I'd known Sam since we were both astronauts with
NASA, riding the old shuttle to the original Mac Dac
Shack—but sue the *Pope?* That's Sam.

At first I thought it was a joke, or at least a grandstand
stunt. Then I began to figure that it was just the latest of
Sam's ploys to avoid marrying me. I'd been chasing him
for years, subtly at first, but once I'd retired from the
Senate, quite openly.

It got to be a game that we both enjoyed. At least, I
did. It was fun to see the panicky look on Sam's Huck
Finn face when I would bring up the subject of marriage.

"Aw, come on, Jill," he would say. "I'd make a lousy
husband. I like women too much to marry one of 'em."

I would smile my most sphinxlike smile and softly reply, "You're not getting any younger, Sam. You need a
good woman to look after you."

And he'd arrange to disappear. I swear, his first ex-
pedition out to the asteroid belt was as much to get away
from me as to find asteroids for mining. He came close
to getting himself killed then, but he created the new
industry of asteroid mining—and just about wiped out
the metals and minerals markets in most of the resource-
exporting nations on Earth. That didn't win him any
friends, especially among the governments of those

nations and the multinational corporations that fed off
them.

I still had connections into the Senate Intelligence
Committee in those days, and I knew that at least three
southern hemisphere nations had put out contracts on
Sam's life. To say nothing of the big multinationals. It
was my warnings that saved his scrawny little neck.

Sam lost the fortune he made on asteroid mining, of
course. He'd made and lost fortunes before that, it was
nothing new to him. He just went into other business
lines; you couldn't keep him down for long.

He was running a space freight operation when he sued
the Pope. And the little sonofagun *knew* that I'd be on
the International Court of Justice panel that heard his suit.

"Senator Meyers, may I have a word with you?" My
Swedish secretary looked very upset. He was always very
formal, always addressed me by my old honorific, the
way a governor of a state would be called "Governor"
even if he's long retired or in jail or whatever.

"What's the matter, Hendrick?" I asked him.

Hendrick was in his office in The Hague, where the
World Court is headquartered. I was alone in my house
in Nashua, sipping at a cup of hot chocolate and watching
the winter's first snow sifting through the big old maples
on my front lawn, thinking that we were going to have a
white Christmas despite the greenhouse warming. Until
Hendrick's call came through, that is. Then I had to look
at his distressed face on my wall display screen.

"We have a very unusual . . . situation here," said
Hendrick, struggling to keep himself calm. "The chief
magistrate has asked me to call you."

From the look on Hendrick's face, I thought somebody
must be threatening to unleash nuclear war, at least.

"A certain . . . person," Hendrick said, with conspic-
uous distaste, "has entered a suit against the Vatican."

"The Vatican!" I nearly dropped my hot chocolate.
"What's the basis of the suit? Who's entering it?"

"The basis is apparently over some insurance claims.
The litigant is an American citizen acting on behalf of
the nation of Ecuador. His name is"—Hendrick looked

down to read from a document that I could not see on the screen—"Samuel S. Gunn, Esquire."

"Sam Gunn?" I did drop the cup; hot chocolate all over my white corduroy slacks and the hooked rug my great-grandmother had made with her very own arthritic fingers.

Sam was operating out of Ecuador in those days. Had himself a handsome suite of offices in the presidential palace, no less. I drove through the slippery snow to Boston and took the first Clipper out; had to use my ex-Senatorial *and* World Court leverage to get a seat amidst all the jovial holiday travelers.

I arrived in Quito half an hour later. Getting through customs with my one hastily packed travel bag took longer than the flight. At least Boston and Quito are in the same time zone; I didn't have to battle jet lag.

"Jill!" Sam smiled when I swept into his office, but the smile looked artificial to me. "What brings you down here?"

People say Sam and I look enough alike to be siblings. Neither Sam nor I believe it. He's short, getting pudgy, keeps his rusty red hair cropped short. Shifty eyes, if you ask me. Mine are a steady brown. I'm just about his height, and the shape of my face is sort of round, more or less like his. We both have a sprinkle of freckles across our noses. But there all resemblance—physical and otherwise—definitely ends.

"You know damned well what brings me down here," I snapped, tossing my travel bag on one chair and plopping myself in the other, right in front of his desk.

Sam had gotten to his feet and started around the desk, but one look at the blood in my eye and he retreated back to his own swivel chair. He had built a kind of platform behind the desk to make himself seem taller than he really was.

He put on his innocent little boy face. "Honest, Jill, I haven't the foggiest idea of why you're here. Christmas vacation?"

"Don't be absurd."

"You didn't bring a justice of the peace with you, did you?"

I had to laugh. Every time I asked myself why in the ever-loving blue-eyed world I wanted to marry Sam Gunn, the answer always came down to that. Sam made me laugh. After a life of grueling work as an astronaut and then the tensions and power trips of Washington politics, Sam was the one man in the world who could make me see the funny side of everything. Even when he was driving me to distraction, we both had grins on our faces.

"I should have brought a shotgun," I said, trying to get serious.

"You wouldn't do that," he said, with that impish grin of his. Then he added a worried, "Would you?"

"Where did you get the bright idea of suing the Vatican?"

"Oh, that!" Sam visibly relaxed, eased back in his chair and swiveled around from side to side a little.

"Yes, that," I snapped. "What kind of a brain-dead nincompoop idea is that?"

"Nincompoop?" He looked almost insulted. "Been a long time since I heard that one."

"What's going on, Sam? You know a private citizen can't sue a sovereign state."

"Sure I know that. *I'm* not suing the Vatican. The sovereign nation of Ecuador is suing. I'm merely acting as their representative, in my position as CEO of Ecuador National Space Systems."

I sank back in my chair, thinking fast. "The Vatican isn't a party to the International Court of Justice's protocols. Your suit is null and void, no matter who the plaintiff may be."

"Christ, Jill, you sound like a lawyer."

"You can't sue the Vatican."

Sam sighed and reached out one hand toward the keyboard on his desk. He tapped at it with one finger, then pointed to the display screen on the wall.

The screen filled with print, all legalese of the densest kind. But I recognized it. The Treaty of Katmandu, the one that ended the three-way biowar between India,

China, and Pakistan. The treaty that established the International Peacekeeping Force and gave it global mandatory powers.

" 'All nations are required to submit grievances to the International Court of Justice,' " Sam quoted from the treaty, " 'whether they are signatories to this instrument or not.' "

I knew it as well as he did. "That clause is in there to prevent nations from using military force," I said.

Sam gave a careless shrug. "Regardless of why it's in there, it's there. The World Court has jurisdiction over every nation in the world. Even the Vatican."

"The Vatican didn't sign the treaty."

"Doesn't matter. The treaty went into effect when two-thirds of the membership of the UN signed it," Sam said. "And any nation that doesn't obey it gets the Peacekeepers in their face."

"Sam, you *can't* sue the Pope!"

He just gave me his salesman's grin. "The nation of Ecuador has filed suit against the Vatican State. The World Court has to hear the case. It's not just my idea, Jill—it's the law."

The little sonofabitch was right.

I expected Sam would invite me to dinner. He did, and then some. Sam wouldn't hear of my staying at a hotel; he had already arranged for a guest suite for me in the presidential palace. Which gave the lie to his supposed surprise when I had arrived at his office, of course. He knew I was coming. It sort of surprised me, though. I wouldn't have thought that he'd want me so close to him. He had always managed to slip away when I'd pursued him before. This time he ensconced me in presidential splendor in the same building where he was sleeping.

I should have been suspicious. I've got to admit that, instead, I sort of half thought that maybe Sam was getting tired of running away from me. Maybe he wanted me to be near him.

He did. But for his own reasons, of course.

When we ate dinner that evening it was with the president of Ecuador himself: Carlos Pablo Francisco Esperanza de Rivera. He was handsome, haughty, and kind of pompous. Wore a military uniform with enough braid to buckle the knees of a Ukranian weightlifter. Very elegant silver hair. A noble profile with a distinguished Castilian nose.

"It is an extremely serious matter," he told me, in Harvard-accented English. "We do not sue the head of Holy Mother Church for trivial reasons."

The fourth person at the table was a younger man, Gregory Molina. He was dark and intense, the smoldering Latino rebel type. Sam introduced him as the lawyer who was handling the case for him.

We sat at a sumptuous table in a small but elegant dining room. Crystal chandelier, heavy brocade napkins, damask tablecloth, gold-rimmed dishes, and tableware of solid silver. Lavish Christmas trimmings on the windows; big holiday bows and red-leafed poinsettias decorating the dining table.

Ecuador was still considered a poor nation, although as the Earthbound anchor of Sam's space operations there was a lot of money flowing in. Most of it must be staying in the presidential palace, I thought.

Once the servants had discreetly taken away our fish course and deposited racks of roast lamb before us, I said, "The reason I came here is to see if this matter can be arbitrated without actually going to court."

"Of course!" said *el Presidente*. "We would like nothing better."

Sam cocked a brow. "If we can settle this out of court, fine. I don't really want to sock the Pope if we can avoid it."

Molina nodded, but his burning eyes told me he'd like nothing better than to get the Pope on the witness stand.

"I glanced through your petition papers on the flight down here," I said. "I don't see what your insurance claims have to do with the Vatican."

Sam put his fork down. "Over the past year and a half, Ecuador National Space Systems has suffered three major accidents: A booster was struck by lightning during launch operations and forced to ditch in the ocean; we were lucky that none of the crew was killed.''

"Why were you launching into stormy weather?" I asked.

"We weren't!" Sam placed a hand over his heart, like a little kid swearing he was telling the truth. "Launchpad weather was clear as a bell. The lightning strike came at altitude, over the Andes, out of an empty sky."

"A rare phenomenon," said Molina. "The scientists said it was a freak of nature."

Sam resumed, "Then four months later one of our unmanned freight carriers was hit by a micrometeor and exploded while it was halfway to our lunar mining base. We lost the vehicle and its entire cargo."

"Seventy million dollars, US," Molina said.

President de Rivera's eyes filled with tears.

"And just six months ago a lunar quake collapsed our mine in the ringwall of Aristarchus."

I hadn't known that. "Was anyone killed?"

"The operation was pretty much automated. A couple technicians were injured," Sam said. "But we lost three mining robots."

"At sixteen million dollars apiece," Molina added.

The president dabbed at his eyes with his napkin.

"I don't see what any of this has to do with the Vatican," I said.

The corners of Sam's mouth turned down. "Our mother-loving insurance carrier refused to cover any of those losses. Claimed they were all acts of God, not covered by our accident policy."

I hadn't drunk any of the wine in the crystal goblet before me, so there was no reason for me to be slow on the uptake. Yet I didn't see the association with the Vatican.

"Insurance policies always have an 'Acts of God' clause," I said.

"Okay," Sam said, dead serious. "So if our losses were God's fault, how do we get Him to pay what He owes us?"

"Him?" I challenged.

"Her," Sam snapped back. "It. Them. I don't care."

President de Rivera steepled his long, lean fingers before his lips, and said, "For the purposes of our discussion, and in keeping with ancient tradition, let us agree to refer to God as Him." And he smiled his handsome smile at me.

"Okay," I said, wondering how much he meant by that smile. "We'll call Her Him."

Molina snickered and Sam grinned. *El Presidente* looked puzzled; either he didn't appreciate my humor, or he didn't understand it.

Sam got back to his point. "If God's responsible for our losses, then we want to get God to pay for them. That's only fair."

"It's silly," I said. "How are you—"

Sam's sudden grin cut me off. "The Pope is considered to be God's personal representative on Earth, isn't he?"

"Only by the Roman Catholics."

"Of which there are more than one billion in the world," Molina said.

"The largest religion on Earth," said the president.

"It's more than that," Sam maintained. "Nobody else claims to be the personal representative of God. Only the Pope, among the major religious leaders. One of his titles is 'the vicar of Christ,' isn't it?"

The two men nodded in unison.

"The Catholics believe that Christ is God, don't they?" Sam asked.

They nodded again.

"And Christ—God Herself—personally made St. Peter His representative here on Earth."

More nods.

"And the Pope is Peter's descendant, with all the powers and responsibilities that Peter had. Right?"

"Exactly so," murmured *el Presidente*.

"So if we want to sue God, we go to his personal representative, the Pope." Sam gave a self-satisfied nod.

Only Sam Gunn would think of such a devious, convoluted scheme.

"We cannot sue the Pope personally," Molina pointed

out, as earnest as a missionary, "because he is technically and legally the head of a state: the Vatican. A sovereign cannot be sued except by his own consent; that is ancient legal tradition."

"So you want to sue the state he heads," I said.

"The Vatican. Yes."

"And since an individual or corporation can't sue a state, the nation of Ecuador is entering the suit."

Sam smiled like a jack-o'-lantern. "Now you've got it."

I picked my way through the rest of the dinner in stunned silence. I couldn't believe that Sam would go through with something so ridiculous, yet there he was sitting next to the president of Ecuador and a fervent young lawyer who seemed totally intent on hauling the Pope before the World Court.

I wondered if the fact that the present Pope was an American—the first US cardinal to be elected Pope—had anything to do with the plot hatching inside Sam's shifty, twisted, Machiavellian brain.

After the servants had cleared off all the dishes and brought a tray of liqueur bottles, I finally gathered enough of my wits to say, "There's got to be a way to settle this out of court."

"Half a billion would do it," Sam said.

He hadn't touched any of the after-dinner drinks and had only sipped at his wine during dinner. So he wasn't drunk.

"Half a billion?"

"A quarter billion in actual losses," Molina interjected, "and a quarter billion in punitive damages."

I almost laughed in his face. "You want to punish God?"

"Why not?" The look on his face made me wonder what God had ever done to him to make him so angry.

President de Rivera took a silver cigarette case from his heavily braided jacket.

"Please don't smoke," I said.

He looked utterly shocked.

"It's bad for your lungs and ours," I added.

Sighing, he slipped the case back into his pocket. "You sound like my daughter."

"Thank you," I said, and made a polite smile for him.

"Do you think we can settle out of court?" Sam asked.

"Where's the Pope going to get half a billion?" I snapped.

Sam shrugged good-naturedly. "Sell some artwork, maybe?"

I pushed my chair from the table. Molina and the president shot to their feet. De Rivera was closer to me; he held my chair while I stood up.

"Allow me to escort you to your room," he said.

"Thank you so much," I replied.

Sam, still seated, gave me a suspicious look. But he didn't move from his chair. The president gave me his arm, and I placed my hand on it, just like we were Cinderella and the Prince at the ball. As we walked regally out of the dining room I glanced back at Sam. He was positively glowering at me.

We took an intimately small elevator up two flights. There was barely room enough in it for the two of us. De Rivera wasn't much taller than I, but he kept bobbing up on his toes as the elevator inched its way up. I wondered if it was some sort of exercise for his legs, until I realized that he was peeking down the front of my blouse. I had dressed casually. Modestly. And there wasn't much for him to see there anyway. But he kept peeking.

I took his proffered arm once again as he walked me to my door. The wide upstairs corridor was lined with portraits, all men, and furniture that looked antique and probably very valuable.

He opened the door to my suite, but before he could step inside I maneuvered myself into the doorway to block him.

"Thank you so much for the excellent dinner," I said, smiling my kiss-off smile.

"I believe you will find an excellent champagne already chilled in your sitting room," said the president.

I gave him the regretful head shake. "It's much too

late at night for me to start drinking champagne."

"Ah, but the night is young, my lovely one."

Lovely? Me? I was as plain as a pie pan, and I knew it. But *el Presidente* was acting as if I was a ravishing beauty. Did he think he could win me over to his side by taking me to bed? I've heard of tampering with a judge, but this was ridiculous.

"I'm really very tired, Mr. President."

"Carlos," he whispered.

"I'm *really* very tired, Carlos."

"Then it would be best for you to go directly to bed, would it not?"

I was wondering if I'd have to knee him in the groin when Sam's voice bounced cheerfully down the corridor, "Hey, Jill, I just remembered that there was another so-called act of God that cost us ten–twenty mill or so."

The president stiffened and stepped back from me. Sam came strolling down the corridor with that imp's grin spread across his round face.

"Lemme tell you about it," he said.

"I'm very tired, and I'm going to sleep," I said firmly. "Good night, Sam. And good night, Carlos."

As I shut the door I saw Carlos glaring angrily at Sam. Maybe I've broken up their alliance, I thought.

Then I realized that Sam had come upstairs to rescue me from Carlos. He was jealous! And he cared enough about me to risk his scheme against the Pope.

Maybe he did love me after all. At least a little.

We tried to settle the mess out of court. And we might have done it, too, if it hadn't been for the other side's lawyer. And the assassins.

All parties concerned wanted to keep the suit as quiet as possible. Dignity. Good manners. We were talking about the Pope, for goodness' sake. Maintain a decent self-control and don't go blabbing to the media.

All the parties agreed to that approach. Except Sam. The instant the World Court put his suit on its arbitration calendar, Sam went roaring off to the newspeople. All of them, from BBC and CNN to the sleaziest tabloids and paparazzi.

Sam was on global television more than the hourly weather reports. He pushed Santa Claus out of the headlines. You couldn't punch up a news report on your screen without seeing Sam's jack-o'-lantern face grinning at you.

"I think that if God gets blamed for accidents and natural disasters, the people who claim to represent God ought to be willing to pay the damages," Sam said gleefully, over and again. "It's only fair."

The media went into an orgy of excitement. Interviewers doggedly tracked down priests, ministers, nuns, lamas, imams, mullahs, gurus of every stripe and sect. Christmas was all but forgotten; seven "holiday specials" were unceremoniously bumped from the entertainment networks so they could put on panel discussions of Sam's suit against the Pope instead.

Philosophers became as commonplace on the news as athletes. Professors of religion and ethics got to be regulars on talk shows all over the world. The Dalai Lama started his own TV series.

It was a bonanza for lawyers. People everywhere started suing God—or the nearest religious establishment. An unemployed mechanic in Minnesota sued his local Lutheran Church after he slipped on the ice while fishing on a frozen lake. An Englishwoman sued the Archbishop of Canterbury when her cat got itself run over by a delivery truck. Ford Motor Company sued the Southern Baptists because a ship carrying electronic parts from Korea sank in a typhoon and stopped Ford's assembly operation in Alabama.

Courts either refused to hear the suits, on the grounds that they lacked jurisdiction over You-Know-Who, or held them up pending the World Court's decision. One way or another, Sam was going to set a global precedent.

The Pope remained stonily silent. He virtually disappeared from the public eye, except for a few ceremonial masses at St. Peter's and his regular Sunday blessing of the crowds that he gave from his usual balcony. There

were even rumors that he wouldn't say the traditional
Christmas Eve mass at St. Peter's.

He even stopped giving audiences to visitors—after the
paparazzi and seventeen network reporters infiltrated an
audience that was supposed to be for victims of a flood
in the Philippines. Eleven photographers and seven Fili-
pinos were arrested after the Swiss Guard broke up the
scuffle that the newspeople started.

The Vatican spokesman was Cardinal Hagerty, a dour-
faced Irishman with the gift of gab, a veteran of the Curia's political infighting who stonewalled the media quite
effectively by sticking to three points:

One: Sam's suit was frivolous. He never mentioned
Ecuador at all; he always pinpointed the notorious Sam
Gunn as the culprit.

Two: This attempt to denigrate God was sacrilegious
and doomed to failure. Cardinal Hagerty never said it in
so many words, but he gave the clear impression that in
the good old days the Church would have taken Sam
by the scruff of his atheistic little neck and burned him
at the stake.

Three: The Vatican simply did not have any money to
spend on malicious lawsuits. Every penny in the Vatican
treasury went to running the Church and helping the poor.

The uproar was global. All across the world people
were being treated to "experts" debating the central
question of whether or not God should be—or could be—
held responsible for the disasters that are constantly as-
sailing us.

There were bloody riots in Calcutta after an earthquake
killed several hundred people, with the Hindus blaming
Allah and the Moslems blaming Kali or Rama or any of
the other hundreds of Hindu gods and goddesses. The
Japanese parliament solemnly declared that the Emperor,
even though revered as divine, was not to be held responsible for natural disasters. Dozens of evangelist ministers in the US damned Sam publicly in their TV
broadcasts and as much as said that anyone who could
stop the little bugger would be a hero in the eyes of God.

"What we need," yowled one TV evangelist, "is a

new Michael the Archangel, who will smite this son of Satan with a fiery sword!''

In Jerusalem, the chief rabbi and Grand Mufti stunned the world by appearing in public side by side to castigate Sam and call upon all good Jews and Moslems to accept whatever God or Allah sends their way.

''Humility and acceptance are the hallmarks of the true believers,'' they jointly told their flocks.

My sources on the Senate Intelligence Committee told me that the chief rabbi added privately, ''May He Who Is Nameless remove this evil man from our sight.''

The Grand Mufti apparently went further. He promised eternal Paradise for anyone who martyred himself assassinating Sam. In a burst of modernism, he added, ''Even if the assassin is a woman, Paradise awaits her.'' I thought he must have been either pretty damned furious at Sam or pretty damned desperate.

Officially, the Vatican refused to defend itself. The Pope would not even recognize the suit, and the Curia—which had been at odds with the new American Pope—backed him on this issue one hundred percent. Even though they knew that the World Court could hear the suit in their absence and then send in the Peacekeepers to enforce its decision, they felt certain that the Court would never send armed troops against the Vatican. It would make a pretty picture, our tanks and jet bombers against their Swiss Guardsmen. Heat-seeking missiles against medieval pikes. In St. Peter's, yet.

But the insurance conglomerate that carried the policy for Ecuador National Space Systems decided that it would step forward and represent the Vatican in the pretrial hearing.

''We've got to put a cork in this bottle right away,'' said their president to me. ''It's a disgrace, a shameful disgrace.''

His name was Frank Banner, and he normally looked cheerful and friendly, probably from the days when he was a salesman who made his living from sweet-talking corporate officials into multimillion-dollar insurance policies. We had known each other for years; Frank had often testified before Senate committees—and donated generously to campaign funds, including mine.

But now he looked worried. He had flown up to Nashua to see me shortly after I returned from Quito. His usual broad smile and easygoing manner were gone; he was grim, almost angry.

"He's ruining the Christmas season," Frank grumbled.

I had to admit that it was hard to work up the usual holiday cheer with this lawsuit hanging over us.

"Look," he said, as we sipped hot toddies in my living room, "I've had my run-ins with Sam Gunn in the past, Lord knows, but this time the little pisser's gone too god-damned far. He's not just attacking the Pope, although that in itself is bad enough. He's attacking the very foundation of Western civilization! That wise-assed little bastard is spitting in the eye of every God-fearing man, woman, and child in the world!"

I had never seen Frank so wound up. He sounded like an old-time politician yelling from a soap box. His face got purple, and I was afraid he'd hyperventilate. I didn't argue with him; I merely snuggled deeper into my armchair and let him rant until he ran out of steam.

Finally, he said, "Well, somebody's got to stand up for what's right and decent."

"I suppose so," I murmured.

"I'm assigning one of our young lawyers to act as an *amicus curiae* in your pretrial hearing."

"I'm not sure that's the proper legal term," I said.

"Well, whatever!" His face reddened again. "*Somebody's* got to protect the Pope's ass. Might as well be us."

I nodded, thinking that if Sam somehow did win his suit against the Pope it would turn the entire insurance industry upside down. *Amicus curiae* indeed.

The moment I laid eyes on the lawyer that Frank sent I knew we'd have nothing but trouble.

Her name was Josella Ecks, and she was a tall, slim, gorgeous black woman with a mind as sharp as a laser beam. Skin the color of milk chocolate. Almond-shaped eyes that I would have killed for. Long silky legs, and she didn't mind wearing slitted skirts that showed them off cunningly.

I knew Sam would go ape over her; the little juvenile delinquent always let his hormones overpower his brain.

Sure enough, Sam took one look at her and his eyes started spinning like the wheels in a slot machine. I felt myself turning seventeen shades of green. If Sam had seemed a little jealous of Carlos de Rivera, I was positively bilious with envy over Josella Ecks.

The four of us met ten days before Christmas in my formal office in the World Court building in The Hague: Sam, his lawyer Greg Molina, the delectable Ms. Ecks, and my plain old self. I settled into my desk chair, feeling shabby and miserable in a nubby tweed suit. Josella sat between the two men; when she crossed her long legs her slitted skirt fell away, revealing ankle, calf, and a lot of thigh. I thought I saw steam spout out of Sam's ears.

She didn't seem to affect Greg that way, but then Gregory Molina was a married man—married to President de Rivera's daughter, no less.

"This pretrial hearing," I said, trying to put my emotions under some semblance of control, "is mandated by the International Court of Justice for the purpose of trying to come to an amicable agreement on the matter of *Ecuador v. Vatican* without the expense and publicity of an actual trial."

"Fine by me," Sam said breezily, his eyes still on the young woman sitting beside him. "As long as we can get it over with by eleven. I've gotta catch the midnight Clipper. Gotta be back at Selene City for the Christmas festivities."

I glowered at Sam. Here the future of Christianity was hanging in the balance, and he was worried about a Christmas party.

Greg was more formal. His brows knitting very earnestly, he said, "The nation of Ecuador would be very much in favor of settling this case out of court." He was looking at me, not Josella. "Providing, of course, that we can arrive at a reasonable settlement."

Josella smiled as if she knew more than he did. "Our

position is that a reasonable settlement would be to throw this case in the trash bin, where it belongs.''

Sam sighed as if someone had told them there is no Santa Claus. ''A reasonable settlement would be a half billion dollars, US.''

Josella waggled a finger at him. I saw that her nails were done in warm pink. ''Your suit is without legal basis, Mr. Gunn.''

''Then why are we here, oh beauteous one?''

I resisted the urge to crown Sam with the meteoric iron paperweight on my desk. He had given it to me years earlier, and at that particular moment I really wanted to give it back to him—smack between his leering eyes.

Josella was unimpressed. Quite coolly, she answered, ''We are here, Mr. Gunn, because you have entered a frivolous suit against the Vatican.''

Greg spoke up. ''I assure you, Ms. Ecks, the nation of Ecuador is not frivolous.''

''Perhaps not,'' she granted. ''But I'm afraid that you're being led down the garden path by this unscrupulous little man.''

''Little?'' A vein in Sam's forehead started to throb. ''Was Napoleon little? Was Steinmetz little? Did Neil Armstrong play basketball in college?''

Laughing, Josella said, ''I apologize for the personal reference, Mr. Gunn. It was unprofessional of me.''

''Sam.''

''Mr. Gunn,'' she repeated.

''I still want half a bill,'' Sam growled.

''There isn't that much money in the entire Vatican,'' she said.

''Baloney. They take in a mint and a half.'' Sam ticked off on his fingers. ''Tourists come by the millions. The Vatican prints its own stamps and currency. They're into banking and money exchange, with no internal taxes and no restrictions on importing and exporting foreign currencies. Nobody knows how much cash flows through the Vatican, but they must have the highest per capita income in the solar system.''

"And it all goes to funding the Church and helping the poor."

"The hell it does! They live like kings in there," Sam growled.

"Wait," I said. "This is getting us nowhere."

Ignoring me, Sam went on, "And the Pope has *absolute* authority over all of it. He's got all the executive, legislative, and judicial powers in his own hands. He's an absolute monarch, responsible to nobody!"

"Except God," Greg added.

"Right," Sam said. "The same God who owes me half a billion dollars."

I repeated, "This is getting us nowhere."

"Perhaps I can set us on a useful course," Greg said.

I nodded hopefully at him.

Greg laid out Sam's case, chapter and verse. He spent nearly an hour tracing the history of the Petrine theory that is the basis for the Pope's claim to be "the vicar of Christ." Then he droned on even longer about the logic behind holding the Pope responsible for so-called acts of God.

"If we truly believe in a God who is the cause of these acts," he said, with implacable logic, "and we accept the Pope's claim to be the representative of God on Earth, then we have a firm legal, moral, and ethical basis for this suit."

"God owes me," Sam muttered.

"The contract between God and man implied by the Ten Commandments and the Scriptures," said Greg, solemnly, "must be regarded as a true contract, binding on both parties, and holding both parties responsible for their misdeeds."

"How do you know they're misdeeds?" Josella instantly rebutted. "We can't know as much as God does. Perhaps these acts of God are part of His plan for our salvation."

With an absolutely straight face, Greg said, "Then He must reveal his purposes to us. Or be held responsible for His acts in a court of law."

Josella shook her head slowly. I saw that Sam's eyes were riveted on her.

She looked at me, though, and asked, "May I present the defendant's argument, Your Honor?"

"Yes, of course."

Josella started a careful and very detailed review of the legal situation, with emphasis on the absurdity of trying to hold a person or a state responsible for acts of God.

"Mr. Gunn is attempting to interpret literally a phrase that was never so meant," she said firmly, with a faint smile playing on her lips.

Sam fidgeted in his chair, huffed and snorted as she went on and on, cool and logical, marshaling every point or precedent that would help her demolish Sam's case.

She was nowhere near finished when Sam looked at his wristwatch, and said, "Look, I've got to get to Selene. Big doings there, and I'm obligated to be present for them."

"What's happening?" I asked.

"Christmas stuff. Parties. We've brought in a ballet troupe from Vancouver to do *The Nutcracker*. Nothing that has anything to do with this legal crapola." He turned to Greg. "Why don't you two lawyers fight it out and lemme know what you decide, okay?"

Sam had to lean toward Josella to speak to Greg, but he looked right past her, as if she weren't there. And he was leaving Greg to make the decision? That wasn't like Sam at all. Was he bored by all these legal technicalities?

He got to his feet. Then a slow grin crept across his face, and he said, "Unless the three of you would like to come up to Selene with me, as my guests. We could continue the hearing there."

So that was it. He wanted Josella to fly with him to the Moon. Greg and I would be excess baggage that he would dump the first chance he got.

And Josella actually smiled at him, and replied, "I've never been to the Moon."

Sam's grin went ear-to-ear. "Well, come on up! This is your big chance."

"This is a pretrial hearing," I snapped, "not a tourist agency."

Just then the door burst open and four women in janitorial coveralls pushed into my office. Instead of brooms they were carrying machine pistols.

"On your feet, all of you, godless humanists!" shouted their leader, a heavyset blonde. "You are the prisoners of the Daughters of the Mother!" She spoke in English, with some sort of accent I couldn't identify. Not Dutch, and certainly not American.

I stabbed at the panic button on my phone console. Direct line to security. The blonde ignored it and hustled the four of us out into the corridor to the bank of elevators. The corridor was empty; I realized it was well past quitting time, and the Court's bureaucrats had cleared out precisely at four-thirty.

But security should be here, I thought. No sign of them. They must have been out Christmas shopping, too. The Daughters of the Mother pushed us into an elevator and rode up to the roof. It was dark and cold up there; the wind felt as if it came straight from the North Pole.

A tilt-rotor plane sat on the roof, its engines swiveled to their vertical position, their big propellers swinging slowly like giant scythes, making a whooshing sound that gave the keening sea wind a basso counterpoint.

"Get in, all of you." The hefty blonde prodded me with the snout of her pistol.

We marched toward the plane's hatch.

"Hey, wait a minute," Sam said, pulling his sports jacket tight across his shivering body. "I'm the guy you want; leave these others out of it. Hell, they'd just as soon shoot me as you would."

"I said all of you!" the blonde shouted.

Where was security? They couldn't be so lax as to allow a plane to land on our roof and kidnap us. They *had* to be coming to our rescue. But when?

I decided to slow us down a bit. As we approached the plane's hatch, I stumbled and went down.

"Ow!" I yelled. "My ankle!"

The big blonde wrapped an arm around my waist,

hauled me off the concrete, and tossed me like a sack of potatoes through the open hatch of the plane. I landed on the floor plates with a painful thump.

Sam jumped up the two-step ladder and knelt beside me. "You okay? Are you hurt?"

I sat up and rubbed my backside. "Just my dignity," I said.

Suddenly the whole roof was bathed in brilliant light, and we heard the powerful throbbing of helicopter engines.

"YOU ARE SURROUNDED!" roared a bullhorn voice. "THIS IS THE POLICE. DROP YOUR WEAPONS AND SURRENDER."

I scrambled to the nearest window, Sam pressing close behind me. I could see two helicopters hovering near the edge of the roof, armored SWAT policemen pointing assault rifles at us.

"What fun," Sam muttered. "With just a little luck, we could be in the middle of a firefight."

The blonde came stumping past us, heading for the cockpit. Greg and Josella were pushed into the plane by the other three Daughters. The last one slammed the hatch shut and dogged it down.

"YOU HAVE THIRTY SECONDS TO THROW DOWN YOUR WEAPONS AND SURRENDER!" roared the police bullhorn.

"WE HAVE FOUR HOSTAGES ABOARD, INCLUDING SENATOR MEYERS." The blonde had a bullhorn, too. "IF YOU TRY TO STOP US, WE WILL SHOOT HER FIRST."

Sam patted my head. "Lucky lady."

They bellowed threats back and forth for what seemed like an eternity, but finally the police allowed the plane to take off. With us in it. There were four police helicopters, and they trailed after us as our plane lifted off the roof, swiveled its engines to their horizontal position, and began climbing into the dark night sky. The plane was much faster than the choppers; their lights dwindled behind us, then got lost altogether in the clouds.

"The Peacekeepers must be tracking us by radar,"

Sam assured me. "Probably got satellite sensors watching us, too. Jet fighters out there someplace, I bet."

And then I realized he was speaking to Josella, not me.

We rode for hours in that plane, Sam jabbering across the aisle to Josella while I sat beside him, staring out the window and fuming. Greg sat on the window seat beside Josella, but as I could see from their reflections in the glass, Sam and Josella had eyes only for each other. I went beyond fuming; I would have slugged Sam if we weren't in so much trouble already.

Two of the Daughters sat at the rear of the cabin, guns in their laps. Their leader and the other one sat up front. Who was in the cockpit I never knew.

Beneath my anger at Sam I was pretty scared. These Daughters of the Mother looked like religious fanatics to me, the kind who were willing to die for their cause— and therefore perfectly willing to kill anybody else for their cause. They were out to get Sam, and they had grabbed me and the other two as well. We were hostages. Bargaining chips for the inevitable moment when the Peacekeepers came at them with everything in their arsenal.

And Sam was spending his time talking to Josella, trying to ease her fears, trying to impress her with his own courage.

"Don't worry," he told her. "It's me they want. They'll let you and the others loose as soon as they turn me over to their leader, whoever that might be."

*And the others.* I seethed. As far as Sam was concerned, I was just one of the others. Josella was the one he was interested in, tall and willowy and elegant. I was just a sawed-off runt with as much glamour as a fire hydrant, and pretty much the same figure.

Dawn was just starting to tinge the sky when we started to descend. I had been watching out the window during the flight, trying to puzzle out where we were heading from the position of the Moon and the few stars I could see. Eastward, I was pretty certain. East and south. That was the best I could determine.

As the plane slowed down for its vertical landing, I

mentally checked out the possibilities. East and south for six hours or so could put us somewhere in the Mediterranean. Italy, Spain—or North Africa.

"Where in the world have they taken us?" I half whispered, more to myself than anyone who might answer me.

"Transylvania," Sam answered.

I gave him a killer stare. "This is no time to be funny."

"Look at my wristwatch," he whispered back at me, totally serious.

Its face showed latitude and longitude coordinates in digital readout. Sam pressed one of the studs on the watch's outer rim, and the readout spelled RUMANIA. Another touch of the stud: TRANSYLVANIA. Another: NEAREST MAJOR CITY, VARSAG.

I showed him my wristwatch. "It's got an ultrahigh-frequency transponder in it. The Peacekeepers have been tracking us ever since we left The Hague. I hope."

Sam nodded glumly. "These Mother-lovers aren't afraid of the Peacekeepers as long as they've got you for a hostage."

"There's going to be a showdown, sooner or later," I said.

Just then the plane touched down with a thump.

"Welcome," said Sam, in a Hollywood vampire accent, "to Castle Dracula."

It wasn't a castle that they took us to. It was a mine shaft.

Lord knows how long it had been abandoned. The elevator didn't work; we had to climb down, single file, on rickety wooden steps that creaked and shook with every step we took. And it was *dark* down there. And cold, the kind of damp cold that chills you to the bone. I kept glancing up at the dwindling little slice of blue sky as the Daughters coaxed us with their gun muzzles down those groaning, shuddering stairs all the way to the very bottom.

There were some dim lanterns hanging from the rough stone ceiling of the bottom gallery. We walked along in gloomy silence until we came to a steel door. It took two of the Daughters to swing it open.

The bright light made my eyes water. They pushed us into a chamber that had been turned into a rough-hewn office, of sorts. At least it was warm. A big, beefy redheaded woman sat scowling at us from behind a steel desk.

"You can take their wristwatches from them now," she said to the blonde. Then she smiled at the surprise on my face. "Yes, Senator Meyers, we know all about your transponders and positioning indicators. We're not fools."

Sam stepped forward. "All right, you're a bunch of geniuses. You've captured the most-wanted man on Earth—me. Now you can let the others go and the Peacekeepers won't bother you."

"You think not?" the redhead asked, suspiciously.

"Of course not!" Sam smiled his sincerest smile. "Their job is to protect Senator Meyers, who's a judge on the World Court. They don't give a damn about me."

"You're the blasphemer, Sam Gunn?"

"I've done a lot of things in a long and eventful life," Sam said, still smiling, "but blasphemy isn't one of them."

"You don't think that what you've done is blasphemy?" The redhead's voice rose ominously. I realized that her temper was just as fiery as her hair.

"I've always treated God with respect," Sam insisted. "I respect Her so much that I expect Her to honor her debts. Unfortunately, the man in the Vatican who claims to be Her special representative doesn't think She has any sense of responsibility."

"The man in the Vatican." The redhead's lips curled into a sneer. "What does he know of the Mother?"

"That's what I say," Sam agreed fervently. "That's why I'm suing him, really."

For a moment the redhead almost bought it. She looked at Sam with eyes that were almost admiring. Then her expression hardened. "You *are* a conniving little sneak, aren't you?"

Sam frowned at her. "Little. Is everybody in the world worried about my height?"

"And fast with your tongue, too," the redhead went on. "I think that's the first part of you that we'll cut off." Then she smiled viciously. "But only the first part."

Sam swallowed hard, but recovered his wits almost immediately. "Okay, okay. But let the others go. They can't hurt you, and if you let them go, the Peacekeepers will get out of your hair."

"Liar."

"Me?" Sam protested.

The redhead got to her feet. She was huge, built like a football player. She started to say something but the words froze in her throat. Her gaze shifted from Sam to the door, behind us.

I turned my head and saw half a dozen men in khaki uniforms, laser rifles in their hands. The Peacekeepers, I thought, then instantly realized that their uniforms weren't right.

"Thank you so much for bringing this devil's spawn to our hands," said one of the men. He was tall and slim, with a trim moustache and an olive complexion.

"Who in hell are you?" the redhead demanded.

"We are the Warriors of the Faith, and we have come to take this son of a dog to his just reward."

"Gee, I'm so popular," Sam said.

"He's ours!" bellowed the redhead. "We snatched him from The Hague."

"And we are taking him from you. It is our holy mission to attend to this pig."

"You can't!" the redhead insisted. "I won't let you!"

"We'll send you a videotape of his execution," said the leader of the Warriors.

"No, no! *We've* got to kill him!"

"I am so sorry to disagree, but it is our sacred duty to execute him. If we must kill you also, that is the will of God."

They argued for half an hour or more, but the Warriors outnumbered and outgunned the Daughters. So we were marched out of that underground office, down the mine gallery, and through another set of steel doors that looked an awful lot like the hatches of airlocks.

The underground corridors we walked through didn't look like parts of a mine anymore. The walls were smoothly finished and lined with modern doors that had numbers on them, like a hotel's rooms.

Sam nodded knowingly as we tramped along under the watchful eyes of the six Warriors.

"This is the old shelter complex for the top Rumanian government officials," he told me as we walked. "From back in the Cold War days, when they were afraid of nuclear attack."

"But that was almost a century ago," Josella said.

Sam answered, "Yeah, but the president of Rumania and his cronies kept the complex going for years afterward. Sort of an underground pleasure dome for the big shots in the government. Wasn't discovered by their taxpayers until one of the bureaucrats fell in love with one of the call girls and spilled the beans to the media so he could run off with her."

"How do you know?" I asked him.

"The happy couple works for me up in Selene City. He's my chief bookkeeper now, and she supervises guest services at the hotel."

"What kind of hotel are you running up there in Selene?" Greg asked.

Sam answered his question with a grin. Then he turned back to me, and said, "This complex has several exits, all connected to old mine shafts."

Lowering my voice, I asked, "Can we get away from these Warriors and get out of here?"

Sam made a small shrug. "There's six of them and they've all got guns. All we've got is trickery and deceit."

"So what—"

"When I say 'beans,'" Sam whispered, "shut your eyes tight, stop walking, and count to ten slowly."

"Why . . . ?"

"Tell Greg," he said. Then he edged away from me to whisper in Josella's ear. I felt my face burning.

"What are you saying?" one of the Warriors demanded.

Sam put on a leering grin. "I'm asking her if she's
willing to grant the condemned man his last request."

The Warrior laughed. "We have requests to make
also."

"Fool!" their leader snapped. "We are consecrated to
the Faith. We have foresworn the comforts of women."

"Only until we have executed the dog."

"Yes," chimed another Warrior. "Once the pig is
slain, we are free of our vows."

A third added, "Then we can have the prisoners." He
smiled at Greg.

"Now wait," Sam said. He stopped walking. "Let me
get one thing straight. Am I supposed to be a pig or a
dog?"

The leader stepped up to him. "You are a pig, a dog,
and a piece of camel shit."

The man loomed a good foot over Sam's stubby form.
Sam shrugged good-naturedly, and said, "I guess you're
entitled to your opinion."

"Now walk," said the leader.

"Why should I?" Sam stuffed his hands into the pockets of his slacks.

A slow smile wormed across the leader's lean face.
"Because if you don't walk, I will break every bone in
your face."

They were all gathered around us now, all grinning, all
waiting for the chance to start beating up on Sam. I realized we were only a few feet away from another airlock
hatch.

"You just don't know beans about me, do you?" Sam
asked sweetly.

I squeezed my eyes shut, but the glare still burned
through my closed lids so brightly that I thought I'd go
blind. I remembered to count . . . six, seven . . .

"Come on!" Sam grabbed at my arm. "Let's get going!"

I opened my eyes and still saw a burning afterimage,
as if I had stared directly into the sun. The six Warriors

were down on their knees, whimpering, pawing madly at their eyes, their rifles strewn across the floor.

Sam had Josella by the wrist with one hand. With the other he was pulling me along.

"Let's *move!*" he commanded. "They won't be down for more than a few minutes."

Greg stooped down and took one of the laser rifles.

"Do you know how to use that?" Sam asked.

Greg shook his head. "I feel better with it, though."

We raced to the hatch, pushed it open, squeezed through it, then swung it shut again. Sam spun the control wheel as tightly as he could.

"That won't hold them for more than a minute," he muttered.

We ran. Of the four of us I was the slowest. Josella sprinted ahead on her long legs, with Greg not far behind. Sam stayed back with me, puffing almost as badly as I was.

"We're both out of shape," he panted.

"We're both too old for this kind of thing," I said.

He looked surprised, as if the idea of getting old had never occurred to him.

"What did you do back there?" I asked, as we staggered down the corridor.

"Miniaturized high-intensity flash lamp," Sam said, puffing. "For priming minilasers."

"You just happened . . ." I was gasping. ". . . to have one . . . on you?"

"Been carrying a few," he wheezed, "ever since the fanatics started making threats."

"Good thinking."

We found a shaft and climbed up into the sweet, clean air of a pine forest. It was cold; there was a dusting of snow on the ground. Our feet got thoroughly soaked, and we were shivering as Sam pushed us through the woods.

"Clearing," he kept telling us. "We gotta get to a clearing."

We found a clearing at last, and the thin sunshine filtering through the gray clouds felt good after the chill shadows of the forest. Sam made us close our eyes again and he set off another of his flashbulbs.

"Surveillance satellites oughtta see that," he said. "Now it's just a matter of time to see who gets us first, the Peacekeepers or the dog-pig guys."

It was the Peacekeepers, thank goodness. Two of their helicopters came clattering and whooshing down on that little clearing while a pair of jump-jets flew cover high overhead. I was never so happy to see that big blue-and-white symbol in my life.

The Peacekeepers had mounted a full search-and-rescue operation. Their helicopter was spacious, comfortable, and even soundproofed a little. They thought of everything. While Sam filled in one of their officers on the layout of the Rumanian shelter complex, two enlisted personnel brought us steaming-hot coffee and sandwiches. It made me realize that we hadn't eaten or slept in close to twenty-four hours.

I was starting to drowse when I heard Sam ask, over the muted roar of the 'copter's turbines, "Who were those guys?"

The Peacekeeper officer, in her sky-blue uniform, shook her head. "Neither the Daughters of the Mother nor the Warriors of God are listed in our computer files."

"Terrorists," Greg Molina said. "Religious fanatics."

"Amateurs," said Josella Ecks, with a disdainful curl of her lip.

That startled me. The way she said it. But the need for sleep was overpowering my critical faculties. I cranked my seat back and closed my eyes. The last thing I saw was Sam holding Josella's hand and staring longingly into her deep, dark, beautifully lashed eyes.

I wanted to murder her, but I was too tired.

Sam went to Selene the next day and, sure enough, Josella went with him. Greg Molina returned to Quito, dropping in at my office just before he left.

"Will the trial be held in The Hague or at Selene?" he asked.

"Wherever," I groused, seething at the thought of Sam

and Josella together a quarter million miles away.

"I assume there will be a trial, since there was no agreement at the pretrial hearing," he said.

Grimly, I answered, "It certainly looks that way."

Looking slightly worried, he asked, "If it's on the Moon, will I have to go there? Or can I participate electronically?"

"It would be better if you were there in person."

"I've never been in space," he admitted.

"There's nothing to it," I said. "It's like flying in an airplane."

"But the lack of gravity . . ."

"You'll get used to it in a day or so. You'll enjoy it," I assured him.

He looked unconvinced.

It took me a whole day of fussing and fuming before I bit the bullet and rocketed to the Moon after Sam. And Josella. Pride is one thing, but I just couldn't stand the thought of Sam chasing that willowy young thing—and catching her. Josella Ecks might think she was smart and cool enough to avoid Sam's clutches, but she didn't know our sawed-off Lothario as well as I did.

And it would be just like Sam to try to get the other side's lawyer to fall for him. Even if he wasn't bonkers about Josella, he'd want to sabotage her ability to represent his adversary in court.

So I told myself I was doing my job as a judge of the International Court of Justice as I flew to Selene.

I hadn't been to the Moon in nearly five years, and I was impressed with how much bigger and more luxurious the underground city had grown.

Selene's main plaza had been mostly empty the last time I'd seen it, an immense domed structure of bare lunar concrete rumbling with the echoes of bulldozers and construction crews. Now the plaza—big enough to hold half a dozen football fields—was filled with green trees and flowering shrubbery. On one side stood the gracefully curved acoustical shell of an open-air theater. Small shops and restaurants were spotted along the pleasant winding walk that led through the plaza, all of them decked out

with Christmas ornaments. The trees along the walk twin-
kled with lights.

There were hundreds of people strolling about, tourists
walking awkwardly, carefully, in their weighted boots to
keep them from stumbling in the one-sixth gravity. A
handful of fliers soared high up near the curving dome,
using colorful rented plastic wings and their own muscle
power to fly like birds. For years Sam had said that tourism would become a major industry in space, and at last
his prediction was coming true. Christmas on the Moon:
the ultimate holiday trip.

The lobby of the Selene Hotel was marvelous, floored
with basalt from Mare Nubium polished to a mirror finish. The living quarters were deeper underground than the
lobby level, of course. There were no stairs, though; too
easy for newcomers unaccustomed to the low gravity to
trip and fall. I walked down a wide rampway, admiring
the sheets of water cascading noiselessly down tilted
panes of lunar glass on either side of the central rampway
into spacious fish ponds at the bottom level. Freely flowing water was still a rare sight on the Moon, even though
aquaculture provided more of the protein for lunar meals
than agriculture did.

Soft music wafted through hidden speakers, and tourists tossed chunks of bread to the fish in the pools, not
realizing that sooner or later the fish would be feeding
them. I saw that others had thrown coins into the water
and laughed to myself, picturing Sam wading in there
every night to collect the loose change.

I hadn't told Sam I was coming, but he must have
found out when I booked a suite at the hotel. There were
real flowers and Swiss chocolates waiting for me when I
checked in. I admired the flowers and gave the chocolates
to the concierge to distribute to the hotel's staff. Let them
have the calories.

Even before I unpacked my meager travel bag I put in
a call to Sam's office. Surprisingly, he answered it himself.

"Hi, there!" Sam said brightly, his larger-than-life
face grinning at me from the electronic window that cov-

ered one whole wall of my sitting room. "What brings you to Selene?"

I smiled for him. "I got lonesome, Sam."

"Really?"

"And I thought that I'd better make certain you're not suborning an officer of the court."

"Oh, you mean Josella?"

"Don't put on your innocent face for me, Sam Gunn," I said. "You know damned well I mean Josella."

His expression went serious. "You don't have to worry about her. She's got more defenses than a porcupine. Her arms are a lot longer than mine, I found out."

He actually looked sad. I felt sorry for him, but I didn't want him to know it. Not yet. Sam had a way of using your emotions to get what he wanted.

So I said, "I presume you're free for dinner."

He sighed. "Dinner, lunch, breakfast, you call it."

"Dinner. Seven o'clock in the hotel's restaurant." All the lunar facilities kept Greenwich Mean Time, which was only an hour off from The Hague.

I had expected Sam to be downcast. I'd seen him that way before, moping like a teenaged Romeo when the object of his desire wouldn't go along with him. Usually his pining and sighing only lasted until he found a new object of desire; I think twenty-four hours was the longest he'd ever gone, in the past. Like a minor viral infection.

But when I got to the restaurant Sam was practically bouncing with excitement. As the maître d' led me to the table, Sam jumped to his feet so hard that he rose clear above the table and soared over it, landing on his toes right in front of me like a star ballet dancer. People stared from their tables.

Gracefully, Sam took my hand and bent his lips to it. His lips were curved into a tremendously self-satisfied smile.

Alarm bells went off in my head. Either he's finally scored with Josella, or he's found a new love. I knew he couldn't possibly be this happy just to see me again.

Sam shooed the maître d' away and helped me into my chair. Then he chugged around the table and sat down,

folded his hands, rested his chin on them, and grinned at
me as if he was a cat who'd just cornered the canary
market.

I saw that there was a chilled bottle of French champagne in a silver bucket next to the table. A waiter immediately brought a dish of caviar and placed it in the
center of the table.

"What's going on?" I asked.

Sam cocked an eyebrow at me. "Going on? What do
you mean?"

"The champagne and caviar. The grin on your face."

"Couldn't that be just because I'm so happy to see
you?"

"No it couldn't," I said. "Come on, Sam, we've
known each other too long for this kind of runaround."

He laughed softly and leaned closer toward me. "He's
coming here."

"Who's coming here?"

"*Il Papa* himself," Sam whispered.

"The Pope?" My voice squeaked like a surprised
mouse.

His head bobbing up and down, Sam said, "William
I. The bishop of Rome. Vicar of Christ. Successor to the
prince of the Apostles. Supreme pontiff of the universal
church. Patriarch of the west, primate of Italy, archbishop
and metropolitan of the Roman province, sovereign of the
state of Vatican City, servant of the servants of God."

He took a breath. "That one."

"The Pope is coming here? To the Moon? To Selene?"

"Just got the word from Cardinal Hagerty himself.
Pope Bill is coming here to deal with me personally."

I felt as if I was in free fall, everything inside me sink-
ing. "Oh my God," I said.

"Nope," said Sam. "Just His representative."

It was supposed to be very hush-hush. No news reporters. No leaks. The Pope came incognito, slipping out
of Rome in plain clothes and riding to the Moon in a
private rocket furnished by Rockledge Industries and paid

for by Frank Banner's insurance consortium.

For once in his life Sam kept a secret that wasn't his own. He bubbled and jittered through the two days it took for the Pope to arrive at Selene. Instead of putting him up in the hotel, where he might be recognized, Sam ensconced Pope William, Cardinal Hagerty, and their retinue of guards and servants—all male—in a new wing of Selene's living quarters that hadn't been opened yet for occupancy.

Their quarters were a little rough, a little unfinished. Walls nothing but bare stone. Some of the electrical fixtures hadn't been installed yet. But there was comfortable furniture and plenty of room for them.

Suddenly I was a World Court judge in charge of a pretrial hearing again. I set up the meeting in the Pope's suite, after a half day of phone discussions with Sam and Cardinal Hagerty. Greg Molina reluctantly came up from Quito; Sam provided him with a special high-energy boost so he could get to us within twenty-four hours.

So there we were: Sam, the Pope, Cardinal Hagerty, Greg, Josella, and me, sitting around a circular table made of lunar plastic. Of the six of us, only Sam and I seemed truly at ease. The others looked slightly queasy from the low gravity. Cardinal Hagerty, in particular, gripped the arms of his chair as if he was afraid he'd be sucked up to the bare stone ceiling if he let go.

I was surprised at Josella's uneasiness. She was seated next to me—I made certain to place myself between her and Sam. She had always seemed so cool and self-possessed that I felt almost pained for her.

While Greg went through the formality of reading the précis of Sam's suit against the Vatican, I leaned over, and whispered to Josella, "Are you having trouble adjusting to the gravity?"

She looked surprised, almost shocked. Then she tried to smile. "It's . . . not that. It's this room. I feel . . . it must be something like claustrophobia."

I wondered that she hadn't been bothered before, but then I figured that the other rooms of the hotel had big electronic window walls and green plants and decorations that tricked the eye into forgetting that you were buried deep underground. This conference room's walls were bare, which made its ceiling seem low. Like a monk's cell, I thought.

Halfway through Greg's reading of the précis, Cardinal Hagerty cleared his throat noisily, and asked, "If there's nothing new in this travesty, could we be dispensing with the rest of this reading?"

Hagerty was by far the oldest person in the group. His face was lined and leathery; his hair thin and white. He looked frail and cranky, and his voice was as creaky as a rusted door hinge.

Sam nodded agreement, as did Josella. Greg tapped his hand-sized computer and looked up from its screen.

"Now then," said the Pope, folding his hands on the tabletop, "let's get down to the nitty-gritty."

He was smiling at us. Pope William looked even younger in person than on TV. And even more dynamic and handsome. A rugged and vigorous man with steel gray hair and steel gray eyes. He looked more like a successful corporate executive or a lawyer than a man of God. Even in his white Papal robes, it was hard for me to think of him as a priest. And a celibate.

He had the knack of making you feel that he was concentrating all his attention on you, even when he wasn't looking directly at you. And when his eyes did catch mine, I got goose bumps, so help me. Dynamic? He was *dynamite*.

Of course, he didn't affect Sam the way he hit me.

"You want the nitty-gritty?" Sam replied, with no hint of awe at speaking face-to-face with the Pope. "Okay. God owes me half a billion dollars."

"Ridiculous," Cardinal Hagerty croaked.

"Not according to the insurance industry," Sam countered. He jabbed a finger toward Josella. "Tell 'em, kid."

Josella looked startled. "Tell them what?"

"Your employers claim that the accidents that've almost wrecked Ecuador National Space Systems were acts of God. Right?"

"Yes," Josella answered warily.

Sam spread his hands. "See? *They're* the ones who put the blame on God, not me. All I'm trying to do is collect what's owed me."

Pope William turned his megawatt smile on Sam. "Surely you don't expect the Church to pay you for industrial accidents."

"Don't call me Shirley," Sam mumbled.

"What?"

Barely suppressing his glee, Sam said, "We've been through all this. The insurance industry says God's responsible. You claim to be God's representative on Earth. So you owe Ecuador National Space Systems half a billion dollars."

Pope William's smile darkened just a bit. "And what will you do if we refuse to pay—assuming, that is, that the World Court should decide in your favor."

"Which is ridiculous," said Hagerty.

Sam was unperturbed. "If the World Court really is an International Court of Justice, as it claims to be"—he gave me the eye—"then it has to decide in my favor."

"I doubt that," said the Pope.

"Ridiculous," uttered Cardinal Hagerty. It seemed to be his favorite word.

"Think about it," Sam went on, sitting up straighter in his chair. "Think of the reaction in the Moslem nations if the World Court seems to treat the Vatican differently from other nations. Or India or China."

Pope William's brows knit slightly. Hagerty's expression could have soured milk.

"Another thing," Sam added. "You guys have been working for a century or so to heal the rifts among other Christians. Imagine how the Protestants will feel if they see the Vatican getting special treatment from the World Court."

"Finding the Vatican innocent of responsibility for your industrial accidents is hardly special treatment," said Pope William.

"Maybe you think so, but how will the Swedes feel about it? Or the Orthodox Catholics in Greece and Russia and so on? Or the Southern Baptists?"

The Pope said nothing.

"Think about the publicity," Sam said, leaning back easily in his chair. "Remember what an American writer once said: 'There is no character, howsoever good and fine, but can be destroyed by ridicule.' "

" 'By ridicule, howsoever poor and witless,' " the Pope finished the citation. "Mark Twain."

"That's right," said Sam.

Cardinal Hagerty burst out, "You can't hold the Vatican responsible for acts of the Lord! You can't expect the Church to pay every time some daft golfer gets struck by lightning because he didn't have sense enough to come in out of the rain!"

"Hey, *you're* the guys who claim you're God's middle-man. You spent several centuries establishing that point, too, from what I hear."

"All right," said Pope William, smiling again, "let's grant for the sake of argument that the World Court decides against the Vatican. We, of course, will refuse to pay. It would be impossible for us to pay such a sum, in fact. Even if we could, we'd have to take the money away from the poor and the starving in order to give it to you."

"To the nation of Ecuador," Sam corrected.

"To Ecuador National Space Systems," grumbled Cardinal Hagerty.

"Which is you," said the Pope.

Sam shrugged.

Pope William turned to me. "What would happen if we refused to pay?"

I felt flustered. My face got hot. "I . . . uh—the only legal alternative would be for the Court to ask the Peacekeepers to enforce its decision."

"So the Peacekeepers will invade the Vatican?" Cardinal Hagerty sneered. "What will they do, cart away the *Pietà*? Hack off the roof of the Sistine Chapel and sell it at auction?"

"No," I admitted. "I don't see anything like that happening."

"Lemme tell you what'll happen," Sam said. "The world will see that your claim to be God's special spokes-

man is phony. The world will see that you hold yourselves above the law. Your position as a moral leader
will go down the toilet. The next time you ask the nations
to work for peace and unity the whole world will laugh
in your face.''

Cardinal Hagerty went white with anger. He sputtered,
but no words came past his lips. I thought he was going
to have a stroke, right there at our conference table.

But the Pope touched him on the shoulder, and the
Cardinal took a deep, shuddering breath and seemed to
relax somewhat.

Pope William's smile was gone. He focused those steel
gray eyes on Sam, and said, ''You are a dangerous man,
Mr. Gunn.''

Sam stared right back at him. ''I've been called lots of
things in my time, but never dangerous.''

''You would extort half a billion dollars out of the
mouths of the world's neediest people?''

''And use it to create jobs so that they wouldn't be
needy anymore. So they won't have to depend on you or
anybody else. So they can stand on their own feet and
live in dignity.''

Sam was getting worked up. For the first time in my
life, I saw Sam becoming really angry.

''You go around the world telling people to accept
what God sends them. You'll help them. Sure you will.
You'll help them to stay poor, to stay miserable, to be
dependent on Big Daddy from Rome.''

''Sam!'' I admonished.

''I've read the Gospels. Christ went among the poor
and shared what he had with them. He told a rich guy to
sell everything he had and give it to the poor if he wanted
to make it into heaven. I don't see anybody selling off
the Papal jewels. I see Cardinals jet-setting around the
world. I see the Pope telling the poor that they're God's
chosen people—from the balconies of posh hotels.''

Greg Molina smiled grimly. He must be a Catholic
who's turned against the Church, I thought.

Sam kept on. ''All my life I've seen the same old story:
big government or big religion or big corporations telling

the little guys to stay in their places and be grateful for whatever miserable crumbs they get. And they stay in their places and take what you deign to give them. And their children grow up poor and hungry and miserable and listen to the same sad song and make more children who grow up just as poor and hungry and miserable.''

"That's not his fault," I said.

"Isn't it?" Sam was trembling with rage. "They're all the same, whether it's government or corporate or religion. As long as you *stay* poor and miserable they'll help you. And all they do is help you to stay dependent on them.''

Pope William's expression was grim. But he said, "You're entirely right."

Sam's mouth opened, then clicked shut. Then he managed to utter, "Huh?"

"You are entirely right," the Pope repeated. He smiled again, but now it was almost sad, from the heart. "Oh, maybe not *entirely*, but right enough. Holy Mother Church has struggled to help the world's poor for centuries, but today we have more poor people than ever before. It is clear that our methods are not successful."

Sam's eyes narrowed warily, sensing a trap ahead. Cardinal Hagerty grumbled something too low for me to hear.

"For centuries we have ridden on the horns of a dilemma, a paradox, if you will," the Pope continued. "The goal of Holy Mother Church—the task given to Peter by Christ—was to save souls, not bodies. The Church's eyes have always been turned toward Heaven. Everything we have done has been done to bring souls to salvation, regardless of the suffering those souls must endure on Earth."

Before Sam could object, the Pope added, "Or so we have told ourselves."

Cardinal Hagerty let out his breath in what might have been a sigh. Or a hiss.

Pope William smiled at the old man, then continued, "The news media have hinted at . . . frictions between myself and the Curia—the bureaucracy that actually runs the Vatican.''

"I've heard such rumors,'' I said.

Clasping his hands together, the Pope said, ''The differences between myself and the Curia are based on the assessment that you have just made, Mr. Gunn. The Church has indeed told its faithful to ignore the needs of this world in order to prepare for the next. I believe that such an attitude has served us poorly. I believe the Church must change its position on many things. We can't save souls who have given themselves to despair, to crime and drugs and all kinds of immorality. We must give our people *hope*.''

"Amen to that,'' Sam muttered.

"Hope for a better life here on Earth.''

Ordinarily Sam would have quipped that we weren't on Earth at the moment. But he remained quiet.

"So you see,'' Pope William said, ''we are not so far apart as you thought.''

Sam shook himself, like a man trying to break loose from a hypnotic spell. "I still want my half bill,'' he said.

Pope William smiled at him. ''We don't have it, and even if we did, we wouldn't give it to you.''

"Then you're going to go down the tubes, just like I said.''

"And the changes I am trying to make within the Vatican will go down the tubes with me,'' Pope William replied.

Sam thought a moment, then said, ''Yeah, I guess they will.''

Leaning toward Sam, Pope William pleaded, ''But don't you understand? If you press your case, all the reforms that the Church needs will never be made. Even if you don't win, the case will be so infamous that I'll be blocked at every turn by the Curia.''

"That's your problem,'' Sam replied, so low I could barely hear him.

"Why do you think I came up here?'' the Pope continued. ''I wanted to make a personal appeal to you to be reasonable. I need your help!''

Sam said nothing.

Cardinal Hagerty recovered his voice. "I thought from the beginning that this trip was a waste of precious time."

Pope William pushed his chair back from the table. "I'm afraid you were right all along," he said to the Cardinal.

"So we'll have a trial," Sam said, getting to his feet.

"We will," said the Pope. He was nearly six feet tall; he towered over Sam.

"You'll lose," Sam warned.

The Pope's smile returned, but it was only a pale imitation of the earlier version. "You're forgetting one thing, Mr. Gunn. God is on our side."

Sam gave him a rueful grin. "That's okay. I'm used to working against the big guys."

Sam and I walked slowly along the corridor that led from the Pope's quarters to the main living section of Selene. Josella trudged along on Sam's other side; Greg was a few steps ahead of us.

"Sam," I said, "I'm going to recommend against a trial."

He didn't look surprised.

"You can't do this," I said. "It's not right."

Sam seemed subdued, but he still replied, "You can recommend all you want to, Jill. The Court will still have to hear the case. The law's on my side."

"Then the law is an ass!"

He grinned at me. "Old gray-eyes got to you, didn't he? Sexy guy, for a Pope."

I glared at him. There's nothing so infuriating as a man who thinks he knows what's going on inside your head. Especially when he's right.

Josella said, "I'll have to report this meeting to my superiors back in Hartford."

"How about having supper with me?" Sam asked her. Right in front of me.

Josella glanced at me. "I don't think so, Sam. It might be seen as a conflict of interest."

Sam laughed. "We'll bring the judge along. We'll discuss the case. Hey, Greg," he called up the corridor, "you wanna have dinner with the rest of us?"

So the four of us met at the hotel's restaurant after freshening up in our individual rooms. I made certain to follow Sam to his suite, down the corridor from Josella's, before going to my own.

"Bodyguarding me?" he asked mischievously.

"Protecting my interest," I said. Then I added loftily, "In the integrity of the World Court and the international legal system."

Sam gave me a wry smile.

"I don't want you tampering with the opposition's lawyer," I said.

"Tamper? Me? The thought never entered my mind."

"I know what's in your mind, Sam. You can't fool me."

"Have I ever tried to?" he asked.

And I had to admit to myself that he never had. To the rest of the world Sam might be a devious womanizing rogue, a sly underhanded con man, even an extortionist, but he'd always been up-front with me. Damn him!

The restaurant was crowded, but Sam got us a quiet table in a corner. He and Greg were already there when I arrived. Shortly after me, Josella swept in, looking like an African princess in a long, clinging gold-mesh sheath. Sam's eyes went wide. He had barely flickered at my Paris original, but I didn't have Josella's figure or long legs.

Sam sat Josella on one side of him, me on the other. Greg was across the table from him. I think he was enjoying having two women next to him. I only hoped he couldn't see how jealous I was of Josella.

Trying to hide that jealousy, I turned to Greg. I was curious about him. Over predinner cocktails, I asked him, "You're a Catholic, aren't you? How do you feel about all this?"

Greg looked down into his drink as he stirred it with his straw. "I am a Catholic, but not the kind you may think. There are many of us in Latin America who recognized ages ago that the bishops and cardinals and all the 'official' Church hierarchy were in the service of the big landlords, the government, the tyrants."

"Greg was a revolutionary," Sam said, with a smirk.

"I still am," he told us. "But now I work from inside the system. I learned that from Sam. Now I help to create jobs for the poor, to educate them and help them break free of poverty."

"And free of the Church?" Josella asked.

Greg said, "Most of us remain Catholics, but we do not support the hierarchy. We have worker priests among us, men of the people."

"Isn't that what Pope William wants to encourage?" I asked.

"Perhaps so," Greg said. "His words sound good. But words are not deeds."

"You're really going to insist on a trial?" I asked Sam.

He didn't look happy about it, but he said softly, "Got to. Ecuador National is close to bankruptcy. We need that money."

Greg nodded. I believed him, not Sam.

Dinner was uncomfortable, to say the least. Pope William had gotten to all of us, even Sam.

But by the time dessert was being served, at least Sam had brightened up a bit. He turned his attention to Josella.

"Is your last name Dutch?" he asked her.

She smiled a little. "Actually, its derivation is Greek, I believe."

"You don't look Greek."

"Looks can be deceiving, Mr. Gunn."

"Call me Sam."

Josella seemed to consider the proposition for a few moments, then decided. "All right—Sam."

"Did you call your bosses in Hartford, Josie?" he asked her.

"Did I! Old man Banner himself got on the screen. Is he pissed with you!"

Sam laughed. "Good. He's the sonofabitch who shifted the blame to God."

"That's a standard clause in every policy, Sam."

"Yeah, but I asked him personally to reconsider in my case, and he laughed in my face."

"He said if you took this case to trial, he'd personally break your neck," Josella said, very seriously. "He used a lot of adjectives to describe you, your neck, and how much he'd enjoy doing it."

"Great!" Sam grinned. "Did you make a copy of the conversation?"

Josella gave him a slow, delicious smile. "I did not. I even erased the core memory of it in my computer. You won't be subpoenaing *my* boss's heated words, Mr. Gunn."

Sam feigned crushing disappointment.

"This Mr. Banner hates Sam so much?" Greg asked.

"I think he truly does," said Josella.

"Perhaps he is the one who sent the assassins after Sam," Greg suggested. "At least one set of them."

"Mr. Banner?" she looked shocked.

A thought struck me. "You said the assassins were amateurs, Josella. Have you had much experience with terrorists?"

"Only what I read in the news media," she answered smoothly. "It seems to me that *real* terrorists blow you away as soon as they get the chance. They don't drag you across the landscape and gloat at you."

"Then let's be glad they were amateurs," Sam said.

"Professionals would have killed us all, right there in your office," Josella said to me. Flatly. As if she knew exactly how it was done.

"Without worrying about getting caught?" Greg asked.

"Considering the response time of the Dutch security people," Josella said, "they could have iced the four of us and made it out of the building with no trouble. If they had been professionals."

"Pleasant thought," Sam said.

There was plenty of night life in Selene, but as we left the restaurant Sam told us that he was tired and going to his quarters. It sounded completely phony to me.

Then Josella said she was retiring for the night, too. Greg looked a little surprised.

"I understand there's a gaming casino in the hotel," he said. "I think I'll try my luck."

We said good night to Greg and headed for the elevator to take us down to the level where our rooms were. On Earth, the higher your floor, the more prestigious and expensive. On the Moon, where the surface is pelted with micrometeors and bathed in hard radiation, prestige and expense increase with your distance downward.

Sam made a great show of saying good night to Josella. She even let him kiss her hand before she closed her door. I walked with him as far as the door to my own suite.

"Want to come in for a nightcap?" I asked.

Sam shook his head. "I'm really pretty pooped, kid. This business with the Pope's hit me harder than I thought it would."

But his eyes kept sliding toward Josella's door, down the corridor.

"Okay, Sam," I said, trying to make it sound sweet and unsuspecting. "Good night."

He pecked me on the cheek. A brotherly kiss. I hadn't expected more, but I still wanted something romantic or at least warm.

I closed my door and leaned against it. Suddenly I felt really weary, tired of the whole mess. Tired of chasing Sam, who was interested in every female in the solar system except me. Tired of this legal tangle with the Vatican. And scared of the effect that Pope William had on me. I wondered if one of the changes he wanted to make in the Church was to allow priests to marry. Wow!

I honestly tried to sleep. But I just tossed and fussed until I finally admitted that I was wide awake. I told the phone beside the bed to get Sam for me.

It got his answering routine. "I'm either sleeping or doing something else important. Leave your name, and I'll get back to you, promise."

Sleeping or doing something else important. I knew what "something else" was. I pulled on a set of coveralls and tramped down the corridor to Sam's door. I knocked.

No answer. Knocked harder. Still no answer. Pounded on it. He wasn't there.

I knew where he was. Steaming with rage, I stomped down the corridor to Josella's door and banged on it with both fists. I even kicked it.

"I know you're in there, Sam!" I shouted, not giving a damn who in the hotel could hear me. "Open up this goddamned door!"

Josella opened it. She was wearing nothing but the sheerest of nightgowns. And she had a pistol in her hand.

"Senator Meyers," she said, with a sad kind of resignation in her voice. "I had hoped to avoid this."

Puzzled, I pushed past her and into her room. Sam was sitting on the bed, buck naked, a sheet wrapped around his middle.

"Aw, shit, Jill," he said, frowning. "Now she's got you, too."

It hit me at last. Turning to Josella, I said, "*You're* an assassin!"

She nodded, her face very serious.

"She wants to waste me," Sam said gloomily, not moving from the bed.

"But why?" I blurted.

Josella kept the pistol rock-steady in her hand. "Because the ayatollahs are unanimous in their decision that this unbeliever must die."

"You're a Moslem?"

She smiled tightly. "Not all Moslem women wear veils and chadors, Senator Meyers."

"But why would the Moslems want to kill Sam? He's suing the Pope, not Islam."

"He is making a travesty of all religions. He is mocking God. The Church of Rome has yet to see the light of true revelation, but we slaves of Allah can't allow this blasphemy to continue."

"It's Islam's contribution to global religious solidarity," Sam said, disgust dripping from his words.

"I had wanted to do it cleanly, professionally," Josella said, "without any complications."

"That's why you let Sam into your room," I said.

"Yes," she said. "To give the condemned man his last wish. Although Sam didn't know he was condemned when I granted his wish."

"So you made it with her, after all," I said to Sam, angrily.

He made a sour face. "She screwed me, all right."

"And now what?" I asked Josella. "You kill us both?"

"I'm afraid so."

"And how do you get away?"

She shrugged. Inside that sheer nightgown it looked delicious, even to me. "There's a shuttle leaving for Earth orbit at midnight. Passage on it has already been booked for a young man named Shankar. By the time your bodies are discovered I will be Mr. Shankar, complete with moustache and beard."

"It'll have to be a damned good disguise," Sam groused. Almost smiling, Josella said, "It will be. Even my fingerprints will be different."

"You said you're a professional." I stalled for time. "You mean you've done this kind of thing before?"

Josella nodded slowly. "For six years. My job has been to assassinate policyholders whose estates would go to Islamic causes."

"You've worked for insurance companies, and they never knew?"

"Of course not."

"She's a lawyer, for Chrissake," Sam snapped. "She's trained to lie."

The phone rang. We heard Josella's taped voice say sweetly, "I am not able to answer your call right now. Please leave your name, and I'll call you back as soon as I possibly can."

"Josella?" I recognized that bombastic voice. It was Frank Banner. "This is Banner. Haven't been able to sleep for the past two nights. This damned business with Sam Gunn is driving me nuts. He's actually going ahead with his suit in the World Court, is he? Damned little pissant jerk! We can't let him drag the Pope through the mud the way he wants to. We just can't! Tell him we'll settle with him. Not his damned half billion, that's out-rageous. But tell him we'll work out something reasonable if he'll drop this damned lawsuit.''

I felt my mouth drop open. I looked at Sam, and he was grinning as if he'd been expecting this all along.

''And tell him that if I ever see him in the same room with me, I'll break every bone in his scrawny goddamned neck! Tell him that, too!''

The phone connection clicked dead. Sam flopped back on the bed and whooped triumphantly.

''I knew it!'' he yelled. ''I knew that Francis Xavier Banner couldn't let the Pope come to trial. I knew the tightfisted sonofabitch would finally break down and offer to settle my insurance claims!'' He laughed wildly, kicking his bare hairy legs in the air and pounding the mattress with his fists.

I just stood there, dumbfounded. Had this whole complex procedure been nothing more than an elaborate scheme by Sam to get his insurance carrier to accept his accident claims? Yes, I realized. That was Sam Gunn at his wiliest: threaten the Pope to get what he considered he was owed.

The gun in Josella's hand wavered, then she let her arm drop to her side.

''You don't have to kill Sam now,'' I said. ''There's not going to be a court case after all.''

''No,'' she said. ''The blasphemer must still die.''

Sam got to his bare feet, clutching the bedsheet around his middle like a Roman senator who didn't quite know how to drape his toga properly.

''You're a fraud,'' Sam said.

Josella's dark eyes snapped at him. ''Fraud?''

''You're about as professional a killer as that fat blond Daughter.''

''You think so?'' Josella's voice went hard and cold, like an ice pick. She still had the gun in her hand.

''You said professionals do the job without hesitation,'' Sam said. ''No talk, just boom, you're dead.''

Josella nodded.

''So you're an amateur,'' Sam said, grinning at her.

"You did a lot more than talk before you hauled out your gun."

"I did that with all the others, too," Josella said. It was a flat statement, neither a boast nor an excuse. "It's my trademark. Two of the older men I didn't even have to kill; they died of natural causes."

"Bullshit all the others. You've never killed anybody, and we both know it."

"You're wrong—"

"Yeah, sure. I'm going to start believing what a lawyer tells me, at my advanced age."

Josella looked confused. I know I was.

But Sam knew exactly what he was doing. "Put your gun back wherever the hell you were hiding it and get out of here," he told her. "Get on the midnight shuttle and don't come back."

"I can't do that," said Josella. "My mission is to kill you—or die. If I let you go, they'll kill me."

"Oh shit," Sam muttered.

"You mean that your own people will murder you if you don't kill Sam?"

Josella nodded. "I must succeed or die. That is what I promised them."

With a disgusted frown, Sam clutched his bedsheet a little tighter and reached for the phone with his free hand.

"Don't!" Josella warned, raising her gun.

"I'm not calling security."

"Then who . . . ?"

Sam called Pope William. The Pope looked shocked, even on the tiny screen of the Picturephone, and even more surprised when Sam told him what his call was about.

"Sanctuary," he said. "This lady here needs your protection."

Blinking sleep from his steely eyes, Pope William said, "Maybe you'd better come over here to explain this to me."

It was almost comical watching Sam and Josella get dressed while she still tried to keep her pistol on us. Then the three of us trotted down the nearly empty corridors,

back to the Pope's quarters. Two of his own security men,
Swiss guards in plain coveralls, were waiting for us.

They brought us to a kind of sitting room, a bare little
cell with four chairs grouped around a coffee table. Nothing else in the room: not a decoration or any refreshments
or even a carpet on the stone floor. Josella sat down warily, put her pistol on her lap.

Pope William entered the room a few moments after
we did. He was wearing a white sweatshirt and an old
pair of Levis, and he still filled the room with a warm
brilliance.

It was long past midnight before Sam got the whole
thing explained to the Pope. Josella didn't help, insisting
that she wanted no help from unbelievers.

"I won't try to convert you," William said, smiling at
her. "But I can offer you protection and help you create
a new persona for yourself."

"A kind of witness protection plan," Sam said, trying
to encourage her. "See, we're bringing the Vatican into
the twenty-first century."

Me? I was stewing. The two of them were falling all
over themselves trying to help Josella and ignoring me
altogether.

Josella was starting to nod, seeing that maybe there
was a way out of the blind corner she'd trapped herself
in. She took the gun from her lap, popped open its magazine, and laid the pieces on the coffee table.

"All right," she said. "I'll go along with you."

"But what about those other killings?" I heard myself
blurt out. "She's admitted to murdering God knows how
many men!"

Sam glowered at me.

Pope William smiled. "How do we know, Senator
Meyers, that this entire episode—Sam's lawsuit, my coming to the Moon, the various assassination attempts—how
do we know that all of this hasn't been God's way of
bringing this one woman to repentance and salvation?"

"I won't convert," Josella snapped. "I'm a Moslem."

"Of course," said the Pope. "I only want you to
change your life, not your religion."

"All this," I heard the disbelief in my own voice, "just for her?"

"There is more joy in heaven over one sinner who's redeemed than there is over one of the faithful," Pope William said.

Even God was concentrating on Josella, I thought, ashamed of my jealousy but feeling it seething inside me nonetheless.

Sam grinned at him. "So you think this whole thing has been an act of God, huh?"

"Everything is an act of God," said Pope William. "Isn't that right, Josella?"

She nodded silently.

Sam and I left Josella with the Pope. As we walked back along the corridors I tried to stop feeling so damned jealous. But the thought of her with Pope William just plain boiled me. All of a sudden it struck me that Josella might be more of a threat to William than she was to Sam. His soul, that is; not his body.

I started to laugh.

"What's so funny?" Sam asked.

"Nothing," I said. "It's just—everything's turned upside down and inside out."

"Nope," Sam said. "Everything worked out just the way I thought it would. Ol' Francis X. was an altar boy, y'know. Went to Notre Dame and almost became a priest, before he found out how much he enjoyed making money."

"You knew that all along?"

"I was counting on it," Sam answered cheerfully.

We were at my door. I realized I was very weary, drained physically and emotionally. Sam looked as chipper as a sparrow, despite the hour.

"Tomorrow's Christmas Eve," he said.

I tapped my wristwatch. "You mean today; it's well past midnight."

"Right. I gotta get a high-gee boost direct to Rome set up for Billy Boy if he's gonna say Christmas Eve mass in St. Peter's. Even then it's gonna be awful close. See ya!"

He hustled down the corridor to his own suite, whistling shrilly off-key. And that's the last I saw of Sam until Christmas.

Pope William was overjoyed, of course. He invited me to breakfast that morning, just before his high-boost shuttle was set to take off. Even Cardinal Hagerty managed to smile, although it looked as if the effort might shatter his stony face. Josella was nowhere in sight, though.

"My prayers have been answered," the Pope told me.

"The Lord certainly moves in mysterious ways," I said.

"Indeed She does," said the Pope, with a mischievous wink.

More mysterious than either of us realized at the time. Sam set up a direct high-gee flight to Rome for the Papal visitors, so that Pope William could get back in time for his Christmas Eve mass in St. Peter's. But all of a sudden an intense solar flare erupted and raised radiation levels in cislunar space so high that all flights between the Earth and the Moon had to be canceled. All work on the lunar surface stopped and everybody had to stay underground for forty-eight hours. It was as if God was forcing all of Selene's residents and visitors to observe the Christmas holiday.

Which is how William I became the first Pope to celebrate a public mass on the Moon. On Christmas Eve, in Selene's main plaza. The whole population turned out, even Sam.

"I figure about five percent of this crowd is Roman Catholic," Sam said, looking over the throng. We were seated up on the stage of the theater shell, behind the makeshift altar. Several thousand people jammed the theater's tiers of seats and spilled out onto the grass of the plaza's greenway.

"That doesn't matter," I said. "For one hour, we're all united."

Sam grinned. The Pope didn't have his best ceremonial robes with him; he offered the mass in a plain white outfit. "They're doing *The Nutcracker* this evening," Sam whispered to me. "Wanna see it?"

Low-gravity ballet. Once I had dreams of becoming a dancer on the Moon. "I wouldn't miss it."

"Good," said Sam.

We watched the elaborate ritual of the mass, and the thousands of transfixed men and women and children standing out on the plaza, their eyes on the Pope. I spotted a slim, dark-skinned young man in a trim moustache and beard who looked awfully familiar.

"Y'know," Sam whispered, "maybe I've been wrong about this all along."

I nodded.

"I mean," he went on, "if a guy really wants to make a fortune, he ought to start a religion."

I turned and stared at him. "You wouldn't!"

"Maybe that's what I ought to do."

"Oh Sam, you devil! Start a religion? You?"

"Who knows."

I tried to glare at him but couldn't.

"And another thing," he whispered. "If we ever do get married, you'll have to live here on the Moon with me. I'm not going back to Earth; it's too dangerous down there."

My heart skipped a couple of beats. That was the first time Sam had ever admitted there was any kind of chance he'd marry me.

He shrugged good-naturedly. "Merry Christmas, Jill."

"Merry Christmas," I replied, thinking that it might turn out to be a very interesting new year indeed.

## Statement of Juanita Carlotta Maria Rivera y Molina
## (Recorded at Mt. Esperanza, Ecuador)

I have no time to speak to you about Sam Gunn. That phase of my life ended long ago. Believe me, directing the construction of the first space elevator on the Earth keeps me quite busy, thank you.

Look at it! Even in its half-finished condition, is it not magnificent? A tower to the heavens, an elevator that rises from this mountaintop all the way up to the geosynchronous orbit, more than twenty-two thousand miles high! Ah, these are wonderful times to be alive.

Yes, my husband is the former president of Ecuador, as was my father. But I have never been involved in politics, except for that brief time when Sam Gunn intruded into my life. In fact the first time I heard of the idea of a space elevator, it was Sam who told me about it. He called it a "skyhook." I thought it was foolishness then, but now I know better.

What can I tell you that you do not already know? Sam was a whirlwind, a force of nature. He was constantly in motion, always tumbling and jumbling everything and everyone around him. It was like living in a perpetual hurricane, being near Sam.

I am not interested in him, whether he is dead or alive. My interest is in this space elevator, which you in the media call the Skyhook Project. When it is finished, people will be able to ride from our site in my native Ecuador all the way up to the geostationary orbit for pennies!

Merely the price of electricity to operate the elevator, plus a modest profit for our company.

Yes, it is costing billions to build the elevator, but we have had no trouble in finding investors.

What? Ah, if Sam were here among us, he would be one of our biggest investors, of course. But what chaos he would cause! We are much better off without him.

Oh, I suppose I really do hope he is not dead. I miss him, to tell the truth. But I'm glad he is not here! This project is too important to have him involved in it.

Still . . . all right, we will have one *café con leche* and I will speak of the time I worked for Sam Gunn. And the revolution. But only one cup! Then I must get back to the construction project.

 **SAM'S WAR**

I KNOW IT IS INCREDIBLE TO BELIEVE THAT SAM GUNN, OF all people, saved civilization-as-we-know-it. But the chauvinistic little gringo did. Although he never got the credit for it.

Yet he was lucky, at that. After all, I was supposed to murder him.

Not that I am a professional assassin, you understand. The daughter of *el Presidente* is no common thug. I followed a higher calling: national honor, patriotism, love of my people and my father. Especially, love of my father.

Ecuador was, and still is, a democracy. My beloved father was, but sadly is no longer, its *Presidente*. Above all else, you must realize that Ecuador was, and always had been, among the poorest nations of the Earth.

Ah, but we owned something of inestimable value. Or at least, we owned a part of it. Or at the very least, we claimed ownership of a part of it.

The equator. It runs across our noble country. Our nation's very name is equatorial. An imaginary line, you say. Not entirely imaginary. For above the equator, some thirty-five thousand kilometers above it, lies the only region of space where satellites may be placed in stationary orbits. The space people call it the *geostationary orbit*, or GEO.

A satellite in GEO rotates around the Earth in precisely

58

the same twenty-three hours, fifty-six minutes and few odd seconds that the Earth itself takes to turn one revolution. Thus a satellite in GEO will appear to hover over one spot above the equator. Communications satellites are placed in GEO so that antennas on the ground can lock onto them easily. They do not wander around the sky, as satellites at lower or higher altitudes do.

It was my father's genius to understand the value of the equator. It was also his sad destiny to have Sam Gunn as his nemesis.

"The gringos and the Europeans get rich with their satellites," my father told the other eleven delegations to the meeting.

"And the Japanese, too," said the representative from Zaire.

"Exactly so."

As host to this meeting of the Twelve Equatorial Nations, my father stood at the head of the long polished conference table and gave the opening speech. He was a majestic figure in the captain-general's uniform of sky blue that he had chosen to wear. With the lifts in his gleaming boots he looked almost tall. The uniform tunic's shoulders were broad and sturdy, the medals gleaming on its breast looked impressive even though they were decorations he had awarded himself. He had long been darkening his hair, but now it was thinning noticeably. He had brought in specialists from North America, from Europe, and even China; there was nothing they could do except recommend an operation to replace his disappearing hair. My father was brave in many ways, but the thought of personal pain made him hesitate.

So he stood before the other delegates with a receding hairline. I thought his high forehead made him look more handsome, more intellectual. Yet he longed for the full leonine mane of his younger days.

My father had spent the better part of two years working, pleading, cajoling to bring these Twelve together. They had come reluctantly, grudgingly, I thought. But they had come. There was much to gain if we could capture the geostationary orbit for ourselves.

I served my father as his personal secretary, so I sat against the wall to one side of his imposing figure, together with the other secretaries and aides and body-guards. The delegates were of all hues and sizes: the massive Ugandan so dark his skin seemed almost to shine; the Brazilian dapper and dainty in his white-silk suit; the silver-haired representative from Kiribati dressed in the colorful robes of his Pacific atolls. One could say that these Twelve truly represented the entire human race in all its variety, except for the fact that they were all male. I was the only woman present. Not even one of the other aides was a woman.

Although Ecuador was a poor nation, my father had spared no expense for this conference. The table was sumptuously set with decanters of wine and stronger spirits, trays of Caspian caviar and Argentine beef. The people may be poor, my father often said, but the *Presidente* must rise above their shortcomings. After all, what are taxes for? The miserable revolutionaries in the mountains vowed to put an end to my father's displays of wealth, and the sour-faced journalists in the cities coined slogans against him, but the people accepted their *Presidente* as they have always accepted the forces of nature over which they have no control.

My father thundered on, his powerful voice making the wines vibrate in their crystal decanters. "The corporations of the northern hemisphere use *our* territory and give us nothing for it. Imperialism! That's what it is, nothing but naked imperialism!"

The representatives applauded his words. They were stirred, I could see. They all agreed with my father, each and every one of them. The rich and powerful corporations had taken something that we wanted for ourselves.

But the Indonesian, slim and dark, with the big soulful eyes of a frightened child, waited until the applause ended, then asked softly, "But what can we do about it? We have tried appeals to the United Nations, and they have done nothing for us."

"We have a legal right to the equatorial orbit," insisted the Kenyan, preaching to the choir. "Our territorial rights are being violated."

The Brazilian shook his head. "Territorial rights end at the edge of the atmosphere." The Brazilians had their own space operations running, although they claimed they were not making any profits from it. Rumor had it that key members of their government were siphoning the money into their own pockets.

"They most certainly do not!" my father snapped. "Territorial rights extend to infinity."

Two-thirds of the men around the table were lawyers, and they immediately fell to arguing. I knew the legal situation as well as any of them. Historically, a nation's territorial rights extended from its boundaries out to infinity. But such legal rights became a shambles once satellites began orbiting the Earth.

The Russians started it all back in 1957 with their original Sputnik, which sailed over virtually every nation on Earth without obtaining prior permission from any of them. No one could shoot down that first satellite, so it established the *de facto* precedent. But now things were different; antisatellite weapons existed. True, the big nations refused to sell them to their smaller neighbors. But such weapons were built by corporations, and there were ways to get what one wanted from the corporations—for money.

My father's strong voice cut through the babble of argument. "To hell with the legalities!"

That stunned them all into silence.

"When a nation's vital interests are being usurped by foreigners, when a nation's legal rights are being trampled under the heels of imperialists, when a nation's wealth is being stolen from its people and their chosen leaders—then that nation must fight back with any and every means at its disposal."

The Indonesian paled. "You are speaking of war."

"Exactly so!"

"War?" echoed the Ugandan, dropping the finger sandwich he had been nibbling.

"We have no other course," my father insisted.

"But . . . war?" squeaked the slim and timid representative from the Maldives. "Against the United States? Europe? Japan?"

My father smiled grimly. "No. Not against any nation. We must make war against the corporations that are operating in space."

The Brazilian ran a fingertip across his pencil-thin moustache. "It should be possible to destroy a few satellites with ASATs." He was showing that he knew not only the political and military situation, but the technical jargon, as well.

"Fire off a single antisatellite weapon and the UN Peacekeepers will swoop down on you like avenging angels," warned the delegate from Gabon.

"The same UN that refuses to consider our request for justice," my father grumbled.

The Colombian representative smiled knowingly. "There are many ways to make war," he said. "Space facilities are extremely fragile. A few well-placed bombs, they can be very small, actually. A few very public assassinations. It can all be blamed on the Muslims or the ecologists."

"Or the feminists," snapped the Indonesian, himself a Muslim and a devoted ecologist. Everyone else in the room laughed.

"Exactly so," said my father. "We pick one corporation and bend it to our will. Then the others will follow."

Thus we went to war against Sam Gunn.

My father was no fool. Making war—even the limited kind of terrorists' war—against one of the giant multinational corporations would have been dangerous, even suicidal. After all, a corporation such as Rockledge International had an operating budget larger than the gross national product of most of the Twelve Nations. Their corporate security forces outgunned most of our armies.

But Sam Gunn's corporation, VCI, was small and vulnerable. It looked like a good place to start.

So our meeting ended with unanimous agreement. The Twelve Equatorial Nations issued the Declaration of

Quito, proclaiming that the space over the Equator was our sovereign territory, and we intended to defend it against foreign invaders just as we would defend the sacred soil of our homelands.

The Declaration was received with nearly hysterical fervor all through Latin America. In Ecuador, even the revolutionaries and the news media reluctantly praised my father for his boldness. North of the Rio Grande, however, it was ignored by the media, the government, and the people. Europe and Japan received it with similar iciness.

My farseeing father had expected nothing more. A week after the meeting of the Twelve he told me over dinner, "The gringos choose to ignore us. Like ostriches, they believe that if they pay us no attention, we will go away."

"What will be your next move, Papa?" I asked.

He smiled a fatherly smile at me. "Not my move, Juanita, my beautiful one. The next move will be yours."

I was stunned. Flattered. And a bit frightened.

My father had chosen me for the crucial task of infiltrating VCI. I had been educated at UCLA and held a degree in computer programming, despite my father's grumbling that a daughter should study more feminine subjects, such as nutrition (by which he meant cooking). I also had a burning fervor to help my people. Now I received a rapid course in espionage and sabotage from no less than the director of our secret police himself.

"You must be very careful," my father told me, once my training was concluded.

"I will be, Papa," I said. I had joined him for breakfast on the veranda of the summer palace, up in the foothills where the air was clean and deliciously cool.

He looked deep into my eyes, and his own eyes misted over. "To send my only child to war is not an easy thing, you know." He was being slightly inaccurate. I was his only legitimate child, and it was obvious that he had been planning to use me this way for some time.

"Yet," he went on, "I must think and act as *el Presidente*, rather than as a loving father."

"I understand, Papa."

"You will be a heroine for your people. A new Mata Hari."

The original Mata Hari had been a slut and so poor at espionage that she was caught and executed. I realized that my father did not know that. He was a politician, not a student of history.

Turning his head to look out over the balcony to the terraced hillsides where the *peons* were hard at work on the coca fields, he murmured, "There is much money to be made in space."

There was much money being made from the coca, I knew. But since the cocaine trade was still illegal, the money that came from it could not be put into the national treasury. My father had to keep it for himself and his family, despite his heartfelt desire to help the destitute *peons* who were forced to labor from sunrise to sunset.

The rebels in the hills claimed that my father was corrupt. They were radical ecologists, I was told, who wanted to stop the lumbering and mining and coca cultivation that provided our poor nation's pitiful income. My father saw our seizure of the equatorial orbit as a means of making more money for our country, money that he desperately needed to buy off the rebels—and the next election.

He dabbed at his eyes with his damask napkin, then rose from the breakfast table. I got up, too. The servants began clearing the dishes away as we walked side by side from the veranda into the big old house, heading for the door and the limousine waiting for me.

"Be a good soldier, my child," he said to me once we had reached the front door. The butler was waiting there with my packed travel bag. "Be brave. Be fearless."

"I will do my best, Papa."

"I know you will." He gripped me in a full embrace, unashamed of the tears that streamed from his eyes or the fact that he was so much shorter than I that I had to bend almost double to allow him to kiss my cheeks.

My own eyes were misty, as well. Finally he let go of me and I went quickly down the steps to the waiting

limousine. While the butler put my bag into the trunk, I
turned back to my father, came to attention, and snapped
a military salute to him. He returned my salute, then
turned away, unable to watch me step into the limo and
start the long ride to the airport.

Thus I went to war.

I had been surprised, at first, that Sam Gunn's company
had hired me on nothing more than the strength of the
faked university credentials of the fictitious person that
my father's secret police had created for me. Of course,
I knew enough computer programming to pass—I hoped.
And of even more course, it would never do for the VCI
people to know that I was the daughter of the man who
had issued the Declaration of Quito. Even if they ignored
our Declaration, I reasoned, they could not possibly be
ignorant of it.

VCI was a surprisingly small operation. I reported to
their headquarters in Orlando, a modest office building
quite near the vast Disney World complex. There were
only a couple of dozen employees there, including the
company's president, a lanky silver-haired former astronaut named Spencer Johansen.

"Call me Spence," he said when I met him, my first
day at VCI. I had just sat down at my own desk in my
own office—actually nothing more than a cubbyhole
formed by movable plastic partitions that were only
shoulder high.

Johansen strolled in, smiling affably, and sat casually
on the corner of my bare desk. He offered his hand, and
I took it in a firm grip.

You must understand that, by any reasonable standard,
I was quite an attractive young lady. My hair is the honey
blond of my Castilian ancestry. My figure is generous. I
have been told that my eyes are as deep and sparkling as
a starry midnight sky. (The young lieutenant who told me
that was quickly transferred to a remote post high in the
Andes to fight the rebels.) I am rather tall for a woman
in my country, although many North American women
are as tall as I, and even taller. Nonetheless, I was not

that much shorter than Spence, whom I judged to be at least 190 centimeters in height.

"Welcome aboard," he said. His smile was dazzling.

"Thank you," I answered in English. "I am happy to be here." I had worked hard to perfect the Los Angelino accent that my fictitious *persona* called for.

His eyes were as blue as a Scandinavian summer sky. Despite his smile, however, I got the impression that he was probing me, searching for my true motives.

"We had planned to start you off on some of the more routine stuff, but we've got a bit of an emergency cooking and we're kinda short-handed—as usual."

Before I could reply he went on, "Can you handle a VR-17 simulator? Reprogram it?"

I nodded cautiously, wondering if this was a true emergency or some kind of a test.

"Okay," Spence said. "Come on down to the simulations center." He headed for the opening in the partitions that was the doorway to my cubicle. There was no door to it.

I followed him, stride for stride, as he hurried along the corridor. He was wearing a soft blue open-necked, short-sleeved shirt and denim jeans. I wore a simple modest blouse of salmon pink and comfortable russet slacks. He glanced at me and grinned. "You play tennis?"

"A little." I had won every tournament I had ever entered; the daughter of *el Presidente* had to win, but I thought it would be best to be modest with him.

"Thought so."

"Oh?"

"You're not puffing," he said. "Not many of these desk-jockeys can keep up with me."

"I am curious," I said, as we entered the simulations center. It was nothing more than a large windowless room, empty except for the big mainframe computer standing in its center and the desks with terminals atop them set up in a ring around the mainframe. The four corners of the room were bare but for a single cheap plastic chair in each corner.

A man was sitting in one of those chairs, with a virtual-realty helmet covering his face and data gloves on both his hands, which twitched in the empty air, manipulating controls that existed only in the VR programming.

"Curious about what?" Spence asked as he showed me to one of the computer terminals.

I slid into the little wheeled chair. "You are the president of this company, right?"

"Yep."

"But I had the impression that the company belonged to someone named Sam Gunn."

Before Spence could answer, the man in the VR helmet began swearing horribly at the top of his voice. He called down the wrath of God on everyone connected with the machinery he was supposed to be operating, on the person or persons who had programmed the VR simulation, on Isaac Newton and Albert Einstein and all the mathematicians in the world. All the while his hands gesticulated wildly, as if he were desperately trying to ward of a host of devils.

Strangely, Spence grinned at the interruption. Then he turned back to me, and said, loud enough to be heard over the continuing tirade of abuse, "I'm the president of VCI, but Sam Gunn is the founder and owns more stock than anybody else. He doesn't like to sell shares to anyone who isn't an employee."

"I can become a stockholder?"

"We have a very generous stock option plan," Spence replied, almost yelling to be heard over the continuing screaming. "Didn't you watch your employee orientation video?"

In truth, I had not. It had never occurred to me that employees might become partial owners of the company. A very clever gringo, this Sam Gunn. He undoubtedly keeps the majority of shares in his own hands and doles out a pittance to his employees, thereby gaining their loyalty.

As if he could read my thoughts, Spence said, "Sam's a minority stockholder now. My wife and I own more shares than anybody else except Sam, but no individual owns more than a few percent."

Wife? Spence was married. For some reason I felt a pang of disappointment.

"Sam Gunn must be an unusual man," I said, loud enough to be heard over the rantings from the corner of the room. But the instant I started to speak, the ravings stopped, and my voice shrilled stupidly. I felt my face flame red. Spence's grin widened but he said nothing.

"I would like to meet him someday," I said, more softly, as I turned to the computer terminal.

"You can meet him right now," said Spence. "That's him in the VR rig."

My mouth must have dropped open. I spun the little chair around to see Spence looking off toward the corner. The man there was pulling off his VR helmet, still muttering obscenities.

I stared at Sam Gunn as he got up from the chair and tugged the data gloves off. He was short, much shorter than I. His torso was stocky, solid, although I could see that his belly bulged the faded blue coveralls he wore. His face was round, with a little snub of a nose and a sprinkling of freckles. Hair the color of rusted wire, cut very short, and sprinkled with gray—which he insisted (I soon learned) was due to exposure to cosmic radiation in space, not from age. From this distance, halfway across the room, I could not tell the color of his eyes. But I could easily see that he was angry, blazing furious, in fact.

"Goddammit, Spence," he said, stamping toward us, "if we don't get this simulation fixed and fixed damned soon, somebody's gonna lose his ass out there."

Spence put a fatherly hand on my shoulder. "Here's the gal who's going to fix it. Just started with us this morning." My shoulder tingled from his touch.

Sam gave me a stern look. "This kid?"

"Juanita O'Rourke," Spence introduced me. It was my alias, of course.

Sam stared at me. Standing, he was about the same height as I was, sitting. I saw that his eyes were a bluish green hazel color, flecked with golden highlights.

"From Los Angeles," Spence added. "Computer programming degree from—"

"I don't care where you're from or where you went to school," said Sam Gunn. "I love you."

I had heard that he was a womanizer of the worst sort. Some of his escapades had been included in the dossier my father's secret police had given me to study. The dossier hinted at much more. Strangely, my father never mentioned the danger that Sam Gunn might pose to me. Perhaps he did not know of it. After all, his attention was focused on affairs of state, not affairs of the bedroom.

I got to my feet and put on a modest smile. Partly it was because I towered nearly thirty centimeters over Sam Gunn. The feeling gave me joy.

"You give your heart quickly," I said, adding to myself silently, and very often.

His round, freckled face turned into an elf's delighted countenance. "Will you have dinner with me tonight?"

I hesitated just long enough to let him think I seriously considered his invitation. "Not tonight," I said. "I just arrived here and there's so much to do . . ."

Spence cleared his throat, and said, "You want this simulation checked out, don't you?"

All Sam's anger and frustration had disappeared as quickly as a dry leaf is blown away by a gust of wind. "Okay, Esmeralda—"

"Juanita," I corrected.

Sam shook his head. "To me you're Esmeralda, the beautiful gypsy girl that Quasimodo loves."

"I am not a gypsy."

"But you're beautiful," he said.

"And you will be Quasimodo?"

Sam dropped into a crouch and twisted his head up at a bizarre angle. "I'll be whoever you want me to be, Esmeralda."

He made me laugh.

"The simulation," Spence reminded him.

"Oh. Yeah. That."

Fortunately, the problem was simple enough for me to solve, although it took several days' intense work. VCI's major business was removing old commsats that had ceased to function from the geosynchronous orbit so that new commsats could be placed there. There were only a finite number of slots available in GEO, and they were strictly allocated by the International Telecommunications Authority. VCI crews flew from space stations in low Earth orbit (LEO) to GEO and removed the dead commsats to make room for new ones.

It was a small part of the satellite communications industry, but a key factor. VCI also had contracts to sweep debris out of the lower orbits where the space stations flew. I learned that the company's name originally stood for Vacuum Cleaners, Incorporated. Sam's company cleaned up the vacuum of orbital space.

More recently, Sam had begun sending people up to GEO to repair malfunctioning commsats. It was cheaper to fix them than to replace them—in theory, at least. In practice, the costs of sending astronauts to GEO even for a few hours was almost as much as replacing a malfunctioning satellite.

The virtual-reality simulation that Sam was frustrated over was one in which an operator could remain aboard the space station in LEO and remotely direct an unmanned spacecraft to repair a malfunctioning satellite in GEO.

"Bring the dead back to life," as Sam put it.

"It would be much safer for our people if they could stay in the space station rather than fly up to GEO," Spence explained to me. "GEO's in the middle of the outer Van Allen belt. Astronauts can't stay there very long because of the radiation."

"I see," I said.

"We could save a bundle of money if we could do this job remotely," said Sam eagerly. "Just the drop in our insurance costs could pay for the whole program."

Spence added, "In the long run we could operate right here from the ground. No need to send people to one of the space stations, even."

"That'd save even more money," Sam agreed happily.

"But the simulation keeps glitching," said Spence.

"And until we get it right in the simulator we can't try it in the real world."

Thus the burden of their hopes was placed on my young shoulders. I thought it strange that something so vital would be entrusted to a totally new and untried employee. Was this a trap of some sort? Or a test? Soon enough I learned that it was typical of the way Sam Gunn ran his company. He kept his staff as small as he possibly could, hiring only when there was no other way to get a necessary job done. And make no mistake about it, Sam Gunn ran VCI. Despite his lofty title, Spence took orders from Sam. Most of the time.

The problem with the simulation was not terribly difficult. If Sam had not been so impatient, his own staff personnel or a consultant would eventually have found it. But what Sam wanted was instant results, which meant that I spent virtually twenty-four hours a day working on the problem. Except for the hour or so each day I spent fending off Sam's invitations to dinner, to lunch, to a suite in the zero-gravity honeymoon hotel he wanted to build in orbit.

Within a few days I had the program running so smoothly that Sam was willing to try a test in orbit. And I realized that I could sabotage his operation quite easily. In fact, I planted a bug in the program that I could activate whenever I chose to.

I discussed my accomplishment with my father on the direct phone link from our consulate in Orlando. I drove to the consulate in the dark of night, well past midnight, to make certain that no one from VCI would see me.

I had feared that I would wake my father from his justly earned sleep. As it turned out, he was in bed, but not asleep. At first he did not activate the phone's video, which puzzled me. When he finally did, I realized that he was not alone in his bed. He tried to hide her, but I could see that a tousle-haired young trollop lay beside him, bundled under the sheets. She peeked out from behind my father's back, showing a bare shoulder, a pair of flashing dark eyes, and piles of raven black hair.

My father was delighted with the progress I had made in little more than a week.

"I can sabotage their mission to repair satellites," I reported to him, trying to ignore his companion. She could not have been much older than I. "And they will never even know that sabotage has occurred."

"Good!" He beamed at me. "Excellent! But do not attack them just yet. Let them run a successful mission or two. Wait until the strategic moment to strike."

"I understand, Papa."

"You are doing well, my child."

I looked past him to the young woman sharing his bed. My mother had been dead for many years, and my father was still a man of vigor. Yet I felt angry. I did not tell him that Sam Gunn was attracted to me.

"And you are well, Papa?" My question sounded acidly cynical to my own ears.

Yet my beloved father obviously did not feel my anger. "I am in good health," he reported smilingly. "Although the rebels have surrounded the army base at Zamora."

"What?" I felt a double pang of alarm. The lieutenant who had been infatuated with me was at the Zamora base.

"Not to worry, my daughter. We are reinforcing the base by helicopter and will soon drive the scum back to their caves in the mountains."

Yet I did worry. The rebels seemed to get bolder, stronger, each year. I went back to work, angry with my father yet frightened for him. We needed to wrest control of the equatorial orbit from the gringo corporations, quickly. I began to look for more ways to sabotage VCI. I even let Sam take me out to dinner several times, although each evening ended at the front door of my apartment building with nothing more romantic than a handshake. Sam was not exactly a perfect gentleman: He was as persistent as a goat in mating season. I fended him off, however. My arms were longer than his.

"Esmeralda," he complained one evening, "you're turning my love life into the petrified forest."

We were at the entrance to my apartment building. I

thought of it as my castle, its walls and electronic door locks my defense against Sam's assaults.

"I agreed to have dinner with you," I said, "nothing more."

He sighed heavily. "I guess I'm paying you too much."

"Paying me . . . ?"

With an almost wicked grin he said, "If you were broke and hungry, you'd appreciate me more, I betcha."

"What an evil thing to say!"

"Well, look at this apartment building," he went on. "It's a frigging luxury palace! I'm just paying you too much money. You're living too well—"

I had to cut off his line of thought before he realized that my salary could never pay the rent on my apartment. Before he began to ask himself how a poor computer programmer from Los Angeles could afford the clothes and the sports car I had.

"So you want women to be starving and poor," I snapped at him. "Or perhaps you prefer them barefoot and pregnant?"

He shrugged good-naturedly. "Barefoot is okay."

I did not have to pretend to be angry. I could feel the blood heating my cheeks. "Sam, the days of male domination over women were finished long ago," I told him. "Don't you understand that?"

"I'm not interested in domination. All I want is a little cooperation."

"You are a hopeless chauvinist, Sam."

He broke into an impish grin. "Not quite hopeless, Esmeralda. I still have some hope."

It was impossible to dislike Sam, even though I tried. But at least I stopped him from asking himself how I could afford my lifestyle on the salary he was paying me.

Yet it was Spence that I felt drawn to. He was quietly competent, always even-tempered, extremely capable. I knew he was married, but somehow I felt that his marriage was not all that happy for him. Perhaps it was because I wanted to believe so. Perhaps it was because he was a kind, fatherly, caring, truly gentle man.

And then I met Spence's wife. Her name was Bonnie Jo. Apparently she had once been engaged to marry Sam Gunn but somehow had married Spence instead. The story I gathered from my fellow workers was that her father had provided the money for Sam to start VCI. Spence had mentioned that he and his wife were both stockholders, which made me wonder if her father was still a financial backer of the company.

But it was not her finances that stunned me. It was her beauty. Bonnie Jo's hair was the color of lustrous gold, her eyes a rich, deep, mysterious grayish green. She was almost as tall as I, her figure slim and athletic, her clothes always impeccably stylish. Compared to her, I felt fat and stupid. Her voice was low, melodious; not the piercing high-pitched shrill of so many gringo women. But her eyes were hard, calculating; her beauty was cold, like an exquisite statue or a fashionably draped mannequin.

It quickly became clear to me that she no longer loved Spence, if she ever had. She was cool to him, sometimes cruelly so, as when she bought herself a sapphire ring for her own birthday and loudly announced that Spence could not have afforded it on the salary Sam gave him.

For his part, Spence buried himself in his work, driving himself deeper and deeper into the technical side of VCI, leaving the administration to Bonnie Jo and the office staff. This brought us together every day. I realized that I was falling in love with this handsome, kind, suffering older man. I also realized that he saw me as nothing more than another employee, almost young enough to be his daughter.

Spence traveled to Space Station Alpha to personally test the program for remotely repairing satellites in GEO. I remained in Orlando, at VCI's mission control center. It was a tiny room, big enough only for three monitoring stations. Windowless, it would have been unbearably stuffy if the air-conditioning had not been turned up so high that it became unbearably frigid. The front wall was one huge display screen, which could be broken into smaller displays if we desired.

I sat at the right-hand monitor, almost shivering despite

the sweater I wore, ready to give whatever assistance I could to the man who was actually controlling Spence's mission. We both wore earphones clamped over our heads, with pin-sized mikes at our lips. However, the mission controller was supposed to do all the talking; I was told to remain silent. Sam took the third seat, on the left, but it was empty most of the time because Sam hardly sat still for two seconds at a time. He was constantly bouncing out of his chair, pacing behind us, muttering to himself.

"This has gotta work, guys," he mumbled. "The whole future of the company's riding on this mission."

I thought he was being overly dramatic. Only later did I come to realize that he was not.

The big display screen before us showed a telescope view from Alpha of our Orbital Transfer Vehicle as it approached the satellite that needed repair. The OTV was an ugly contraption: clusters of spherical tanks and ungainly metal struts. At its front a pair of mechanical arms poked out stiffly. Ridiculously small rocket nozzles studded the vehicle fore and aft and around its middle; they reminded me of the bulbous eyes of a mutant iguana.

I could feel Sam's breath on my neck as Spence's voice said, "Shifting to onboard camera view."

"Roger, onboard view," said the mission controller, sitting at my elbow.

The screen abruptly showed a close-up view of the malfunctioning satellite. It seemed huge as it hung serenely against the black backdrop of space.

"Starting rendezvous sequence," Spence's voice said. Calmly, quietly, as unruffled as a man tying his shoelaces.

Sam was just the opposite. "Keep your eyes glued on the readouts," he snapped. "And your finger on the abort button. The *last* thing we want is a collision out there."

He was speaking to the mission controller, I knew, but his words applied to me as well. I had inserted a subroutine into the automatic rendezvous program that would fire an extra burst of thrust at the critical moment. Not only would the OTV be destroyed, but the communications satellite, too. VCI would be sued by the commsat's insurer, at the very least. All I had to do was touch one keypad on the board in front of me. Despite the frigid air-conditioning I began to perspire.

But I kept my hands in my lap as calmly, methodically, Spence achieved the rendezvous and then directed the OTV's machinery to remove the malfunctioning power conditioner from the commsat and insert the new one. I watched the screen, fascinated, almost hypnotized, as the robot arms did their delicate work, directed by Spence's fingers from more than thirty thousand kilometers' distance.

At last the mission controller said into his microphone, "I copy power conditioning checkout in the green. Move off for communications test."

"Moving off for comm test." The mission plan called for the OTV to back away from the commsat while its owners in Tokyo tested the new power conditioner to make certain it properly fed electrical power to the satellite's forty transponders.

The display screen showed the commsat dwindling away. And then the great glowing blue curve of the Earth swung into view, speckled with dazzling white clouds. I felt my breath gush from me. It was overwhelming.

I heard Spence chuckle in my earphone. "I'll bet that's Juanita."

"Yes," I replied without thinking. I glanced at the mission controller. Instead of frowning at my breaking the mission protocol, he was grinning at me.

"Never seen the view from orbit before, huh?" Spence asked.

"Only photographs in magazines or videos," I said.

"Welcome to the club," said Spence. "It still gets me, every time."

"Let's get back to work, shall we?" Sam said. But his voice was strangely subdued.

The word came from Tokyo that the power conditioner functioned perfectly. A seventy-million-dollar commsat had been saved by replacing one faulty component.

Now it was Sam who gushed out a heartfelt sigh.

"Good work, guys. C'mon, I'm gonna buy you all the best dinner in town."

I wanted to stay at my monitoring station and talk with Spence. But I could not. The mission controller cut the link to him even before I could say *adios*.

For some reason, Sam insisted that Bonnie Jo join us. So he bundled the four of us into his leased Mercedes and drove us to a Moroccan restaurant on the strip just outside Disney World.

"You're gonna love this place," Sam assured us as our turbaned host guided us to a table by the dance floor, a big round engraved brass table, barely a few centimeters off the floor. There were no chairs, only pillows scattered around the table.

"Relax, kick your shoes off," Sam said as he flopped onto one of the big pillows. "The belly dancers start in a few minutes."

The restaurant was small, almost intimate. Although smoking in restaurants had been outlawed for decades, the management filtered a thin gray haze (nontoxic, the menu assured us) through the air-conditioning system. For "atmosphere," the menu said. The food was surprisingly good, roasted goat and couscous and a tangy sauce that reminded me of the best Mexican dishes. But it was clear that Sam had come to see the dancers. And that he had seen them many times before. They all seemed to recognize him and to spend most of their performances close enough to our table for me to smell the heavy perfumes they used.

Our mission controller's name was Gene Redding. He was well into his forties, balding, portly, and very competent at his job. As he sat on the pillows gazing up at the dancers gyrating within arm's reach, his face turned redder and redder and his bald pate began to glisten with perspiration. His glasses kept fogging, and he constantly removed them to wipe them clear, squinting at the dancers all the while. From the silly grin on his face it was obvious that he was enjoying the entertainment.

Conversation was impossible while the dancers were on. The reedy music and thumping percussion were too

loud, and the men were too engrossed. I saw that Bonnie
Jo was just as interested in the dancers as the men were.
I must admit that they were fascinating: erotic without
being vulgar. God knows what fantasies they stirred in
the men's minds.

It was on the drive back to the office that the argument
began.

"We turned the corner today," Sam said happily as he
drove along Interstate 4. "Now the money's gonna start
pouring in."

"And you'll pour it all out again, won't you, Sam?"
said Bonnie Jo.

She was sitting in the backseat, with me. Gene was up
front with Sam.

"I'm gonna invest it in the company's growth," Sam
said lightly.

"You're going to sink it into your idiotic orbital hotel
scheme." It sounded to me as if Bonnie Jo was speaking
through gritted teeth.

"Idiotic?" Sam snapped. "Whattaya mean, idiotic?
People are gonna pay good money for vacations in zero
g. It's gonna be the honeymoon capital of the world!"

"Sam, if just for once you'd think with your brain
instead of your testicles, you'd see what a damned fool
scheme this is!"

"Yeah, sure. They laughed at Edison, too."

"We can't piss away our profits on your harebrained
schemes, Sam!"

"As long as I'm the biggest stockholder I can."

I noticed that we were going faster as the argument got
hotter. Sam was using neither the highway's electronic
guidance system nor the car's cruise control; his rising
blood pressure made his foot lean harder on the car's
accelerator.

Bonnie Jo said, "Not if I can get a bloc to outvote you
at the annual meeting."

"You tried that before, and it didn't get you very far,
did it?"

"Spence will vote on my side this time," she said.

The other cars were blurring past us, streaks of headlights on one side, streaks of red taillights on the other. I felt like a crew member in a relativistic starship.

"The hell he will," Sam yelled back. "Spence is solidly behind me on this. So's your father."

"My father has already given me his proxy."

Sam was silent for several moments. We sped past a huge double trailer rig like a bullet passing a tortoise.

"So what," he said at last. "Most of the employees'll vote my way. And that includes Spence."

"We'll see," said Bonnie Jo.

"We sure as hell will."

So there were internal strains within VCI's top management. My discovery of this pleased me very much; mainly, I must confess, because I realized that Spence and Bonnie Jo were truly unhappy with one another. I began to think that I might use their differences to destroy VCI—and their marriage.

But Sam had other ideas. So did my father. And also, so did the rebels.

The following Friday afternoon Sam popped into my cubbyhole of an office, whistling off-key and grinning at the same time. It made him look rather like a lopsided jack-o'-lantern.

"Got any plans for this weekend?" he asked me as he pulled up the only other chair in my cubicle, turned it backwards, and straddled it.

I certainly did. I was planning to spend the weekend at my desk, studying every scrap of data I could call up on my computer about VCI's finances. I already knew enough about the technical operations of the company. Sam's argument with Bonnie Jo had opened my eyes to the possibilities of ruining the corporation by financial manipulations.

"I will be working all weekend," I said.

"You sure will," said Sam, crossing his arms over the back of the little plastic chair and leaning his chin on them.

His mischievous grin told me that he had something unusual in mind. I merely stared at him, saying nothing, knowing that he was bursting to tell me whatever it was.

Sure enough, Sam could not remain silent for more than two heartbeats. "Ever been in orbit?" he asked. Quickly he added, "Literally, I mean. In space."

I blinked with surprise. "No. Never."

His grin widened. "Okay, then. Pack an overnight bag. You're going up tomorrow morning. I'll have you back here in time to be at your desk first thing Monday morning."

"You're taking me into space?"

"Space Station Alpha," he said. "You'll love it."

"With you?"

He tried to put on a serious expression. "Strictly business, Esmeralda. Strictly business. You'll have a private compartment in the one-g section."

"But why?"

"Company policy. Everybody who works for VCI gets a chance to go into orbit."

"This is the first time anyone's told me about it," I said.

His grin returned. "Well . . . it's a new company policy. I just made it, as a matter of fact."

I realized his intention. "So you merely want to get *me* into space with you."

"It'll be business, I swear," Sam said, trying to look innocent.

"What business?" I asked. All my instincts were ringing alarm bells within me.

"I need a woman's opinion about my plans for the orbital hotel. Can't ask Bonnie Jo, she's dead set against the idea."

I must have frowned, because he swiftly added, "I'm talking about the way the compartments are done up, the facilities and the decorations and all that. The food service. I need a woman's point of view, honest."

He almost sounded reasonable.

But his grin would not fade away. "Of course, if the mood strikes you and you start to feel romantic, I could show you the zero-g section of the station and we could accomplish feats that could never be done on Earth."

"No!" I snapped. "Never!"

"Aw, come on," Sam pleaded like a little boy. "I'll behave myself, honest. I really do need your opinion. It's business, really it is."

My mind was racing furiously. The more I knew about Sam's operations the easier it would be to trip him up, I reasoned. However, I knew that no matter how much he protested, his lecherous male mind still entertained the hope that he could seduce me, still harbored fantasies of making love with me in zero gravity. I had to admit to myself that I harbored a similar fantasy—except that it was Spence I fantasized about, not Sam.

"Listen," Sam said, interrupting my train of thought, "I know you think I'm a male chauvinist and all that. Okay, maybe I am. But I'm not a rapist. If anything happens between us, it'll be because you want it to happen as much as I do."

"I should be perfectly safe, then."

He laughed. "See? You've got nothing to fear."

Still I hesitated. His reputation worried me. Apparently he could be irresistibly charming when he wanted to be.

He heaved a great, disappointed sigh, threw his hands up over his head, and said, "All right, all right. You want a chaperon to go with us? You got it. I'll ask Spence to come along, too. How's that?"

I had to exert every iota of self-control I possessed to keep myself from leaping out from behind my desk and shouting, Yes! Yes! Very deliberately, I turned my gaze away from Sam's eager eyes and studied the blank wall behind him, pretending to think mightily.

At last I said, "A chaperon is proper. But it should be a woman. A *dueña.*"

Sam sighed again, this time from exasperation. "Look, I can't shuttle people up and back to a space station just to keep your Hispanic proprieties. D'you know how much it costs?"

"But you are taking me," I said.

"I need your mother-loving feminine opinion about the hotel accommodations, dammit! And Spence has useful work to do for the company at Alpha. That's it!"

"Very well," I said with as much reluctance as I could feign. "Spence is a married gentleman. He is not as good as a proper *dueña*, but I suppose he can be trusted to act as our chaperon."

Sam jumped to his feet, bowed deeply, and pranced out of my cubicle. Only when I was certain that he could not see me did I allow myself to smile.

Less than a quarter hour later a young man appeared at my open doorway. He looked like a Latino: somber dark eyes, thick curly black hair, skin the color of smoked parchment. He was handsome, in a smoldering, sullen way. Sensuous lips.

"Ms. O'Rourke?" he asked.

"Yes."

"I'm supposed to give you an orientation tour. For your ride up to Alpha." His tone was little short of insolent.

"Right now? I'm busy . . ."

He shrugged disdainfully. "Whenever you're ready, princess. Sam told me to hang around until you've got an hour of free time."

Princess? I seethed inwardly, but maintained a calm exterior. I would not give this sneering youth the satisfaction of seeing that he could anger me.

"I won't be ready until sometime after six," I said.

Again he shrugged. "Then I'll hafta hang around until after six."

"Where will I find you?"

A spark of something glinted in his eyes. Perhaps it was anger. "I'll be in the simulations lab, back down the main corridor, past—"

"I know where the simulations lab is," I said.

"Okay. See you whenever you get there." He turned and started to leave.

"Wait!" I called. "What is your name?"

"Gregory Molina," he answered over his shoulder. "Extension 434."

It was close to seven-thirty before I finished my day's work and made my way to the simulations lab. Although quitting time at VCI was nominally six, there were still plenty of people in the corridors and offices. Many of Sam's employees worked long hours. Most of them, in fact.

But the simulations lab seemed deserted. The computer in its center was dark and silent. The overhead lights were dimmed. I stood in the doorway frowning with uncertainty. He had said he would be here. How dare he leave without informing me?

"You ready for your orientation spin?"

The voice behind me startled me. I turned and saw that it was Molina. He held a frosted can of cola in one hand.

"Dinner," he said, hoisting the can before my face. "Want some?"

"No thank you. Let's get this over with."

"Okay. It's pretty simple," he said as he ushered me inside the lab. The ceiling lights brightened automatically. "IAA safety regulations require anyone flying into orbit for the first time to have an orientation simulation and lecture. The lecture is taped, and you can see it on one of the display screens here or take a copy home with you and view it at your leisure. Which do you prefer?"

"I'll see it here," I said.

He nodded. "Sure. There's another half hour I'll have to hang around twiddling my thumbs."

His attitude angered me. "Really!" I snapped. "If it's your job to do this, why are you so nasty about it?"

He stared straight into my eyes. "My *job, señorita,* is maintaining these goddamned computers. What I'm doing now is extra."

"Maintaining the computers? But I've never seen you here."

"You haven't noticed," he replied sullenly. "I've been here. I've seen you plenty of times. But you just look right past the hired help, like some goddamned princess or something."

"That's no reason to be angry with me."

"That's not why I'm pissed off."

"And there's no need for such vulgar language!"

"*Dispense Usted perdón, princesa,*" he said, with a horrible accent.

"Where are you from?" I demanded.

"Los Angeles," he said as he guided me to one of the monitoring desks that ringed the computer.

"And what makes you so angry?"

He snorted. "The thought that a refined lady like you would willingly ride into a tryst in space with an Anglo."

"A tryst? Is that what you think I'm doing?"

"What else?"

I wanted to slap his sullen, accusing face. But I decided that I would not dignify his anger with any response whatsoever.

"Let's get this orientation over with," I said, barely controlling my temper. "Then we can both go home."

I watched the taped lecture. Then he silently led me to one of the simulation areas and helped me don the VR helmet and gloves. I "rode" in virtual reality aboard a Delta Clipper from Cape Canaveral to Space Station Alpha. The simulation did not provide the physical sensations of acceleration or zero gravity: It was strictly a safety review, showing the interior layout of the Clipper's passenger cabin, the escape hatches, and the emergency oxygen system.

At last it was finished, and I pulled the helmet off. Molina was standing beside me; he took the helmet from my hands.

"I am not engaging in a tryst with Sam Gunn," I heard myself mutter as I wormed off the VR gloves.

He gave me a smoldering look. "I'm glad to hear it, even if it's not true."

"I do not tell lies!"

For the first time, he smiled at me. It was only half a smile, really, but it made him look much better. "I'm sure you're telling the truth. But you don't know Sam."

I almost wanted to tell him that I loved Spence, not Sam. But that would have been foolish. Apparently the rumors flew thick and fast through the whole company. Already it was taken for granted that Sam and I would make out in zero g. Besides, telling him how I felt about Spence would have made him angry all over again.

So I tried to shift the conversation as we walked along

the corridor to the building's front entrance. The halls were mostly deserted now. Even Sam's most dedicated employees eventually went home to their families and friends.

"I am from Los Angeles, too, you know," I said.

"Really? What part?"

Quickly I realized I had put my foot into a quagmire. "Oh, I went to UCLA," I said. "I lived just off the campus."

"Westwood, huh?"

Actually I had lived in a leased condominium in Pacific Palisades, with a magnificent view of the beach and the sunsets over the ocean.

"When I said Los Angeles," he told me as we reached the front door, "I meant the city. The *barrio*. Downtown."

"Oh." I had heard about the squalor and crime in the downtown area, but had never visited such a slum.

We stepped out into the soft warm breeze of a balmy Florida evening.

"You were born there?" I asked, as we walked toward our cars.

It was dark in the parking lot. Suddenly I was glad of his companionship.

"No," he answered. "My parents came to Los Angeles when I was an infant."

"And where were you born?" I asked.

"In Quito."

I felt stunned. Quito!

"That's the capital of Ecuador," he explained, misunderstanding my silence. "My father was a university professor there but he was driven out by the dictator."

"Dictator?" I snapped. "Ecuador is a democracy."

"Democracy, hell! It's a dictatorship, run by a little clique of fascist bastards."

I felt myself shaking from head to toe. My throat went dry with suppressed anger.

"Someday I'll go back to Ecuador," Gregory Molina said. "Someday there's going to be a reckoning. The peo-

ple won't stand for this corrupt regime much longer. Revolution is on the way, you'll see.''

In the shadows of the parking lot I could not make out
the expression on his face or the fire in his eyes. But I
could hear it in his voice, his passionate, fervent voice,
filled with hatred for my father. And if he knew who I
really was, he would hate me, too.

I slept hardly at all that night, worrying about my father and the rebels and the seething hatred I had heard in
young Gregory Molina's voice. When I did manage to
close my eyes I was racked by terrifying nightmares in
which I was struggling to climb the sheer face of a high
cliff with Sam up above me and Spence below. I saw the
rope connecting me to Sam begin to fray. I tried to shout,
but no sound would come from my throat. I tried to
scream, but I was helpless. The rope snapped, and I
plunged down into the abyss, past Spence, who reached
out to save me, but in vain.

I woke screaming, bathed in perspiration, tangled in
my bedsheets. And I realized that in the last moment of
my nightmare the man who reached toward me was not
Spence after all. It was Gregory.

Dawn was breaking. Time to get up anyway.

I was applying the final dab of mascara when the apartment's intercom chimed. I called out to it, and Sam's
voice rasped, ''Arise, Esmeralda. Your knight in shining
armor is here to whisk you away to the promised land.''

I had seldom heard such a mixture of metaphors.

We drove to the Cape in Spence's reconditioned antique Mustang, gleaming silver, with me crammed into
the tiny rear seat and the top down. My careful hairdo
was blown to tatters once we hit the highway but I did
not care; it was glorious to race in the early-morning sunlight.

Despite my VR orientation, I gulped as we strapped
ourselves into the contoured chairs of the Delta Clipper.
It was a big, conical-shaped craft, sitting in the middle
of a concrete blast pad. It reminded me of the ancient
round pyramids of Michoacán, in Mexico: massive, tall

and enduring. But this "pyramid" was made of light-weight alloys and plastics, not stone. And it was intended to fly into space.

After all my fears, the actual takeoff was almost mild. The roar of the rocket engines was muffled by the cabin's acoustical insulation. The vibration was less than my orientation simulation had led me to believe. Before I fully realized we were off the ground, the ship had settled down into a smooth, surging acceleration.

And then the engines shut off, and we were coasting in zero gravity. My stomach felt as if it were dropping away to infinity and crawling up my throat, both at the same time. The medicinal patch Sam had given me must have helped, though, because in a few moments my feeling of nausea eased. It did not disappear entirely, but it sank to a level where I could turn to Spence, sitting beside me, and make a weak grin.

"You're doing fine," he said, treating me to that dazzling smile of his. I did not even mind that the loose end of his shoulder belt was floating in the air, bobbing up and down like a flat gray snake.

Sam, of course, unclipped his harness as soon as the engines cut off and floated up to the padded ceiling.

"This is the life!" he announced to the ten other passengers. Then he tucked his knees up under his chin and did a few zero-g spins and tumbles.

The other passengers were mostly experienced engineers and technicians riding up to Alpha for a stint of work on the space station. One of them, however, must have been new to zero gee. I could hear him retching into one of the bags that had been thoughtfully placed in our seatbacks. The sound of it made me gag.

"Ignore it," Spence advised me, placing a cool, calm hand on my arm. With his other hand he pointed at the acrobatic Sam. "And ignore him, too. He does this every trip, just to see who he can get to throw up."

Once we docked with Alpha and got down to the main wheel of the station, everyone felt much better. Except Sam. I believe he truly preferred zero g to normal gravity.

Alpha station was a set of three nested wheels, each at

a different distance from the center to simulate a different level of gravity. The outermost wheel was at one g, normal Earthly gravity. The second was at one-third g, roughly the same as Mars. The innermost was at the Moon's level of one-sixth g. The hub of the station was, of course, effectively zero gravity, although some of the more sensitive scientific and industrial experiments were housed in "free flyers" that floated independently of the space station's huge, rotating structure.

Much of the main wheel was unoccupied, I saw. Long stretches of the sloping corridor stood bare and empty as Sam and I walked through them. Nothing but bare structural ribs and dim overhead lights. Not even any windows.

"Plenty room for hotel facilities here," Sam kept muttering.

Spence had disappeared into the area on the second wheel that VCI had leased from Alpha's owner, Rockledge Industries. He had come up to work on the satellite-repair facility we had established there, not merely to chaperon me.

"But Sam," I asked as we strolled through the dismally empty corridor, "why would anyone pay the price of a ticket to orbit just to be cooped up in cramped compartments in a space station? It's like being in a small ocean liner, down in steerage class, below the waterline."

He smiled as if I had stepped into his web. "Two reasons, Esmeralda. One—the view. You can't imagine what it's like to see the Earth from up here until you've done it for yourself."

"I've seen photos and videos. They're breathtaking, yes, but—"

"But not the real experience," Sam interrupted. "And then there's the second reason." He broke into a lecherous leer. "Making love in zero gravity. It's fantastic, lemme tell you."

I did not respond to that obvious ploy.

"Better yet, lemme show you."

"I think not," I said coolly. But I wondered what it

would be like to make love in zero gravity. Not with Sam, of course. With Spence.

Sam's expression turned instantly to wounded innocence. "I mean, lemme show you the zero-g section of the station."

"Oh."

"Did you think I was propositioning you?"

"Of course."

"How could you? This is a business trip," he protested. "I even brought you a chaperon. My intentions are honorable, cross my heart." Which he did, and then raised his right hand in a Boy Scout's salute.

I trusted Sam as far as I could throw the cathedral of Quito, but I followed him down the long passageway to the hub of the space station. It was a strange, eerie journey. The passageway was nothing more than a long tube studded with ladderlike rungs. With each step we ascended, the feeling of gravity lessened until it felt as if we were floating, rather than climbing. Sam showed me how to let go of the rungs altogether, except for the faintest touch against them now and then to propel myself up the tube. Soon we were swimming, hardly touching the rungs at all, hurtling faster and faster along the long metal tube.

I realized why the standard uniform for the space station was one-piece coveralls that zipped at the cuffs of the trousers and sleeves. Anything else would have been undignified, perhaps even dangerous.

The tube was only dimly lit, but I could see up ahead a brighter glow coming from an open hatch at the end. We were whipping along by now, streaking past the rungs like a pair of dolphins.

And then we shot into a huge, empty space: a vast hollow sphere with padded walls. Sam zoomed straight across the center and dived headfirst into the curving wall. It gave, and he bounced back toward me. I felt as if I had been dropped out of an airplane. I was falling, and there was no way I could control myself.

Then Sam grabbed me as we passed each other. His hands gripped my flailing arms, and I was surprised at how strong he was. We spun around each other, two astronomical bodies suddenly caught in a mutual orbit. I was breathless, unable to decide whether I should scream or laugh. Slowly we drifted to the wall and nudged against it. Sam flatted his back against the padding, gaining enough traction to bring us both to a stop.

"Fun, huh?"

It took me several moments to catch my breath. Once I did, I realized that Sam was holding me in his arms and his lips were almost touching mine.

I pushed away, gently, and floated toward the middle of the huge enclosure. "Fun, yes," I admitted.

We spent nearly an hour playing games like a pair of schoolchildren let loose for recess. We looped and dived and bounced off the padded walls. We played tag and blindman's bluff, although I was certain that Sam cheated and peeked whenever he felt like it.

Finally we hovered in the middle of the empty sphere, sweating, panting, an arm's length from one another.

"Well," Sam said, running a hand over his sweaty brow, "whattaya think? Worth the price of a ticket to orbit?"

"Yes! Well worth it. I believe people will gladly pay to come here for vacations."

"And honeymoons," Sam added, with his impish grin. "You haven't even tried the best part of it yet."

I laughed lightly. There was no sense getting angry at him. "I think I can imagine it well enough."

"Ah, but the experience, that's the thing."

I looked into his devilish hazel eyes and, for the first time, felt sad for Sam Gunn. "Sam," I said as gently as I could, "you must remember that Esmeralda loves the young poet, not Quasimodo."

His eyes widened with surprise for a moment. Then his grin returned. "Hell, you don't have to follow the script *exactly*, do you?"

He was truly incorrigible.

"It must be time for dinner," I said. "We should get back to the galley, shouldn't we?"

So we started up the tube and, as the gravity built up,

found ourselves clambering down the rungs of the ladder like a pair of firefighters descending to the street.

"You mean you're in love with somebody else?" Sam's voice echoed along the metal walls of the tube.

He was below me. I could see his face turned up toward me, like a round ragamuffin doll with scruffy red hair. I pondered his question for a few moments.

"I think I am," I answered.

"Somebody younger? Somebody your own age?"

"What difference does it make?"

He fell silent for several moments. At last he said softly, "Well, he better treat you right. If he gives you any trouble you tell me about it, understand?"

I was so surprised at that I nearly missed my step on the next rung. Sam Gunn being fatherly? I found it hard to believe, yet that was what he seemed to be saying.

Spence was already in the galley when we got there.

Sam showed me how to work the food dispensers as he explained, "This glop is barely fit for human consumption. I think Rockledge has some kind of experiment going about how lousy the food has to be before people stop eating it and let themselves starve."

I accepted a prepared tray from the machine and went to the table where Spence was sitting. There were only ten tables in the galley, and most of them were empty.

"Experienced workers bring their own food up with them and microwave it," Sam kept rattling on. "Of course, when I open the hotel I'll have a *cordon bleu* chef up here and the best by-damn food service you ever saw. Cocktail lounge, too, with real waitresses in cute little outfits. None of those idiot robots like they have down at the Cape . . ."

He chattered and babbled straight through our meager dinner. In truth, the food was not very appetizing. The soyburger was too cool and the iced tea too warm. I am sure it was nutritious, but it was also bland and dull.

Spence could barely get a word in, the way Sam was nattering. I was content to let him do the talking. Suddenly I felt extremely tired, worn-out. It had been a demanding day, with the flight from the Cape and Sam's zero-g acrobatics. I had barely slept the night before and had arisen with the dawn.

I yawned in Sam's face. And immediately felt terribly embarrassed. "Sorry," I apologized. "But I am very tired."

"Or bored," Sam said, without a trace of resentment.

"Tired," I repeated. "Fatigued. I didn't sleep well last night."

"Too much excitement," Sam said.

Spence said nothing.

"I must get some sleep," I said, pushing my chair back.

"Can you find your room all right?" Spence asked.

"I think so."

"I'll walk you to your door," he said, getting to his feet.

Sam remained seated, but he glanced first at me and then at Spence. "I've got a few things to attend to," he said, "soon as I finish this glorious Rockledge repast."

So Spence walked with me along the sloping corridor toward the area where the sleeping compartments were.

"Sam works very long hours, even up here," I said.

Spence chuckled. "He's working on a couple of Rockledge people. Of the female variety."

"Oh?"

"The little guy's always got something going. Although I've got to admit," Spence added, "that he gets a lot of dope about what Rockledge is doing from his— uh, contacts."

"A sort of masculine Mata Hari?" I asked.

Spence laughed outright.

As we neared the door to my compartment I heard myself asking Spence, "Why don't they have windows in the compartments? It makes them feel so small and confined."

Even as I spoke the words I wondered if I wanted to delay the moment I must say good night to Spence, or if there was another reason.

"The station's spinning, you know," he replied, completely serious. "If you had a window in your compart-

ment, you'd see the stars looping around, and then the
Earth would slide past, and maybe the Moon, if it was in
the right position. Could make you pretty queasy, everything spinning by like that.''

"But Sam said the view was magnificent.''

"Oh, it is! Believe me. But that's the view from outside, or down at the observation blister in the hub.''

"I see.''

"Sam plans to put a video screen in each of his hotel
rooms. It'll look like a window that gives you a steady
view of the Earth or whatever else you'd like to see.''

So after all his talk about seeing "the real thing,'' Sam
was prepared to show his hotel guests little more than
video images of the Earth from space. That was just like
the gringo capitalist exploiter, I told myself.

Yet I heard myself asking Spence, "Is the view truly
magnificent?''

"Sam didn't show you?''

"No.''

His face lit up. "Want to see it now? You're not too
tired, are you? It'll only take—''

"I'm not too tired," I said eagerly. "I would like very
much to see this fabulous view.''

All the way along the long tube leading to the station's
hub a voice in my mind reprimanded me. You know why
you asked him about the windows, it scolded. You
*wanted* Spence to take you to the zero-gee section.

We floated into the big padded gym. Spence propelled
himself to a particular piece of the padding and peeled it
back, revealing a small hatch. He opened it and beckoned
me to him. I pushed off the curving wall and swam to
him, my heart racing so hard I feared it would break my
ribs.

Spence helped me wriggle through the narrow hatch,
then followed me into a small, cramped dome. There was
barely room enough for the two of us. He swung the
hatch shut and we were in total darkness.

"Hang on a minute . . .'' he mumbled.

I heard a click and then the whir of an electric motor.

The dome seemed to split apart, opening like a clamshell. And beyond it—

The Earth. A huge brilliant blue curving mass moving slowly, with ponderous grace, below us. The breath gushed out of me.

Spence put his arm around my shoulders, and whispered, "Lord, I love the beauty of thy house, and the place where thy glory dwells."

It was—there are no words to do it justice. We huddled together in the transparent observation blister and feasted our eyes on the world swinging past, immense and glorious beyond description. Deep blue seas and swirling purest white clouds, the land brown and green with wrinkles of mountains and glittering lakes scattered here and there. Even the dark night side was spectacular, with the lights of cities and highways outlining the continents.

"No matter how many times you've seen it," Spence said, "it still takes your breath away. I could watch it for hours."

"It's incredible," I said.

"We'll have to build more observation blisters for the hotel guests. Stud the whole zero-section with them."

The panorama was ever-changing, one spectacular scene blending imperceptibly into another. We saw the sun come up over the curving horizon, shooting dazzling streamers of red and orange through the thin layer of the atmosphere. I recognized the isthmus of Panama and the curving bird's head of the Yucatán.

"Where is Ecuador?" I asked.

"Too far south for us to see on this swing. Why do you want to see Ecuador?"

In my excitement I had forgotten that I was supposed to be from Los Angeles.

"Gregory Molina," I temporized quickly. "He told me was born in Ecuador."

By the time we were watching our second sunrise, nearly two hours later, I had melted into Spence's arms. I turned my face up to his, wanting him to kiss me.

He understood. He felt the same passion that I did.

But he said, very gently, "I'm a married man, Juanita."

"Do you love Bonnie Jo?"

"I used to. Now . . ." He shook his head. In the light from the glowing Earth I could see how troubled and pained he was.

"I love you, Spence," I told him.

He smiled sadly. "Maybe you think you do, but it isn't a smart move. I wouldn't be very good for you, kid."

"I know my own heart," I insisted.

"Don't make it any tougher than it has to be, Juanita. I'm old enough to be your father, and I'm married. Not happily, true enough, but that's my fault as much as Bonnie Jo's."

"I could make you happy."

"You shouldn't be getting yourself involved with old married men. Pay some attention to guys your own age, like Greg."

"Molina? That . . . that would-be revolutionary?"

He looked totally surprised. "Revolutionary? What are you talking about?"

"Nothing," I snapped. "Nothing at all."

The mood was shattered, the spell broken. I had confessed my love to Spence, and he had treated me like a lovesick child.

"We'd better leave," I said coldly.

"Yeah," Spence said. "We could both use some sleep."

But I did not sleep. Not at all. I seethed with anger all night. Spence had not only rejected me, he had belittled me. He did not see me as a desirable woman; he thought of me as a child to be lectured, to be palmed off on some young puppy dog whose only passion was to avenge his miserable family's supposed honor.

What a fool I had been! I did not love Spence. I hated him! I spent the whole night telling myself so.

When we boarded the Clipper for the return flight to Florida, Sam was not with us.

"Where is he?" I asked Spence.

"He left a message. Went off to visit a buddy of his in the old Mac Dac Shack."

"The what?"

"One of the smaller stations. It's a medical center now."

"Sam needs medical attention?"

Spence broke into a grin. "Maybe after last night, he does, after all."

I did not find that funny.

Sam did not appear at the office until three days later, and when he did finally show up he was grinning like a cat who had feasted on canaries.

He breezed into the mission control center while I was monitoring our latest repair mission. Gregory Molina sat in the left-hand chair, busily removing a set of computer boards that had to be replaced with upgrades.

"I've got everything lined up for the hotel," Sam announced loudly, plopping himself into the chair on my right.

"Congratulations," I said.

"Yep. Finally got Rockledge to agree to a reasonable leasing fee. Got my buddy Omar set to handle the logistics up in orbit. Contractors, a personnel outfit to hire the staff—everything's in place."

He smiled contentedly and leaned back in the little swivel chair. "All I need is the money."

I had to smile at him. "That would seem to me to be a major consideration."

"Nah." Sam waved an arm in the air. "I'll get the board to approve it at the next stockholders' meeting. That's only six weeks away."

He popped to his feet and strode confidently out of the center, whistling in his usual off-key fashion.

"Gringo imperialist," muttered Gregory Molina.

"You accept his paychecks," I taunted.

He gave me a dark look. "So do you."

"I don't call him names."

"No. But you don't need his money, do you? You live in a fine condo and drive a fancy sports car. Your clothing costs more than your salary."

"You've been spying on me?"

He laughed bitterly. "No need for spying. You are as obvious as an elephant in a china shop."

"So my family has money," I said. "What of it?"

"You don't come from Los Angeles, and you don't need this job, that's what of it. Why are you here?"

I could not answer. My brain froze in the laser beams of his dark eyes.

"Is it because you are Sam's mistress?"

"No!"

He smiled tightly. "But you are in love with Spence, aren't you?"

"No I am not!"

"It's obvious," Gregory said.

"I *hate* him!"

"Yes," he said. "Anyone can see that."

The annual stockholders' meeting took place six weeks later. In that time I had become quite expert at running the mission control board. During my first weeks on the job I merely sat alongside Gene Redding and watched how he handled the job. Within two weeks he was allowing me to take over when he took a break. Within a month we were sharing the duty on long, ten- and even twelve-hour shifts.

Sam needed more mission controllers because the volume of work was increasing rapidly. As he had predicted, the money was beginning to pour in to VCI. The ability to repair malfunctioning commsats and to replenish the fuel they used for their attitude-control thrusters suddenly made VCI a major force in the communications satellite industry. Instead of replacing aging commsats, the corporations could get VCI to refurbish them, at a fraction of the replacement cost.

Spence worked closely with us, handling most of the remotely controlled missions himself, operating the unmanned OTVs that now ran regular repair-and-refurbishment missions to GEO.

Sam practically danced with joy. "I'll be able to declare a dividend for the stockholders," he told us, "and *still* have a wad of moolah to get the hotel started.''

Bonnie Jo frowned at him. ''We could give the stockholders a bigger dividend if you'd forget about your orbital sex palace.''

Sam laughed. ''Are you kidding? My hotel's gonna be the biggest moneymaker you've ever seen in space. I've even got an advertising motto for it: 'If you like water beds, you're gonna *love* zero g!' ''

Bonnie Jo huffed.

Spence spent more time in the simulator than at home with Bonnie Jo. Sam was frugal when it came to hiring more staff; he might take on a very junior computer programmer from Los Angeles, but astronauts and mission controllers carried much higher price tags, and he refrained from hiring them. We worked extremely long hours, and Sam himself ''flew'' many of the remote missions; Spence did the rest of them—more than Sam did, by actual count.

It seemed to me that Spence was glad of the excuse to spend so much time away from his wife. Anyone could sense that their marriage was ripping apart. It made me sad to see him so unhappy, and I had to remind myself often that he had treated me like a schoolgirl and I hated him. For her part, Bonnie Jo seemed perfectly content to have Spence spend most of his time on the remote missions. She herself began to fly back to Salt Lake City every weekend.

Naturally, with my duties as the second mission controller and his as principal operator of the remote satellite repairs, we were together quite a bit.

Well, not together in the physical sense, precisely. Spence was in another room, some twenty meters down the hall from my mission control desk. But somehow, when I was not on duty, I often found myself walking down that hallway to watch him at work. He sat in an astronaut's contoured couch, his hands covered with metallic gloves that trailed hair-thin fiber-optic cables, the top half of his handsome face covered by the stereo screens that showed him what the OTV's cameras were seeing.

I told myself that I was studying his moves, learning

how to sabotage the repair missions. When the time came
I would strike without mercy. When I was not hanging
by the doorway to the remote manipulator lab, studying
him like an avenging angel, I was at my mission control
console, actually speaking with Spence, connected electronically to him, closer to him than anyone else in the
world. Including his wife. I wanted to be close to him;
that made it easier to find a way to sabotage his work,
his company, his life.

"You planning to attend the stockholders' meeting?"
Spence asked me, during a lull in one of the missions.

I was startled that he asked a personal question. "Say
again?" I asked, in the professional jargon of a mission
controller.

Spence chuckled. "It's okay, Juanita. The OTV's still
in coast mode. It'll be another hour before we have to
get to work. Loosen up."

"Oh. Yes. Of course."

"You bought some stock, didn't you?"

"A few shares," I said. In actuality I was spending
my entire salary on shares of VCI. If there had been a
way to buy up all the existing shares, I would have done
it, using my father's treasury to deliver the company into
his hands.

As fate would have it, the annual stockholders' meeting
took place on the same day that my father gave his famous speech at the United Nations.

He told me about the speech the night before the meeting. As usual, I had driven to the consulate late at night
and called him on the videophone. At least he had the
good sense to receive my calls in his office, when he
knew I was going to contact him.

My father was glowing with pride. His smile was brilliant, the shoulders of his suit wider than ever. He had
even faced the necessity of replacing his thinning hair.
Although his new mane of curly brown hair looked as if
it had been stolen from a teenage rock star, it was so wild
and thick, it obviously made him feel younger and more
vigorous.

"With Brazil in the chair at the Security Council and

the Committee of the Twelve Equatorial Nations lining up support among the small nations in the General Assembly, I have high hopes for our cause.''

"And your speech?'' I asked him. "What will you say?''

His smile became even wider, even more radiant. "You must watch me on television, little one. I want you to be just as surprised as the rest of the world will be.''

He would tell me no more. I, of course, reported in full to him about VCI's continuing success in repairing and refurbishing satellites remotely. And of the growing strains in the company's management.

"You still have the capability of destroying their spacecraft?'' he asked me.

"Yes,'' I replied, thinking of how much damage I could do to Spence.

"Good,'' said my father. "The time is fast approaching when we will strike.''

"Will it be necessary—''

But his attention was suddenly pulled away from me. I heard an aide shouting breathlessly at him, "The rebels have ambushed General Quintana's brigade!''

"Ambushed?'' my father snapped, his eyes no longer looking at me. "Where? When?''

"In the mountains of Azuay, south of Cuenca. The general has been captured, and his troops are fleeing for their lives!''

My father's face went gray, then red with fury. He turned back to me. "Excuse me, daughter. I have urgent business to attend to.''

"Go with God,'' I mumbled, feeling silly at using such an archaic phrase. But it was all I could think to say.

The rebels were very clever. They must have known that my father was scheduled to fly to New York to deliver his speech to the United Nations. Now he either had to cancel his speech and admit to the world that his nation was in the throes of a serious internal conflict, or go to New York and leave his army leaderless for several days.

\*      \*      \*

I could not sleep that night. When I arrived at the stockholders' meeting my eyes were red and puffy, my spirits low. How can I help my father? I kept asking myself. What can I do? He had sent me here to help him triumph over Sam Gunn and these other gringos. But he was being threatened at home, and I was thousands of kilometers away from him. I felt miserable and stupid and helpless.

Spence noticed my misery.

More than a hundred people were filing into the room in the big hotel where the stockholders' meeting was being held. Employees and their spouses, all ages, all colors. Blacks and Hispanics and Asians, women and men, Sam had brought together every variety of the human species in his company. He hired for competence; VCI was truly a company without prejudice of any kind. Except that it helped if you were female and young and attractive. That was Sam's one obvious weakness.

Out of that throng Spence noticed me. He made his way through the crowd that was milling around the coffee and doughnuts and came to my side.

"What's the matter, Juanita?"

I looked up into his clear blue eyes and saw that he, too, was sad-faced.

"Family problems," I muttered. "Back home."

He nodded grimly. "Me too."

"Oh?"

Before he could say more, Sam's voice cut through the hubbub of conversations. "Okay, let's get this show on the road. Where's our noble president? Hey, Spence, you silver-haired devil, come on up here and preside, for God's sake, will ya?"

Spence lifted my chin a centimeter and gave me a forced grin. "Time to go to work," he said. Then he turned and almost sprinted up to the front of the room and jumped up onto the makeshift dais.

Bonnie Jo, Sam, and two other men flanked Spence at the long table set up on the dais. The board of directors, I realized. Each of them had a microphone and a name card in front of them. I was fairly certain that the older of the two strangers—Eli G. Murtchison—was Bonnie Jo's father.

There were two mammoth television sets on either side of the dais, as well. I wondered if the hotel kept them there all the time, or if they had been brought in for some specific reason.

The rest of us took the folding plastic chairs that the hotel had set along the floor of the meeting room. They were hard and uncomfortable: a stimulus to keep the meeting short, I thought. The meeting began with formalities. Spence asked that the minutes of the last meeting be accepted. Bonnie Jo read her treasurer's report so fast that I could not understand a word of it.

Then Sam, as chairman of the board, began his review of the year's business and plans for the coming year.

I could feel the tension in the air. Even as Sam spoke glowingly to the stockholders about VCI's new capabilities in remote satellite repair, even while they loudly applauded his announcement of a dividend, the room seemed to crackle with electricity.

And all the while I wondered where my father was, what he was doing, what decisions he was making.

A stockholder—Gene Redding, of all people—rose to ask a question. "Uh, Sam, uh, why isn't our dividend bigger, if we're, uh, making such good profits now?"

I turned in my chair to see Gene better. He was standing: portly, bald, looking slightly flustered. I had never before seen him in a suit and tie; he had always worn jeans and sports shirts at the office. But his suit was rumpled and his tie hung loosely from his unbuttoned shirt. It seemed to me that he felt guilty about asking his question. He was on Bonnie Jo's side, I realized.

Sam said tightly, "We have always plowed our profits back into the company, to assure our growth. This year the profits have been big enough to allow a dividend. But we are still plowing some of the profits back into growth."

Gene got red in the face, but he found the strength to ask, "Back into the growth of VCI's existing projects, or, uh, some other program?"

Sam shot a glance along the head table toward Bonnie Jo. Then he grinned at Gene. "You can sit down, Gene. This is gonna take some time, I can see that."

Bonnie Jo said, "Sam wants to put our profits—*your* profits—into building an orbital tourist hotel."

"A honeymoon hotel," Sam corrected.

A few chuckles arose from the stockholders.

"And we don't have to build it," Sam added. "We can lease space aboard Alpha from Rockledge International."

"Didn't you try that once before, when Global Technologies first built Space Station Alpha?" asked another stockholder, a woman I did not recognize.

"And it didn't work out?" asked another.

"You went broke on that deal, didn't you?" still another asked. I realized that Bonnie Jo had recruited her troops carefully.

"Yeah, yeah," Sam answered impatiently. "That was years ago. Rockledge has taken over Alpha now, and they're looking for customers to lease space."

"Under what terms?" Bonnie Jo asked.

"It's a bargain," said Sam enthusiastically. "A steal!"

I looked at Spence, sitting between Sam and Bonnie Jo. His face was a mask, his usual smile gone, his features frozen as if he wished to betray not even the slightest sign of emotion or partisan bias.

Gene Redding rose to his feet once again. I could see that his hands were trembling, he was so nervous.

"I . . ." He cleared his throat. "I want to make a, uh, a motion."

Spence said grimly, "Go ahead."

"I move . . . that the board of directors . . ." he seemed to be reciting a memorized speech, "refuse to allocate, uh, any monies . . . for any programs . . . not directly associated with VCI's existing lines of business." Gene said the last words in a rush, then immediately sat down.

"Second!" cried Bonnie Jo.

Spence stared at the back wall of the meeting room as he said automatically, "Movement made and seconded. Discussion?"

I had expected Sam to jump up on the table and do a war dance. Or at least to rant and scream and argue until we all dropped from exhaustion. Instead, he glanced at his wristwatch and said:

"Let's postpone the discussion for a bit. There's a speech coming up at the UN that we should all take a look at."

Spence agreed to Sam's suggestion so quickly that I knew the two of them had talked it over beforehand. Bonnie Jo looked surprised, nettled, but her father laid a hand on her arm, and she refrained from objecting.

The UN speech was by my father, of course, although no one in the room knew that I was the daughter of Ecuador's *el Presidente*. I felt a surge of pride when his handsome face appeared on the giant TV screens. If only his new hair had matched his face better! He wore a civilian's business suit of dark blue, with the red sash of his office slanting across his chest. He looked bigger than normal, his chest broader and deeper. I realized he must have been wearing a bulletproof vest. Was he worried that the rebels would try to assassinate him? Or merely wary of New York?

My father's speech was marvelous, although I had to listen to the English translation instead of hearing his dramatic, flowery Spanish. Still, it was dramatic enough. My father explained the legal origins of our claim to the equatorial orbit, the injustice of the rich corporations who refused to share their wealth with the orbit's rightful owners, and the complicity of the United Nations for allowing this terrible situation to persist.

I sat in my hard little folding chair and basked in the glow of my father's unassailable logic and undeterrable drive.

"Is there no one to help us?" he asked rhetorically, raising his hands in supplication. "Cannot all the apparatus of international law come to the aid of the Twelve nations who have seen their territory invaded and usurped? Will no one support the Declaration of Quito?"

Suddenly his face hardened. His hands balled into fists. "Very well, then! The Twelve Equatorial Nations will defend their sacred territory by themselves, if necessary. I serve notice, on behalf of the Twelve Equatorial Nations, that the equatorial orbit belongs to *us*, and to no other nation, corporation, or entity. We are preparing to send an international team of astronauts to establish permanent residence in the equatorial orbit. Once there, they will dismantle or otherwise destroy the satellites that the invaders have placed in our territory.''

The audience in the UN chamber gasped. So did we, in the hotel's meeting room. I felt a thrill of hot blood race through me.

''We will defend our territory against the aggressors who have invaded it,'' my father declared. ''If this means war, then so be it. To do anything less would be to bow to the forces of imperialism!''

The people around me stared at one another, stunned into silence.

All except Sam, who yelled, ''Jesus H. Christ on a motorcycle!''

As the TV picture winked off, one of the stockholders shouted, ''What the hell are we going to do about *that?*''

All sense of order in our meeting room dissolved. Everyone seemed to talk at once. Spence rapped his knuckles on the table, but no one paid any attention to him. The argument about Sam's orbital hotel was forgotten. My father had turned our meeting into chaos.

Until Sam jumped up on the table and waved his arms excitedly. ''Shut the hell up and listen to me!'' he bellowed.

The room silenced. All eyes turned to the pudgy rust-haired elf standing on the head table.

''We're gonna get there before they do,'' Sam told us. ''We're gonna put a person up there in GEO before they can, and we're gonna claim the orbit for ourselves. They wanna play legal games, we can play 'em, too. Faster and better!''

Spence objected, ''Sam, nobody can stay in GEO for long. It's in the middle of the outer Van Allen belt, for gosh sakes.''

''Pull a couple of OTVs together, fill the extra propellant tanks with water. That'll provide enough shielding for a week or so.''

''How do you know? We've got to do some calculations, check with the experts—''

''No time for that,'' Sam snapped. ''We're in a race, a land rush, we gotta go *now*. Do the calculations afterward. Right now the vital thing is to get somebody parked up there in GEO before those greedy sonsofbitches get there!''

''But who would be nuts enough to—''

''I'll do it,'' Sam said, as if he had made up his mind even before Spence asked the question. ''Let's get busy!''

That broke up our meeting, of course. Spence officially called for an adjournment until a time to be decided. Everyone raced for their cars and drove pell-mell back to the office. Except for Sam and Spence, who jumped into Spence's convertible Mustang and headed off toward Cape Canaveral.

Despite my feelings of patriotism and love of my father, I felt thrilled. It was tremendously exciting to dash into the mission control center and begin preparations for launching Sam to GEO. Spence went with him as far as Space Station Alpha. Together they hopped up to the station where our OTVs were garaged on the next available Delta Clipper, scarcely thirty-six hours after my father's speech.

Even Bonnie Jo caught the wave of enthusiasm. She came into the control center as Sam and Spence were preparing the two OTVs for Sam's mission. It was night; I was running the board, giving Gene a rest after he had put in twelve hours straight. Bonnie Jo slid into the chair beside me and asked me to connect her with Sam, up at Alpha.

''We've been monitoring the Brazilian launch facility,'' she said, once Sam's round, freckled face appeared on the screen. ''They're counting down a manned launch. They claim it's just a scientific research team going up to the *Nôvo Brasil* space station. But get this, Sam: The Brazilians are also counting down an unmanned launch.''

"With what payload?"

"An old storm cellar that the U.S. government auctioned off five years ago."

"A what?"

"A shielded habitat module, like the ones the scientists used on their first Mars missions to protect themselves from solar flare radiation," Bonnie Jo said.

Sam looked tired and grim. "They ain't going to Mars."

"According to the flight plan they filed, they're merely going to the Brazilian space station."

"My ass. They're heading for GEO."

"Can you get there first?" Bonnie Jo asked.

He nodded. "Got the second OTV's tanks filled with water. Rockledge bastards charged us two arms and a leg for it, but the tanks are filled. Spence is out on EVA now, rigging an extra propulsion unit to the tanker."

"Where did you get an extra propulsion unit?"

"Cannibalized from a third OTV."

Bonnie Jo tried not to, but she frowned. "That's three OTVs used for this mission. We only have two left for our regular work."

"There won't be any regular work if we don't get to GEO and establish our claim."

Her frown melted into a tight little smile. "I think I can help you there."

"How?"

"The Brazilians haven't filed an official flight plan with the IAA safety board."

The International Astronautical Administration had legal authority over all flights in space.

"Hell, neither have we," said Sam.

"Yes, but you didn't have that fatheaded Ecuadorian spouting off about sending a team to occupy GEO."

Fatheaded Ecuadorian! I almost slapped her. But I held on to my soaring temper. There was much to be learned from her, and I was a spy, after all.

Sam was muttering, "I don't see what—"

With a smug, self-satisfied smile, Bonnie Jo explained, "I just asked my uncle, the senator from Utah, to request that our space-agency people ask the IAA if they've inspected the Brazilian spacecraft to see if it's properly fitted out for long-term exposure to high radiation levels.''

Sam grinned back at her. ''You're setting the lawyers on them!''

''The safety experts,'' corrected Bonnie Jo.

''Son of a bitch. That's great!''

Bonnie Jo's smile shrank. ''But you'd better get your butt off the space station and on your way to GEO before the IAA figures out what you're up to.''

''We'll be ready to go in two shakes of a sperm cell's tail,'' Sam replied happily.

If Bonnie Jo was worried about Sam's safety up there in the Van Allen radiation, she gave no indication of it. I must confess that I felt a twinge of relief that it was Sam who was risking himself, not Spence. But still I smoldered at Bonnie Jo's insulting words about my father.

And suddenly I realized that I had to tell Papa about her scheme to delay the Brazilian mission. But how? I was stuck here in the mission control center until 8:00 A.M.

I could risk a telephone call, I thought. Later, in the dead of night, when there was little chance of anyone else hanging around.

The hours dragged by slowly. At midnight Molina and another technician were in the center with me, helping Sam and Spence to check out their jury-rigged OTV prior to launch. By one-thirty they were almost ready to start the countdown.

I found myself holding my breath as I watched Sam and Spence go through the final inspection of the OTV, both of them encased in bulky space suits as they floated around the ungainly spacecraft, checking every strut and tank and electrical connection. Their suits had once been white, I suppose, but long use had turned them both dingy gray. Over his years in space Sam had brightened his with decorative patches and pins, but they, too, were frayed and faded. I could barely read the patch just above his

name stencil. It said, *The meek shall inherit the Earth.
The rest of us are going to the stars.*

"Hey, Esmeralda," Sam called to me, "why don't you
come up here with me? It's gonna be awful lonesome up
there all by myself."

"Pay attention to your inspection," I told him.

But Sam was undeterred, of course. "We could practice different positions for my zero-g hotel."

"Never in a million years," I said.

He grinned, and said, "I'll wait."

At last the inspection was finished, and we finally began the final countdown. I cleared my display screen of
the TV transmission from Alpha and set up the OTV's
interior readouts. For the next half hour I concentrated
every molecule of my attention on the countdown. A man
could be killed by the slightest mistake now.

A part of my mind was saying, so what if Sam is
killed? That would stop his mission to GEO and give
your father the chance he needs to triumph. But I told
myself that my father would not condone murder or even
a political assassination. He would triumph and keep his
hands clean. And mine. It was one thing to tinker with a
computer program so that an unmanned spacecraft would
be destroyed. I was not a murderer, and neither was my
father. Or so I told myself.

"Thirty seconds," said Gregory Molina, sitting on my
left.

Sam had become very quiet. Was he nervous? I wondered. I certainly was. My hands were sweaty as I stared
at the readouts on my display screen.

"Fifteen seconds."

Everything seemed right. All systems functioning normally. All the readouts on my screen in the green.

"Separation," the tech announced.

The launch was not dramatic. I cleared my display
screen for a moment and switched to a view from one of
the space station's outside cameras and saw Sam's ungainly conglomeration move away, without so much as a
puff of smoke, and dwindle into the star-filled darkness.

I felt inexpressibly sad. He was my enemy, the sworn

foe of my people. I should have hated Sam Gunn. Yet, as he flew off into the unknown dangers of living in the radiation belt for who-knew-how-long, I did not feel hatred for him. Admiration, perhaps. Respect for his courage, certainly.

Suddenly I blew him a kiss. To my shock, I found that I actually *liked* Sam Gunn.

"It's a good thing he couldn't see that," Gregory growled at me. "He would turn the OTV around and come to carry you off with him."

I leaned back in my chair, my head throbbing from the tension, glad that this Molina person was there to remind me of my true responsibilities.

"Sam is a rogue," I said loftily. "One can admire a rogue without being captivated by him."

Gregory snorted his disdain and got up from his chair, leaving me alone in the control center.

I waited until almost dawn before daring to phone my father. The mission was going as planned: Sam was coasting out to GEO, all systems were within nominal parameters, there was nothing for anyone to do. We had not even chatted back and forth since the launch; there was no need to, although I found myself wondering if Sam was so worried about his brash jaunt into the radiation dangers of GEO that he had finally lost the glibness of his tongue.

Somewhere a band of university scientists that Spence had hired as consultants were figuring out how long Sam could remain in GEO safely. Molina and the other technicians went home. The second shift came in and sat on either side of me. After an hour of nothing to do, I told them to take a break, take a nap if they liked. I could monitor the controls by myself. I promised to call them if I needed them.

I phoned my father, instead. He was still in New York, where he planned to wait for the success of the Brazilian mission. I woke him, of course, but at least this time he was alone in his bed. Or so it seemed.

"He is already on his way?" My father's sleepy eyes opened wide once I told him about Sam.

"Yes," I said. "And the United States is asking the IAA to make a safety investigation of the Brazilian spacecraft."

He seemed confused by that.

"It will delay the Brazilian mission for days!" I hissed, not daring to raise my voice. "Sam will be in GEO and claim the territory before they even get off the space station."

My father lapsed into a long string of heartfelt curses so foul that even today I blush at the memory.

He raged at me, "And what have you done about it? Nothing!"

"There is nothing I can do, Papa."

"Bah! I am surrounded by traitors and incompetents! My own daughter cannot raise a finger to help me."

"But Papa—"

"Do you realize what this gringo is doing? He is turning our own position against us! He is using my speech as a pretext for taking the equatorial orbit away from us! I will look like a fool! Before the United Nations, before the news media, before the whole world—I will be made to appear like a fool!"

I was shocked and saddened to realize that my father's concern was not for his people or for the injustice of the situation. His first concern was about his own image.

"But Papa," I asked tearfully, "what can we do about it?"

"You must act!" he said. "You said you were prepared to sabotage their spacecraft. Now is the time to do it. Strike! Strike now!"

I stared at his image in horror. My father's face was contorted with fury and hate.

"Kill that gringo bastard!" he snarled at me. "He must never reach the equatorial orbit alive."

The bug that I had inserted into the mission control program merely allowed me to fire an OTV's thrusters when I chose to. Originally I had thought that I could send an unmanned OTV crashing into a communications satellite, a neat piece of sabotage.

Sam was not planning to park his spacecraft close enough to a commsat for my plan to work, however. He merely wanted to establish himself in GEO long enough to make the territorial claim that my father wanted for the Twelve—and for the UN to recognize that claim.

I could not send him crashing into a satellite, I realized. But what if I used my bug to fire his thrusters as he approached GEO? He would go careening past the orbit, farther out into space. His trajectory would undoubtedly carry him into a wildly looping orbit that would either fling him into deep space forever, or send him hurtling back toward the Earth, to plunge into the atmosphere and burn up like a meteor.

Yes, I told myself, I could kill Sam Gunn with the touch of a finger. I was alone in the mission control center. No one would see me do it. I could then erase the bug in the program, and no one would ever know why Sam's thrusters misfired.

But—murder Sam? Only a few hours earlier I had been telling myself that my father was too good a man to stoop to murder. And now—

"They're going to assassinate him."

I whirled in my chair to see Gregory standing just inside the control center's doorway. His face was grim, his eyes red and sleepless.

"I thought you had gone home," I said.

"Didn't you hear me?" He stalked toward me, angry or frightened or both, I could not tell. "They're going to kill him! Assassinate him!"

"No . . . I can't . . ." My voice choked in my throat.

"It's all set up," Gregory said, padding to the chair beside me like a hunting cat. "There's nothing you can do about it."

"I can't kill Sam," I said, nearly breaking into sobs.

"Sam?" Gregory's brows knit. "I'm not talking about Sam. It's your father. The rebels are going to assassinate him in New York."

"What? How do you know?"

"Because I'm one of them," he snapped. "I've been

with them all along. And now I've been assigned to kidnap you."

"Kidnap me?" My voice sounded like a stranger's to me: pitched high with surprise and fear. Yet inwardly I was not afraid. Shocked numb, perhaps, but not frightened.

Gregory's expression was unfathomable, but he seemed to be in torment. "Kidnap you," he repeated. "Or assassinate you if kidnapping becomes impossible."

"You wouldn't dare!"

He made a bitter, twisted smile. "This is our moment, princess. Your father is in New York, where we have enough people to get past his security team. You are his only living relative—or the only one he admits to. General Quintana is already storming the main army barracks in the capital."

"General Quintana? But he's . . ." The words choked in my mouth as I realized that Quintana was a traitor.

"He will be our next president," Gregory said, then added, "he thinks."

I could feel my eyes widening.

Still with his twisted smile, Gregory explained, "Do you think we are fools enough to trust a traitor? Or to put a general in the president's chair?"

"No, I suppose you are not."

Gregory fell silent for a long moment, then he asked, "Will you allow me to kidnap you? It will be merely for long enough to keep you from warning your father."

"So that you can murder him."

"I didn't want them to do that. I thought we could overthrow him without bloodshed, but the others want to make certain that he won't be able to stop us."

I said nothing. I was desperately trying to think of something to do, some way to escape Gregory and warn my father.

"After we finish Sam's mission I'll have to take you with me." His expression changed. He seemed almost shy, embarrassed. "I promise you that you will not be harmed in any way. Unless you try to resist, of course."

"Of course," I snapped.

He pointed to my display screen. "It's almost time for you to activate your bug."

"You know about that?"

"Of course I know about it," he said. "I have been watching you very closely since the first day you came here, pretending to be from Los Angeles."

My heart sank. I had not fooled him for a moment. Yet, somehow, I was forced to admire how clever Gregory had been, even though he was my enemy. Or rather, my father's enemy.

"It will be a shame to kill Sam," he said, with real regret in his voice. "Maybe his trajectory will bring him close enough to one of the space stations so that somebody can rescue him."

"Not much chance of that," I said.

He shrugged. Unhappily, I thought. "It must be done. We can't allow Sam to claim the equatorial orbit."

"So your glorious rebels want the orbit for themselves," I taunted.

"Yes! Why not? It is the one chance that a poor nation such as Ecuador has to gain some of the wealth these corporations are making in space."

"So you will kill Sam as well as my father."

"No," he said grimly. "*You* will kill Sam."

At that instant Spence's voice came through the radio receiver, "Preparing for OIB."

Spence's voice. Not Sam's.

Greg looked surprised. I felt a flame of shock race through me. I whirled my chair back to the console and toggled the radio switch.

"Spence! Where are you?"

"Aboard the OTV, Juanita honey. Sam got a brilliant idea at the last minute, and we switched places."

"Where is Sam?"

"He ought to be in New York by now."

"New York?" we both said in unison.

"Yeah. Anyway, I'm five minutes away from OIB. You copy?"

Orbital insertion burn. The final firing of the OTV's thrusters to place the spacecraft in the geosynchronous orbit. The time when my bug would make the thrusters fire much longer than they should and fling the craft into a wild orbit that would undoubtedly kill its pilot.

But the pilot was Spence! I had found it troubling to think of killing Sam, but it was Spence inside that OTV! No matter how angry I was with him, no matter how much I told myself I hated him, I could not knowingly, willingly, send him to his death.

"For what it's worth," Spence reported cheerfully, "the radiation monitors in this ol' tin can show everything's in the green. Radiation's building up outside, but the shielding's protecting me just fine. So far."

I turned from the display screen to Greg. His face looked awful.

"I can't do it," I whispered. "I can't kill him."

He reached out his hand toward my keyboard, then let it drop to his side. "Neither can I."

"OIB in three minutes," Spence's voice called out. "You copy?"

I looked at the mission time-line clock as I flicked the radio switch again. "We copy OIB in two minutes, fifty-six seconds."

Greg sank down onto the chair next to me, his head drooping. "Some revolutionary," he muttered.

"Let me warn my father," I pleaded. "You don't want his blood on your hands."

"No," he said, shaking his head stubbornly. "I can't go that far."

"But Sam will be with him, don't you understand?"

"Sam? Why would—"

"Sam went to New York! That's what Spence told us. The only reason for Sam to go to New York is to see my father. Sam will be in the line of fire when your assassins strike. They'll kill him, too!"

Greg looked miserable, but he said in a hoarse croak, "That can't be helped. There's nothing I can do."

"Well, I can," I said, reaching for the telephone.

"Don't!"

"What will you do? Kill me?"

He grabbed my arm. I tried to pull free but he was

stronger. I struggled but he held me in his powerful arms and pulled me to him and kissed me. Before I realized what I was doing I was kissing him, wildly, passionately, with all the heat of a jungle beast.

At last Greg pulled loose. He stared into my eyes for a long, timeless moment, then said, "Yes. Call your father. Warn him. I can't be a party to murder. It's one thing to talk about it, plan for it. But I just can't go through with it."

"OIB in one minute," Spence's voice chirped.

"Copy OIB in fifty-nine seconds," I said as I took up the telephone. My eyes were still on Greg. He smiled at me, the sad smile of a man who has given up everything. For me.

"You are not a killer," I said to him. "That is nothing to be ashamed of."

"But the revolution—"

"To hell with the revolution and all politics!" I snapped as I tapped out the number for my father's hotel room.

"We are sorry," said a computer-synthesized voice, "but the number you have called is not in service at this time."

Cold terror gripped my heart.

I called the hotel's main number. It was busy. For half an hour, while Spence's OTV settled into its equatorial orbit and he read off all the radiation monitors inside and outside the spacecraft, the hotel's main switchboard gave nothing but a busy signal.

I was ready to scream when Greg suddenly bolted from the control center and came back a moment later with a hand-sized portable TV. He turned it to the all-news channel.

". . . hostage situation," said a trench-coated reporter standing in front of a soaring hotel tower. It was drizzling in New York, but a huge throng had already gathered out on the streets.

"Is the president of Venezuela still in there?" asked an unseen anchor woman.

"It's the president of Ecuador, Maureen," said the reporter on the street. "And, yes, as far as we know he's still in his suite with the gunmen who broke in about an hour ago."

"Do you know who's in there with him?"

The reporter, bareheaded in the chilly drizzle, squinted into the camera. "A couple of members of his staff. The gunmen let all the women in the suite go free about half an hour ago. And there is apparently an American businessman in there, too. The hotel security director has identified the American as a Sam Gunn, from Orlando, Florida."

"How could the rebels get past my father's security guards?" I wondered out loud.

"Bribes," said Greg. He spoke the word as if it were a loathsome thing. "Some men will sell their souls for money."

I told Spence what was happening, of course. He seemed strangely nonchalant.

"Sam's been in fixes like this before. He always talks his way out of 'em."

He was trying to keep my spirits up, I thought. "But these men are killers!" I said. "Assassins."

"If they haven't shot anybody yet, the chances are they won't. Unless the New York cops get trigger-happy."

That was not very encouraging.

"For what it's worth," Spence added, "the radiation monitors inside my cabin are still in the green."

We had not had time to link the radiation monitors to the telemetry system, so there was no readout for them on my console.

"Maybe you could pipe the television news up to me," he suggested. "I've got nothing else to do for a stretch."

I did that. We watched the tiny television screen until Gene Redding and his assistants showed up at 8:00 A.M. A murky morning was breaking through the clouds in New York. I thought about hiring a jet plane to fly up there, but realized it would do no good. The hostage crisis dragged on, with the hotel surrounded by police and no one entering or leaving the penthouse suite of my father.

All the employees of VCI were watching the TV scene

by now. It seemed as if at least half of them were jammed into the mission control center. Gene Redding had taken over as controller; I had moved to the right-hand chair, a headset still clamped over my ear.

"Want to make a bet Sam talks them out of whatever they came for?" Spence asked me.

I shook my head, then realized that he could not see me. "No," I said. "Not even Sam could—"

"Wait a minute!" said the news reporter. Like the rest of us, he had been on the scene all night without relief. "Wait a minute! There seems to be some action up there!"

The camera zoomed up to the rooftop balcony of my father's suite. And there stood Sam, grinning from ear to ear, and my father next to him, also smiling—although he looked drawn and pale, tired to the point of exhaustion. Behind them, three of the rebel gunmen were pulling off their ski masks. They, too, were laughing.

I rented the fastest jet available at the Orlando airport and flew to New York. With Greg at my side.

By the time we reached my father's hotel suite the police and the crowds and even the news reporters had long since gone. Sam was perched on the edge of one of the big plush chairs in the sitting room, looking almost like a child playing in a grown-up's chair. He was still wearing the faded coveralls that he had put on for the space mission.

My father, elegantly relaxed in a silk maroon dressing gown and white-silk ascot, lounged at his ease in the huge sofa placed at a right angle to Sam's chair. The coffee table before them was awash with papers.

My father was smoking a cigarette in a long ivory holder. He was just blowing a cloud of gray smoke up toward the ceiling when Greg and I burst into the room.

"Papa!" I cried.

He leaped to his feet and put the cigarette behind him like a guilty little boy. Sam laughed.

"Papa, are you all right?" I rushed across the room to him. Awkwardly, he balanced the long cigarette holder on the arm of the sofa as I flung my arms around his neck.

"I am unharmed," he announced calmly. "The rebels have gone back to Quito to form the new government."

"New government?"

"General Quintana will head the provisional government," my father explained, "until new elections are held."

"Quintana?" I blurted. "The traitor?"

Greg's face clouded over. "The army will run the government and find excuses not to hold elections. It's an old story."

"What else could I do?" my father asked sadly.

Still seated in the oversize chair, Sam grinned up at us. "You didn't do too badly, Carlos, old buddy."

Sam Gunn, on a first-name basis with my father?

Getting to his feet, Sam said to me, "Meet the new co-owner of OrbHotel, Inc."

One shock after another. It took hours for me to get it all straight in my head. Gradually, as my father and Sam told me slightly conflicting stories, I began to put the picture together.

Sam had barged into my father's hotel suite just as the rebel assassination team had arrived, guns in hand.

"They had bribed two of my security guards," my father said grimly. "They just walked in through the front door of the suite, wearing those ridiculous ski masks."

Sam added, "They were so focused on your father and the other two guys in his security team that I walked in right behind them and they never even noticed. Some assassins. A trio of college kids with guns."

Once they realized that an American citizen was in the suite the student-assassins became confused. Sam, of course, immediately began bewildering them with a non-stop monologue about how rich they could become if they would merely listen to reason.

"They're all shareholders in my new corporation," Sam told us happily. "Sam Gunn Enterprises, Unlimited. Neat title, isn't it?"

"They refrained from assassinating my father in

exchange for shares in a nonexistent corporation?'' I asked.

''It'll exist!'' Sam insisted. ''It's going to be the holding company for all my other enterprises—VCI, Orb-Hotel, I got lots of other ideas, too, you know.''

My father's face turned somber. ''They did not settle merely for shares in Sam's company.''

''Oh? What else?''

''I had to resign as president of Ecuador and name Quintana as head of the interim government.''

''Until elections can be held,'' Greg added sarcastically.

''Who is this young man?'' my father asked.

''I am Gregorio Esteban Horacio Molina y Diego, son of Professor Molina, who fled from your secret police the year you became president.''

''Ah.'' My father sagged down onto the sofa and picked up his cigarette holder once again. ''Then you want to murder me, too, I suppose.''

''Papa, you're murdering yourself with those cigarettes!''

''No lectures today, little one,'' he said to me. Then he puffed deeply on his cigarette. ''I have been through much these past twenty hours.''

''Greg did not condone assassinating you,'' I told my father. ''He wanted me to warn you.'' That was stretching the truth, of course, and I wondered why I said it. Until I took a look at Greg, so serious, so handsome, so brave.

For his part, Greg said, ''So you have joined forces with this gringo imperialist.''

''Imperialist?'' Sam laughed.

''I have invested my private monies in the orbital hotel project, yes,'' my father admitted.

''Drug money,'' Greg accused. ''Cocaine money squeezed from the sweat of the poor farmers.''

''We're going to make those farmers a lot richer,'' Sam said.

''Yes, of course.'' Greg looked as if he could murder them both.

''Listen to me, hothead,'' said Sam, jabbing a stubby

finger in Greg's direction. "First of all, I'm no flogging imperialist."

"Then why have you claimed the equatorial orbit for yourself?"

"So that nobody else could claim it. I don't give a crap whether the UN recognizes our claim or not, I'm *giving* all rights to the orbit to the UN itself. That orbit belongs to the people of the world, not any nation or corporation."

"You're giving . . . ?"

"Yeah, sure. Why let the lawyers spend the next twenty years wrangling over the legalities? I claim the orbit, then voluntarily give up the claim to the people of the world, as represented by the United Nations. So there!" And Sam stuck his tongue out at Greg, like a self-satisfied little boy.

Before either of us could reply, Sam went on, "There's big money to be made in space, kids. VCI's just the beginning. OrbHotel's gonna be a winner, and with Carlos bankrolling it, I won't have to fight with VCI's stockholders for the start-up cash."

"And how are you going to make the farmers of Ecuador rich?" Greg asked, still belligerent.

Sam leaned back in the plush chair and clasped his hands behind his head. His grin became enormous.

"By making the government of Ecuador a partner in Sam Gunn Enterprises, Unlimited."

Greg's face went red with anger. "That will make Quintana rich, not the people!"

"Only if you let Quintana stay in office," Sam said smugly.

"A typical gringo trick."

"Wait a minute. Think it out. Suppose I announce that I'm willing to make a *democratically elected* government of Ecuador a partner in my corporation? Won't that help you push Quintana out of power?"

"Yes, of course it would," I said.

Greg was not so enthusiastic. "It might help," he said warily. But then he added, "Even so, how can a partnership in your corporation make millions of poor farmers rich?''

''It won't make them poorer,'' replied Sam. ''It may put only a few *sucres* into their pockets, but that'll make life a little sweeter for them, won't it?''

Sam had made a bilingual pun! I was impressed, even if Greg was not.

''And we'll be buying all our foodstuffs for OrbHotel from Ecuadorian producers, naturally,'' Sam went on. ''And I'll sell Ecuadorian produce to the other orbital facilities, too. Make a nice profit from it, I betcha. Sure, there's only a few hundred people living in orbit right now, but that's gonna grow. There'll be thousands pretty soon, and once the Japanese start building their solar-power satellites they're going to need food for a lot of workers.''

Without seeming to draw a breath, Sam went on, ''Then there's the hotel training facility we're gonna build just outside Quito. We'll hire Ecuadorians preferentially, of course. Your father drove a hard bargain, believe me, Esmeralda.''

My father smiled wanly.

''And one of these days we could even build a sky-hook, an elevator tower up to GEO,'' Sam continued. ''That'd make Ecuador the world's center for space transportation. People won't need rockets; they'll ride the elevator, starting in Ecuador. It'll cost peanuts to get into space that way.''

He talked on and on until even Greg was at least half-way convinced that Sam would be good for the people of Ecuador.

It was growing dark before Sam finally said, ''Why don't we find a good restaurant and celebrate our new partnership?''

I looked at Greg. He wavered.

So I said, for both of us, ''Very well. Dinner tonight. But tomorrow Greg and I leave for Quito. We have much work to do if Quintana is to be prevented from cementing his hold on the government.''

Sam smiled at us both. ''You'll be going to Quito as

representatives of Sam Gunn Enterprises, Unlimited. I don't want this Quintana character to think you're revolutionaries and you kids getting into trouble."

"But we are revolutionaries," Greg insisted.

"I know," said Sam. "The best kind of revolutionaries. The kind that're really going to change things."

"Do you think we can?" I asked.

My father, surprisingly, said, "You must. The future depends on you."

"Don't look so gloomy, Carlos, old buddy," Sam said. "You've got to understand the big picture."

"The big picture?"

"Sure. There's money to be made in space. Lots of money."

"I understand that," said my father.

"Yeah, but you gotta understand the rest of it." And Sam looked squarely at Greg as he said, "The money is made in space. But it gets spent here on Earth."

My father brushed thoughtfully at his moustache with a fingertip. "I see."

"So let's spread it around and do some good."

Greg almost smiled. "But I think you will get more of the money than anyone else, won't you?"

Sam gave him a rueful look. "Yeah, that's right. And I'll spend it faster than anybody else, too."

So Greg and I returned to Ecuador. General Quintana reluctantly stepped aside and allowed elections. Democracy returned to Ecuador, although Greg claimed it arrived in our native land for the first time. Quintana retired gracefully, thanks to a huge bribe that Sam and my father provided. My father actually was voted back into the presidency, in an election that was mostly fair and open.

Spence and Bonnie Jo eventually were divorced, but that happened years later. By that time I had married Greg and he was a rising young politician who would one day be president of Ecuador himself. The country was slowly growing richer, thanks to its investment in space industries. Sam's orbital hotel was only the first step in the constantly growing commerce in space.

I never saw Sam again. Not face-to-face. Naturally, we

all saw him in the news broadcasts time and again. Just as he said, he spent every penny of the money he made on OrbHotel and went broke.

But that is another story. And, *gracias a dios*, it is a story that does not involve me.

# Statement of Lawrence V. Karsh
## (Recorded aboard Solar Power Satellite 4, in Mercury orbit)

I worked for Sam for several years back in the old days. In a way, he was a big factor in my marriage. But my wife and I could never forgive him for kidnapping our baby. That ended it between Sam and me, for good.

Oh, T.J.'s none the worse for the experience. He was still in diapers when it happened. Now he's heading up the Ecological Protection Service on Mars, making sure that the tourists don't do any harm to the Martian environment so the scientists can keep on studying the lifeforms in the rocks. He's a bright young man, my son is.

You know, the power we generate from these sunsats here in Mercury orbit will be beamed to the Mars stations. We'll be providing electrical power for most of the inner solar system, how about that? And we'll still have plenty left over to power the sailships out to Alpha Centauri and Lalande 21185.

Sam? I kinda miss him, sure. But don't let my wife hear that! She'd just as soon boil Sam in molten sulfur, even after all these years.

Well sure, Sam felt pretty bad about what happened. Or so he said. He even sent me a long letter explaining his side of it. Not a written letter, Sam never liked to commit very much to writing. It's an audiotape, from his diary.

That's right, Sam kept an audio diary. Like a running log of everything he did. No, I haven't the faintest idea of where he stored it. Probably carried it with him wherever he went, knowing Sam. Editing it every day, most likely, changing it to suit his mood or the needs of the moment, you know.

The only part of the diary I've got is the bit he sent me, which deals with the time he kidnapped my son. Yeah, sure, I've got it here in my stuff someplace. Always carry it with me. Figured it might be a valuable historical document someday.

Wanna hear it?

 **NURSERY SAM**

I WAS TRYING TO GET AWAY FROM THE SENATOR WHO wanted to marry me. So I'm sitting in the Clipper—riding tourist fare—waiting for the engines to light off and fly us to my zero-gee hotel, when who traipses into the cabin but Jack Spratt and his wife.

With a baby.

I scrunched *way* down in my seat. I didn't want them to see me. I had enough troubles without a pissed-off former employee staring daggers at me for the whole ride up to orbit.

His name wasn't really Jack Spratt, of course. It was Larry Karsh, and he had been a pretty key player in my old company, VCI. But that goddamnable Pierre D'Argent, the silver-haired slimeball, had hired him away from me, and Larry wouldn't have gone to work at Rockledge if he hadn't been sore at me for some reason. Damned if I knew what.

Okay, maybe I shouldn't have called them the Spratts. But you know, Larry was so skinny he hardly cast a shadow and Melinda was—well, the kindest word is *zaftig*, I guess. She could just look at a potato chip and gain two kilos. Larry could clean out a whole shopping mall's worth of junk food and never put on an ounce. So with him such a classic ectomorph and Melinda so billowy despite every diet in the world, it just seemed natural to call them Jack Spratt and his wife.

127

I guess it irritated Larry.

Well, I didn't like the idea of bringing a baby up to my zero-gee hotel. Business was lousy enough up there without some mewling, puking ball of dirty diapers getting in everybody's way. Heaven—that was my name for the hotel—was supposed to be for honeymooners. Oh, I'd take tourists of any sort, but I always thought of Heaven as primarily a honeymoon hotel. You know, sex in free fall, weightless lovemaking.

For the life of me, I couldn't figure out why people didn't flock to Heaven. I thought I had a terrific motto for the hotel: "If you like water beds, you'll love zero gee."

Okay, okay, so most people got sick their first day or so in weightlessness. It's a little like seasickness: You feel kind of nauseous, like you're coming down with the flu. You feel like you're falling all the time; you want to upchuck and just generally die. Of course, after a while it all goes away and you're floating around in zero gee and you start to feel terrific. Scientists have even written reports about what they call "microgravity euphoria." It's wonderful!

But first you've got to get over the miseries. And I knew damned well that Rockledge was working on a cure for space sickness, right there in the same space station as my Hotel Heaven. But even if they found the cure, who do you think would be the *last* person in the solar system that Pierre D'Argent would sell it to?

That's right. Sam Gunn, Esq. Me.

Me, I love weightlessness. God knows I've spent enough time in zero gee. The idea for the honeymoon hotel came out of plenty of practical experience, believe me. In fact, the senator who wanted to marry me had been one of my first datum points in my research on zero-gee sex, years ago. She had been a fellow astronaut, back in the days when we both worked for the old NASA.

But it only takes a few newlyweds tossing their cookies when free fall first hits them to sour the whole damned travel industry on the idea of honeymooning in Heaven. As one travel agent from North Carolina told me, sweetly,

"Even if you don't get sick yourself, who wants to spend a vacation listening to other people puking?"

I tried beefing up the acoustical insulation in the suites, but Heaven got the reputation of being like an ocean liner that's always in rough seas. And to this day I'm still convinced that D'Argent used Rockledge's high-powered public-relations machine to bad-mouth Heaven. D'Argent hated my guts, and the feeling was mutual.

And now Jack Spratt and his wife are bringing a baby up to Heaven. Perfect.

They sat two rows in front of me: Larry Karsh, Melinda, and a squirming dribbling baby that couldn't have been more than nine or ten months old. Larry had filled out a little in the couple of years since I had last seen him, but he still looked like an emaciated scarecrow. Melinda had slimmed down a trace. Maybe. They still looked like Jack Spratt and his wife. And baby.

I could feel my face wrinkling into the grandfather of all frowns. A baby aboard a space station? That's crazy! It's sabotage! Yet, try as I might, I couldn't think of any company rules or government regulations that prohibited people from bringing babies to Heaven. It just never occurred to me that anybody would. Well, I'll fix *that*, I told myself. What the hell kind of a honeymoon hotel has a baby running around in it? Upchucking is bad enough; we don't need dirty diapers and a squalling brat in orbit. They're going to ruin the whole idea of Heaven.

The Clipper took off normally; we pulled about three gees for a minute or so. The cabin was less than half-full; plenty of empty seats staring at me like the Ghost of Bankruptcy to Come. I scrunched deeper in my seat so Jack Spratt and his wife wouldn't see me. But I was listening for the yowling that I knew was on its way.

Sure enough, as soon as the engines cut off and we felt weightless, the baby started screaming. The handful of paying passengers all turned toward the kid, and Larry unbuckled himself and drifted out of his seat.

"Hey, T.J., don't holler," he said, in the kind of voice that only an embarrassed father can put out. While he talked, he and Melinda unbuckled the brat from his car seat.

The baby kicked himself free of the last strap and floated up into his father's arms. His yowling stopped. He gurgled. I knew what was coming next: his breakfast.

But instead the kid laughed and waved his chubby little arms. Larry barely touched him, just sort of guided him the way you'd tap a helium-filled balloon.

"See?" he cooed. "It's fun, isn't it?"

The baby laughed. The passengers smiled tolerantly. Me, I was stunned that Jack Spratt had learned how to coo.

Then he spotted me, slumped down so far in my seat I was practically on the floor. And it's not easy to slump in zero gee; you really have to work at it.

"Sam!" he blurted, surprised. "I didn't know you were on this flight." And Melinda turned around in her chair and gave me a strained smile.

"I didn't know you had a baby," I said, trying not to growl in front of the paying customers.

Larry floated down the aisle to my row, looking so proud of his accomplishment you'd think nobody had ever fathered a son before. "Timothy James Karsh, meet Sam Gunn. Sam, this is T.J."

He glided T.J. in my direction, the baby giggling and flailing both his arms and legs. For just the flash of a second I thought of how much fun it would be to play volleyball with the kid, but instead I just sort of held him like he was a Ming vase or something. I didn't know what the hell to do with a baby!

But the baby knew. He looked me straight in the eye and spurted out a king-size juicy raspberry, spraying me all over my face. Everybody roared with laughter.

I shoved the kid back to Larry, thinking that baseball might be more fun than volleyball.

In the fifty-eight minutes it took us to go from engine cutoff to docking with the space station, T.J. did about eleven thousand somersaults, seventy-three dozen midair pirouettes, and God knows how many raspberries. Everybody enjoyed the show, at first. The women especially gushed and gabbled and talked baby talk to the kid. They reached out to hold him, but little T.J. didn't want to be held. He was having a great time floating around the tourist cabin and enjoying weightlessness.

I had feared, in those first few moments, that seeing this little bundle of dribble floating through the cabin would make some of the passengers queasy. I was just starting to tell myself I was wrong when I heard the first retching heave from behind me. It finally caught up with them; the baby's antics had taken their minds off that falling sensation you get when zero gee first hits you. But now the law of averages took its toll.

One woman. That's all it took. One of those gargling groans, and inside of two minutes almost everybody in the cabin was grabbing for their whoopie bags and making miserable noises. I turned up the air vent over my seat to max, but the stench couldn't be avoided. Even Melinda started to look a little green, although Larry was as unaffected as I was, and little T.J. thought all the noise was hysterically funny. He threw out raspberries at everybody.

When we finally got docked we needed the station's full medical crew and a fumigation squad to clean out the cabin.

Three couples flatly refused to come aboard Heaven; green as guacamole, they canceled their vacations on the spot, demanded their money back, and rode in misery back to Earth. The other eight couples were all honeymooners. They wouldn't cancel, but they looked pretty damned unhappy.

I went straight from the dock to my cubbyhole of an office in the hotel.

"There's gotta be a way to get rid of that baby," I muttered as I slid my slippered feet into their restraint loops. I tend to talk to myself when I'm upset.

My office was a marvel of zero-gee ergonomic engineering: compact as a fighter plane's cockpit, cozy as a squirrel's nest, with everything I needed at my fingertips, whether it was up over my head or wherever. I scrolled through three hours' worth of rules and regulations, insurance, safety, travel rights, even family law. Nothing there that would prevent parents from bringing babies onto a space station.

I was staring bleary-eyed at old maritime law statutes on my display screen, hoping that as owner of the hotel I had the same rights as the captain of a ship and could make unwanted passengers walk the plank. No such luck. Then the phone light blinked. I punched the key, and growled, "What?"

A familiar voice said coyly, "Senator Meyers would like the pleasure of your company."

"Jill? Is that you?" I cleared my display screen and punched up the phone image. Sure enough, it was Senator Jill Meyers (R-NH).

Everybody said that Jill looked enough like me to be my sister. If so, what we did back in our youthful NASA days would have to be called incest. Jill had a pert round face, bright as a new penny, with a scattering of freckles across her button of a nose. Okay, so I look kind of like that, too. But her hair is a mousy brown and straight as a plumb line, while mine is on the russet side and curls so tight you can break a comb on it.

Let me get one thing absolutely clear. I am taller than she. Jill is not quite five-foot-three, whereas I am five-five, no matter what my detractors claim.

"Where are you?" I asked.

"Roughly fifty meters away from you," she said, grinning.

"Here? In Heaven?" That was not the best news in the world for me. I had come up to my zero-gee hotel to get away from Jill.

See, I had been sort of courting her down in Washington because she's a ranking member of the Senate Commerce Committee, and I needed a favor or two from her. She was perfectly happy to do me the favor or two, but she made it clear she was looking for a husband. Jill had been widowed maybe ten years earlier. I had never been married and had no intention of starting now. I like women way too much to marry one of them.

"Yes, I'm here in Heaven," Jill said, with a big grin. "Came up on the same flight you did."

"But I didn't see you."

"Senators ride first-class, Sam."

I made a frown. "At the taxpayers' expense."

"In this case, it was at the expense of Rockledge International Corporation. Feel better?"

No, I didn't feel better. Not at all. "Rockledge? How come?"

"I've been invited to inspect their research facilities here at their space station," Jill said. "Pierre D'Argent himself is escorting me."

I growled.

Maybe I should tell you that the Rockledge space station was built of three concentric wheels. The outermost wheel spun around at a rate that gave it the feeling of regular Earth gravity: one gee. The second wheel, closer to the hub, was at roughly one-third gee: the gravity level of Mars. The innermost wheel was at one-sixth gee, same as the Moon. And the hub, of course, was just about zero gravity. The scientists call it microgravity, but it's so close to zero gee that for all intents and purposes you're weightless at the hub.

I had rented half the hub from Rockledge for my Hotel Heaven. Zero gee for lovers. Okay, so it's not exactly zero gee, so what? I had built thirty lovely little mini-suites around the rim of the hub and still had enough room left over to set up a padded gym where you could play anything from volleyball to blindman's bluff in weightlessness.

Once I realized that most tourists got sick their first day or so in orbit, I tried to rent space down at the outermost wheel, so my customers could stay at normal Earth gravity and visit the zero-gee section when they wanted to play—or try weightless sex. No dice. D'Argent wouldn't rent any of it to me. He claimed Rockledge was using the rest of the station—all of it—for their research labs and their staff. Which was bullcrap.

I did manage to get them to rent me a small section in the innermost wheel, where everything was one-sixth gee.

I set up my restaurant there, so my customers could at least have their meals in some comfort. Called it the Lunar Eclipse. Best damned restaurant off Earth. Also the only one, at that time. Lots of spilled drinks and wine, though. Pouring liquids in low gravity takes some training. We had to work hard to teach our waiters and waitresses how to do it. I personally supervised the waitress training. It was one of the few bright spots in this black hole that was engulfing me.

"How about lunch?" Jill asked me, with a bright, happy smile.

"Yeah," I said, feeling trapped. "How about it?"

"What a charming invitation," said Jill. "I'll see you at the restaurant in fifteen minutes."

Now here's the deal. The first big industrial boom in orbit was just starting to take off. Major corporations like Rockledge were beginning to realize that they could make profits from manufacturing in orbit.

They had problems with workers getting space sick, of course, but they weren't as badly affected as I was with Heaven. There's a big difference between losing the first two days of a week-long vacation because you're nauseous and losing the first two days of a ninety-day work contract. Still, Rockledge was searching for a cure. Right there on the same space station as my Hotel Heaven.

Anyway, I figured that the next step in space industrialization would be to start digging up the raw materials for the orbital factories from the Moon and the asteroids. A helluva lot cheaper than hauling them up from Earth, once you get a critical mass of mining equipment in place. The way I saw it, once we could start mining the Moon and some of the near-approach asteroids, the boom in orbital manufacturing would really take off. I'd make zillions!

And I was right, of course, although it didn't exactly develop the way I thought it would.

I wanted to get there first. Start mining the Moon, grab an asteroid or two. Megafortunes awaited the person who could strike those bonanzas.

But the goddamned honeymoon hotel was bleeding me

to death. Unless and until somebody came up with a cure for space sickness, Heaven was going to be a financial bottomless pit. I was losing a bundle trying to keep the hotel open, and the day D'Argent became Rockledge's CEO he doubled my rent, sweetheart that he is.

But I knew something that D'Argent didn't want me to know. Rockledge was working on a cure for space sickness. Right here aboard the space station! If I could get my hands on that, my troubles would be over. Pretty much.

It occurred to me, as I headed for the Lunar Eclipse, that maybe Jill could do me still another favor. Maybe her being here on the station might work out okay, after all.

I pushed along the tube that went down to the inner ring. You had to be careful, heading from the hub toward the various rings, because you were effectively going downhill. Flatlanders coming up for the first time could flatten themselves but good if they let themselves drop all the way down to the outermost wheel. The coriolis force from the station's spin would bang them against the tube's circular wall as they dropped downward. The farther they dropped, the bigger the bangs. You could break bones.

That's why Rockledge's engineers had designed ladder rungs and safety hatches in the tubes that connected the hub to the wheels, so you had something to grab on to and stop your fall. I had even thought about padding the walls but D'Argent nixed my idea: too expensive, he claimed. He'd rather see somebody fracture a leg and sue me.

I was almost at the lunar level. In fact, I was pulling open the hatch when I hear a yell. I look up and a bundle of screaming baby comes tumbling past me like a miniature bowling ball with arms and legs.

"Catch him! Stop him!"

I look around and here comes Larry Karsh, flailing around like a skinny spider on LSD, trying to catch up with his kid.

"Sam! Help!"

If I had thought about it for half a microsecond I would've let the kid bounce off the tube walls until he splattered himself on the next set of hatches. And Larry after him.

But, no—instinct took over, and I shot through the hatch and launched myself after the baby like a torpedo on a rescue mission. S. Gunn, intrepid hero.

It was a long fall to the next set of hatches. I could see the kid tumbling around like a twenty-pound meteoroid, bare-ass naked, hitting the wall and skidding along it for a moment, then flinging out into midair again. His size worked for him, a little guy like he was didn't hit the wall so hard—at first. But each bump down the tube was going to be harder, I knew. If I didn't catch him real fast, he'd get hurt. Bad.

There was nobody else in the damned tube, nobody there to grab him or break his fall or even slow him down a little.

I started using the ladder rungs to propel myself faster, grabbing the rungs with my fingertips and pushing off them, one after another, faster and faster. Like the Lone Ranger chasing a runaway horse. Damned coriolis force was getting to me, though, making me kind of dizzy.

As I got closer and closer, I saw that little T.J. wasn't screaming with fear. He was screeching with delight, happy as a little cannonball, kicking his arms and legs and tumbling head over bare ass, laughing as hard as he could.

Next time he hits the wall he won't be laughing anymore, I thought. Then I wondered if I could reach him before he slammed into the hatch at the bottom of this level of the tube. At the speed I was going I'd come down right on top of him, and the kid wouldn't be much of a cushion.

Well, I caught up with him before either of us reached the next hatch, tucked him under one arm like he was a wriggling football, and started trying to slow my fall with the other hand. It wasn't going to work, I saw, so I flipped myself around so I was coming down feetfirst and kept grabbing at rungs with my free hand, getting dizzier and dizzier. Felt like my shoulder was going to come off, and my hand got banged up pretty good, but at least we slowed down some.

The baby was crying and struggling to get loose. He'd been having fun, dropping like an accelerating stone. He didn't like being saved. I heard Larry yelling and looked up; he was clambering down the ladder, all skinny arms and legs, jabbering like a demented monkey.

I hit the hatch feetfirst like I'd been dropped out of an airplane. I mean, I did my share of parachute jumps back when I was in astronaut training, but this time I hit a hell of a lot harder. Like my shinbones were shattering and my knees were trying to ram themselves up into my rib cage. I saw every star in the Milky Way, and the wind was knocked out of me for a moment.

So I was sprawled on my back, kind of dazed, with the kid yelling to get loose from me, when Larry comes climbing down the ladder, puffing like *he'd* been trying to save the kid, and takes the yowling little brat in his arms.

"Gee, thanks, Sam," he says. "I was changing his diaper when he got loose from me. Sorry about the mess."

That's when I realized that the ungrateful little so-and-so had peed all down the front of my shirt.

So I was late for my lunch date with Senator Meyers. My hand was banged up and swollen, my legs ached, my knees felt like they were going to explode, and the only other shirt I had brought with me was all wrinkled from being jammed into my travel bag. But at least it was dry. Even so, I got to the restaurant before she did. Jill was one of those women who has a deathly fear of arriving anywhere first.

I was so late, though, that she was only half a minute behind me. I hadn't even started for a table yet; I was still in the restaurant's teeny little foyer, talking with my buddy Omar.

"Am I terribly late?" Jill asked.

I turned at the sound of her voice and, I've got to admit, Jill looked terrific. I mean, she was as plain as vanilla, with hardly any figure at all, but she still looked bright and attractive and, well, I guess the right word is *radiant*. She was wearing a one-piece zipsuit, almost like the coveralls that we used to wear back on the NASA shuttle. But now her suit was made of some kind of shiny stuff and decorated with color accents and jewels. Like Polonius said: rich, not gaudy.

Her hair was a darker shade than I remembered it from the old days, and impeccably coiffed. She was dyeing it, I figured. And getting it done a lot better than she did when she'd been a working astronaut.

"You look like a million dollars," I said, as she stepped through the hatch into the restaurant's foyer.

She grinned that freckle-faced grin of hers, and said, "It costs almost that much to look like this."

"It's worth it," I said.

Omar, my buddy from years back, was serving as the maître d' that afternoon. He was the general manager of the hotel, but everybody was pulling double or triple duty, trying to keep the place afloat. He loomed over us, painfully gaunt and tall as a basketball star, his black pate shaved bald, a dense goatee covering his chin. In the easy lunar gravity Omar could walk normally with nothing more than the lightest of braces on his atrophied legs. Omar had more to lose than I did if the hotel went bust. He'd have to go back to Earth and be a cripple.

As he showed us to our table, all dignity and seriousness, Jill cracked, "You're getting gray, Sam."

"Cosmic rays," I snapped back at her. "Not age. I've been in space so much that primary cosmic rays have discolored my pigmentation."

Jill nodded as if she knew better but didn't want to argue about it. The restaurant was almost completely empty. It was the only place aboard the station to eat, unless you were a Rockledge employee and could use their cafeteria, yet still it was a sea of empty tables. I mean, there wasn't any other place for the tourists to eat, it was lunch hour for those who came up from the States, but the Eclipse had that forlorn look. Three tables occupied, seventeen bare. Twelve human waiters standing around with nothing to do but run up my salary costs.

As Omar sat us at the finest table in the Eclipse (why not?), Jill said, "You ought to get some new clothes, Sam. You're frayed at the cuffs, for goodness' sake."

I refrained from telling her about T.J.'s urinary gift. But I gave her the rest of the story about my thrilling rescue, which nobody had witnessed except the butterfingered Jack Spratt.

"My goodness, Sam, you saved that baby's life," Jill said, positively glowing at me.

"I should've let him go and seen how high he'd bounce when he hit the hatch."

"Sam!"

"In the interest of science," I said.

"Don't be mean."

"He's supposed to be a bouncing baby boy, isn't he?"
She did not laugh.

"Dammit, Jill, they shouldn't have brought a kid up here," I burst out. "It's not right. There ought to be a regulation someplace to prevent idiots from bringing their lousy brats to my hotel!"

Jill was not helpful at all. "Sam," she told me, her expression severe, "we made age discrimination illegal almost a century ago."

"This isn't age discrimination," I protested. "That baby isn't a voting citizen."

"He's still a human being who has rights. And so do his parents."

I am not a gloomy guy, but it felt like a big raincloud had settled over my head. Little T.J. was not the only one pissing on me.

But I had work to do. As long as Jill was here, I tried to make the best of it. I started spinning glorious tales of the coming bonanza in space manufacturing, once we could mine raw materials from the Moon or asteroids.

I never mentioned our weightless escapades, but she knew that I held that trump card. Imagine the fuss the media would make if they discovered that the conservative senator from New Hampshire had once been a wild woman in orbit. With the notorious Sam Gunn, of all people!

"What is it you want, Sam?" Jill asked me. That's one of the things I liked best about her. No bull-hickey. She came straight to the point.

So I did, too. "I'm trying to raise capital for a new venture."

Before I could go any farther, she fixed me with a leery eye. "Another new venture? When are you going to stop dashing around after the pot of gold at the end of the rainbow, Sam?"

I gave her a grin. "When I get my hands on the gold."

"Is that what you're after, money? Is that all that you're interested in?"

"Oh no," I said honestly. "What I'm really interested in is the things money can buy."

She frowned; it was part annoyance, part disappointment, I guess. Easy for her. She was born well-off, married even better, and now was a wealthy widowed United States Senator. Me, I was an orphan at birth, raised by strangers. I've always had to claw and scrabble and kick and bite my way to wherever I had to go. There was nobody around to help me. Only me, all five-foot-three—excuse me, five-foot-five inches of me. All by myself. You're damned right money means a lot to me. Most of all, it means respect. Like that old ballplayer said, the home-run hitters drive the Cadillacs. I also noticed, very early in life, that they get the best-looking women.

"Okay," I backpedaled. "So money can't buy happiness. But neither can poverty. I want to get filthy rich. Is there anything wrong with that?"

Despite her New England upbringing, a faint smile teased at the corners of Jill's mouth. "No, I suppose not," she said softly.

So I went into the details about my hopes for lunar mining and asteroid prospecting. Jill listened quietly, attentively, I thought, until I finished my pitch.

She toyed with her wineglass as she said, "Mining the Moon. Capturing asteroids. All that's a long way off, Sam."

"It's a lot closer than most people realize," I replied, in my best-behaved, serious man-of-business attitude. Then I added, "It's not as far in the future as our own space-shuttle missions are in the past."

Jill sighed, then grinned maliciously. "You always were a little bastard, weren't you?"

I grinned back at her. "What's the accident of my birth got to do with it?"

She put the wineglass down and hunched closer to me. "Just what are you after, Sam, specifically?" I think she was enjoying the challenge of dealing with me.

I answered, "I want to make sure that the big guys like Rockledge and Yamagata don't slit my throat."

"How can I help you do that?"

"You're on the Commerce Committee and the Foreign Relations Committee, right? I need to be able to assure my investors that the Senate won't let my teeny little company be squashed flat by the big guys."

"Your investors? Like who?"

I refused to be rattled by her question. "I'll find investors," I said firmly, "once you level the playing field for me."

Leaning back in her chair, she said slowly, "You want me to use my influence as a United States Senator to warn Rockledge and the others not to muscle you."

I nodded.

Jill thought about it for a few silent moments, then she asked, "And what's in it for me?"

Good old straight from the shoulder Jill. "Why," I said, "you get the satisfaction of helping an old friend to succeed in a daring new venture that will bring the United States back to the forefront of space industrialization."

She gave me a look that told me that wasn't the answer she had wanted to hear. But before I could say anything more, she muttered, "That might win six or seven votes in New Hampshire, I guess."

"Sure," I said. "You'll be a big hero with your constituents, helping the little guy against the big, bad corporations."

"Cut the serenade, Sam," she snapped. "You've got

something else going on in that twisted little brain of yours; I can tell. What is it?''

She was still grinning as she said it, so I admitted, ''Well, there's a rumor that Rockledge is developing an antinausea remedy that'll stop space sickness. It could mean a lot for my hotel.''

''I hear your zero-gee sex palace is on its way to bankruptcy.''

''Not if Rockledge will sell me a cure for the weightless whoopsies.''

''You think they'd try to keep it from you?''

''Do vultures eat meat?''

She laughed and started in on her plate of soyburger.

After lunch I took Jill down to her minisuite in the hub and asked how she liked her accommodations.

''Well,'' she said, drawing the word out, ''it's better than the old shuttle mid-deck, I suppose.''

''You suppose?'' I was shocked. ''Each one of Heaven's rooms is a luxurious, self-contained minisuite.'' I quoted from our publicity brochure.

Jill said nothing until I found her door and opened it for her, with a flourish.

''Kind of small, don't you think?'' she said.

''Nobody's complained about the size,'' I replied. Then I showed her the controls that operated the minibar, the built-in sauna, the massage equipment, and the screen that covered the observation port.

''A real love nest,'' Jill said.

''That's the idea.''

I opened the observation port's screen and we saw the Earth hanging out there, huge and blue and sparkling. Then it slid past as the station revolved and we were looking at diamond-hard stars set against the velvet black of space. It was gorgeous, absolutely breathtaking.

And then we heard somebody vomiting in the next compartment. The hotel's less than one-quarter full and my crackbrained staff books two zero-gee compartments next to one another!

But Jill just laughed. ''This hotel isn't going to prosper

until somebody comes up with a cure for space sickness.''

"That's what Rockledge is doing,'' I grumbled. "Right aboard this station.''

"You're sure?''

"I'm sure.''

Jill pursed her lips. Then, "Let me ask D'Argent about that. Unofficially, of course. But maybe I can find out something for you.''

My eyes must have widened. "You'd do that for me?''

Jill touched my cheek with cool fingertips. "Of course I would, Sam. You have no idea of the things I'd do for you, if you'd only let me.''

That sounded dangerous to me. So I bid her a hasty adieu and pushed through her doorway, heading for my cubbyhole of an office. Jill just gave me a sphinxlike inscrutable smile as I floated out of her compartment.

When I got back to my office there was more depressing news on my computer screen. A contingent of Rockledge board members and junior executives was scheduled for a tour of the station and its facilities. They would be staying for a week and had booked space in my hotel—at the discount prices Rockledge commanded as my landlord. Those prices, negotiated before I had ever opened Heaven, were lower than the rent D'Argent was now charging me. If I filled the hotel with Rockledge people I could go bankrupt even faster than I was.

And they were all bringing their wives. And children! Larry, Melinda, and their bouncing baby boy were just the first wave of the invasion of the weightless brats. I began to think about suicide. Or murder.

I can't describe the horrors of that week. By actual count there were only twenty-two kids. The oldest was fifteen and the youngest was little T.J., ten months or so. But it seemed like there were hundreds of them, thousands. Everywhere I turned there were brats getting in my way, poking around the observation center, getting themselves stuck in hatches, playing tag along the tubes that connected the station's hub with its various wheels, yelling, screaming, tumbling, fighting, throwing food around, and just generally making my life miserable.

Not only my life. Even the honeymooners started checking out early, with howls of protest at the invasion of the underage monsters and dire threats about lawsuits.

"You'll pay for ruining our honeymoon," was the kindest farewell statement any of them made.

The brats took over the zero-gee gym. It looked like one of those old martial-arts films in there, only in weightlessness. They were swarming all over the padded gym, kicking, thrashing, screaming, arms and legs everyplace, howls and yelps and laughing and crying. One five-year-old girl, in particular, had a shriek that could cleave limestone.

I tried to get the three teenagers among them to serve as guardians—guards, really—for the younger tots. I offered them damned good money to look after the brats. The two girls agreed with no trouble. The one boy—fourteen, sullen, face full of zits—refused. He was the son of one of the board members. "My mother didn't bring me up here to be a baby-sitter," he growled.

As far as I could see, the only thing the pizza-faced jerk did was hang around the hub weightlessly and sulk.

I couldn't blame the honeymooners for leaving. Who wants to fight your way through a screaming horde of little monsters to get to your zero-gee love nest? It was hopeless. I could see D'Argent smiling that oily smile of his; he knew I was going down in flames and *he* was enjoying every minute of it.

And right in the middle of it were Larry and Melinda and their bouncing baby boy—who really did bounce around a lot off the padded walls of the gym. T.J. loved it in there, especially with all the other kids to keep him company. The two teenage girls made him their living doll. And T.J. seemed to look out with his ten-month-old eyes at the whole noisy, noisome gang of kids as if they were his personal play toys, a swirling, riotous, colorful mobile made up of twenty-two raucous, runny-nosed, rotten kids.

Make that twenty-one kids and one fourteen-year-old moper.

I found that Larry and Melinda started feeding the baby in the gym. "It's easier than doing it in the restaurant or in our own quarters," Melinda said, as T.J. gummed away at some pulpy baby goop. "Practically no mess at all."

I could see what she meant. They just hovered in mid-air with the baby. Three-fourths of what they aimed at the brat's mouth wound up in his ear or smeared over his face or spit into the air. Being weightless, most of the stuff just broke into droplets or crumbs and drifted along in the air currents until they stuck on one of the intake ventilator screens. At the end of the meal Larry would break out a hand vacuum and clean off the screens while Melinda cleaned the baby with premoistened towels. Not bad, I had to admit. Didn't have to mop the floor or clean any furniture.

The other kids liked to eat in zero gee, too. Made their food fights more interesting. It was okay with me; anything that kept them out of the restaurant or the other areas where adult human beings lived and worked was a score for our side, far as I was concerned. But zero-gee sex was a thing of the past as long as they held the station's gym in their grubby little paws. My honeymoon hotel had turned into an orbital camp for tots.

"You were right, Sam," Jill told me over dinner the third or fourth night of Hell Week.

The restaurant was almost empty. Nearly every one of Rockledge's junior executives took their meals in their rooms. Too cheap for the restaurant, they used the fast-food dispensers and the cafeteria in the Rockledge research facility.

At least the Eclipse was quiet. No kids. I had thought about trying to make a rule that nobody under twenty-one was allowed into the Lunar Eclipse, but Omar, my long-suffering hotel manager, had convinced me that it would just cause a ruckus with the parents. They were happy as Torquemada in a synagogue to be in the restaurant without their little darlings. But if I said they weren't allowed to bring their kids to the Eclipse they'd get pissed off and *demand* their rights.

So the restaurant was nice and quiet and civilized with all the kids up in the gym dashing around and playing zero-gee games.

"I was right about what?" I asked. I must have looked as miserable as I felt. My mind was echoing with the screeches of all those brats yowling at the top of their lungs and the somber prediction of my accountant that the hotel would sink beneath the financial waves in another two weeks. All day long I had been receiving cancellation notices from travel agencies. The word was going around at the speed of light.

Jill nudged her chair a little closer to mine. "Rockledge really is working on a preventative for space sickness. Pierre D'Argent showed me the laboratory studies they've done so far. It looks as if they've got it."

No sooner had she mentioned D'Argent's name than the silver-haired sonofabitch showed up at the restaurant's door, leading a contingent of six senior Rockledge board members and their trophy wives. The men all looked like grumpy old farts, white-haired or bald; the women were heavy with jewelry. I wondered which one of them owned that fourteen-year-old sourpuss.

"What lovely women," Jill said.

I made no response.

"Don't you think they're beautiful, Sam?"

I grunted. "Who cares."

Jill gave me a funny expression. I didn't realize it at the time, but her expression was a mixture of surprise and admiration. She thought I had finally matured to the point where I didn't salivate like one of Pavlov's dogs every time I saw a good-looking woman. What Jill didn't realize was that I was too down in the dumps to be interested in a bevy of expensively dressed advertisements for cosmetic surgery who were already married. I never chased married women. Never. That's a point of honor with me. It also saves you a lot of threats, fights, lawsuits, and attempts on your life.

Jill returned to her original subject. "Didn't you hear me, Sam? Rockledge is going to market a skin patch that prevents space sickness."

"Yeah," I said gloomily. "The day after this hotel closes, that's when they'll put it on the market."

I was watching D'Argent and his troupe as they sat at the biggest table in the restaurant. Laughing softly among themselves, happy, relaxed, their biggest worry was how to evade the taxes that were due on their enormous profits. The more they ate and drank, at their discount prices, the deeper into the red they pushed me.

Jill shook me by my wrist and made me look at her. She had a kind of pixie grin on her face. Almost evil. "Suppose I could get D'Argent to use your hotel customers as a field trial for their new drug?"

"Suppose you could get the Pope to pee off the roof of the Vatican."

"Wouldn't that help you?" she insisted.

I had to admit that it might.

"Then that's what I'll do," Jill said, as firmly as a US Senator announcing she was running for reelection.

I had no romantic interest in Jill, and for the life of me I couldn't figure out why she was interested in me. What did it matter? I was in such a funk over those brats infesting my hotel that I wouldn't have noticed if Helen of Troy had been sitting naked in my bed with her arms out to me. Well, maybe.

What was going through my mind was an endless vicious circle. The hotel is failing. When the hotel goes down the tubes it'll drag my company, VCI, down with it. VCI was technically in the black, making steady money selling magnetic bumpers that protected space facilities from orbiting debris. But legally, VCI owned Hotel Heaven and the hotel's accumulated debts would force VCI into bankruptcy. I would be broke. Nobody would lend me a cent. There went my dreams for mining the Moon and making myself the tycoon of the asteroids. I'd have to find a job someplace.

Unless—there was only one way I could see out of the black pit that was staring at me. I had to swallow hard several times before I could work up the nerve to even put out a feeler. But it was either that or bankruptcy, the end of all my dreams. So the next morning I gritted my teeth (having swallowed hard several times) and took the first little step on the road to humiliation.

"Hi, Larry old pal, how's it going?" The words almost stuck in my throat, but I had to get started somehow.

Oh, that's right, I haven't told you about Larry and Melinda and the Gunn Shield. Here's the story.

I had first started VCI, years earlier, to build magnetic bumpers for space stations, to protect them against the orbiting junk whizzing around up there. Larry designed them for me. They're called Gunn Shields, of course. Without them, a space station would get dinged constantly from the crap zipping around in orbit. Even a chip of paint hits with the impact of a high-power bullet, and there's a helluva lot more than paint chips flying around in the low orbits.

The Russians finally had to abandon their original *Mir* space station because it was starting to look like a target in a shooting gallery. And the more stations and factories people built in orbit, the more debris they created and the more they needed Gunn Shields. A nice, steady, growing market. Not spectacular, not enough to bring in the kind of cash flow I needed, but dependable.

Back in those days Melinda had a crush on me. Just a kid's crush, that's all it was, but Larry loved her madly and hated me for it. She was kind of pretty underneath her avoirdupois, but not my type.

That surprises you? You heard that Sam Gunn chases all types of women, didn't you. No discrimination at all. Well, that's about as true as all the rest of the bull manure they spread about me.

Melinda was not my type. But she had this thing about me and Larry had his heart set on her. So I hired Melinda to come to work for me at VCI, and then kind of offhand asked Larry if he'd like to come along, too. Larry was the guy I needed, the one I had to have if VCI was going to be a success. He was the semigenius who thought up the idea for magnetic bumpers in the first place. Poor fish rose to the bait without even stopping to think. They both moved to Florida, and together we put VCI into business.

So while Larry was designing the original bumper, I

was touting Melinda off me and onto Larry. Cyrano de
Gunn, that's me. Made her fall in love with him. *Voilà*.
Once we tested the original bumper, and it worked, I got
it patented and Larry got Melinda to marry him. Everybody was happy, I thought. Wrong!

For some unfathomable reason, Larry got pissed at me
and went off to work for D'Argent, the sneaky sleazoid,
over at Rockledge. And when he quit VCI, Melinda did,
too.

Oh, yeah, we almost got into a shooting war over the
rights to the geocentric orbit. But that's another story.
Larry only played a minor role in that one.

Anyway, I had spent a sleepless night tussling over my
problems and couldn't see a way out. Except to sell the
goddamned hotel to Rockledge. And the rights to the
Gunn Shield, too. Dump it all for cash. D'Argent had
tried before to sneak the magnetic bumper design away
from me. He had tried bribery and even theft. Hell, he
had hired Larry with the idea of getting the kid to figure
out a way to break my patent. I knew that, even if Larry
himself didn't.

So now I toadied up to Larry, in the middle of the
mayhem of the station's gym. The kids had taken it over
completely. Larry and I were the only adults among the
yowling, zooming, screeching, barfing little darlings.
Even the two teenage girls who were supposed to be
watching the kids were busy playing free-fall tag and
screaming at the top of their considerable voices.

Larry gave me a guarded look. He was feeding T.J.,
who was happily spraying most of his food into weightless droplets that hovered around him like tiny spheres of
multicolored glop before drifting slowly toward the nearest ventilator grid.

"Where's Melinda?" I asked, trying to radiate good
cheer and sincerity while dodging the goo that the baby
was spewing out.

"She's down in the second wheel, doing aerobics," he
said. He spooned a bit of puke-colored paste out of a jar
and stuck it in front of T.J.'s face. The baby siphoned it
off with a big slurping noise and even managed to get

some of it past his two visible teeth and into his mouth.

Gradually, with every ounce of self-control and patient misdirection I could muster, I edged the topic of conversation to the Gunn Shields. All the time we were both dodging flying kids and the various missiles they were throwing at each other, as well as T.J.'s pretty constant spray of food particles. And I had to shout to make myself heard over the noise the brats were making.

I only hoped that none of them figured out the combinations for the electronic locks on the zero-gee minisuites. I could just see the little SOBs breaking into the minibars and throwing bottles all over the place or scalding themselves in the saunas. Come to think of it, boiling a couple of them might have been fun.

But I had work to do.

The more I talked to Larry about the magnetic shields, though, the more he seemed to drift away from me. I mean, literally move away. He kept floating backward through the big, padded zero-gee compartment, and I kept pushing toward him. We slowly crossed the entire gym, with all those kids whooping and zooming around us. Finally I had him pinned against one of the padded walls, T.J. floating upside down above him and the jar of baby food hovering between us. It was only then that I realized Larry was getting red in the face.

"What's the matter?" I asked, earnestly. "Are you getting sick?"

"Dammit, Sam, they shouldn't be called Gunn Shields!" Larry burst out. "I designed the bumpers, not you! They ought to be called Karsh Shields!"

I was stunned. I had never even thought of that. And he certainly had never mentioned it to me before.

"You mean, all this time you've been sore at me over a public-relations title?"

"It means a lot to me," he said, as surly as that teenage grump.

"Is that why you left me for Rockledge?"

Larry nodded petulantly.

It was my big chance. Maybe my only chance. I let

my head droop as if I had suddenly discovered religion and was ashamed of my past life.

"Gee, Larry," I said, just loudly enough to be heard over the screams of the kids, "I never realized how much it meant to you."

"Well, it's my invention, but you took out the patent and took all the credit, too."

I noticed that he had not spoken a word about money. Not a syllable. Larry was pure of heart, bless his unblemished soul.

I looked him in the eye with the most contrite expression I could manage. It was hard to keep from giggling; this was going to be like plucking apples off a blindman's fruit stand.

"If that's the way you feel about it, kid," I said, trying to keep up the hangdog expression, "then we'll change the name. Look—I—I'll even license Rockledge to manufacture and sell the shields. That's right! Let Rockledge take it over completely! Then you can call them Karsh Shields with no trouble at all!"

His eyes goggled. "You'd do that for me, Sam?"

I slid an arm around his shoulder. "Sure I would. I never wanted to hurt you, Larry. If only you had told me sooner . . ." I let my voice fade away. Then I nodded, as if I had been struggling inside myself. "I'll sell Rockledge the hotel, too."

"No!" Larry gasped. "Not your hotel."

"I know D'Argent wants it." That wasn't exactly the truth. But I had a strong suspicion the silver-haired bastard would be happy to take the hotel away from me— as long as he thought it would break my heart to part with it.

Larry's face turned red again, but this time he looked embarrassed, not angry. "Sam . . ." He hesitated, then went on, "Look, Sam, I'm not supposed to tell you this, but the company's been working on a cure for space sickness."

I blinked at him, trying to generate a tear or two. "Really?"

"If it works, it should help to make your hotel a success."

"If it works," I said, with a big sigh.

The way I had it figured, Rockledge would pay a nice royalty for the license to manufacture and sell the magnetic bumpers. Not as much as VCI was making in profits from the shields, but the Rockledge royalties would go to me, personally, as the patent holder. Not to VCI. The damned hotel's debts wouldn't touch the royalties. VCI would go down the tubes, but what the hell, that's business. I'd be moving on to lunar mining and asteroid hunting. ET Resources, Inc. That's what I would call my new company.

Let Larry call them Karsh Shields, I didn't give a fart's worth about that. Let D'Argent do everything he could to make the world forget I had anything to do with them, as long as he sent me the royalty checks on time. What I really wanted, what I desperately needed, was the money to start moving on ET Resources, Inc.

"Maybe I can talk D'Argent into letting you use their new drug," Larry suggested. "You know, try it out on your hotel customers."

I brightened up a little. "Gee," I said, "that would be nice. If only I could keep my hotel." I sighed again, heavier, heavy enough to nudge me slightly away from Larry and the baby. "It would break my heart to part with Heaven."

Larry gaped at me while T.J. stuck a sticky finger in his father's ear.

"It would make both of us happy," I went on. "I could keep the hotel, and Rockledge could take over the magnetic bumpers and call them Karsh Shields."

That really turned him on. "I'll go find D'Argent right now!" Larry said, all enthusiasm. "Would you mind looking after T.J. for a couple of minutes?"

And he was off like a shot before I could say a word, out across the mayhem of all those brats flinging themselves around the gym. Just before he disappeared through the main hatch he yelled back at me, "Oh, yeah,

T.J.'s going to need a change. You know how to change a diaper, don't you?''

He ducked through the hatch before I could answer. The kids swarmed all through the place, and little T.J. stared after his disappearing father.

I was kind of stunned. I wasn't a baby-sitter! But there I was, hanging in midair with twenty crazed kids zipping all around me and a ten-month-old baby hanging a couple of feet before my eyes, his chin and cheeks smeared with baby food and this weird expression on his face.

"Well," I said to myself, "what the hell do I do now?"

T.J. broke into a bawling cry. He wanted his father, not this stranger. I didn't know what to do. I tried talking to him, tried holding him, even tried making faces at him. He didn't understand a word I said, of course; when I tried to hold him he squirmed and shrieked so loud even the other kids stopped their games to stare at me accusingly. And when I made a few faces at him he just screamed even louder.

Then I smelled something. His diaper.

One of the teenage girls gave me a nasty look, and said firmly, "I'm going to call his mother!"

"Never mind," I said. "I'll bring the kid to her myself."

I nudged squalling T.J. weightlessly toward the hatch and started the two of us down the connector tube toward the second-level wheel, where the Rockledge gym was. It had been a stroke of genius (mine) to put their exercise facility in the wheel that rotated at about one-third gee, the gravity you'd feel on Mars. You can lift three times the weight you'd be able to handle on Earth and feel like you've accomplished something without straining yourself. But do you think D'Argent or any of his Rockledge minions would give me credit for the idea? When hell freezes over—maybe.

T.J. stopped yowling once I got his flailing little body through the hatch and into the tube. This was a different-enough place for his curiosity to override the idea that his father had abandoned him and whatever discomfort his loaded diaper might be causing him. He was fascinated with the blinking lights on the hatch control panel. I opened and shut the damned hatch half a dozen times, just to quiet him down. Then I showed him the color-coded guide-lines on the tube's walls, and the glowing light strips. He pointed and smiled. Kind of a goofy smile, with just two teeth to show. But it was better than crying.

By the time we reached the second wheel we were almost pals. I let him smear his greasy little hands over the hatch control panel; like I said, he liked to watch the lights blink, and there wasn't much damage he could do to the panel except make it sticky. I even held his hand and let him touch the keypads that operated the hatch. He laughed when it started to swing open. After we went through he pointed at the control panel on the other side and made it clear he wanted to play with that one, too.

There was enough of a feeling of gravity down at this level for me to walk on the floor, with T.J. crawling along beside me. I tried to pick him up and carry him, despite his smell, but he was too independent for that. He wanted to be on his own.

Kind of reminded me of me.

Melinda was sweaty and puffing and not an ounce lighter than she had been when she entered the exercise room. T.J. spotted her in the middle of all the straining, groaning women doing their aerobics to the latest top-forty pop tunes. He let out a squeal, and all the women stopped their workout to surround the kid with cooing gushing baby talk. Melinda was queen of them all, the mother of the center of their attention. You'd think the brat had produced ice cream.

I beat a hasty retreat, happy to be rid of the kid. Although, I've got to admit, little T.J. was kind of fun to be with. When he wasn't crying. And if you held your breath.

True to his naive word, Larry arranged a meeting between D'Argent and me that very afternoon. I was invited to the section of the station where Rockledge had its lab, up in the lunar wheel, alongside my restaurant.

You might have thought we were trying to penetrate a top-secret military base. Between the Lunar Eclipse and the hatch to the Rockledge laboratory was a corridor no more than ten meters long. Rockledge had packed six uniformed security guards, an X-ray scanner, three video cameras, and a set of chemical sniffers into those ten meters. If we didn't have a regulation against animals, they would have probably had a few Dobermans in there, too.

"What're you guys doing in here?" I asked D'Argent, once they had let me through the security screen and ushered me into the compartment he was using as an office. "You've got more security out there than a rock star visiting the emperor of Japan."

D'Argent never wore coveralls or fatigues, like the rest of us. He was in a spiffy silk suit, pearl gray with pencil-thin darker stripes, just like he wore Earthside. He gave me one of his oily little smiles. "We need all that security, Sam," he said, "to keep people like you from stealing our ideas."

I sat at the spindly little chair in front of his desk and gave him a sour look. "The day you have an idea worth stealing, the Moon will turn into green cheese."

He glared at me. Larry, sitting at the side of D'Argent's desk, tried to cool things off. "We're here to discuss a business deal, not exchange insults."

I looked at him with new respect. Larry wasn't a kid anymore. He was starting to turn into a businessman. "Okay," I said. "You're right. I'm here to offer a trade."

D'Argent stroked his pencil-thin moustache with a manicured finger. "A trade?"

Nodding, I said, "I'll license Rockledge to manufacture and market the magnetic bumpers. You let me buy your space-sickness cure."

D'Argent reached for the carafe on his desk. Stalling for time, I thought. He poured himself a glass of water, never offering any to Larry or me. In the soft lunar gravity of the inner wheel, the water poured at a gentler angle than it would on Earth. D'Argent managed to get most of the water into his glass; only a few drops messed up his desk.

He pretended not to notice it. "What makes you think we've developed a cure for space sickness?" And he gave Larry a cold eye.

"Senator Meyers told me," I said calmly. D'Argent looked surprised. "Jill and I are old friends. Didn't you know?"

"You and Senator Meyers?" I could read the expression on his face. A new factor had entered his calculations.

We went around and around for hours. D'Argent was playing it crafty. He wanted the magnetic bumper business, that was clear to see. And Larry was positively avid to call them Karsh Shields. I pretended that I wanted the space-sickness cure to save my hotel, while all the time I was trying to maneuver D'Argent into buying Heaven and taking it off my hands.

But he was smarter than that. He knew that he didn't have to buy the hotel; it was going to sink of its own weight. In another two weeks I'd be in bankruptcy court.

So he blandly kept insisting, "The space-sickness cure isn't ready for public use, Sam. It's still in the experimental stage."

I could see from the embarrassed red of Larry's face that it was a gigantic lie.

"Well then," I suggested, "let me use it on my hotel customers as a field trial. I'll get them to sign waivers, take you off the hook, legally."

But D'Argent just made helpless fluttering gestures and talked about the Food and Drug Administration, this law, that regulation, scientific studies, legal red tape, and enough bullcrap to cover Iowa six feet deep.

He was stalling, waiting for my hotel to collapse so he could swoop in, grab Heaven away from me, and get the magnetic bumper business at a bargain.

But while he talked in circles, I started to think. What if I could get my hands on his space-sickness cure and try it out on a few of my customers? What if I steal the damned cure right out from under D'Argent's snooty nose and then get a tame chemist or two to reproduce whatever combination of drugs they've got in their cure? That would put me in a better bargaining position, at least. And it would drive the smooth-talking sonofabitch crazy!

So I decided to steal it.

It was no big deal. D'Argent and his Rockledge security types were too Earthbound in their attitudes. They thought that by guarding the corridor access to the laboratory area, they had the lab adequately protected. But there were four emergency airlocks strung along that wheel of the station. Two of them opened onto the restaurant; the other two opened directly into the Rockledge research laboratory.

All I had to do was wait until night, get into a space suit, and go EVA to one of those airlocks. I'd be inside the lab within minutes, and the guards out in the corridor would never know it.

Then I had a truly wicked idea. A diversion that would guarantee that the Rockledge security troops would be busy doing something else instead of guarding the access to their lab.

The meeting with D'Argent ran out of steam with neither one of us making any real effort to meet the other halfway. Halfway? Hell, neither D'Argent nor I budged an inch. Larry looked miserably unhappy when we finally decided to call it quits. He saw his Karsh Shield immortality sliding away from him.

I went straight from D'Argent's office to the station's gym. Nothing had changed there, except that T.J. was gone. The place still looked like a perpetual-motion demonstration, kids flapping and yelling everywhere. All except that surly teenage boy.

I glided over to him.

"Hi!" I said brightly.

He mumbled something.

"You don't seem to be having a good time," I said.

"So what?" he said sourly.

I made a shrug. "Seems a shame to be up here and not enjoying it."

"What's to enjoy?" he grumbled. "My mother says I have to stay here with all these brats and not get in anybody's way."

"Gee, that's a shame," I said. "There's a lot of really neat stuff to see. You want a tour of the place?"

For the first time his face brightened slightly. "You mean, like the command center and all?"

"Sure. Why not?"

"They threw me out of there when I tried to look in, a couple days ago."

"Don't worry about it," I assured him. "I'll get you in with no trouble."

Sliding an arm across his skinny shoulders as we headed for the command center, I asked him, "What's your name, anyway, son?"

"Pete," he said.

"Stick with me, Pete, and you'll see stuff that hardly any of the adults ever see."

So I took him on a tour of the station. I spent the whole damned afternoon with Pete, taking him all over the station. I showed him everything from the command center to my private office. While we were in the command center I booted up the station security program and found that Rockledge didn't even have intruder alarms or motion sensors inside their lab area. Breaking in through the airlock was going to be easy.

It would have been nifty if I could've used Pete as an excuse to waltz through the Rockledge lab, just to get a look at the layout, but it was off-limits, of course. Besides, Pete grandly informed me that he had already seen them. "Just a bunch of little compartments with all kinds of weird glass stuff in them," he said.

He wasn't such a bad kid, it turned out. Just neglected by his parents, who had dragged him up here, shown off Daddy's place of work, and then dumped him with the other brats. Like any reasonable youth, he wanted to be an astronaut. When he learned that I had been one, he started to look up to me, at least a little bit. Well, actually he was a teeny bit taller than I, but you know what I mean.

We had a great time in one of the escape pods. I sat Pete at the little control panel and he played astronaut for more than an hour. It only took a teeny bit of persuasion to get him to agree to what I wanted him to do. He even liked the idea. "It'll be like being a real astronaut, won't it?" he enthused.

"Sure it will," I told him.

While he was playing astronaut in the escape pod I ducked out to my office and made two phone calls. I invited Jill to an early dinner at the Eclipse. She accepted right away, asking only why I wanted to eat at five o'clock.

"I'll be baby-sitting later," I said.

Her face on my display screen looked positively shocked. "Baby-sitting? You?"

"There are more things in Heaven and Earth, Horatio, than are dreamed of in your philosophy." That was all I could think of to say. And at that, it was probably too much.

Then I tracked down Melinda by phone and invited her and Larry to have dinner, on me, in the Eclipse at eight o'clock.

She was back in the damned exercise room, walking on one of the treadmills. "Dinner?" she puffed. "I'd love to, Sam, but by eight T.J.'s usually in bed for the night."

"Oh, that's all right," I said as casually as I could manage. "I'll take care of him."

"You?" Her eyes went round.

"Sure. We're old pals now. I'll baby-sit while you and Larry have a decent meal, for a change. Why should D'Argent and the old farts on his board of directors be the only ones to enjoy good food?"

"I don't know . . ." She wavered.

"The best cooking in the solar system," I tempted her. "My chef is *cordon bleu*." Which was almost true. He had worked in Paris one summer. As a busboy.

"I'll have to check with Larry," she said.

"Sure. Do that."

I noticed that she turned up the speed on her treadmill. Like I said, taking apples off a blindman's fruit stand.

So I had a nice, relaxed dinner with Jill early that evening. Then I escorted her back to her minisuite in the zero-gee section. Some of the kids were still in the gym area, whizzing around and screaming at each other.

"You're not going to get much sleep until they get put away," I said to Jill.

She gave me a crooked grin as she opened the door to her suite. "I wasn't planning to sleep—not yet."

I didn't like the sly look in her eye. "Uh, I promised Larry and Melinda I'd watch their baby . . ."

"When do you have to be there?" Jill asked, gliding through the doorway and into her zero-gee love nest.

I glided in after her, naturally, and she maneuvered around and shut the door, cutting off the noise of the kids playing outside.

I can recognize a trap when I see one, even when the bait is tempting. "Jill—uh, I've got to go. Now."

"Oh, Sam." She threw her arms around my neck and kissed me passionately. I've got to admit that while I was kissing her back a part of my brain was calculating how much time I had left before I had to show up at Larry and Melinda's door. Which was just on the opposite side of the wailing banshees in the gym.

Reluctantly I disengaged from Jill, and said, "I don't have the time. Honest." My voice sounded odd, like some embarrassed acne-faced teenager's squeak.

Jill smiled glumly, and said, "A promise is a promise, I suppose."

"Yeah," I answered weakly. And I didn't want to make any promises to a United States Senator that I didn't intend to keep.

So I left Jill there in her suite, looking sad and disappointed, and zipped through the gym area, heading straight for the Karshes' suite.

Larry and Melinda were waiting for me. He was wearing an actual suit, dark blue, and a tie that kept floating loose from his shirt front. Melinda had a dress full of flounces that billowed in zero gee like a waterfall of lace. Jack Spratt and the Missus. They'd look better in the restaurant's lunar gravity.

Melinda floated me into the bedroom of their suite, where T.J. was zippered into a sleep cocoon. They had stuffed it with pillows because it was way too big for him. The kid was sound asleep with a thumb in his mouth. I've got to admit, he looked like a little angel.

"He won't wake up for at least four hours," she assured me. "We'll be back by then." Still, she gave me the whole orientation demonstration: bottle, milk, diapers, ass wipes, the whole ugly business.

I kept a smile on my face and shooed them out to their dinner. Then I went back into T.J.'s room.

"Okay, kid," I whispered, "it's you and me now."

I fidgeted around their suite for more than an hour, waiting for Larry and Melinda to get through most of their meal, thinking that I might swing back to Jill's suite and—no, no; there lay madness. Finally I went into the baby's room and gently, gently picked up T.J., blankets and all, and headed for the escape pod where I had stashed Pete.

The baby stirred and half woke up when I lifted him, but I shushed and rocked him. He kind of opened one eye, looked at me, and made a little smile. Then he curled himself into my arms and went back to sleep. Like I said, we were old pals by then.

I've got to admit that I felt a slight pang of conscience when I thought about how Larry and especially Melinda would feel when they came back from dinner and found their darling baby missing. I'd be missing, too, of course, and probably at first they'd be more miffed than scared. They'd phone around, trying to find me, figuring I had their kid with me, wherever I was. But after fifteen minutes, half an hour at most, they would panic and call for the security guards.

I grinned to myself at that. While the goons were searching the station I'd be in a space suit, breaking into the Rockledge lab from the outside. The one place nobody would bother looking for me because it was already so heavily guarded. Hah!

Okay, so Larry and Melinda would have a rough hour or two. They'd forget it when I returned their kid to them, and they saw he was none the worse for wear. And if Larry wants to call the bumpers Karsh Shields, he owes me some kind of payment, doesn't he?

Pete was in the escape pod waiting for me. I had told him only that he could play astronaut in the pod for a couple of hours, as long as he watched the baby. I had some work to do, but I'd be back when I was finished. The kid was as happy as an accordion player in a Wisconsin polka bar. Little T.J. was snoozing away, the picture of infant innocence.

"I'll take good care of him, Mr. Gunn," Pete assured me. He had come a long way from the surliness he had shown earlier. He was even grinning at the thought of playing inside the pod for hours.

I'm not a complete idiot, though. I carefully disconnected the pod's controls. Pete could bang on the keyboard and yank at the T-yokes on the control panel till his arms went numb; nothing would happen—except in his imagination. I disconnected the communications link, too, so he wouldn't be able to hear the commotion that was due to come up. Wouldn't be able to call to anybody, either.

"Okay, Captain," I said to Pete. "You're in charge until I return."

"Aye, aye, sir!" And he snapped me a lopsided salute. The grin on his face told me that he knew what we were doing was not strictly kosher, and he loved it.

I carefully sealed the pod's hatch, then closed the connecting airlock hatch and sealed it. I hustled down the corridor to the emergency airlock and my personal space suit, which I had stashed there. It was going to be a race to get into a suit and out the airlock before any of the security types poked their noses in this section of the corridor. I had disabled the surveillance cameras earlier in the afternoon and duly reported the system malfunction in the station's log. By the time they got them fixed I'd be long gone.

As if on cue, the intercom loudspeakers in the corridor started blaring, "SAM GUNN, PLEASE REPORT TO

SECURITY AT ONCE. SAM GUNN, PLEASE RE-
PORT TO SECURITY AT ONCE.''

They had found that T.J. was missing, and had called
security. The panic was on.

You know, the more you hurry the slower things seem
to go. Felt like an hour before I had the suit sealed up,
the helmet screwed on, and was opening the emergency
airlock.

But once I popped outside, I got that rush I always get
when I'm back in space, on my own. My suit was old
and smelled kind of ripe, but it felt homey inside it. And
there was the big curving ball of Earth, huge and blue
and sparkling in the sunlight. I just hung there for a minute or so and watched the sunset. It happens fast from
orbit, but the array of colors are dazzling.

Now we were in shadow, on the night side. All the
better to sneak around in. The controls to my maneuvering pack were on the equipment belt of my suit. I worked
them as easily and unconsciously as a pianist playing
scales and jetted over to the laboratory airlock on the
innermost wheel.

I kept my suit radio tuned to the station's intercom
frequency. Plenty of jabbering going on. They were
looking for me and T.J. Starting a compartment-to-
compartment search. There would be plenty more dis-
gruntled customers before this night was through, but
most of them were Rockledge people staying at my hotel
at a ruinous discount, so what the hell did I care?

I got to the lab's emergency airlock with no trouble.
The light was dim, and I didn't want to use my helmet
lamp. No sense advertising that I was out here. Over my
shoulder the lights of night-side cities and highways twin-
kled and glittered like a connect-the-dots map of North
America.

I was just starting to work the airlock's control panel
when the station shuddered. At first I thought I had hic-
cupped or something, but almost immediately I realized
that the airlock hatch had shaken, shivered. Which meant
that the whole damned station must have vibrated, quiv-
ered for some reason.

Which meant trouble. The station was big, massive. It wouldn't rattle unless it had been hit by something dangerous, or somebody had set off an explosion inside it, or—

I spun around, and my eyes damn near popped out of my head. An escape pod had just fired off! Somebody had set off the explosive separation bolts and detached it from the station. It was floating away like a slow-motion cannonball.

And I knew exactly which pod it was. Pete must have figured out how to override my disconnect and booted up the pod's mother-loving systems. Now he was riding off into the sunrise, on an orbit of his own, with T.J. aboard. Son of a motherless she-dog!

I jetted after the goddamned pod. I didn't stop to think about it, I just went out after it. Everything else dropped out of my mind. All I could think of was that little T.J. and Pete were in there, and they stood a better than even chance of getting themselves killed if somebody didn't get to them before they sailed out beyond reach. And it was all my fault.

If I had been really smart, I would have just reported the loose pod over my suit radio and gone about my business of burglarizing the Rockledge lab. The security people would have fired up another pod to go out and rescue the kids, everybody in the station would be plastered to the viewports or display screens to watch the scene, and I could pilfer away inside the lab without being disturbed.

But I'm not that smart. I went chasing after the damned pod. It was only after I had been barreling toward it for a few minutes that I realized I had damned well better reach it because I didn't have enough juice in my jet pack to get me back to the station again.

Pete must be scared purple, I thought, floating off into his own orbit. He apparently hadn't figured out how to reconnect the radio, because I heard nothing from the pod when I tapped into its assigned frequency. Maybe he's yelling himself hoarse into the microphone, but he's getting no response. Poor kid must be crapping his pants by now.

Fortunately, he hadn't lit off the pod's main thruster. That would've zoomed him out so far and so fast that I wouldn't have a prayer of reaching him. He had just fired the explosive disconnect bolts, which blew the pod away from the station. If he fired the main thruster without knowing how to use the pod's maneuvering jets, he'd either blast the damned cannonball down into the atmosphere so steeply that he'd burn up like a meteor, or he'd rocket himself out into a huge looping orbit that would take days or even weeks to complete.

As it was, he was drifting in an independent orbit, getting farther from the station every second. And I was jamming along after him, hard as I could.

I knew I had to save enough of my fuel to slow myself down enough to latch on to the pod. Otherwise I'd go sailing out past them like some idiotic jerk and spend the rest of my numbered hours establishing my own personal orbit in empty space. I wondered if anybody would bother to come out and pick up my body, once they knew what had happened to me.

Okay, I was on course. The pod was growing bigger, fast, looming in front of me. I turned myself around and gave a long squirt of my maneuvering jet to slow me down. Spun around again and saw the pod coming up to smack me square in the visor. I was still coming on too fast! Christ, was my flying rusty.

I had to jink over sideways a bit, or splatter myself against the pod. As the jets slid me over, I yanked out the tether from my equipment belt and whipped it against the curving hull of the pod as I zoomed by. Its magnetized head slid along the hull until it caught on a handhold. The tether stretched a bit, like a bungee cord, and then held.

As I pulled myself hand over hand to the pod, I glanced back at the station. It was so far away now it looked like a kid's toy hanging against the stars.

Grunting, puffing, totally out of shape for this kind of exercise, I finally got to the pod's airlock and lifted open its outer hatch. I was pouring sweat from every square inch of my skin. Got the hatch shut again, activated the pump, and as soon as the telltale light turned green I popped the inner hatch with one hand and slid my visor up with the other.

There sat Pete at the controls, ecstatic as a Hungarian picking pockets. And little T.J. was snoozing happily in the arms of Senator Jill Meyers.

"Hello, Sam," she said sweetly to me. "What kept you?"

It was then that I realized I had been nothing but the tool of a superior brain.

Jill had reconnected the pod's systems and blown the explosive bolts. She had known exactly what I was doing because she had stuck a microminiaturized video homing beacon on the back of my shirt when she had clutched me so passionately there in the doorway of her suite.

"It's standard equipment for a US Senator," she quipped, once she had plucked it off my shirt.

For once in my life I was absolutely speechless.

"When you told me you were baby-sitting—*voluntarily*—I started to smell a rodent," Jill said as she almost absently showed Pete how to maneuver the pod back to the station. "I knew you were up to something," she said to me.

I just hung there in midair, all my hopes and plans in a shambles.

"I've got to be invisible now," Jill said as we neared the station. She glided over to the equipment locker built into the pod's curving bulkhead and slid its hatch open. "It'll be a snug fit," she said, eyeing it closely. "Glad I didn't have dessert tonight."

"Wait a minute!" I burst. "What's going on? How did you—I mean, why—what's going on?" I felt like a chimpanzee thrown into a chess tournament.

As she squeezed herself into the equipment locker, Jill said, "It's simple, Sam. You were walking with the baby when Pete here accidentally set off the pod."

Pete turned in his pilot's chair and grinned at me.

"And then you got into your suit, with little T.J., and

rescued Pierre D'Argent's only son. You're going to be a hero.''

"Pete is D'Argent's son?" I must have hit high C.

"In return for your bravery in this thrilling rescue, D'Argent will let you have the space-sickness cure. So everything works out fine."

Like I said, I was just the tool of a superior brain.

"Now," said Jill, "you'd better help Pete to make rendezvous with the station and reberth this pod." And with that she blew me a kiss, then slid the hatch of the equipment locker shut.

It didn't work out exactly as Jill had it figured. I mean, D'Argent was furious, at first, that I'd let his kid into one of the pods and then left him alone. But his wife was enormously grateful, and Pete played his role to a tee. He lied with a straight face to his own father and everybody else. I figured that one day, when D'Argent realized how his son had bamboozled him, he'd be truly proud of the lad. Probably send him to law school.

In the meantime, D'Argent did indeed let me have the space-sickness cure. Grudgingly. "Only for a limited period of testing," he growled. Mrs. D'Argent had prodded him into it, in return for my heroic rescue of their only son. She got a considerable amount of help from Jill— who sneaked off the pod after all the commotion had died down.

Larry and Melinda didn't know whether they should be sore at me or not. They had been scared stiff when T.J. turned up missing, and then enormously relieved when I handed him their little bundle of joy, safe and sound, gurgling happily. I knew Larry had forgiven me when he reminded me, almost sheepishly, about changing the name of the magnetic bumpers to Karsh Shields.

So we all got what we wanted. Or part of it, at least.

The space-sickness cure helped Heaven a lot. The hotel staggered into the black, not because honeymooners took a sudden fancy to it, but because the word started to spread that it was an ideal spot for children! It still cost more than your average luxury vacation, but wealthy families started coming up to Heaven. My zero-gee sex palace eventually became a weightless nursery. And—many years later—a retirement home. But that's another story.

I licensed the *Karsh* Shields to Rockledge. A promise is a promise, and the money was good because Rockledge had the manufacturing capacity to make three times as many of the shields as I could. And, once the hotel started showing a profit, I let D'Argent buy it from me. He's the one who turned it into a nursery. I was long gone by then.

With Jill's help I raised enough capital to start a shoe-string operation in lunar mining. It was touch-and-go for a while, but the boom in space manufacturing that I had prophesied actually did come about, and I got filthy rich.

Of course, I more or less had to marry Jill. I owed her that, she had been so helpful. Why she wanted to marry me was a mystery to me, but she was damned determined to do it.

Of course, I was just as damned determined not to get married. So I—but that's another story.

## Statement of Clark Griffith IV
## (Recorded at Lunar Retirement Center,
## Copernicus)

That's right, I've known Sam Gunn longer than anybody still living. Except maybe for Jill Meyers.

How long? I knew the little sonofabitch when he was a NASA astronaut, back in the days when we were first setting up a permanent base here on the Moon, over at Alphonsus.

I was his boss, believe it or not. It was like trying to train a cat—Sam always went his own way, fractured the rules left and right, and somehow managed to come out smelling like a rose. Most of the time. He stepped into the doggie-doo now and then, but usually he was too fast on his feet for it to matter. By the time we'd catch up to him he was off somewhere else, raising more hell and giving us more trouble back in Washington.

Another thing about Sam. He's not that much younger than I am, yet he's off flitting around the goddamned solar system like some kid on pills. How's he do that? And from what I hear he's still chasing women from here to Pluto and back. At his age! Well, maybe it's because he's spent so much of his life in low-gravity environments. Keeps you young, so I hear. That's why I retired here to the Moon, but it doesn't seem to be helping me much.

Digressing? I'm digressing? I was talking about Sam. That's what you want, isn't it?

No, I never believed he was dead. Never believed he

fell into that mini–black hole out there past Pluto, either. It was all a fraud. A load of bullcrap. Pure Sam Gunn, another one of his tricky little gambits.

So he's on his way back, is he? What'd I tell you. Mini–black hole my great-grandmother! And he claims he fell into a space-time warp and found aliens on the other side? Well, I can almost believe that. Sure! That's why he's coming back, the aliens don't want the little bastard around their planets!

When did I first meet Sam? God, let me think. It was back . . . never mind. Let me tell you about Sam's last days with NASA. I got to fire the little pain-in-the-butt. Bounced him right out of the agency, good and proper. Happiest day of my life.

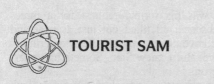 **TOURIST SAM**

WHY DID NASA FIRE SAM GUNN? IT'D BE BETTER TO ASK why we didn't fire the little SOB out of a cannon and get rid of him once and for all. Would've been a service to the human race.

I'm no detective, but I smelled a rat when Sam put in a formal request for a three-month leave of absence. I just stared at my desktop screen. Sam Gunn, going through regular channels? Something was fishy. I mean, Sam *never* did things according to regulations. Give him a road map with a route on the interstates plotted out by AAA and he'd go down every dirt road and crooked alley he could find, just to drive my blood pressure up to the bursting point.

Trouble was, the sawed-off little runt was a damned good astronaut. About as good as they come, as a flyer and ingenious troubleshooter. Like the time he saved the lunar mission by jury-rigging a still and getting all the stranded astronauts plastered so they'd be unconscious most of the time and use up less oxygen.

That was typical of Sam Gunn. A hero who left the rules and regulations in a shambles every time.

He had just come off his most notorious stunt of all, getting the first skipper of space station *Freedom* to punch the Abandon Ship alarm and riding back down to Earth in an emergency escape capsule with some young woman from a movie studio. He had to be hospitalized after they landed; he claimed it was from stress during reentry, but everybody at the Cape was wondering who was reentering what.

Anyway, there was his formal request for a three-month leave of absence, all filled out just as neat and precise as I would have done it myself. He was certainly entitled to the leave. But I knew Sam. Something underhanded was going on.

I called him into my office and asked him point-blank what he was doing. A waste of time.

"I need a rest," he said. Then he added, "Sir."

Sam's face was as round and plain as a penny, and his wiry hair was kind of coppery color, come to think of it. Little snub of a nose with a scattering of freckles. His teeth had enough spaces between them so that he reminded me of a jack-o'-lantern when he grinned.

He wasn't grinning as he sat in front of my desk. He was all perfectly polite earnestness, dressed in a *tie* and a real suit, like an honest-to-Pete straight-arrow citizen. His eyes gave him away, though: They were as crafty as ever, glittering with visions that he wanted to keep secret from me.

"Going any place special?" I asked, trying to make it sound nonchalant.

Sam nonchalanted me right back. "No, not really. I just need to get away from it all for a while."

Yeah, sure. Like Genghis Khan just wanted to take a little pony ride.

I had no choice except to approve his request. But I had no intention of letting the sneaky little sumbitch pull one over on me. Sam was up to something; I knew it, and the glitter in his eyes told me that he knew I knew it.

As I said, I'm no detective. So I hired one. Well, she really wasn't a detective. My niece, Ramona Perkins, was an agent with the Drug Enforcement Agency—a damned stupid name, if you ask me. Makes it sound like the government is *forcing* people to do drugs.

Well, anyway, Ramona wasn't too thrilled with the idea of trailing a furloughed astronaut for a few weeks.

"Yes, Uncle Griff, I have three weeks of vacation time coming, but I was going to wait until December and go to Alaska."

That was Ramona, as impractical as they come. She was pretty, in a youngish, girl-next-door way. Nice sandy blond hair that she always kept pinned up; made her look even younger than she was. And there was no doubt about her courage. Anybody who makes a career out of posing as an innocent kid and infiltrating drug gangs has more guts than brains, if you ask me.

She had just gone through a pretty rough divorce. No children, thank Pete, but her ex-husband made a big to-do about their house and cars. Seemed to me he cared more about their damned stereo and satellite TV setup than he did about my niece.

I made myself smile at her image in my phone screen. "Suppose I could get you three weeks of detached duty, assigned to my office. Then you wouldn't use up any of your vacation time."

"I don't know . . ." She sort of scrunched up her perky face. I figured she was trying to bury herself in her work and forget about her ex.

"It'd do you good to get away from everything for a while," I said.

Ramona's cornflower blue eyes went curious. "What's so important about this one astronaut that you'd go to all this trouble?"

What could I tell her? That Sam Gunn had been driving me nuts for years, and I was certain he was up to no good? That I was afraid Sam would pull some stunt that would reflect dishonorably on the space agency? That if and when he got himself in trouble the agency management would inevitably dump the blame on me, since I was in charge of his division.

I wasn't going to have Sam botch up my record, dammit! I was too close to retirement to let him ruin me. And don't think the little SOB wasn't trying to do me dirt. He'd slit my throat and laugh about it, if I let him.

But to my sweet young niece, I merely said, "Ramona, this is a matter of considerable importance. I wouldn't be asking your help if it weren't. I really can't tell you any more than that.''

Her image in my phone screen grew serious. "Does it involve narcotics, then?''

I took a deep breath and nodded. "That's a possibility.'' It was a lie, of course; Sam was as straight as they come about drugs. Wasn't even much of a drinker. His major vice was women.

''All right,'' she said, completely businesslike. "If you can arrange the reassignment, I'll trail your astronaut for you.''

''That's my girl!'' I said, really happy with her. She'd always been my favorite niece. At that point in time it never occurred to me that sending her after Sam might put her in more danger than the entire Colombian cartel could throw at her.

The three weeks passed. No report from her. I began to worry. Called her supervisor at DEA and he assured me she'd been phoning him once a week, just to tell him she was okay. I complained that she should've been phoning me, so a few days later I got an e-mail message: EVERYTHING IS FINE BUT THIS IS GOING TO TAKE LONGER THAN WE THOUGHT.

It took just about the whole three damned months. It wasn't until then that Ramona popped into my office, sunburned and weary-looking, and told me what Sam had been up to. This is what she told me:

I know this investigation took a lot longer than you thought it would, Uncle Griff. It was a lot more complicated than either one of thought it'd be. *Nothing* that Sam Gunn does is simple!

To begin with, by the time I started after him, Sam had already gone to Panama to set up the world's first space-tourist line.

That's right, Uncle Griff. A tourist company. In Panama.

He called his organization Space Adventure Tours and registered it as a corporation in Panama. All perfectly legal, but it started alarm bells ringing in my head right from the start. I knew that Panama was a major drug-transshipment area, and a tourist company could be a perfect front for narcotics smuggling.

By the time I arrived in Colón, on the Caribbean side of the Panama Canal, Sam had established himself in a set of offices he rented on the top floor of one of the three-story stucco commercial buildings just off the international airport.

As I said, my first thought was that he was running a smuggling operation, probably narcotics, and his wild-sounding company name was only a front. I spent a week watching his office, seeing who was coming and going. Nobody but Sam himself and a couple of young Panamanian office workers. Now and then an elderly guy in casual vacation clothes or a silver-haired couple. Once in a while a blue-haired matronly type would show up. Seldom the same people twice. No sleazebags in five-hundred-dollar suits. No Uzi-toting maniacs of enforcers.

I dropped in at the office myself to look the place over. It seemed normal enough. An anteroom with a couple of tacky couches and armchairs, divided by a chest-high counter. Water stains on the ceiling tiles. On the other side of the counter sat the two young locals, a male and a female, both working at desktop computers. Beyond them was a single door prominently marked S. GUNN, PRESIDENT AND CEO.

Most smuggling operators don't put their own names on doors.

The young woman glanced up from her display screen and saw me standing at the counter. Immediately she came out from behind her desk, smiling brightly, and asked in local-accented English, "Can I help you?"

I put on my best Dorothy-from-Kansas look, and said, "What kind of tours do you offer?"

"An adventure in space," she said, still smiling.

"In space?"

"Yes. Like the astronauts."

"For tourists?"

"*Sí*—Yes. Our company is the very first in the world to offer a spaceflight adventure."

"In space?" I repeated.

She nodded and said, "Perhaps Mr. Gunn himself should explain it to you."

"Oh, no, I wouldn't want to bother him."

"No bother," she said sweetly. "He enjoys speaking to the customers."

She must have pressed a buzzer, because the S. GUNN door popped open and out walked Sam, smiling like a used-car salesman.

The first thing about him to strike me was how short he was. I mean, I'm barely five-five in my flats and Sam was a good two inches shorter than I. He seemed solidly built, though, beneath the colorful flowered short-sleeved shirt and sky-blue slacks he was wearing. Good shoulders, a little thick in the midsection.

His face was, well . . . *cute*. I thought I saw boyish enthusiasm and charm in his eyes. He certainly didn't look like your typical drug lord.

"I'm Sam Gunn," he said to me, sticking his hand out over the counter. "At your service."

I got the impression he had to stand on tiptoe to get his arm over the counter.

"Ramona Perkins," I said, taking his hand in mine. He had a firm, friendly grip. With my free hand I activated the microcassette recorder in my shoulder bag.

"You're interested in a space adventure?" Sam asked, opening the little gate at the end of the counter and ushering me through.

"I really don't know," I said, as if I were taking the first step on the Yellow Brick Road. "It all seems so new and different."

"Come into my office and let me explain it to you."

Sam's office was much more posh than the outer room. He had a big modernistic desk, all polished walnut and chrome, and two chairs in front of it that looked like reclinable astronaut's seats. I learned soon enough that they were reclinable, and Sam liked to recline in them with female companions.

No windows, but the walls were lined with photographs of astronauts hovering in space, with the big blue curving Earth as a backdrop. Behind Sam's desk, on a wide walnut bookcase, there were dozens of photos of Sam in astronaut uniform, in a space suit, even one with him in scuba gear with his arm around a gorgeous video starlet in the skimpiest bikini I've ever seen.

He sat me in one of the cushioned, contoured recliners and went around behind his desk. I realized there was a platform back there, because when Sam sat down he was almost taller than he had been standing up in front of the desk.

"Ms. Perkins . . . may I call you Ramona?"

"Sure," I said, in a valley-girl accent.

"That's a beautiful name."

"Thank you."

"Ramona, until now the thrill of flying in space has been reserved to a handful of professional astronauts like myself—"

"Haven't some politicians and video stars gone into orbit?" I asked, with wide-eyed innocence.

"Yes indeed they certainly have," Sam answered. "And if *they've* flown in space, there's no good reason why *you* shouldn't have the experience, too. You, and anyone else who wants the adventure of a lifetime!"

"How much does it cost?" I asked.

Sam hiked his rust-red eyebrows at me and launched into a nonstop spiel about the beauties and glories and excitement of space travel. He wasn't really eloquent, that wasn't Sam's style. But he was persistent and energetic. He talked so fast and so long that it seemed as if he didn't take a breath for half an hour. I remember thinking that he could probably go out for an EVA space walk without oxygen if he put his mind to it.

For the better part of an hour Sam worked up and down the subject.

"And why shouldn't ordinary people, people just like you, be allowed to share in the excitement of spaceflight? The once-in-a-lifetime adventure of them all! Why do government agencies and big, powerful corporations refuse to allow ordinary men and women the chance to fly in space?"

I batted my baby blues at him, and asked, in a breathless whisper, "Why?"

Sam heaved a big sigh. "I'll tell you why. They're all big bureaucracies, run by petty-minded bureaucrats who don't care about the little guy. Big corporations like Rockledge could be running tourists into orbit right now, but their bean-counting bureaucrats won't let that happen for fear that some tourist might get a little nauseous in zero gravity and sue the corporation when he comes back to Earth."

"Maybe they're afraid of an accident," I said, still trying to sound naive. "I mean, people have been killed in rocket launches, haven't they?"

"Not in years," Sam countered, waggling a hand in the air. "Besides, the launch system we're gonna use is supersafe. And gentle. We take off like an airplane and land like an airplane. No problems."

"But what about space sickness?" I asked.

"Likewise, no problem. We've developed special equipment that eliminates space sickness just about completely. In fact, you feel just as comfortable as you would in your own living room for just about the entire flight."

"Really?"

"Really," he said, with a *trust-me* nod of his head.

"Wouldn't you be better off operating in the States?" I probed. "I mean, like, I just ran across your office kind of by accident while I was checking on my flight back home."

Sam scowled at me. "The US government is wrapped up with bureaucrats and—worse—lawyers. You can't do *anything* new there anymore. If I tried to start a space-tourist company in the States, I'd have sixteen zillion bozos from NASA, OSHA, the Department of Transportation, the Commerce Department, the State Department, the National Institutes of Health, and St. Francis of Assisi knows who else coming down on my head. I'd be filling out forms and talking to lawyers until I was old and gray!"

"It's easier to get started in Panama, then."

"Much easier."

I sat there, gazing at Sam, pretending to think it all over.

Then I asked again, "How much does it cost?"

Sam looked at his wristwatch and said, "Hey! It's just about time for our first space cruiser to land! Let's go out and see it come in!"

I felt a little like the first time I went out to buy a car on my own, without Daddy or any of my big brothers with me. But I let Sam take me by the hand to his own car—a leased fire-engine red BMW convertible—and drive me out to an immense empty hangar with a newly painted SPACE ADVENTURE TOURS sign painted across its curved roof.

"Used to be a blimp hangar," Sam said over the rushing wind as we drove up to the hangar. "US Navy used 'em for antisubmarine patrol. It was falling apart from neglect. I got it for a song."

The DEA had considered asking the Navy to use blimps to patrol the sea-lanes that drug smugglers used, I remembered.

"You're going into space in a blimp?" I asked, as we braked to a gravel-spitting stop.

"No no no," Sam said, jumping out of the convertible and running over to my side to help me out. "Blimps wouldn't work. We're using . . . well, look! Here it comes now!"

I turned to look where he was pointing and saw a huge, lumbering Boeing 747 coming down slowly, with ponderous grace, at the far end of the long concrete runway. And attached to its back was a space shuttle orbiter.

"That's one of the old shuttles!" I cried, surprised.

"Right," said Sam. "That's what we ride into space in."

"Gosh." I was truly impressed.

The immense piggyback pair taxied right up to us, the 747's four jet engines howling so loud I clapped my hands over my ears. Then it cut power and *loomed* over us, with the shuttle orbiter riding high atop it. It was certainly impressive.

"NASA sold off its shuttle fleet, so I got a group of

investors together and bought one of 'em," Sam said,
rather proudly, I noticed. "Bought the piggyback plane
to go with it, too."

While the ground crew attached a little tractor to the
747's nosewheel and towed it slowly into the old blimp
hangar, Sam explained that he and his technical staff had
worked out a new launch system: The 747 carries the
orbiter up to more than fifty thousand feet, and then the
orbiter disconnects and lights up its main engines to go
off into space.

"The 747 does the job that the old solid rocket boost-
ers used to do when NASA launched shuttles from Cape
Canaveral," Sam explained to me. "Our system is
cheaper and safer."

The word *cheaper* reminded me. "How much does a
tour cost?" I asked still again, determined this time to
get an answer.

We had walked into the hangar by now. Technicians
were setting up ladders and platforms up and down the
length of the plane. The huge shadowy hangar echoed
with the clang of metal equipment and the clatter of their
voices, yelling back and forth in Spanish.

"Want to go aboard?" Sam asked, with a sly grin.

I sure did, but I answered, "Not until you tell me how
much a flight costs."

"Ten thousand dollars," he said, without flicking an
eyelash.

"Ten thou . . ." I thought I recalled that the shuttle cost
ten thousand dollars *a pound* when NASA was operating
it. Even the new Clipperships, which were entirely reus-
able, cost several hundred dollars per pound.

"You can put it on your credit card," Sam suggested.

"Ten thousand dollars?" I repeated. "For a flight into
orbit?"

He nodded solemnly. "You experience two orbits and
then we land back here. The whole flight will last a little
more than four hours."

"How can you do it so cheap?" I blurted.

Sam spread his arms. "I'm not a big, bloated government agency. I keep a very low overhead. I don't have

ten zillion lawyers looking over my shoulder. My insurance costs are much lower here in Panama than they'd be in the States. And . . ." He hesitated.

"And?" I prompted.

With a grin that almost bashful, Sam told me, "I want to do good for the people who'll never be able to afford spaceflight otherwise. I don't give a damn if I make a fortune or not: I just want to help ordinary people like you to experience the thrill and the wonder of flying in space."

I almost believed him.

In fact, right then and there I really *wanted* to believe Sam Gunn. Even though I had a pretty good notion that he was laying it on with a trowel.

I told Sam that even though ten thousand was a bargain for orbital flight, it was an awfully steep price for me to pay. He agreed and invited me to dinner. I expected him to keep up the pressure on me to buy a ticket, but Sam actually had other things in mind. One thing, at least.

He was charming. He was funny. He kept me laughing all through the dinner we had at a little shack on the waterfront that served the best fish in onion sauce I've ever tasted. He told me the story of his life, several times, and each time was completely different. I couldn't help but like him. More than like him.

Sam drove me back to my hotel and rode up the creaking elevator with me to my floor. I intended to say good night at the door to my room, but somehow it didn't work out that way. I never said good night to him at all. What I said, much later, was good morning.

Now, Uncle Griff, don't go getting so red in the face! It was the first time I'd let anybody get close to me since the divorce. Sam made me feel attractive, wanted. I needed that. It was like . . . well, like I'd run away from the human race. Sam brought me back, made me alive again. He was thoughtful and gentle and somehow at the same time terrifically energetic. He was great fun.

And besides, by the time we were having breakfast together in the hotel's dining room he offered to let me fly on his space cruiser for free.

"Oh no, Sam, I couldn't do that. I'll pay my own way," I said.

He protested faintly, but I had no intention of letting him think I was in his debt. Going to bed with Sam once was fun. Letting him think I *owed* him was not.

So I phoned Washington and told my boss to expect a ten-grand charge to come through—which you, Uncle Griff, will be billed for. Then I got into a taxi and drove out to the offices of Space Adventure Tours and plunked down my credit card.

Sam took me to lunch.

But not to dinner. He explained over lunch that he had a business conference that evening.

"This space-tour business is brand-new, you gotta understand," he told me, "and that means I have to spend most of my time wining and dining possible customers."

"Like me," I said.

He laughed, but it was bitter. "No, honey, not like you. Old folks, mostly. Little old widows trying to find something interesting to do with what's left of their lives. Retired CEOs who want to think that they're still on the cutting edge of things. They're the ones with the money, and I've got to talk forty of 'em out of some of it."

"Forty?"

"That's our orbiter's passenger capacity. Forty is our magic number. For the next forty days and forty nights I'm gonna be chasing little old ladies and retired old farts. I'd rather be with you, but I've gotta sell those seats."

I looked rueful and told him I understood. After he left me back at my hotel, I realized with something of a shock that I really was rueful. I missed Sam!

So I trailed him, telling myself that it was stupid to get emotionally involved with the guy I'm supposed to be investigating. Sam's business conference turned out to be a dinner and show at one of Colón's seamier night clubs. I didn't go in, but the club's garish neon sign. *The Black Hole*, was enough for me to figure out what kind of a place it was. Sam went in with two elderly gentlemen from the States. To me they looked like middle-class retired businessmen on a spree without their wives.

Sure enough, they were two more customers, I found out later.

Sam was busy most evenings, doing his sales pitch to potential customers over dinners and nightclub shows. He squired blue-haired widows and played tour guide for honeymooning couples. He romanced three middle-aged woman on vacation from their husbands, juggling things so well that the first time they saw one another was at the one-day training seminar in Sam's rented hangar.

It didn't quite take forty days and forty nights, but Sam gave each of his potential customers the full blaze of his personal attention. As far as I know, each and every one of them signed on the dotted line.

And then he had time for me again.

I had extended my stay in Colón, waiting for the flight that Sam promised. Once he had signed up a full load of paying customers, he brought us all out to the hangar for what he called an "orientation."

So there we were, forty tourists standing on the concrete floor of the hangar with the big piggyback airplane *cum* orbiter looming in front of us like a freshly painted aluminum mountain. Sam stood on a rusty, rickety metal platform scrounged from the maintenance equipment.

"Congratulations," he said to us, his voice booming through the echo chamber of a hangar. "You are the very first space tourists in the history of the world."

Sam didn't need a megaphone. His voice carried through to our last row with no problem at all. He started off by telling us how great our flight was going to be, pumping up our expectations. Then he went on to what he said were the two most important factors.

"Safety and comfort," he told us. "We've worked very hard to make absolutely certain that you are perfectly safe and comfortable throughout your space adventure."

Sam explained that for safety's sake we were all going to have to wear a full space suit for the whole four-hour flight. Helmet and all.

"So you can come in your most comfortable clothes," he said, grinning at us. "Shorts, tee shirts, whatever you feel happiest in. We'll all put on our space suits right here in the hangar before we board the orbiter.''

He explained, rather delicately, that each suit was equipped with a waste-disposal system, a sort of high-tech version of the pilot's old relief tube, which worked just as well for women as it did for men.

"Since our flight will be no more than four hours long, we won't need the FCS—fecal containment system—that NASA's brainiest scientists have developed for astronauts to use." And Sam held up a pair of large-sized diapers.

Everybody laughed.

"Now I'm sure you've heard a great deal about space sickness," Sam went on, once the laughter died away. "I want to assure you that you won't be bothered by the effects of zero gravity on this flight. Your space suits include a special antisickness system that will protect you from the nausea and giddiness that usually hits first-time astronauts.''

"What kind of a system is it?" asked one of the elderly men. He looked like a retired engineer to me: shirt pocket bristling with ballpoint pens.

Sam gave him a sly grin. "Mr. Artumian, I'm afraid I can't give you any details about that. It's a new system, and it's proprietary information. Space Adventure Tours has developed this equipment, and as soon as the major corporations learn how well it works they're going to want to buy, lease, or steal it from us.''

Another laugh, a little thinner than before.

"But how do we know it'll work?" Artumian insisted.

Very seriously, Sam replied, "It's been thoroughly tested, I assure you.''

"But we're the first customers you're trying it on.''

Sam's grin returned. "You're the first customers we've had!''

Before Artumian could turn this briefing into a dialogue, I spoke up. "Could you tell us what we'll feel when we're in zero gravity? Give us an idea of what to expect?''

Sam beamed at me. "Certainly, Ms. Perkins. When we first reach orbit and attain zero gee, you'll feel a moment or two of free fall. You know, that stomach-dropping sensation you get when an elevator starts going down. But it'll only last a couple of seconds, max. Then our proprietary antidisequilibrium system kicks in, and you'll feel perfectly normal.''

Artumian muttered "Ah-hah!" when Sam used the term antidisequilibrium system. As if that meant something to his engineer's brain.

"Throughout the flight," Sam went on, "you may feel a moment now and then of free fall, kind of like floating. But our equipment will quickly get your body's sensory systems back to normal.''

"Sensory systems," Artumian muttered knowingly.

Sam and two people in flight attendants' uniforms showed us through the orbiter's passenger cabin. The attendants were both really attractive: a curvaceous little blonde with a megawatt smile and a handsome brute of a Latino guy with real bedroomy eyes.

We had to climb a pretty shaky metal ladder to get up there because the orbiter was still perched on top of the 747. The plane and the orbiter were gleaming with a fresh coat of white paint and big blue SPACE ADVENTURE TOURS running along their sides. But the ladder was flaking with rust.

It made me wonder just what kind of shoestring Sam was operating on: this big airplane with a NASA surplus space-shuttle orbiter perched atop it, and we all had to clamber up this rusty, clattery ladder. Some of Sam's customers were pretty slow and feeble; old, you know. I heard plenty of wheezing going up that ladder.

The orbiter's cabin, though, was really very nice. Like a first-class section aboard an airliner, except that the seats were even bigger and more plush. Two seats on either side of the one central aisle. I saw windows at each row, but they were covered over.

"The windows are protected by individual opaque heat shields," Sam explained. "They'll slide back once we're in orbit so you can see the glories and beauties of Earth and space.''

There were no toilets in the cabin, and no galley. The

passengers would remain strapped into their seats at all times, Sam told us. "That's for your own safety and comfort," he assured us.

"You mean we won't get to float around in zero gravity like they do in the videos?" asked one of the elderly women.

" 'Fraid not," Sam answered cheerfully. "Frankly, if you tried that, you'd most likely get so sick you'd want to upchuck. Even our very sophisticated antidisequilibrium equipment has its limitations."

I wasn't close enough to hear him, but I saw Artumian's lips mouth the word, "Limitations."

That evening all forty of us, plus Sam, had a festive dinner together on the rooftop of the local Hyatt Hotel. It was a splendid night, clear and filled with stars. A crescent Moon rose and glittered on the Caribbean for us.

Sam flitted from table to table all through the dinner; I doubt that he got to swallow more than a few bites of food. But he ended the evening at my table and drove me to my hotel himself, while all the other customers rode to their hotels in a rattletrap gear-grinding, soot-puffing big yellow school bus that Sam had rented.

"Tomorrow's the big day," Sam said happily as we drove through the dark streets. "Space Adventure's first flight."

My romantic interest in Sam took a backseat to my professional curiosity.

"Sam," I asked over the rush of the night wind, "how can you make a profit if you're only charging ten thousand per passenger? This flight must cost a lot more than four hundred thousand dollars."

"Profit isn't everything, my blue-eyed space beauty," he said, keeping his eyes on his driving.

"But if it costs more to fly than you make from ticket sales, you'll go out of business pretty quickly, won't you?"

He shot a glance at me. "My pricing schedule is pretty flexible. You got the bargain rate. Others are paying more; a lot more."

"Really?"

"Uh-huh. That's another reason I'm operating here in Panama. Let the fat cats open their wallets wider than ordinary folks. If I tried that in the States, I'd have a ton of lawyers hitting me with discrimination suits."

I thought about that as we pulled up in front of my hotel.

"Then how much will you make from this flight?" I asked, noticing that Sam kept the motor running.

"Gross? About a million-two."

"Is that enough to cover your costs?"

Sam grinned at me. "I won't go bankrupt. It's like the old story of the tailor who claims that he sells his clothing at prices *below* his own costs. 'On each and every individual sale we lose money,' he tells a customer. 'But on the volume we make a modest profit.' "

I didn't see anything funny in it. It didn't make sense.

Suddenly Sam shook me out of my musing. He grabbed me by the shoulders, kissed me on the lips, and then announced, "I'd love to go up to your room and make mad, passionate love to you, Ramona, but I've got an awful lot to do between now and takeoff tomorrow morning. See you at the hangar!"

He leaned past me, and opened my door. Kind of befuddled, I got out of the car and waved good-bye to him as he roared off in a cloud of exhaust smoke.

Alone in my room, I started to wonder if our one night of passion had merely been Sam's way of closing the sale.

The next day, Space Adventure Tours' first flight was just about everything Sam had promised.

All forty of us gathered at the hangar bright and early. It took nearly two hours to get each of us safely sealed up inside a space suit. Some of the older tourists were almost too arthritic to get their creaky arms and legs into the suits, but somehow—with Sam and his two flight attendants pushing and pulling—they all managed.

Instead of that rickety ladder Sam drove a cherry picker across the hangar floor and lifted us in our space suits, two by two like Noah's passengers, up to the hatch of the orbiter. The male attendant went up first and was there at the hatch to help us step inside the passenger cabin and clomp down the aisle to our assigned seats.

Sam and I were the last couple hoisted up. With the visor of my suit helmet open, I could smell the faint odor of bananas in the cherry picker's cab. It made me wonder where Sam had gotten the machine, and how soon he had to return it.

After we were all strapped in, Sam came striding down the cabin, crackling with energy and enthusiasm. He stood up at the hatch to the flight deck and grinned ear-to-ear at us.

"You folks are about to make history. I'm proud of you," he said. Then he opened the hatch and stepped into the cockpit.

Three things struck me, as I sat strapped into my seat, encased in my spacesuit. One: Sam didn't have to duck his head to get through that low hatch. Two: he wasn't wearing a space suit. Three: he was probably going to pilot the orbiter himself.

Was there a copilot already in the cockpit with him? Surely Sam didn't intend to fly the orbiter into space entirely by himself. And why wasn't he wearing a space suit, when he insisted that all the rest of us do?

No time for puzzling over it all. The flight attendants came down the aisle, checking to see that we were all firmly strapped in. They were in space suits, just as we passengers were. I felt motion: the 747 beneath us was being towed out of the hangar. The windows were sealed shut, so we couldn't see what was happening outside.

Then we heard the jet engines start up; actually we felt their vibrations more than heard their sound. Our cabin was very well insulated.

"Please pull down the visors on your helmets," the blond flight attendant singsonged. "We will be taking off momentarily."

I confess I got a lump in my throat as I felt the engines whine up to full thrust, pressing me back in my seat. With our helmet visors down I couldn't see the face of the elderly woman sitting beside me, but we automatically clasped our gloved hands together, like mother and daughter. My heart was racing.

I wished we could see out the windows! As it was, I had to depend on my sense of balance, sort of flying by the seat of my pants, while the 747 raced down the runway, rotated its nosewheel off the concrete, and then rose majestically into the air—with us on top of her. Ridiculously, I remembered a line from an old poem: *With a sleighful of toys and St. Nicholas, too.*

"We're in the air," came Sam's cheerful voice over our helmet earphones. "In half an hour we'll separate from our carrier plane and light up our main rocket engines."

We sat in anticipatory silence. I don't know about the others—it was impossible to see their faces or tell what was going through their minds—but I twitched every time the ship jounced or swayed.

"Separation in two minutes," Sam's voice warned us.

I gripped my seat's armrests. Couldn't see my hands through the thick space-suit gloves, but I could feel how white my knuckles were.

"You're going to hear a banging noise," Sam warned us. "Don't be alarmed; it's just the explosive bolts separating the struts that're clamping us to the carrier plane."

Explosive bolts. All of a sudden I didn't like that word *explosive.*

The bang scared me even though I knew it was coming. It was a really loud, sharp noise. But the cabin didn't seem to shake or shudder at all, thank goodness.

Almost immediately we felt more thrust pushing us back into our seats again.

"Main rocket engines have ignited on schedule," Sam said evenly. "Next stop, LEO!"

I knew that he meant low Earth orbit, but I wondered how many of the tourists were wondering who this person Leo might be.

The male flight attendants's voice cut in on my earphones. "As we enter Earth orbit you will experience a few moments of free fall before our antidisequilibrium equipment balances out your inner sensory systems.

Don't let those few moments of a falling sensation worry you; they'll be over almost before you realize it.''

I nodded to myself inside my helmet. Zero gee. My mouth suddenly felt dry.

And then I was falling! Dropping into nothingness. My stomach floated up into my throat. I heard moans and gasps from my fellow tourists.

And just like that it was over. A normal feeling of weight returned, and my stomach settled back to where it belonged. Sam's equipment really worked!

''We are now in low Earth orbit,'' Sam's voice said, low, almost reverent. ''I'm going to open the viewport shutters now.''

Since I had paid the lowest price for my ride, I had an aisle seat. I leaned forward in my seat harness and twisted my shoulders sideways as far as I could so that I could peer through my helmet visor and look through the window.

The Earth floated below us, huge and curving and so brightly blue it almost hurt my eyes. I could see swirls of beautiful white clouds and the sun gleaming off the ocean and swatches of green ground and little brown wrinkles that must have been mountains and out near the curving sweep of the horizon a broad open swath of reddish tan that stretched as far as I could see.

''That's the coast of Africa coming up. You can see the Sahara a little to our north,'' Sam said.

The cabin was filled with gasps and moans again, but this time they were joyous, awestruck. I didn't care how much the ticket price was; I would have paid my own way to see this.

I could see the Horn of Africa and the great rift valley where the first protohumans made their camps. Sinbad's Arabian Sea glittered like an ocean of jewels before my eyes.

Completely around the world we went, not in eighty days but a little over ninety minutes. The Arabian peninsula was easy to spot, not a wisp of a cloud anywhere near it. India was half-blotted out by monsoon storms, but we swung over the Himalayas and across China. It was night on that side of the world, but the Japanese islands were outlined by the lights of their cities and highways.

"Mount Everest's down there under the clouds," Sam told us. "Doesn't look so tall from up here."

Japan, Alaska, and then down over the heartland of America. It was an unusually clear day in the Midwest; we could see the Mississippi snaking through the nation's middle like a coiling blood vessel.

Twice we coasted completely around the world. It was glorious, fascinating, an endless vision of delights. When Sam asked us how we were enjoying the flight the cabin echoed with cheers. I didn't want the flight to end. I could have stayed hunched over in that cumbersome space suit and stared out that little window for the rest of my days. Gladly.

But at last Sam's sad voice told us, "I'm sorry, folks, but that's it. Time to head back to the barn."

I could feel the disappointment that filled the cabin.

As the window shutters slowly slid shut Sam announced casually, "Now comes the tricky part. Reentry and rendezvous with the carrier plane."

Rendezvous with the carrier plane? He hadn't mentioned that before. I heard several attendant call buttons chiming. Some of the other tourists were alarmed by Sam's news, too.

In a few minutes he came back on the intercom. In my earphones I heard Sam explain, "Our flight plan is to rendezvous with the carrier plane and reconnect with her so she can bring us back to the airport under the power of her jet engines. That's much safer than trying to land this orbiter by herself.

"However," he went on, "if we miss rendezvous, we'll land the orbiter just the way we did it for NASA, no sweat. I've put this ninety-nine-ton glider down on runways at Kennedy and Edwards, no reason why I can't land her back at Colón just as light as a feather."

A ninety-nine-ton feather, I thought, can't be all that easy to land. But reconnecting to the carrier plane? I'd never heard of that even being tried before.

Yet Sam did it, smooth as pie. We hardly felt a jolt or rattle. Sam kept up a running commentary for us, since our window shutters had been closed tight for reentry into the atmosphere. There were a few tense moments, but only a few.

"Done!" Sam announced. "We're now connected again to the carrier plane. We'll be landing at Colón in twenty-seven minutes."

And that was it. I felt the thud and bounce of the 747's wheels hitting the concrete runway, and then we taxied back to the hangar. Once we stopped and the engines whined down, the flight attendants opened the hatch and we went down to the ground in the same banana-smelling cherry picker.

The plane had stopped outside the hangar. There were a couple of photographers at the base of the cherry picker taking each couple's picture as they stood on terra firma once again, grinning out from their space-suit helmets. The first tourists in space.

Sam popped out of the cockpit and personally escorted me to the hatch and went down the cherry picker with me and my seat companion. He posed for the photographer between us, his arms on our shoulders, standing on tiptoe.

The thirty-nine other tourists went their separate ways that afternoon, clutching their photographs and smiling with their memories of spaceflight the way a new saint smiles at the revelation of heaven. They were converts, sure enough. They would go back home and tell everyone they knew about their space adventure. They were going to be Sam's best sales force.

I had a decision to make. I had started out investigating Sam for you, Uncle Griff, with the probability that his so-called tourist operation was a front for narcotics smuggling. But it sure didn't look that way to me.

Besides, I really liked the little guy. He was a combination of Huckleberry Finn and Long John Silver, with a bit of Chuck Yeager thrown in.

Yet I had come on to Sam as a wide-eyed tourist. If I hung around Colón, sooner or later he'd realize that I hadn't told him the exact truth about myself. I discovered, to my own surprise—shock, really—that I didn't want to hurt Sam's feelings. Worse, I didn't want him to know that I had been spying on him. I didn't want Sam Gunn to hate me.

So I had to leave. Unless Sam *asked* me to stay.

Like a fool, I decided to get him to ask me.

He invited me to dinner that evening. "A farewell dinner," he called it. I spent the afternoon shopping for the slinkiest, sexiest, black lace drop-dead dress I could find. Then I had my hair done: I usually wore it pinned up or in a ponytail, part of my sweet-sixteen pose. Now I had it sweeping down to my bare shoulders, soft and alluring.

I hoped.

Sam's eyes bugged out a bit when he saw me. That was good.

"My god, Ramona, you're . . ." he fished around for a compliment, ". . . you're *beautiful*!"

"Thank you," I said, and swept past him to settle myself in his convertible, showing plenty of thigh in the process.

Don't growl, Uncle Griff. I was emotionally involved with Sam. I know I shouldn't have been, but at the time there wasn't much I could do about it.

Sam was bouncing with enthusiasm about his first flight, of course.

"It worked!" he shouted, exultant, as he screeched the convertible out of my hotel's driveway. "Everything worked like a mother-loving charm! Nothing went wrong. Not one thing! Not a transistor or a data bit out of place. Perfect! One thousand batting average. Murphy's Law sleeps with the fishes."

He was so excited about the successful flight that he really wasn't paying much attention to me. And the breeze as we drove through the twilight was pulling my carefully done coiffure apart.

Sam took me to a quiet little restaurant out in a suburban shopping mall, of all places. The food was wonderful, but our conversation—over candlelight and wine—continued to deal with business instead of romance.

"If we start the flights at seven in the morning instead of nine, we can get in an afternoon flight, too," Sam was musing, grinning like an elf on amphetamines. "Double our income."

"Will your customers be able to get up that early?" I heard myself asking, intrigued by his visions of success despite myself. "Some of them are pretty old and creaky."

Sam waved a hand in the air. "We'll schedule the oldest ones for afternoon flights. Take the spryer ones in the morning. Maybe give 'em a slight break in the price for getting up so early."

I wanted Sam to pay attention to me, but his head was filled with plans for the future of Space Adventure Tours. Feeling a little downhearted, I decided that if I couldn't beat him, I might as well join him.

"It was a great flight," I assured him. Not that he needed it; I did. "I'd love to go again, if only I could afford it."

Either Sam didn't hear me or he paid me no attention.

"I was worried something would go wrong," he rattled on. "You know, something always gets away from you on a mission as tricky as this one. But it all worked fine. Better than fine. Terrific!"

It took a while before Sam drew enough of a breath for me to jump into his monologue. But at last I said:

"Sam, I've been thinking. Your antidisequilibrium system—"

"What about it?" he snapped, suddenly looking wary.

"It worked so well . . ."

His expression eased. His elfin grin returned. "Sure it did."

"Why don't you license it to NASA or some of the corporations that are building space stations in orbit? It could be a steady source of income for you."

"No," he said. Flat and final.

"Why not? You could make good money from it—"

"And let Masterson or one of the other big corporations compete with Space Adventure Tours? They'd drive us out of business in two months."

"How could they do that?" I really was naive, I guess.

Sam explained patiently, "If I let them get their foot in the door, they'll just price tours so far below cost that I'll either lose all my customers or go bankrupt trying to compete with 'em."

"Oh."

"Besides," he added, his eyes avoiding mine, "if they ever got their hands on my system, they'd just duplicate it and stop paying me."

"But you've patented the system, haven't you?"

His eyes became really evasive. "Not yet. Patents take time."

Suddenly our celebration dinner had turned glum. The mood had been broken, the charm lost, the enchantment gone. Maybe we were both tired from the excitement of the day, and our adrenaline rush had petered out. Whatever the reason, we finished dinner, and Sam drove me back to my hotel.

"I guess you're going back to the States," he said. once he stopped the convertible at the hotel's front entrance.

"I guess," I said.

"It's been fun knowing you, Ramona. You've been a good-luck charm for me."

I sighed. "Wish I didn't have to leave."

"Me too."

"Maybe I could find a job here," I hinted.

Sam didn't reply. He could have said he'd find a position for me in his company, but it's probably better that he didn't, the way things worked out.

The hotel doorman came grudgingly up to the car and opened my door with a murmured, *"Buenas noches."*

I went up to my room, feeling miserable. I couldn't sleep. I tossed in the bed, wide-awake, unhappy, trying to sort out my feelings and take some control of them. Didn't do me one bit of good. After hours of lying there in the same bed Sam and I had made love in, I tried pacing the floor.

Finally, in desperation, I went back to bed and turned on the TV. Most of the channels were in Spanish, of course, but I flicked through to find some English-speaking movie or something else that would hypnotize me to sleep.

And ran across the weather channel.

I almost missed it, surfing through the channels the way I was. But I heard the commentator say something about a hurricane as I surfed through. It took a couple of seconds for the words to make an impression on my conscious mind.

Then I clicked back to the weather. Sure enough, there was a monster hurricane roaring through the Caribbean. It was too far north to threaten Panama, but it was heading toward Cuba and maybe eventually Florida.

When we orbited over the region, not much more than twelve hours ago, the Caribbean had been clear as crystal. I remember staring out at Cuba; I could even see the little tail of the Keys extending out from Florida's southern tip. No hurricane in sight.

I punched up my pillows and sat up in bed, watching the weather. The American Midwest was cut in half by a cold front that spread early-season snow in Minnesota and rain southward all the way to Louisiana. The whole Mississippi Valley was covered with clouds.

But the Mississippi was clearly visible for its entire length when we'd been up in orbit that morning.

Could the weather change that fast?

I fell asleep with the weather channel bleating at me. And dreamed weird, convoluted dreams about Sam and hurricanes and watching television.

The next morning I packed and left Colón, but only flew as far as Panama City, on the Pacific side of the canal. I was determined to find out how Sam had tricked me. Deceived all forty of us. But I was taking no chances on bumping into Sam in Colón.

Within a week Sam was doing a roaring business in space tours. He hadn't gotten to the point where he was flying two trips per day, but a telephone call to his company revealed that Space Adventure Tours was completely booked for the next four months. The smiling young woman who took my call cheerfully informed me that she could take a reservation for early in February, if I liked.

I declined. Then I phoned my boss at the DEA in Washington, to get him to find me an Air Force pilot.

"Someone who's never been anywhere near NASA," I told my boss. I didn't want to run the risk of getting a pilot who might have been even a chance acquaintance of Sam's.

"And make sure he's male," I added. Sam was just too heart-meltingly charming when he wanted to be. I would take no chances.

What they sent me was Hector Dominguez, a swarthy, broad-shouldered, almost totally silent young pilot fresh from the Air Force Academy. I met him in the lobby of my hotel, the once-elegant old Ritz. It was easy to spot him: he wasn't in uniform, but he might as well have been, with a starched white shirt, knife-edged creases on his dark blue slacks, and a military buzz cut. He'd *never* make it as an undercover agent.

I needed him for flying, thank goodness, not spying. I introduced myself and led him to the hotel's restaurant, where I explained what I wanted over lunch. He nodded in the right places, and mumbled an occasional, "Yes, ma'am." His longest conversational offering was, "Please pass the bread, ma'am."

He made me feel like I was ninety! But he apparently knew his stuff, and the next morning when I drove out to the airport he was standing beside a swept-wing jet trainer, in his flier's sky-blue coveralls, waiting for me.

He helped me into a pair of coveralls, very gingerly. I got the impression that he was afraid I'd complain of sexual harassment if he actually touched me. Once I had to lean on his shoulder, when I was worming into the parachute harness I had to put on; I thought he'd break the Olympic record for long jump, the way he flinched away from me.

The ground crew helped me clamber up into the cockpit, connected my radio and oxygen lines, buckled my seat harness, and showed me how to fasten the oxygen mask to my plastic helmet. Then they got out of the way and the clear bubble of the plane's canopy clamped down over Hector and me.

Once we were buttoned up in the plane's narrow cockpit, me up front and him behind me, he changed completely.

"We'll be following their 747," Hector's voice crackled in my helmet earphones, "up to its maximum altitude of fifty thousand feet."

"That's where the orbiter is supposed to separate from it," I said, needlessly.

"Right. We'll stay within visual contact of the 747 until the orbiter returns."

If it ever actually leaves the 747, I thought.

Hector was a smooth pilot. He got the little jet trainer off the runway and arrowed us up across the Panama Canal. In less than fifteen minutes we spotted the lumbering 747 and piggybacking orbiter, with their bright blue SPACE ADVENTURE TOURS stenciled across their white fuselages.

For more than three hours we followed them. The orbiter never separated from the 747. The two flew serenely across the Caribbean, locked together like Siamese twins. Far below us, on the fringe of the northern horizon, I could see bands of swirling gray-white clouds: the edge of the hurricane.

Sam's 747-and-orbiter only went as high as thirty thousand feet, then leveled out.

"He's out of the main traffic routes," Hector informed me. "Nobody around for a hundred miles, except us."

"They can't see us, can they?"

"Not unless they have rear-looking radar."

Hector kept us behind and slightly below Sam's hybrid aircraft. Then I saw the 747's nose pull up; they started climbing. Hector stayed right on station behind them, as if we were connected by an invisible chain.

Sam's craft climbed more steeply, then nosed over into a shallow dive. We did the same, and I felt my stomach drop away for a heart-stopping few moments before a feeling of weight returned.

In my earphones I heard Hector chuckling. "That's

how he gave you a feeling of zero gee,'' he said. ''It's the old Vomit Comet trick. They use it at Houston to give astronauts-in-training a feeling for zero gravity.''

''What do you mean?'' I asked.

''You fly a parabolic arc: up at the top of the arc you get a few seconds of pretty-near zero gravity.''

''That's when we felt weightless!'' I realized.

''Yeah. And when they leveled off you thought his anti–space-sickness equipment was working. All he did was start flying straight and level again.''

Magic tricks are simple when you learn how they're done.

''What did you say about a vomit something or other?''

Hector laughed again. It was a very pleasant, warm sound. ''At Houston, they call the training plane the Vomit Comet. That's because they fly a couple dozen parabolic arcs each flight. You go from regular gravity to zero gee and back again every few minutes. Makes your stomach go crazy.''

So Sam's entire space adventure was a total shuck. A sham. A hoax. I had felt disappointed when I'd first suspected Sam. Now that I had the evidence, I felt even worse: bitter, sad, miserable.

I know, Uncle Griff! You told me he was no good. But—well, I still felt awful.

That evening I just couldn't bear the thought of eating alone, so I invited Hector to have dinner with me. He was staying at the Ritz, too, so we went to the hotel's shabby old restaurant. It must have once been a splendid place, but it was tacky and run-down and not even half-filled. The waiters were all ancient, and even though the food was really good, the meal left me even more depressed than I had been before.

To make it all worse, Hector reverted to his monosyllabic introversion once we left the airport.

Is it me? I wondered. Is he naturally shy around women? Is he gay? That would've been a shame, I thought. He was really handsome, in a dark, smoldering sort of way. Gorgeous big midnight eyes. And I imagined that his hair would grow out curly if he ever allowed it to. His voice was low and dreamy, too—when he chose to say a word or two.

I tried to make conversation with him, but it was like pulling teeth. It took the whole dinner to find out that he was from New Mexico, he wasn't married, and he intended to make a career of the Air Force.

"I like to fly." That was his longest sentence of the evening.

I went to bed wanting to cry. I dreamed about Sam; I dreamed that I was a hired assassin and I had to kill him.

Hector and I trailed Sam's plane again the next day, but this time I brought a video camera and got his entire flight sequence on tape. Evidence.

A job is a job, and no matter how much I hated doing it, I was here to get the goods on Sam Gunn. So he wasn't smuggling drugs. What he was doing was still wrong: bilking people of their hard-earned money on phony promises to fly them into space. Scamming little old widows and retired couples living on pensions. Swindling honeymoon couples.

And let's face it, he swindled me, too. In more ways than one.

That afternoon I had Hector fly me over to Colón and, together, we went to the offices of Space Adventure Tours.

Sam seemed truly delighted to see us. He ushered us into his elegant office with a huge grin on his apple-pie face, shook hands with Hector, bussed me on the cheek, and climbed the ramp behind his walnut-and-chrome desk and sat down in his high-backed leather swivel chair. Hector and I sat on the two recliners.

"Are you two a thing?" Sam asked, archly.

"A thing?" I asked back.

"Romantically."

"No!" I was surprised to hear Hector blurt the word out just as forcefully as I did. Stereophonic denial.

"Oh." Sam looked slightly disappointed, but only for a moment. "I thought maybe you wanted to take a honeymoon flight in space."

"Sam, you never go higher than thirty-five thousand feet and I have a videotape to prove it."

He blinked at me. It was the first time I'd ever seen Sam Gunn go silent.

"Your whole scheme is a fake, Sam. A fraud. You're stealing your customers' money. That's theft. Grand larceny, I'm sure."

The sadness I had felt was giving way to anger: smoldering burning rage at this man who had seemed so wonderful but was really such a scoundrel, such a rat, such a lying, sneaking, thieving bastard. I had trusted Sam! And he had been nothing but deceit.

Sam leaned back in his luxurious desk chair and puckered his lips thoughtfully.

"You're going to jail, Sam. For a long time."

"May I point out, oh righteous, wrathful one, that you're assuming the laws of Panama are the same as the laws of the good old US of A."

"They have laws against fraud and bunko," I shot back hotly, "even in Panama."

"Do you think I've defrauded my customers, Ramona?"

"You certainly have!"

Very calmly, Sam asked, "Did you enjoy your flight?"

"What's that got to do with it?"

"Did you enjoy it?" Sam insisted.

"At the time, yes, I did. But then I found out—"

"You found out that you didn't actually go into orbit. You found out that we just fly our customers around and make them *feel* as if they're in space."

"Your whole operation is a fake!"

He made an equivocal gesture with his hands. "We don't take you into orbit, that's true. The scenes you see through the spacecraft's windows are videos from real spaceflights, though. You're seeing what you'd see if you actually did go into space."

"You're telling your customers that you take them into space!" I nearly screamed. "That's a lie!"

Sam opened a desk drawer and pulled out a slick, multicolored sales brochure. He slid it across the desk toward me.

"Show me where it says we take our customers into orbit."

I glanced at the brochure's cover. It showed a picture of an elderly couple smiling so wide their dentures were in danger of falling out. Behind them was a backdrop of the Earth as seen from orbit.

"Nowhere in our promotional literature or video presentations do we promise to take out customers into space," Sam said evenly.

"But—"

"The contracts our customers sign say that Space Adventure Tours will give them an *experience* of space flight. Which is what we do. We give our customers a simulation: a carefully designed simulation so that they can have the *experience* of their lives."

"You tell them you're taking them into space!"

"Do not."

"You do, too! You told *me* you'd fly me into orbit!"

Sam shook his head sadly. "That may be what you heard. What you wanted to hear. But I have never told any of my customers that Space Adventure Tours would actually, physically, transport them into orbit."

"You did! You did!"

"No I didn't. If you'd taped our conversations, you'd find that I never told you—or anybody else—that I'd fly you into space."

I looked at Hector. He sat like a graven idol: silent and unmoving.

"When we were in the orbiter," I remembered, "you made all this talk about separating from the 747 and going into orbit."

"That was part of the simulation," Sam said. "Once you're on board the orbiter, it's all an act. It's all part of the experience. Like an amusement-park ride."

Exasperated, I said, "Sam, your customers are going home and telling their friends and relatives that they've really flown in space. They're sending new customers to you, people who expect to go into orbit for real!"

With a shrug, Sam answered, "Ramona, honey, I'm not responsible for what people think, or say, or do. If they wanna believe they've really been in space, that's their fantasy, their happiness. Who am I to deny them?"

I was beyond fury. My insides felt bitter cold. "All right," I said icily. "Suppose I go back to the States and let the news media know what you're doing? How long do you think customers will keep coming?"

Sam's brows knit slightly. "Gimme two more months," he said.

"Two more months?"

"Let me operate like this for two more months, and then I'll close down voluntarily."

"You're asking me to allow you to defraud the public for another two months?"

His eyes narrowed. "You know, you're talking like a lawyer. Or maybe a cop."

"What and who I am has nothing to do with this," I snapped.

"A cop," Sam said, with a heavy sigh.

Out of nowhere, Hector spoke up. "Why do you want two months?"

I whirled on the poor guy. "So he can steal as much money as he can from the poor unsuspecting slobs he calls his customers, why else?"

"Yeah," Hector said, in that smoky low voice of his, "okay, maybe so. But why two months?"

Before I could think of an answer, Sam popped in. "Because in two months I'll have proved my point."

"What point?"

"That there's a viable market for tourists in space. That people'll spend a good-sized hunk of change just for the chance to ride into orbit."

"Which you don't really do," I reminded him.

"That doesn't matter," Sam said. "The point I'm making is that there really is a market for space tourism. People have been talking about space tourism for years; I'm doing something about it."

"You're stealing," I said. "Swindling."

"Okay, so I'm faking it. Nevertheless, people are

plunking down their money for a space adventure.''

"So what?" I sneered.

Hunching forward, leaning his forearms on the gleaming desktop, Sam said, "So with three whole months of this operation behind me, I can go back to the States and raise enough capital to lease a Clippership that'll *really* take tourists into orbit."

I stared at him.

Hector got the point before I did. "You mean the financial people won't believe there's a market for space tourism now, but they will after you've operated this fake business for three months?"

"Right," Sam answered. "Those Wall Street types don't open up their wallets until you've got solid numbers to show 'em."

"What about venture capitalists?" Hector asked. "They back new, untried ideas all the time."

Sam made a sour face. "Sure they do. I went to some of 'em. First thing they did was ask me why the big boys like Masterson and Global Technologies aren't doing it. Then they go to the 'experts' in the field and ask their opinion of the idea. And who're the experts?"

"Masterson and Global," I guessed.

Shaking his head, Sam said, "Even worse. They went to NASA. To Clark Griffith IV, my own boss, for crap's sake! By the time he got done scaring the *cojones* off them, they wouldn't even answer my e-mail."

"NASA shot you down?"

"They didn't know it was me. They talked to a team that the venture capitalists put together."

I asked, "But shouldn't NASA be in favor of space tourism? I mean, they're the space agency, after all."

"Some people in NASA are in favor of it, sure," Sam said. "But the higher you go in the agency, the more conservative they get. Up at the top they have nightmares of a spacecraft full of tourists blowing up, like the old *Challenger*. That'd set back everything we do in space by ten years, at least."

"So when the venture capitalists asked . . ."

"The agency bigwigs threw enough cold water on the

idea to freeze the Amazon River," Sam growled.

"And that's when you started Space Adventure Tours," I said.

"Right. Set the whole company up while I was still working at the Cape. Then I took a three-month leave to personally run the operation. I've got two months left to go."

Silence. I sat there, not knowing what to say next. Hector looked thoughtful, or maybe puzzled is a better description of the expression on his face. Sam leaned back in his high chair, staring at me like a little boy who's been caught with his hand in the cookie jar, but is hoping to get a cookie out of it instead of a spanking.

I was in a turmoil of conflicting emotions. I really liked Sam, even though he had quite literally screwed me. But I couldn't let him continue to swindle people; that was wrong any way you looked at it, legally or morally.

On the other hand, Sam wasn't really hurting anybody. Was he? Did any of his customers empty their retirement accounts to take his phony ride? Would any of those retired couples spend their declining years in poverty because Sam bilked them out of their life savings?

I shook my head, trying to settle my spinning thoughts into some rational order. Sam was breaking all kinds of laws, and he'd have to stop. Right now.

"All right," I said, my mind finally made up. "I'm not going to report this back to your superiors at NASA."

Sam's face lit up.

"And I'm not going to blow the whistle on you or bring in the authorities," I continued.

Sam grinned from ear to ear.

"On one condition," I said firmly.

His rusty eyebrows hiked up. "One condition?"

"You've got to shut this operation down, Sam. Either shut down voluntarily, or I'll be forced to inform the authorities here in Panama and the news media in the States."

He nodded solemnly. "Fair enough. In two months I'll close up shop."

"Not in two months," I snapped. "Now. Today. You

go out of business *now* and refund whatever monies you've collected for future flights.''

I expected Sam to argue. I expected him to rant and holler at me. Or at least plead and wheedle. He did neither. For long, long moments he simply sat there staring at me, saying nothing, his face looking as if I'd just put a bullet through his heart.

I steeled myself and stared right back at him. Hector stirred uneasily in his chair beside me, sensing that there was more going on than we had expressed in words, but saying nothing.

At last Sam heaved an enormous sigh, and said, in a tiny little exhausted voice, ''Okay, if that's what you want. I'm in no position to fight back.''

I should have known right there and then that he was lying through his crooked teeth.

Hector flew me back to Panama City, and we repaired to our separate hotel rooms. I felt totally drained, really out of it, as if I'd spent the day fighting dragons or climbing cliffs by my fingernails.

Then things started to get weird.

I had just flopped on my hotel-room bed, not even bothering to take off my clothes, when the phone rang. My boss from DEA headquarters in Washington.

''You're going to have a visitor,'' he told me, looking nettled in the tiny phone screen. ''Her name will be Jones. Listen to what she has to tell you and act accordingly.''

''A visitor?'' I mumbled, feeling thickheaded, confused. ''Who? Why?''

My boss doesn't nettle easily, but he sure looked ticked off. ''She'll explain it all to you. And this is the last goddamned time I let you or any other of my people go off on detached duty to help some other agency!''

With that, he cut off the connection. I was looking at a blank phone screen, wondering what on earth was going on.

The phone buzzed again. This time it was Hector.

''I just got a phone call from my group commander at Eglin,'' he said. ''Some really weird shit has hit the fan,

Ramona. I'm under orders to stay here in Panama with you until we meet with some woman named Jones."

"I got the same orders from my boss," I told him.

Hector's darkly handsome face went into brooding mode. "I don't like the sound of this," he muttered.

"Neither do I," I confessed.

We didn't have long to wait. Ms. Jones arrived bright and early the following morning. In fact, Hector and I were having breakfast together in the hotel's nearly empty dining room, trying to guess what was going on, when she sauntered in.

She didn't hesitate a moment, just walked right up to our table and sat down, as if she'd been studying photographs of us for the past week or two.

"Adrienne Jones," she said, opening her black-leather shoulder bag and pulling out a leather-encased laminated ID card. It said she was with the US Department of State.

She didn't look like a diplomat. Adrienne Jones—if that was really her name—was a tall, sleek, leggy African-American whose skin was the color of polished ebony. She had a fashion model's figure and face: high cheekbones, almond eyes, and a tousled, careless hairdo that must have cost a fortune. Her clothes were expensive, too.

Hector stared at her, too stunned to speak. I felt dismal and threadbare beside her in my shapeless slacks and blouse, with a belly bag strapped around my middle.

I hated her immediately.

"If you're really with the State Department," I said as she snapped her ID closed and put it back in her capacious shoulder bag, "then I'm from Disney World."

She smiled at me the way a snake does. "That's the one in Florida, isn't it?"

Hector found his voice. "CIA, right? You've got to be with the CIA."

Jones ignored his guess. "You both have been informed that you are to cooperate with me, correct?"

"I was told to listen to what you have to say," I said.

"Me too," said Hector.

"Very well, then. Here's what I have to say: Leave

Sam Gunn alone. Let him continue to operate. Do not interfere with him in any way.''

What kind of strings had Sam pulled? He had come across to me as the little guy struggling against the big boys, but here was the State Department or the CIA—or *some* federal agency—ordering me to keep my hands off.

''Why?'' I asked.

''You don't have to know,'' said Jones. ''Just leave Sam be. No interference with his operation.''

Hector scratched his head and glanced at me. He was an Air Force officer, I realized, and had to follow orders. His career depended on it. Me, I had a career, too. But I wasn't going to let this fashion-model stranger order me around, no matter what my boss said.

''Okay,'' I told her, ''I've listened to what you have to say. That doesn't mean I'm going to do what you're asking me to do.''

Jones smiled again, venomously. ''I'm not asking you. I'm telling you.''

''You can tell me whatever you like. I'm not going to go along with it unless I know the whys and wherefores.''

Her smile faded into grimness. ''Look, Ms. Perkins, your superior at DEA has been briefed, and he agreed to cooperate. He's told you to cooperate, and that's what you'd better do, if you know what's good for you.''

''You briefed him? Then brief me.''

She snorted through her finely chiseled nostrils. ''All I can tell you is that this is a high-priority matter, and it has the backing of the highest levels of authority.''

''Highest levels?'' I asked. ''Like the White House?'' She didn't answer.

''The Oval Office? The president himself?''

Jones remained as silent and still as the sphinx.

I heard myself say, ''Not good enough, Ms. Jones. Anybody can claim they're working on orders from the White House. I've heard even fancier stories, in my line of work. What's going on?''

She merely shook her head, just the slightest of motions but clearly a negative.

''Okay then.'' I got up from my chair. ''I'm catching

the next flight to Miami and going straight to the news media. They'll be really interested to hear that the CIA is backing a fraudulent tourist operation in Panama."

"I wouldn't try that if I were you," Jones said.

Hector stood up beside me. "You threaten her, you've got to go through me."

I gaped at him. "You don't have to protect me. I can take care of myself."

"I'm in this, too," he insisted. "We're partners."

Jones threw her head back and laughed. "What you two are," she said, "is a couple of babes in the woods. And if you don't start behaving yourselves, you're going to end up as babes in a swamp, feeding alligators."

I unzipped my belly bag and pulled out my cellphone. "CNN, Atlanta, USA," I said to the phone system's computer. "News desk."

"Put it down," Jones said.

I kept the phone pressed against my ear, listening to the computer chatter as the system made the connection.

"Put it down," she repeated. Her voice was flat, calm, yet menacing. I realized that her black leather shoulder bag was big enough to hold a small arsenal.

"News," I heard a tired voice answer.

Jones said, "We can cut a deal, if you're reasonable."

"News desk," the voice repeated, a little irked.

I put the phone down and clicked it off. "What kind of a deal?"

Jones gestured with both her hands; she had long, graceful fingers, I noticed. I sat down, then Hector took his seat beside me.

"God spare me the righteous amateurs," Jones muttered. "You two have no idea of what you're messing with."

"Then tell us," I said.

"I can't tell you," she replied. "But if you want to, you can come back to Colón with me and watch it happen."

I didn't know what to say.

Jones misinterpreted my silence as reluctance, so she went on, "You give me your word you won't go blowing

off to the media or anybody else, and you can come with
me and see what this is all about. After it's over you can
go back home, safe and sound. Deal?''

I'd seen enough drug deals to know that she was showing us only the tip of the iceberg. But I was curious,
and—to tell the absolute truth—I was wondering how
Sam got himself mixed up with the CIA and whether he
was in danger or not.

So I glanced at Hector, who remained silent, suspicious. But he looked at me, and his expression said that
he'd back whatever move I made. So I said, ''Deal.''

We couldn't squeeze a third body into Hector's training jet, and Jones didn't trust us out of her sight, so we
flew back to Colón again in her plane: a twin-engined
executive jet. I was beginning to feel like a Ping-Pong
ball, bouncing from Colón to Panama City and back
again.

Hector was impressed with the plane's luxurious interior. ''Like a movie,'' he said, awed. Instead of sitting
beside me, he asked to go up into the cockpit. Jones gave
him a friendly smile, and said okay. I didn't see him again
until we landed.

An unmarked Mercedes four-door sedan was waiting
for us at the runway ramp, the kind of luxury car the drug
dealers call a ''cocaine Ford.'' Two men in dark suits
bustled Hector and me into the rear seat. Jones sat up
front with the driver. The other man followed us in another unmarked Mercedes. I felt distinctly nervous.

But all we did is drive across the airport to Sam's con-
verted blimp hangar.

''Mr. Gunn is doing a special flight this afternoon,''
Jones told us cryptically, half-turned in her seat to face
us. ''Once it's finished, you two can go back to the
States—*if* you promise not to blow the whistle on Space
Adventure Tours.''

''And if we don't promise?'' I asked. Instead of strong
and forceful, my voice came out as a little girl's squeak,
which made me disgusted with myself.

Jones didn't answer; she merely reverted to her rattler-
type smile.

We pulled up outside the hangar. Inside, I could see the big 747 with the orbiter clamped atop it. Technicians were swarming all over it.

"Sam had his regular flight this morning," I muttered to Hector. "Now they're getting the plane ready for another flight."

Hector nodded. "Looks like."

We sat and watched, while our Mercedes's engine purred away so the car's air-conditioning could stay on. Sam came out of an office up on the catwalk above the hangar floor, with two slick-looking lawyerly types flanking him. He was grinning and gabbing away a mile a minute, happy as a kid in a candy store. Or so it seemed from this distance.

Jones opened her door. "You stay here," she said—as much to the driver as to us, I thought. "Don't leave this car."

So we sat in the car with the afternoon sun beating down on us and the air conditioner laboring to keep the interior cool. Our driver was old enough to be gray at the temples; solidly built, and I guessed that he was carrying a nine-millimeter automatic in a shoulder holster under his dark suit jacket. He looked perfectly comfortable and prepared to sit and watch over us for hours and hours.

I was bursting to find out what was going on. There were more technicians clambering over the ladders and scaffolds surrounding the piggyback planes than I had ever seen in Sam's employ. Most of them must be Jones's people, I thought. Something very special is being cooked up here.

Then a fleet of limousines drove into view, coming slowly across the concrete rampway until they stopped in front of the hangar. Eleven limos, I counted. One of them had stiff little flags attached to its front fenders: blue with some kind of shield or seal in the middle, surrounded by six five-pointed white stars.

Dozens of men jumped out of the limos, about half of them in olive green army fatigues. They didn't look like Americans. Each soldier carried a wicked-looking assault rifle with a curved magazine. The rest of the men wore business suits that bulged beneath their armpits and the kind of dark sunglasses that just screamed "bodyguard."

They spread out, poking their noses—and rifle muzzles—into every corner of the hangar. A couple of the suits came up to our car, where the glamorous Ms. Jones greeted them with a big toothy smile. I couldn't make out what she was saying to them, but it sounded like she was speaking in Spanish.

Sam came bubbling over, practically drooling once he feasted his eyes on Jones. He didn't notice us inside the car, behind the heavily tinted windows.

At last, the leader of the suits turned to the team of soldiers surrounding the beflagged limo and gave a curt nod. They opened the rear door and out stepped a little girl, with big dark eyes and long hair that just had to be naturally curly. She couldn't have been more than ten years old. She smiled at the soldiers, as if she knew them by name. She was very nicely dressed in a one-piece jumpsuit of butter yellow.

She turned back and said something to someone who was still inside the limo. She reached her hand in to whoever it was. A tall, lean man of about fifty came out of the limo and stretched to his full height. He was wearing army fatigues and smoking an immense cigar.

My jaw fell open. "That's the president of Cuba!" I gasped. "The man who took over when Castro retired."

"No," Hector corrected me. "He's the man who took over after the bloodbath in Havana when Castro retired."

"That must be his daughter."

"What're they doing here?" Hector wondered.

"Taking one of Sam's phony rides into space," I said. "I wonder if they know it's a phony?"

Hector turned to face me. "Maybe it's not."

"Not what?"

"Not a phony," he said grimly. "Maybe they're going to have an accident up there. On purpose."

It hit me like a shot of pure heroin. "They're going to assassinate the president of Cuba!"

"And make it look like an accident."

"Oh my God!"

The driver turned slightly to tell us, "Don't get any crazy ideas—"

He never got any further. I jammed my thumbs into his carotids and held on. In a few seconds he was unconscious.

"Where'd you learn that?" Hector asked, his tone somewhere between amazement and admiration.

"South Philadelphia," I answered as I yanked the nine-millimeter from the driver's holster. "Come on."

Hector grasped my shoulder. "You're not going to get far in a shoot-out."

He was right, dammit. I had to think fast. Outside, I could see Jones leading the president of Cuba and his daughter toward the plane. Half the Cuban security force walked a respectful distance behind them, the other half was deployed on either side of them.

"Most of those ground-crew personnel must be security guys from the States," Hector pointed out. "Must be enough firepower out there to start World War III."

My eye lit on Sam. He was still standing in the sunshine of the ramp, outside the hangar, hardly more than ten meters from our car.

"Come on," I said, leaning past the unconscious driver to pop the door lock.

I stuffed the pistol in my belly bag; kept the bag unzipped so I could grab the gun quickly if I needed to.

Sam turned as we approached him. He looked surprised, then delighted.

"Ramona!" he said with a big grin. "I thought you two had gone back to the States."

"Not yet," I said grimly. "We're taking this flight with you."

For an instant Sam looked puzzled, but then he said, "Great. Come on, you can ride in the 747 with me."

"You're not going aboard the orbiter?"

"Not this flight," Sam said easily.

Of course not, I thought. On this flight the orbiter's really going to be released from the 747. Instead of going into space, as Sam promised, it was going to crash into the Caribbean. With the president of Cuba aboard. And his ten-year-old daughter.

"Sam, how could you do this?" I asked as we walked into the hangar.

"Listen, I was just as surprised as you would be when the State Department asked me to do it."

"With his little daughter, too."

We reached the ladder. "It was his daughter's idea," Sam said. "She wanted to take the space ride. Poppa's only doing this to please his little girl—and for the international publicity, of course."

With Sam leading the way, we climbed up the ladder into the 747. Its interior was strictly utilitarian; no fancy decor. Most of the cavernous passenger cabin was empty. There were only seats up in the first-class section, below the cockpit. Sam, Hector, and I went up the spiral stairs and entered the cockpit, where a young woman in a pilot's uniform was already sitting in the right-hand seat.

"Can you fly this plane?" I asked Hector.

He stared at the control panels; the gauges and buttons and keypads seemed to stretch for miles. Looking out the windshield, I saw we were already so high up we might as well have been on oxygen.

"I've got a multiengine license," Hector muttered.

"But can you fly *this* plane?" I insisted.

He nodded tightly. "I can fly anything."

Sam put on a quizzical look. "Why should he have to fly? I'm going to pilot this mission myself, and I've got a qualified copilot here."

I pulled the pistol from my belly bag and pointed it at the copilot. "Get out," I said. "Hector, you take her place."

She stared at me, wide-eyed, frozen.

"*Vamos*," Sam said, in the most un-Spanish accent I'd ever heard. The woman slipped out of the copilot's chair.

"What's this all about?" Sam asked, more intrigued than scared. "Why the toy cannon?"

I pointed the gun at him. "Sam, you're going to fly this plane just the way you would for any of your tourist flights. No more and no less."

He gave me one of his lopsided grins. "Sure. What else?"

There were two jump seats behind the pilots' chairs. I took one, and Sam's erstwhile copilot the other. I kept the pistol in my hand as we rolled out of the hangar, lit up the engines, and taxied to the runway.

"What do you think is going on here," Sam asked, "that makes you need a gun?"

"You know perfectly well what's going on," I said.

"Yeah," he answered ruefully. "But I don't know what *you* know."

"Who's in the orbiter's cockpit?" I asked.

"Some guy the State Department insisted on. They wanted their own people up there with *el Presidente* and his daughter."

"Do they have parachutes?"

"Parachutes? What for?"

"They're all going down with the president and his daughter?"

"Whither he goest," Sam replied.

We took off smoothly and headed out over the Caribbean. Is this part of the Bermuda Triangle? I asked myself. Will this fatal accident be chalked up as another mystical happening, or the work of aliens from outer space?

"How could you let them use you like this, Sam?" I blurted.

He glanced over his shoulder at me, saw how miserable I felt, and quickly turned back to the plane's controls.

"Ramona, honey, when people that high up in the federal government want to make you jump, you really don't have all that much of a choice."

"You could have said no."

"And miss the chance of a lifetime! No way!"

So despite all his blather about hating bureaucracies and wanting to help ordinary people, the little guy, against the big shots of government and industry, Sam sold out when they put the pressure on him. He probably didn't have much of a choice, at that. Do what they tell you or you're out of business. Maybe they threatened his life. I'd heard stories about the CIA and how they worked both sides of the street. They'd even been involved in the drug traffic, according to rumors around headquarters.

We flew in dismal silence across a sparkling-clear sea. At least, I grew silent. Sam spent the time acquainting Hector with the plane's controls and particular handling characteristics.

"Gotta remember we've got a ninety-nine-ton brick on our backs," he chattered cheerfully, as if he didn't have a care in the world.

Hector nodded and listened, listened and nodded. Sam jabbered away, one pilot to another, oblivious to everything else except flying.

Me, I was starting to worry about what was going to happen when we returned to Colón with the orbiter still intact and the Cuban president very much alive. Jones and her people would probably put the best face they could on it, like that's what they had intended all along: a goodwill flight to help cement friendly relations between Cuba and the US. But I knew that if the CIA didn't get me, some fanatical old anti-Castro nutcake in Miami would come after me.

And Hector, too, I realized. I'd put his life in danger, when all he wanted was to protect me.

I felt really miserable about that. The poor guy was in as much danger as I was, even though none of this was his fault.

I studied his face as he sat in the copilot's chair next to Sam. Hector didn't look worried. Or frightened. Or even tense. He was happy as a clam, behind the controls of this monstrous plane, five miles over the deep blue sea.

"Now comes the tricky part," Sam was telling him, leaning over toward Hector slightly so he could hear him better.

Sitting on the jump seat behind Sam, I tightened my grip on the pistol. "You're not going to separate the orbiter," I said firmly.

Without even glancing back at me, Sam broke into a cackling laughter. "Couldn't even if I wanted to, oh masked rider of the plains. The bird's welded on. You'd need a load of primacord to blast 'er loose.''

"What about the explosive bolts?'' I asked.

Sam cackled again. "That's part of the simulation, kiddo. There aren't any.''

I saw that Hector was grinning, as if he knew something that I didn't.

"Then how do you intend to separate the orbiter?'' I demanded.

"I don't,'' Sam replied.

"Then how . . .'' The question died in my throat. I had been a fool. A stupendous fool. This wasn't an assassination plot; Sam was taking the president of Cuba—and his ten-year-old daughter—for a spaceflight experience, just as he'd taken several hundred other tourists.

I could feel my face burning. Hector, his smile gentle and sweet, turned toward me, and said softly, "Maybe you should unload the gun, huh? Just to be on the safe side.''

I clicked on the safety, then popped the magazine out of the pistol's grip.

I sat in silence for the rest of the flight. There was nothing for me to say. I had been an idiot, jumping to conclusions and suspecting Sam of being a partner in a heinous crime. I felt *awful*.

After the regular routine over the Caribbean, Sam turned us back to Colón, and we landed at the airport without incident. Sam taxied the plane to his hangar, where a throng of news reporters and photographers were waiting.

With his daughter clinging to his side, the president of Cuba gave a long and smiling speech in Spanish to the newspeople. Sam squirmed out of his pilot's chair and rushed down to the hangar floor so he could stand beside the Cuban president and bask in the glow of publicity. Naturally, he grabbed the woman who was supposed to be his copilot and took her along with him.

I stayed in the cockpit with Hector, watching the whole thing. I could see Ms. Jones hovering around the edge of the crowd, together with her people; even she was smiling.

*El Presidente* put his arm around Sam's shoulders and spoke glowingly. It was still in Spanish, but the tone was very warm, very friendly. Cuban-American relations soared almost as high as the president thought he'd flown. Sam signed his autograph for the president's daughter. She was almost as tall as he, I noticed.

Cameras clicked and whirred, vidcams buzzed away, reporters shouted questions in English and Spanish. It was a field day—for everybody but me.

Hector shook his head and gave me a rueful grin. "I guess we were a little wrong about all this," he said, almost in a whisper.

"It's my fault," I said. "I got you into this."

"Don't look so sad. Everything came out okay. Sam's a hero."

All I wanted to do was to stay in that cockpit and hide forever.

At last *el Presidente* and his daughter made their way back to their limousine. The fleet of limos departed, and the crowd of media people broke up. Even the American State Department people started to leave. That's what they were, I reluctantly admitted to myself. Jones and her people really were from the State Department, not the CIA.

Finally Sam came strolling the length of the 747's cabin and climbed up the spiral staircase to the cockpit, whistling horribly off-key every step of the way.

He popped his head through the hatch, grinning like a jack-o'-lantern. "You want me to send some pizzas up here or are you gonna come out and have dinner with me?"

Hector took me by the hand, gently, and got to his feet. He had to bend over slightly in the low-ceilinged cockpit, a problem that Sam didn't have to worry about.

"We're coming out," he said. I let him lead me, like a docile little lamb.

We went straight to Sam's favorite restaurant, the waterfront shack that served such good fish. Jones was already there, sipping at a deadly looking rum concoction and smiling happily.

"I ought to be angry with you two," she said, once we sat at the little round table with her.

"It's my fault," I said immediately. "I'm the one to blame."

Hector started to say something, but Jones shushed him with a gesture of her long, graceful hand. "No harm, no foul. The flight went *beautifully*, and I'm not going to screw up my report by even mentioning your names."

Sam was aglow. He ordered drinks for all of us, and as the waiter left our table, he looked over at the bar.

"Lookit that!" Sam said, pointing to the TV over the joint's fake-bamboo bar.

We saw the president of Cuba smiling toothily, his daughter on one side of him and Sam Gunn on the other.

"Worldwide publicity!" Sam crowed. "I'm a made man!"

Hector shook his head. "If anybody ever finds out that your orbiter never left the 747, Sam, the publicity won't be so good."

For Hector, that was a marathon speech.

Sam grinned at him. "Now who's going to tell on me? The Department of State?"

Jones shook her head. "Not us."

"NASA?" Sam asked rhetorically. "You think some rocket expert in NASA's gonna stand up and declare that you can't remate the orbiter with its carrier plane once it's been separated?"

Before any of us could reply, Sam answered his own question. "In a pig's eye! The word's going through the agency now, from top to bottom: no comment on Space Adventure Tours. Zip. *Nada*. Zilch. The lid is on, and it's on tight."

"What about you two?" Jones asked, arching a perfect brow.

Hector glanced at me, then shrugged. "I'm in the Air Force. If I'm ordered to keep quiet, I'll keep quiet."

"And you, Ms. Perkins?" Jones asked me.

I focused on Sam. "You promised to end this bogus business in two months, Sam."

"Yeah, that's right, I did."

"Did you tell the president of Cuba that all he got was a simulation?" I asked.

Sam screwed up his face, and admitted, "Not exactly."

"What happens to Cuban-American relations when he finds out?"

Jones' smile had evaporated. "Which brings us back to the vital question: Are you going to try to blow the whistle?"

I didn't like the sound of that *try to*.

"No, she's not," Sam said. "Ramona's a good American citizen, and this is a matter of international relations now."

The gall of the man! He had elevated his scam into an integral part of the State Department's efforts to end the generations-old split between Cuba and the US. I wondered who in Washington had been crazy enough to hang our foreign policy on Sam Gunn's trickery and deceit. Probably the same kind of deskbound lunkheads who had once dickered with the Mafia to assassinate Castro with a poisoned cigar.

"I want to hear what you have to say, Ms. Perkins," Jones said, her voice low but hard as steel.

What could I say? What did I *want* to say? I really didn't know.

But I heard my own voice tell them, "Sam promised to close down Space Adventure Tours in two more months. I think that would be a good idea."

Sam nodded slowly. "Sure. By that time I oughtta be able to raise enough capital to buy a Clippership and take tourists into orbit for real."

Jones looked from me to Sam and back again.

Sam added, "Of course, it would help if the State Department ponied up some funding for me."

She snapped her attention to Sam. "Now wait a minute . . ."

"Not a lot," Sam said. "Ten or twenty million, that's all."

Jones's mouth dropped open. Then she yelped, "That's extortion!"

Sam placed both hands on his flowered shirt in a gesture of aggrieved innocence. "Extortion? Me?"

"And that's just about the whole story, Uncle Griff," Ramona said to me.

I leaned back in my desk chair and stared at her. "That business with the president of Cuba happened two months ago. What kept you down there in Panama until now?"

She blushed. Even beneath her deep suntan I could see her cheeks reddening.

"Uh . . . well, I wanted to stay on Sam's tail and make certain he closed up his operation when he promised he would."

Sam hadn't closed Space Adventure Tours, I knew. He had suspended operations in Panama and returned to the agency. Gone back on duty. He was scheduled for a classified Air Force mission, of all things. I had talked myself blue in the face, trying to get the astronaut office in Houston to replace him with somebody else, but they kept insisting Sam was the best man they had for the mission. Lord knows who he bribed, and with what.

"You didn't have to stay in Panama all that time," I pointed out to my niece. "You could have kept tabs on him from here in Washington."

She blushed even more deeply. "Well, Uncle Griff, to tell the truth . . . it was sort of like a, you know, kind of like a honeymoon."

I snorted. Couldn't help it. The thought of my own little niece shacked up with . . .

"You were *living* with him?" I bellowed.

She just smiled at me. "Yes," she said, dreamily.

I was furious. "You let Sam Gunn—"

"Not Sam!" Ramona said quickly. Then she grinned at me. "You thought I was living with Sam?" She laughed at me.

Before I could ask, she told me, "Hector! We fell in love, Uncle Griff! We're going to get married."

That was different. Sort of. "Oh. Congratulations, I suppose. When?"

"Next year," my niece answered. "When Sam starts *real* flights into orbit, Hector and I are going to spend our official honeymoon in space!"

I wanted to puke.

So that's why we had to fire Sam Gunn. Government regulations specifically state that you can't be running a business of your own while you're on the federal payroll. Besides, the little SOB made a shambles of everything he touched.

It wasn't easy, though. Actually firing somebody from a government job is never easy, and Sam played every delaying trick in the book. Just to see if he could give me apoplexy, I'm sure.

The little conniving sneak was even working out an arrangement to rent a section of a new space station and turn it into an orbiting honeymoon hotel before I finally got all the paperwork I needed to fire his butt out of the agency.

And he didn't leave quietly. Not Sam. Know what his final masterstroke was? He left me a prepaid ticket to ride his goddamned Clippership into orbit and spend a full week in his orbiting hotel.

He knew damned well I'd never give him the satisfaction! Probably the little bastard thought I was too old to enjoy sex. Or maybe he expected me to bust a blood vessel while I'm making love in weightlessness.

But I fooled him. Good and proper. I grew a beard. I got hair implants. The little wiseass never recognized me.

When they opened this retirement center here at Copernicus I was one of the first residents. I thought maybe Sam would come here, sooner or later, if and when he finally retired.

That's what I'm waiting for. To have him here, retired, with nothing to do. Then I can drive him nuts, for a change.

That's something worth living for!

## Statement of Steven Achernar Wright
## (Recorded aboard torch ship *Hermes*)

Look, I was the closest thing to a lawyer that Sam ever had. I mean, he *hated* lawyers. Probably that's because he was always getting himself into legal troubles, you know, operating out at the edge of the law the way he always did.

I don't know if he really fell into that black hole or not. And I guess I don't really care. Maybe he found real aliens out there and maybe not. We'll see if he brings any back with him.

Why am I running all the way out to Pluto to meet him when he comes back? Because I feel responsible for the little guy, that's why. He went tootling off to find Planet X with that university geek and left behind, like, a ton and three-quarters of lawsuits. Okay, he's been away for fifteen years, and the statute of limitations on all the suits has run out, right?

Maybe not. That Beryllium Blonde that he's tangled with has come up with the idea that since Sam claims he was in a space-time warp, time hasn't passed for him the way it has for the rest of us and therefore the statutes of limitations should be considered suspended for all the time Sam was allegedly in the warp! You know, if time hasn't elapsed for him, then it shouldn't elapse for the lawsuits. That's what she's contending, and the courts are taking it very seriously.

So I'm going out there to warn the little bugger that

his legal troubles aren't over. Not by a longshot.

The Beryllium Blonde? You don't know about her? Or the Toad, either? Cheez, what kind of a historian are you? Didn't you do any research before you came aboard this torch ship?

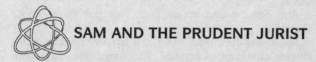 **SAM AND THE PRUDENT JURIST**

YOU MIGHT HAVE KNOWN THAT THE VERY FIRST PERSON TO
be hauled in to trial by the spanking-new Interplanetary
Tribunal would be Sam Gunn. And on trial for his life,
at that.

Things might not have been too bad, even so, if it
weren't for Sam's old nemesis, the Beryllium Blonde.
She wanted Sam's hide tacked onto her office wall. Sam,
of course, wanted her body. Anyplace.

And then there was the Toad, as well.

Sam's voice had been the loudest one in the whole
solar system against letting lawyers get established off-
Earth.

"When it comes to interplanetary jurisprudence," he
often said—at the top of his leathery lungs—"what we
need is less juris and more prudence!"

But it was inevitable that the Interplanetary Astronautical Authority would set up a court to enforce its rulings
and carry Earth-style legalities out to the edge of the fron-
tier. After all, the asteroid belt was being mined by little
guys like Sam and big corporations like Rockledge Industries.

And major consortiums like Diversified Universities &
Laboratories, Ltd. (which Sam called DULL) were already pushing the exploration of Jupiter and its many
moons.

When the scientists announced the discovery of life on

225

the Jovian moon Europa, of course, the environmentalists and theologians and even the right-to-lifers *demanded* that laws—and lawyers—be established in space to protect it.

And Sam wound up on trial. Not just for murder. Genocide.

Me, I was the closest thing to a lawyer in Sam's then-current company, Asteroidal Resources, Inc. Sam had started up and dissolved more corporations than Jupiter has moons, usually making a quick fortune on some audacious scheme and then blowing it on something even wilder. Asteroidal Resources, Inc. was devoted to mining heavy metals from the asteroid belt, out beyond Mars, and smelting them down to refined alloys as his factory ships sailed back to the Earth/Moon system.

The company was based on solid economics, provided needed resources to the Earth/Moon system's manufacturers, and was turning a tidy—if not spectacular—profit. For Sam, this was decidedly unusual. Even respectable.

Sam ran a tight company. His ships were highly automated, with bare-bones skeleton crews. There were only six of us in ARI's headquarters in Ceres, the largest of the asteroids. None of us was a real lawyer; Sam wouldn't allow any of them into his firm. My paralegal certificate was as far as Sam was willing to go. He snarled with contempt when other companies began bringing their lawyers into the belt.

And when I said that the office was *in* Ceres, that's exactly what I mean. Even though it's the biggest chunk of rock in the belt, Ceres is only a little over nine hundred kilometers across; barely big enough to be round, instead of an irregular lump, like the other asteroids. No air, hardly any gravity. Mining outfits like Sam's and big-bad Rockledge and others had honeycombed the rock to set up their local headquarters inside it.

My official title was Director, Human Resources. That meant that I was the guy who handled personnel problems, payroll, insurance, health claims, and lawsuits. Sam always had three or four lawsuits pending; he constantly skirted the fringes of legality—which was why he didn't want lawyers in space, of course. He had enough trouble with the Earthbound variety.

The Beryllium Blonde, by the way, was a corporate lawyer, one of the best, with a mind as sharp and vindictive as her body was lithe and curvaceous. A deadly combination, as far as Sam was concerned.

The entire Human Resources Department in ARI consisted of me and a computer. I had very sophisticated programs to work with, you know, but there was no other human in Human Resources.

Still, I thought things were humming along smoothly enough in our underground offices until the day Sam came streaking back home on a high-gee burn, raced straight from the landing pad to my office without even taking off his flight suit, and announced:

"Orville, you're gonna be my legal counsel at the trial. Start boning up on interplanetary law."

My actual name is Steven. Steven Achernar Wright. But for some reason Sam called me Orville. Sometimes Wilbur, but mostly Orville.

"Legal counsel?" I echoed, bounding out of my chair so quickly that I sailed completely over my desk in the low gravity. "Trial? For what? What're you charged with?"

He shook his head. "Murder, I think. Maybe worse."

And he scooted into his office. All I really saw of the little guy was a sawed-off blur of motion topped with rusty red hair. Huckleberry Finn at Mach 5.

I learned about the charges against Sam almost immediately. My phone screen chimed and the impressive black-and-silver seal of the International Astronautical Authority appeared on its screen, followed an eyeblink later by a very legal-looking summons and an arrest warrant.

The charges were attempted murder, grand larceny, violation of sixteen—count 'em, sixteen—different IAA environmental regulations, and assault and battery with willful intent to cause grievous bodily harm.

Oh yes, and the aforementioned charge of genocide.

All that happened before lunch.

*      *      *

I tapped into the best legal programs on the sys and, after half a day's reading, arranged to surrender Sam to the IAA authorities at Selene City, on the Moon. He yowled and complained every centimeter of the way. Even when we landed on the Moon Sam screeched loud enough to set up echoes through Selene City's underground corridors, right up to the headquarters of the IAA.

The IAA chief administrator cheerfully released Sam on his own recognizance. He and Sam were old virtual billiards buddies, and besides Sam couldn't get away; his name, photo, fingerprints, retinal patterns, and neutron-scattering index were posted at every rocket port on the Moon. Sam was stuck on the Moon, at least until his trial.

Maybe longer. The World Government's penal colony was at Farside, where convicts couldn't even see Earth in their sky, and they spent their time trying to scrounge helium-three from the regolith, competing with nanomachines that did the job for practically nothing for the big corporations like Masterson and Wankle.

The trial started promptly enough. I begged for more time to prepare a defense, interview witnesses, check the prosecution's published statement of the facts of the case ("And scatter a few bribes around," Sam suggested). No go. The IAA refused any and all requests for a delay in the proceedings. Even their cheerful chief administrator gave me a doleful look, and said, "No can do. The trial starts tomorrow, as scheduled."

That worried me. Nobody wanted to appear on Sam's behalf; there were no witnesses to the alleged crimes that weren't already lined up to testify for the prosecution. I couldn't even dig up any character witnesses.

"Testify to Sam's character?" asked one of his oldest friends. "You want them to throw the key away on the little SOB? Or maybe you expect me to commit perjury?"

That was the *kindest* response I got.

What worried me even more was the fact that several hundred "neutral observers" had booked passage to the

Moon to attend the trial; half of them were environmentalists who thirsted for Sam's blood; the other half were various enemies the little guy had made over his many years of blithely going his own way and telling anybody who didn't like it to stuff his head someplace where the Sun doesn't shine.

The media sensed blood—and *Sam's* blood, at that. He had been great material for them for a long time: the little guy who always thumbed his nose at authority and got away with it. But now Sam had gone too far, and the kindest thing being said about him in the media was that he was "the accused mass murderer of an entire alien species, the man who wiped out the harmless green lichenoids of Europa."

If all this bothered Sam, he gave no indication of it. "The media," he groused. "They love you when you win, and they'll use you for toilet paper when you don't."

I studied his round, impish, jack-o'-lantern face for a sign of concern. Or remorse. Or even anger at being hauled into court on such serious charges. Nothing. He just grinned his usual toothy grin and whistled while he worked, maddeningly off-key.

Sam was more worried about the impending collapse of Asteroidal Resources, Inc., than his impending trial. The IAA had frozen all his assets and embargoed all his vehicles. The two factory ships on their way in from the belt were ordered to enter lunar orbit when they arrived at the Earth/Moon system and to stay there; their cargoes were impounded by the IAA, pending the outcome of the trial.

"They want to break me," Sam grumbled. "Whether I win the trial or lose, they want to make sure I'm flat busted by the time it's over."

And then the Toad showed up, closely followed by Beryllium Blonde.

We were sitting at the defendant's table in the courtroom, a very modernistic chamber with severe, angular banc and witness stand of lunar stone, utterly bare smoothed-stone walls and long benches of lunar aluminum for the spectators. The tables and chairs for the defendant and prosecution were also burnished aluminum, cold and hard. No decorations of any kind; the courtroom was functional, efficient, and gave me the feeling of inhuman relentlessness.

"Kangaroo court," Sam muttered as we took our chairs.

The crowd filed in, murmuring and whispering, and filled the rows behind us. Various clerks appeared. No media reporters or photographers were allowed in the courtroom, but there had been plenty of them out in the corridor, asking simple questions like, "Why did you wipe out those harmless little green lichenoids, Sam?"

Sam grinned at them, and replied, "Who says I did?"

"The IAA, DULL, just about everybody in the solar system," came their shouted response.

Sam shrugged good-naturedly. "Nobody's heard my side of it yet."

"You mean you didn't kill them?"

"You claim you're innocent?"

"You're denying the charges against you?"

For once in his life, Sam refused to be baited. All he said was, "That's what this trial is for; to find out who did what to whom. And why."

They were so stunned at Sam's refusal to say anything more that they stopped pestering him and allowed us to go into the courtroom. I was sort of stunned, too. I was used to Sam's nonstop blather on any and every subject under the Sun. Sphinxlike silence was something new, from him.

The courtroom was settling down to a buzzing hum of whispered conversations when the three black-robed judges trooped in to take their seats at the banc. No jury. Sam's fate would be decided by the three of them.

As everybody rose to their feet, Sam looked at the three judges and groaned. "Buddha on ice skates, it's the Toad."

His name was J. Everest Weatherwax, and he was so famous that even I recognized him. Multitrillionaire, captain of industry, statesman, public servant, philanthropist, Weatherwax was a legend in his own time. He had helped to found DULL and funded unstintingly the universities that joined the consortium. He was on the board of directors of so many corporations nobody knew the exact number. He was also on the board of governors of the IAA. His power was truly interplanetary in reach, but he had never been known to use that power except for other people's good.

Yet Sam clearly loathed him.

"The Toad?" I whispered to Sam as we sat down and the chief judge—a comely gray-haired woman with steely eyes—began to read the charges against Sam.

"He's a snake," Sam hissed under his breath. "An octopus. He controls people. He *owns* them."

"Mr. Weatherwax?" I was stunned. I had never heard a harsh word said against him before. His good deeds and public unselfishness were known throughout the solar system.

"Just look at him," Sam whispered back, his voice dripping disgust.

I had to admit that Weatherwax did look rather toadlike, sitting up there, looming over us. He was very old, of course, well past the century mark. His face was fleshy, flabby, his skin was gray and splotchy, his shoulders slumped bonelessly beneath his black robe. His eyes bulged and kept blinking slowly, his mouth was a wide, almost lipless, slash that hung slightly open.

"God help any fly that comes near him," Sam muttered. "Zap! with his tongue."

Weatherwax's money had founded DULL. He had saved the ongoing Martian exploration company when that nonprofit gaggle of scientists had run out of funding. He had made his money originally in biotechnology, almost a century ago, then diversified into agrobusiness and medicine before getting into space exploration and scientific research in a major way. He had received the Nobel Peace Prize for settling the war between India and China. Rumor had it that if he would only convert to Catholicism, the Pope would make him a saint.

As soon as the chief judge finished reading the charges, Sam shot to his feet.

"I protest," he said. "One of the judges is prejudiced against me."

"Mr. Gunn," said the chief judge, glaring at Sam, "you are represented by legal counsel. If you have any protests to make, they must be made by him."

Sam turned to me and made a nudging move with both hands.

I got to my feet slowly, thinking as fast as I could. "Your Honor, my client feels that the panel might be less than unbiased, since one of the judges is a founder of the organization that had brought these charges against the defendant."

Weatherwax just smiled down at us, drooling ever so slightly from the corner of his toadish mouth.

The chief judge closed her eyes briefly, then replied to me, "Justice Weatherwax has been duly appointed by the International Astronautical Authority to serve on this panel. His credentials as a jurist are impeccable."

"Since when is he a judge?" Sam stage-whispered at me.

"The defense was not aware that Mr. Weatherwax had received an appointment to the bench, Your Honor," I said as diplomatically as I could.

"*Justice* Weatherwax received his appointment last week," she answered frostily, "on the basis of his long and distinguished record of service in international disputes."

"I see," I said meekly. "Thank you, Your Honor." There was nothing else I could do.

"Settling international disputes," Sam grumbled. "Like the China-India War. Once he stopped selling bioweapons to both sides they *had* to stop fighting."

"However," the chief judge said, turning to Weatherwax, "if the justice would prefer to withdraw in the face of the defendant's concern . . ."

Weatherwax stirred and seemed to come to life like a large mound of protoplasm touched by a spark of electricity.

"I assure you, Justice Ostero, that I can judge this case with perfect equanimity." His voice was a deep groan, like the rumble of a distant bullfrog.

The chief justice nodded once, curtly. "So be it," she said. "Let's get on with these proceedings."

It was exactly at the point that the Beryllium Blonde entered the courtroom.

It was as if the entire courtroom stopped breathing; like the castle in Sleeping Beauty, everything and everybody seemed to stop in their tracks, just to look at her.

Lunar cities were pretty austere in those days; the big, racy casinos over at Hell Crater hadn't even been started yet. Selene City was the largest of the Moon's communities, but even so it wasn't much more than a few kilometers of rock-walled tunnels. Even the so-called Grand Plaza was just a big open space with a dome sealing it in. Okay, so most of the ground inside the plaza was green with grass and shrubs. After two days, who cared? You could rent wings and go flying on your own muscle power, but there wasn't much in the way of scenery.

The Beryllium Blonde was *scenery*. She stepped into the courtroom and lit up the place, like her golden hair was casting reflections of the bare stone walls. The panel of three judges—two women and the Toad—just stared at her as she walked demurely down the courtroom's central aisle and stopped at the railing that separated the lawyers and their clients from the spectators.

We were all spectators, of course. She was absolutely gorgeous: tall and shapely beyond the dreams of a teenage cartoonist. A face that could launch a thousand rockets—among other things.

She looked so sweet, with those wide blue eyes and that perfect face. Her glittery silver suit was actually quite modest, with a high-buttoned Chinese collar and trousers that looped beneath her delicate little feet. Of course, the suit was form-fitting, it clung to her as if it'd been sprayed onto her body, and there wasn't a man in the courtroom who didn't envy the fabric.

Even Sam could do nothing more than stare at her,

dumbfounded. It wasn't until much later that I learned why he called her the Beryllium Blonde: beryllium, a steel gray metal, quite brittle at room temperature, with a very high melting point, used mostly as a hardening agent.

How true.

"Am I interrupting?" she asked, in a breathy innocent voice.

The chief judge had to swallow visibly before she found her voice. "No, we were just getting started. What can I do for you?" This from the woman who was known, back in Australia, as the Scourge of Queensland.

"I am here to help represent the prosecution, on a pro bono basis."

All four of the prosecution's expensive lawyers shot to their feet and welcomed her to their midst.

Sam just moaned.

"It goes back a long way," Sam told me after the preliminaries had ended and the court had adjourned for lunch. We had scooted back to the hotel suite we were renting, the two of us desperately trying to hold the company together despite the trial and embargo and everything else.

"She tried to screw me out of my zero-gee hotel, 'way back when," he said.

I wondered how literally Sam meant his words. He had the solar system's worst reputation as an insensitive womanizing chauvinist boor. Yet somehow Sam never lacked for female companionship. I've seen ardent feminists succumb to Sam's charm. Once in a while.

"Hell hath no fury like a woman scorned," Sam said, sighing mightily at his memories. "Of course, we spent a pretty intense time together before the doo-doo hit the fan." He sighed again. "All she was after was the rights to my hotel."

"While you were truly and deeply in love," I wise-cracked.

Sam looked shocked. "I think I was," he said, sounding hurt. "At least, while it lasted."

"So she has a personal bias against you. Maybe I can get her thrown off the case—"

"Don't you dare!" Sam shrieked, nearly jumping over the coffee table.

"But—"

He gave me his Huck Finn grin. "If I've got to be raped, pillaged, and burnt at the stake," he said happily, "I couldn't think of anybody I'd prefer to have holding the matches."

Had Sam given up?

I don't know about Sam, but after the first two days of testimony I was ready to give up.

Fourteen witnesses—a baker's dozen plus one—all solemnly testified that Sam had deliberately, with malice aforethought and all that stuff, wiped out the harmless lichenoid colony that dwelled under Europa's ice mantle. And had even bashed one of the DULL scientists on the head with an oxygen tank when the man had tried to stop him.

The spectators on the other side of the courtroom rail sobbed and sighed through the testimony, hissed at Sam, and groaned piteously when the last of the witnesses showed a series of computer graphics picturing the little green lichenoids before Sam and the empty cavity under the ice where the lichenoids had been but were no longer—because of Sam.

"What need have we of further witnesses?" bellowed a heavyset woman from the back of the courtroom.

I turned and saw that she was on her feet, brandishing an old-fashioned rope already knotted into a hangman's noose.

The chief judge frowned at her, rather mildly, and asked her to sit down.

For the first time since his profession of impartiality, Weatherwax spoke up. "We want to give the accused a fair trial," he rumbled, again sounding rather like a bullfrog. "Then we'll hang him."

He made a crooked smile to show that he was only joking. Maybe.

The chief judge smiled, too. "Although we haven't yet decided how a sentence of capital punishment would be carried out," she said, looking straight-faced at Sam, "I'm sure it won't be by hanging. In this low-gravity environment that might constitute cruel and unusual punishment."

"Thanks a lot," Sam muttered.

Then the chief judge turned to me. "Cross-examination?"

The scientist who had shown the computer graphics was still sitting in the witness chair, to one side of the judges' banc. I didn't have any questions for him. In fact, I wanted him and his cute little pictures off the witness stand as quickly as possible.

But just as I started to shake my head I heard Sam, beside me, speak up.

"I have a few questions for this witness, Your Honors."

The three judges looked as startled as I felt.

"Mr. Gunn," said the chief judge, with a grim little smile, "I told you before that you are represented by counsel and should avail yourself of his expertise."

Sam glanced at me. We both knew my expertise consisted of a gaggle of computer programs and not much else.

"There are aspects of this case that my, uh . . . counsel hasn't had time to study. I was on the scene, and I know the details better than he possibly could."

The three judges conferred briefly, whispering and nodding. At last the chief judge said, "Very well, Mr. Gunn, you may proceed." Then she smiled coldly, and added, "There is an old tradition in the legal profession that a man who represents himself in court has a fool for a client."

Sam got to his feet, grinning that naughty-little-boy grin of his. "And a fool for a lawyer, too, I guess."

All three judges nodded in unison.

"Anyway," Sam said, jamming his hands into the pockets of his baby blue coveralls, "there are a couple of things I think the court should know in deeper detail."

I glanced over at the Beryllium Blonde while Sam sauntered up to the witness box. She was sitting back, smiling and relaxed, as if she were enjoying the show. Her four colleagues were watching her, not Sam.

The witness was one of the DULL scientists who'd been on Europa, Dr. Clyde Erskine. He was a youngish fellow, with thinning sandy hair and the beginnings of a potbelly.

Sam gave him his best disarming smile. "Dr. Erskine. Are you a biologist?"

"Uh . . . no, I'm not."

"A geologist?"

"No." Rather sullenly, I thought.

"What is your professional specialty, then?" Sam asked, as amiably as he might ask a bartender for a drink on the house.

Erskine replied warily. "I'm a professor of communications at the University of Texas. In Austin."

"Not a biologist?"

"No, I am not a biologist."

"Not a geologist or a botanist or zoologist or even a chemist, are you?"

"I am a doctor of communications," Erskine said testily.

"Communications? Like, communicating with alien life forms? SETI, stuff like that?"

"No," Erskine said. "Communications between humans. My specialty is mass media."

Sam put on a look of shocked surprise. "Mass media? You mean you're a public-relations flack?"

"I am a doctor of communications!"

"But what you were doing on Europa was generating PR material for DULL, wasn't it?"

"Yes," he admitted. "That was my job."

Sam nodded and took a few steps away from the witness, as if he were trying to digest Erskine's admission.

Turning back to the witness chair, Sam asked, "We've heard fourteen witnesses so far. Were any of them biologists?"

Erskine frowned in thought for a moment. "No, I don't believe any of them were."

"Were any of them scientists of any stripe?"

"Most of them were communications specialists," Erskine answered.

"PR flacks, like yourself."

"I am not a flack!" Erskine snapped.

"Yeah, sure," said Sam. He hesitated a moment, then asked, "How many people were on Europa?"

"Uh ... let me see," Erskine muttered, screwing up his eyes to peer at the stone ceiling. "Must have been upwards of three dozen ... no, more like forty, forty-five."

"How many of 'em were scientists?" Sam asked.

"We all were!"

"I mean biologists, geologists—not PR flacks."

Erskine's face was getting red. "Communications is a valid scientific field—"

"Sure it is," Sam cut him off. "How many biologists among the forty-five men and women stationed on Europa?"

Erskine frowned in thought for a moment, then mumbled, "I'm not quite certain ..."

"Ten?" Sam prompted.

"No."

"More than ten?"

"Uh ... no."

"Five?"

Silence.

"More or less?" Sam insisted.

"I think there were three biologists," Erskine muttered, his voice so low that I could hardly hear him.

"Yet none of them have testified at this trial," Sam said, a hint of wonder in his voice. "Why is that, do you think?"

"I don't know," Erskine replied sullenly. "I guess none of them was available."

"Not available." Sam seemed to mull that over for a moment. "Then who prepared all the slides and graphs you and your cohorts have shown at this trial?"

Erskine glanced up at the judges, then answered, "The communications department of the University of Texas."

"At Austin."

"Yes."

"Not the handful of scientists who were on Europa and are now mysteriously not available?"

"The scientists gave us the input for the computer graphics."

"Oh? They were available to help you prepare your presentations, but they're not available for this trial? Why is that?"

"I don't know."

Sam turned away from the witness. I thought he was coming back to our table, but suddenly Sam wheeled back to face Erskine again. "Do you have any samples of the Europa lichenoids?"

"Samples? Me? No."

"Do any of the biologists have samples of them? Actual physical samples?"

"No," Erskine said, brows knitting. "They were living under more than seven kilometers of ice. We were—"

"Thank you, Dr. Erskine," Sam snapped. Looking up at the judges he said grandly, "No further questions."

Erskine looked slightly confused, then started to get to his feet.

"Redirect, please," said the Beryllium Blonde.

All three judges smiled down at her. I smiled, too, as she walked from behind the prosecution's table toward the witness box. Just watching her move was a pleasure. Even Sam gawked at her. Beads of perspiration broke out on his upper lip as he sat down beside me.

"Dr. Erskine," the Blonde asked sweetly, "which scientists helped you to prepare the graphics you showed us?"

Erskine blinked at her as if he were looking at a mirage that was too good to be true. "They were prepared by Dr. Heinrich Fossbinder, of the University of Zurich."

"Dr. Fossbinder is a biologist?"

"Dr. Fossbinder is a Nobel laureate in biology. He was head of the biology team at Europa."

"All three of 'em," Sam stage-whispered loud enough to draw a warning frown from the judges.

The Blonde proceeded, undeterred. "But if you have no samples of the Europa life-forms, how were these computer images produced?"

Erskine nodded, as if to compliment her on asking an astute question. "As I said, the lichenoids were living beneath some seven kilometers of ice. We very carefully sank a fiber-optic line down to within a few dozen meters of their level and took the photographs you saw through that fiber-optic link."

With an encouraging smile that dazzled the entire courtroom, the Blonde asked, "Was your team drilling a larger borehole, in an effort to extract samples of the life-forms?"

"Yes we were."

"And what happened?"

Erskine shot an angry look at Sam. "He ruined it! He came in with his ore-crushing machinery and chewed up so much of the ice that the entire mantle collapsed. Our borehole was shattered, and the lichenoids were exposed to vacuum."

"What effect did that have on the native life-forms of Europa?" she asked in a near whisper.

"It killed them all!" Erskine answered hotly. "Wiped them out!" He pointed a trembling finger at Sam. "He killed a whole world's biosphere!"

The courtroom erupted in angry shouts. I thought the audience was going to lynch Sam then and there.

The Beryllium Blonde smiled at the raging spectators, and said, barely loud enough to be heard over their yelling, "The prosecution rests."

The chief judge banged her gavel and recessed for the day, but hardly any of the audience paid her any attention. They wanted Sam's blood. A cordon of security guards formed around us, looking worried. But as we headed for the door, I saw that Sam was unperturbed by any of the riotous goings-on; his eyes were locked on the Blonde. It was as if no one else existed for him.

\*          \*          \*

The outlook wasn't brilliant that evening. The prosecution had presented what looked like an airtight case. I had no witnesses except Sam, and in our discussions of the case he hadn't once refuted the prosecution's testimony.

"You really wiped out the colony of lichenoids?" I asked him repeatedly.

His only answer was a shrug and an enigmatic, "They're not there, are they?"

"And you actually banged that scientist on the head with an oxy bottle?"

He grinned at the memory of it. "I sure did," he admitted, impishly.

We were having dinner in our hotel suite. Sam couldn't show his face in a restaurant, that's how much public opinion had turned against him. We had needed six security guards just to walk us from the courtroom to the hotel.

"But he wasn't a scientist," Sam added, heaping broiled scungilli on his plate. Selene's aquaculture produced the best shellfish off-Earth, and the hotel's chef was a Neapolitan master artist.

"He was a science writer for DULL," Sam went on. "Most of the so-called scientists on Europa were public-relations flacks and administrators."

"Like Erskine?"

He nodded. "They weren't doing research. They were busy pumping out media hype about their great green discovery."

"That's neither here nor there, Sam," I said, picking at my own clams posilipo.

"Isn't it?" He made a know-it-all smile.

"Sam, are you keeping something from me?" I asked.

"Me?"

"If you've got some information that will help win this case, some facts, witnesses—anything! We need it now, Sam. I'm supposed to open your defense tomorrow morning, and I don't have a thing to go on."

"Except my testimony," he said.

That's what I was afraid of.

*    *    *

Yet the next morning I put Sam on the witness chair
and asked him one single question:

"Mr. Gunn, can you tell us in your own words what
took place on Europa during the time you were there?"

"Soitinly!" Sam said, grinning.

The judges were not amused. Neither was the Beryllium Blonde, sitting at the prosecution's table, watching
Sam intently, her blue eyes focused on him like twin
lasers.

The whole thing started—Sam said—with the Porno
Twins. Cindy and Mindy.

You gotta understand that working those mining ships
out there in the asteroid belt is hard, lonely work. Sure,
there are women among the crews, but there's always
eight or nine more guys than gals on those factory ships,
and the guys get—well, the polite word for it is horny.

(The chief judge huffed at that but didn't interrupt. The
Toad snorted. The Beryllium Blonde smiled.)

The Porno Twins supplied a needed service for the
miners. Virtual sex, on demand. Oh sure, there were VR
services from Earth/Moon, but the time lag meant that
you couldn't do real-time simulations: you had to buy a
VR program that was prepackaged. It might have a few
variables, but you more or less got a regular routine, take
it or leave it.

The Porno Twins had come out to the belt and established themselves in a spacecraft that could swing around
the area and maneuver close enough to the factory ships
to do real-time simulations. You know, positive feedback
and all that. You could *talk* with 'em, and they'd respond
to you. It was great!

Well, anyway, the guys told me it was great. Some of
the women used them, too, but that's their business. I
never did. Virtual reality is terrific and all that, but I prefer the real thing. I want to feel some warmth instead of
grappling with an electronic fantasy.

I saw the twins' advertisements, of course. They were
really attractive: two very good-looking dolls who were

identical down to their bellybuttons, except that one was right-handed and the other was a lefty. Mindy and Cindy. Geniuses at what they did. They were natural redheads, but with VR they could be any color or shade you wanted.

It was the idea of their being twins that made them so popular. Every guy's got a fantasy about that, and they were happy to fulfill your wildest dreams, anything you asked for. And it was all perfectly safe, of course: They were usually a million kilometers away, feeding your fantasy at the speed of light with a real-time virtual-reality link.

I had thought about dropping in on them for a real visit, you know, in the flesh. Me and every other guy in the belt. But they stayed buttoned up inside their own spacecraft; no visitors. None of us knew what kind of defenses they might have on their craft, but I guess we all realized that their best defense was the threat of leaving the belt.

So nobody molested them. If anybody gave even a hint that he might try to sneak out to their ship, his fellow miners dissuaded him—as they say—forcefully. Nobody wanted the Twins to leave us alone out in the dark and cold between Mars and Jupiter.

It was sheer coincidence that I happened to be the closest ship to theirs when their life-support system malfunctioned. I guess I'm lucky that way, if you can call it lucky when lightning strikes you.

I was trying to repair the mining boat *Clementine* when I heard their distress call. Most mining boats have minimal crews; *Clementine* was the first to be designed to run with no crew at all. Except it didn't work right.

Mining boats attach themselves to an asteroid and grind up the rock or metal, sort it by chemical composition, and store it in their holds until they make rendezvous with a factory boat and unload the ores. *Clementine* was chewing up its target asteroid all right, but there was a glitch in the mass spectrometer and the idiot computer running the boat couldn't figure out which stream of ore should go into which hold, so it stopped all operations halfway into the program and just clung to the asteroid like a scared spider, doing absolutely nothing except costing me money.

So I jetted out to *Clementine* from Ceres in my personal torch ship, leaving the company's important business in the capable and well-trained hands of my crackerjack staff. I figured they could run things for maybe four–five days before driving me into bankruptcy.

So I'm in a battered old hard suit hanging weightless with my head stuck in the computer bay and my feet dangling up near the navigation sensors when the radio bleeps.

"This is *SEX069*," said a sultry female voice. "We have an emergency situation. Our life-support system has suffered a malfunction. Our computer indicates we have only eleven point four days until the air-recycling scrubbers fail completely. We need help immediately."

I didn't have to look up the IAA registry to find out who *SEX069* was. That's the Porno Twins' spacecraft! I pulled my head out of the computer bay, cracking my helmet on the edge of the hatch hard enough to make me see stars, and jackknifed myself into an upright position by the set of navigation sensors. Not easy to do in a hard suit, by the way.

Being designed to operate uncrewed, *Clementine* didn't have an observation port or even cameras outside its dumb hull. But it had a radio, so I squirted off a message to the Twins as fast as my gloved fingers could hit the keypad.

"This is Sam Gunn," I said, in my deepest, manliest voice. "Received your distress call and am on my way to you." Then I couldn't resist adding, "Have no fear, Sam is here!"

I got out of *Clementine* fast as I could and into my personal torch ship, *Joker*. While I was taking off my hard suit I had the Twins squirt me their location and their computer's diagnostic readings.

Their craft was several million kilometers away, coasting in a Sun-centered orbit not far from the asteroid Vesta.

Now, *Joker*'s built for my comfort—and for speed. Her

fusion-MHD drive could accelerate at a full gee contin-
uously, as long as she had reaction mass to fire out her
nozzles. Any other rock jockey in the belt would have
had to coast along for weeks on end to reach the Twins.
I could zip out to Vesta in a matter of hours, accelerating
like a bat out of sheol.

"Spare us the profanity, Mr. Gunn," said the Toad.

"And kindly stick to the facts of the case," the chief
judge added, frowning. "We don't need a sales pitch for
your personal yacht."

Sam shrugged and glanced at me. I realized that if he
was trying to drum up interest in *Joker*, he must be feeling pretty desperate, financially.

The point is—Sam blithely continued—that *Joker* was
the only craft in the belt that had a chance in . . . in the
solar system, of helping the Twins. Nobody else could
get to them in eleven days or less.

But as I sat in the bridge, in my form-accommodating,
reclinable, swiveling command chair, which has built-in
massage and heat units (the chief judge glowered at Sam)
and looked into the details of the Twins' diagnostics, I
realized they were in even deeper trouble than I had
thought. The graphs on the screens showed that not only
had their recycler failed, they were also losing air;
must've been punctured by a centimeter-sized asteroid,
punched right through their armor and sprung a leak in
their main air tank. Maybe it knocked out their recycling
system, too.

Their real problem was with their automated maintenance equipment. How could their system allow the air-
recycling equipment to go down? And their damned
outside robot was supposed to fix punctures as soon as
they happened. Theirs didn't. It was just sitting on the
outer skin of the hull, frozen into immobility. Maybe an
asteroid had dinged it, too. Their diagnostics didn't show
why the robot wasn't working.

They needed air, or at least oxygen. And they needed
it in a hurry. Even if I got to them in a day or so and

fixed the leak and repaired their recycling system, they wouldn't have enough air to survive.

I spent the next few hours chewing on their problem. Or really, getting the best computers I could reach to chew on it. *Joker* has some really sophisticated programs in its access (the chief judge scowled again), but I also contacted my headquarters on Ceres and even requested time on the IAA system. I had to come up with a solution that would work. And fast.

By the time I had showered, put on a fresh set of coveralls, and taken a bite of food, the various analyses started showing up on the multiple display screens in *Joker*'s very comfortable yet efficiently laid-out bridge. ("Mr. Gunn!" all three judges yelped.)

Okay, so here's the situation. The Twins' air is leaking out through the puncture. I can fix the puncture in ten minutes, while their dumb robot sits on its transistors and does nothing, but they'll still run out of air in a couple of days. I can give them oxygen from *Joker*'s water tanks—electrolyze the water, that's simple enough. But then I won't have enough reaction mass to get away, and we'll both be in trouble.

Now, I've got to admit, the thought of being marooned off Vesta with the Porno Twins had a certain appeal to it. But when I thought it over, I figured that although being with them could be great fun, *dying* with them wasn't what I wanted to do.

Besides, they flatly refused to even consider letting me inside their leaking craft.

"Oh, no, Mr. Gunn!" they said, in unison. "We could never allow you to board our ship."

Cindy and Mindy were on my main display screen, two lovely redheads with sculpted cheekbones and emerald green eyes and lips just trembling with emotion.

"That wouldn't be right," said Cindy. Or maybe it was Mindy.

"We've never let anyone into our ship," said the other one.

"If we let you, then all the other miners would want to visit us, too."

"In person!"

"In the flesh."

"But this would be a mission of mercy," I pleaded.

They blushed and lowered their eyes. Beautiful long silky lashes, I noticed.

"Mr. Gunn," said Mindy. Or maybe Cindy. "How would you feel if we allowed one of your miners to board our vessel?"

"You'd want the same privilege, wouldn't you?" the other one asked.

"I sure would," I admitted, feeling deflated and erect at the same time.

"For your information," said Cindy (Mindy?), "we've received calls from seventeen other mining ships, responding to our distress message."

"They're all on their way to us."

"And they all will want to come aboard once they reach us."

"Which we won't allow, of course."

"Of course," I said, downcast. "How soon can they reach you?"

"Not for several weeks, at least."

"We've informed them all that there's no sense in their coming to us, since they can't reach us in time."

"But they've all replied that they'll come anyway."

I wondered who the hell was doing any mining. The Twins could cause a financial collapse of the metals and minerals market, at this rate.

"Mr. Gunn," said the chief judge sharply, "will you please stick to the facts pertaining to this case? We have no prurient interest in your sexual fantasies."

"Or your financial problems," added the Toad.

"But you've gotta understand the situation," Sam insisted. "Unless you can see how the distances and timing were, you won't be able to grasp the reasons for my actions."

The chief judge heaved a long, impatient sigh. "Get on with it, Mr. Gunn," she groused.

\*     \*     \*

Okay, okay. Where was I . . . oh, yeah.

I didn't believe the computer analyses when I first saw them. But each system came up with the same set of alternatives, and the only one that had any chance of helping the Twins was the one I took.

It looked crazy to me, at first. But the computers had taken into account *Joker*'s high-thrust capability; that was the key to their solution.

All I had to do was zip out to Jupiter at three gees acceleration, grab some oxygen from one of the ice-covered Galilean moons, refuel *Joker*'s fusion generator by scooping hydrogen and helium isotopes from Jupiter's upper atmosphere, and then roar back to the belt at another three gees and deliver the oxygen to the Twins.

Simple.

Also impossible.

So that's what I did.

"May I interrupt?" asked the Beryllium Blonde, rising to her feet behind the prosecution's table.

All three judges looked happy to accommodate her. Or maybe they were just getting tired of listening to Sam. His voice had a kind of nervous edge to it; after a while it was like listening to a mosquito whining in your ear.

"Mr. Gunn," she said, smiling ingenuously at Sam, in the witness box, "you told this court that you consulted several computer analyses before deciding on your course of action?"

"That's right," Sam replied, grinning goofily at her. He seemed overjoyed that she was talking to him.

"And did each of these computer analyses specifically direct you to the Jovian moon Europa?"

Sam shifted a little on the chair. "No, they didn't. They all showed that Ganymede would be my best bet."

"Then why did you go to Europa?"

"I was coming to that when you interrupted me."

"Isn't it true, Mr. Gunn, that your entire so-called 'mission of mercy' was actually a clever plot to break the embargo on commercial exploitation of the Jupiter system?"

That's where Sam should have said a simple and emphatic *no!* and let it go at that. But not Sam.

Apparently some things were more important to Sam even than women. He lost his goofy expression and stared straight into her china blue eyes.

"The IAA's embargo on the commercial development of the Jupiter system is a shuck," Sam said evenly.

A general gasp arose. Even the judges—especially the judges—seemed shocked. For the first time since the trial had begun, the Toad looked angry.

Undeterred, Sam went on, "Why embargo commercial enterprises from the entire Jupiter system? What's the sense of it? Even if you want to protect those little green things on Europa, just putting Europa off-limits would be good enough. Why close off the whole system?"

"Why indeed," the Blonde countered, "now that you've killed off those poor little green creatures."

"Would you rather let two human women die?" Sam demanded.

"Two prostitutes?"

"Look who's talking."

The chief judge whacked her gavel so hard its head flew off, nearly beaning the clerk sitting at the foot of the banc.

But before the judge could say anything, Sam exclaimed, "One of the issues at stake here is the moral question of human life versus animal rights."

A rail-thin, bald and bleary-eyed man shot to his feet from the middle of the spectators. "Animals have legal rights! A dog or a cat has just as much right to life and dignity as a human being!"

"Yeah," Sam retorted, "unless the human being's life is in danger. If I'm a fireman rushing into a burning building, who am I gonna grab first, a human baby or a puppy dog?"

"Stop this!" the chief judge bellowed, slapping the top of the banc with the flat of her hand. "I will have order in this courtroom, or I'll clear the chamber!"

The gaunt animal-rights man sat down, muttering to himself.

"And you, Mr. Gunn," said the chief judge, scowling down at Sam, "will not turn this trial into a circus. Stick to the facts of the case!"

"One of the 'facts' of this case," Sam replied evenly, "is the accusation that I wiped out an entire alien life-form. Even if that's true—and I'm not admitting it is— I did what I did to save the lives of two human women."

He turned back to the Blonde. "And they're not prostitutes; they're producers of virtual-reality simulations. Which is more than I can say for some of the broads in this courtroom!"

"Your Honors!" the Blonde cried, her hands flying to her face. But I was close enough to see that her cheeks weren't blushing, and there was pure murder in those deep blue eyes.

The chief judge threw her hands in the air. "Mr. Gunn, if you cannot or will not restrict your testimony to the facts of this case, we will hold you in contempt of court."

For just an instant the expression on Sam's face told me that he was considering a term in the penal colony as better than certain bankruptcy. But the moment passed.

"Okay," he said, putting on his most contrite little boy face. "I'll stick to the facts—if I'm not interrupted."

The Blonde huffed and stamped back to the prosecution table.

As I said, the computer analyses showed that I had to zoom out to the Jupiter system at three gees, grab some oxygen from Ganymede, restock my fusion fuel and re-action mass by scooping Jupiter's atmosphere, and then race back to the Twins—again at three gees. Three point oh two, to be exact.

It was trickier than walking a tightrope over Niagara Falls on your hands, blindfolded; more convoluted than a team of Chinese acrobats auditioning for the Beijing Follies; as dangerous as—

("Mr. Gunn, please!" wailed the chief judge.)

Well, anyway, it was going to be a female dog and a half. Riding for several days at a time in three gees is no fun; you can't really move when every part of your body weighs three times normal. A hiccup can give you a hernia. If you're not *extremely* careful, you could end up with your scrotum hanging down to your ankles. I always wear a lead jockstrap, of course, but even so . . .

(I thought the judges were about to have apoplexy, but Sam kept going without even taking a breath, so by the time they were ready to yell at him he was already miles away, subject-wise.)

I cranked my reclining command chair all the way down so it could work as an acceleration couch. I couldn't take the chance of trying to raise my head and chew solid food and swallow while under three gees, so while the acceleration was building up I set up an intravenous feeding system for myself from *Joker*'s medical systems. The ship has the best medical equipment this side of Lunar University, by the way. That was pretty easy. The tough part was sticking the needle into my own arm and inserting the intravenous feed.

(Half the courtroom groaned at the thought.)

And then there was the waste elimination tubing, but I won't go into that.

(More groans and a couple of gargling, retching sounds.)

I welded the computer keyboard to the end of my command chair's right armrest even though the computer was fully equipped with voice-recognition circuitry. Didn't want to take any chances on the system—as ultrasophisticated as it is—failing to recognize my voice because I was strangling in three gees.

By the time *Joker*'s acceleration passed two gees I was flat on my back in the couch, all the necessary tubes in place, display screens showing me the ongoing analyses of this crazy mission. I had to get everything right, down to the last detail, or end up burning myself to a crisp in Jupiter's atmosphere or nosediving into Ganymede and making a new crater in the ice.

"You keep saying Ganymede," the Toad demanded. "How did you end up at Europa?"

"I'm coming to that, oh saintly one," Sam replied.

\*     \*     \*

I had to drag *Clementine* along with me, because I was going to need the ores she'd managed to store in her holds before her super-duper computer fritzed. Those chunks of metal were going to be my heat shield when I skimmed Jupiter's upper atmosphere. I just hoped there was enough of 'em to make a workable heat shield.

The way the numbers worked out, I would accelerate almost all the way to the Jupiter system, then flip around and start decelerating. I'd still be doing better than two gees when I hit Jupiter's upper atmosphere. Even though the gases are pretty thin at that high altitude, I needed a heat shield if I didn't want *Joker* to get barbecued, with me inside her.

So even though I was flat on my back and not able to move much more than my fingers and toes, I had plenty of work to do. I couldn't trust *Clementine*'s smart-ass computer to handle the heat-shield job; her computer was too glottal-stop sophisticated for such a menial job. I had to manually direct the manipulators to pull chunks of ore from her holds and place them up ahead of *Joker* by a few meters, all the time lying on the flat of my back, spending most of my energy just trying to breathe.

Believe me, breathing in three gees is not fun, even when you're on a padded couch. The gee force is running from your breastbone to your spine, so every time you try to expand your lungs to take in some air, you've got to push your ribs against three times their normal weight. It's like having an asthma attack that never goes away. I was exhausted before the first day was over.

It would've been better if I could've just pumped some sedatives through the IV in my arm and slept my way to Jupiter. But I had to build up the heat shield or I'd be fricasseed when I hit Jupiter's atmosphere. I tapped into the best reentry programs on Earth as I put together those chunks of metal. They had to be close enough to one another so that the shock waves from the heated gases would cancel one another out before they got through the spaces between chunks and heated up *Joker*.

\*     \*     \*

"You did this while on the way to Jupiter?" asked the other woman judge. "While accelerating at three gravities?"

Sam put his right hand over his heart. "I did indeed," he said.

The woman shook her head, whether in admiration or disbelief I couldn't figure out.

"A question, please?" asked the Beryllium Blonde from her seat at the prosecution table.

For the first time, the chief judge looked just a trifle annoyed. "There will be ample time for cross-examination, counselor."

"I merely wanted to ask if Mr. Gunn was aware of the embargo on unauthorized flights into the Jovian system imposed by the Interplanetary Astronautical Authority."

Aware of it?—Sam replied—I sure was. I sent out a message to the research station on Europa to tell 'em I was entering the Jupiter system on a mission of mercy. I set my comm unit to continue sending the message until it was acknowledged. They ignored it for a day and a half, and then finally sent a shi—an excrement-load of legalese garbage that took my computer twenty minutes to translate into understandable English.

("And what was the message from Europa?" the chief judge asked.)

Boiled down to, "Keep out! We don't care who you are or why you're heading this way, just turn around and go back to where you came from."

I got on the horn and tried to explain to them that I was trying to save the lives of two women, and I wouldn't disturb them on Europa, but they just kept beaming their legal ka-ka. Either they didn't believe me, or they didn't give a hoot about human lives.

Well, I couldn't turn around even if I'd wanted to. My flight profile depended on using Jupiter's atmosphere to aerobrake *Joker*, swing around the planet, and make a slowed approach to Ganymede. So I programmed my comm unit to keep repeating my message to Europa. It was really pretty: We're both hollering at each other and paying no attention to what the other guy's hollering back. Like two drivers in Boston yelling at each other over a fender bender.

But while I'm roaring down toward Jupiter I start wondering: why does DULL need the whole Jupiter system roped off, when all they're supposed to be studying is Europa? I mean, they looked at Jupiter's other Galilean moons and didn't find diddly-poo. And if there's any life on Jupiter, it's buried so deep inside those clouds that we haven't been able to find it.

Why embargo the whole Jupiter system when all they're supposed to be studying is Europa?

The question nagged at me like a toothache. Even while I was putting my makeshift heat shield together, I kept wondering about it in the back of my mind. I kept mulling it over, using the question to keep me from thinking about how much my chest hurt and wondering about how many breaths I had left before my ribs collapsed.

Once the heat shield was in place—or as good as a ramshackle collection of rocks can be—I could devote my full attention to the question. Mine, and the computer's.

One thing I've learned over the years of being in business: When you're trying to scope out another company's moves, follow the money trail. So I started sniffing out the financial details of Diversified Universities & Laboratories, Ltd. It wasn't all that easy; DULL is a tax-exempt, nonprofit organization; it isn't publicly owned, and its finances are not on public record.

But even scientists like to see their names in the media, and corporate bigwigs like it even more. So I started scrolling through the media stories about the discovery of life-forms on Europa and DULL's organization of a research station on the Jovian moon.

I learned two very interesting things.

The cost of setting up the research operation on Europa was funded by Wankle Enterprises, Incorporated, of New York, London, and Shanghai.

It was Wankle's lawyers—including a certain gorgeous blonde—who talked the IAA into placing the whole Jupiter system, planet, moons, all of it, under embargo. No commercial development allowed. No unauthorized missions permitted.

Make that three things that I learned: The IAA's embargo order has some fine print in it. DULL is allowed to permit "limited resource extraction" from the Jupiter system as a means of funding its ongoing research activities on Europa. And guess who got permission from DULL to start "limited resource extraction" from Jupiter and its moons? Wankle Enterprises, Inc.

Who else?

The spectators stirred and muttered. The judges were staring at Sam with real interest now, as if he'd suddenly turned into a different species of witness. All five of the prosecution attorneys—including the Beryllium Blonde— were on their feet, making objections.

"Irrelevant and immaterial," said the first attorney.

"Rumor and hearsay," said number two.

"Wankle Enterprises is not on trial here," said number three. "Sam Gunn is."

"He's trying to smear Diversified Universities and Laboratories, Limited," number four bleated.

The Blonde said, "I object, Your Honors."

The chief judge raised an eyebrow half a millimeter. "On what grounds, counselor?"

"Mr. Gunn's statements are irrelevant, immaterial, based on rumor and hearsay, an attempt to shift the focus of this trial away from himself and onto Wankle Enterprises, and a despicable attempt to smear the good name of an organization dedicated to the finest and noblest scientific research."

The chief judge nodded, then glanced briefly at her colleagues on either side of her. They both nodded, much more vigorously.

"Very well," she said. "Objection sustained. Mr. Gunn's last statement will be stricken from the record."

Sam shrugged philosophically. "None of those three facts can stay on the record?"

"None."

"I found out something else, too," Sam said to the judges. "A fourth fact about DULL."

"Unless it is strictly and necessarily relevant to this case," said the chief judge sternly, "it will not be allowed as testimony."

Sam thought it over for a moment, an enigmatic smile on his jack-o'-lantern face. Then, with a shake of his head that seemed to indicate disappointment but not defeat, Sam returned to his testimony.


Okay, I'll save the fourth fact for a while, and then we'll see if it's relevant or not.

Where was I—oh, yeah, I'm dropping into Jupiter's gas clouds at a little three gees, the insides of my chest feeling like somebody's been sandpapering them for the past few days.

I put in a call to the Twins, telling them to hang in there, I'd be back with all the oxygen they needed in less than a week. I didn't tell them how awful I felt, but they must have seen it in my face.

It took about eleven minutes for my comm signal to reach them, and another eleven for their answer to get back to me. So I gave them a brave "Don't give up the ship" spiel and then went about my business checking out my heat shield—and DULL's finances.

Cindy and Mindy both appeared on my comm screen, wearing less than Samoan nudists at the springtime fertility rites. If my eyeballs hadn't weighed a little more than three times normal, they would've popped right out of their sockets.

"We truly appreciate what you're doing for us, Sam," they said in unison, as if they'd rehearsed it. "And we want you to know that we'll be *especially* appreciative when you come back to us."

"Extremely appreciative," breathed Cindy. Mindy?

"Extraordinarily appreciative," the other one added, batting her long lashes at me.

I was ready to jump off my couch and fly to them like Superman. Except that the damned gee load kept me pinned flat. All of me.

Everything would've worked out fine—or at least okay—if my swing through Jupiter's upper atmosphere had gone as planned. But it didn't.

Ever see an egg dropped from the top of a ninety-story tower hit the pavement? That's what *Joker* was doing, just about: dropping into Jupiter's atmosphere like a kamikaze bullet. I had to use the planet's atmosphere to slow down my ship while at the same time I scooped enough Jovian hydrogen and helium isotopes to fill my propellant tanks. With that makeshift heat shield of rocks flying formation in front of *Joker* all the while.

Things started going wrong right away. The heat shield heated up too much and too soon. *Joker*'s skin temperature started rising really fast. One by one my outside cameras started to conk out; their circuitry was being fricasseed by white-hot shock-heated gases. Felt like I was melting, too, inside the ship despite the bridge's absolutely first-rate climate-control system.

The damned heat shield started breaking up, which was something my hotshot computer programs didn't foresee. I should've thought of it myself, I guess. Stands to reason. Each individual rock in that jury-rigged wall in front of me was blazing like a meteor, ablating away, melting like the Wicked Witch of the West when you throw water on her.

(The chief judge frowned, puzzled, at Sam's reference but Weatherwax gave a toadlike smile and even nodded.)

I would've peeled down to my skivvies if I'd been able to, but I was still plastered into my reclined command chair like a prisoner chained to a torture rack. Must've lost twenty pounds sweating. Came as close to praying as I ever did, right there, zooming through Jupiter's upper atmosphere.

The camera on *Joker*'s ass end was still working, and while I sweated and almost prayed I watched Jupiter's swirling clouds whizzing by, far, far below me. Beautiful, really, all those bands of colors and the way they curled and eddied along their edges, kinda like the way—

("Spare us the travelogue," said the Toad, his bulging

eyes blinking with displeasure. The chief judge added, "Yes, Mr. Gunn. Get on with it.")

Well, okay. So I finally pull out of Jupiter's atmosphere with my propellant tanks full and *Joker*'s skin still intact—barely. But the aerobraking hadn't followed the computer's predicted flight path as closely as I'd thought it would. Wasn't off by much, but as I checked out my velocity and position I saw pretty damned quickly that I wasn't going to be able to reach Ganymede.

*Joker* had slowed to less than one gee, all right, and other than the failed cameras and a few strained seams in the skin the ship was okay. I could sit up and even walk around the bridge, if I wanted to. I even disconnected all the tubing that was hooked into me. Felt great to be free and able to take a leak on my own again.

But Ganymede was out of reach.

Now the whole reason for this crazy excursion was to grab oxygen to replenish the Porno Twins' evaporating supply. I checked through the computer and saw that the only ice-bearing body I could reasonably get to was— you guessed it—good ol' Europa.

"Mr. Gunn," the Toad interrupted, his voice a melancholy croak, "do you honestly expect this court to believe that after all your derring-do, Europa was the only possible body that you could reach?"

Sam gave him his most innocent look. "I'm under oath, right? How can I lie to you?"

The chief judge opened her mouth as if she were going to zing Sam, then she seemed to think better of it and said nothing.

"Besides," Sam added impishly, "you can check *Joker*'s computer logs, if you haven't already done that."

The Beryllium Blonde called from the prosecution table, "A point of information, please?"

All three judges smiled and nodded.

Without rising, the Blonde asked, "There are twenty-seven moons in the Jupiter system, are there not?"

"Twenty-nine," Sam snapped, "including the two little sheepdog rocks that keep Jupiter's ring in place."

"Aren't most of these moons composed of ices that contain a goodly amount of oxygen?"

"Yes they are," Sam replied before anyone else could, as politely as if he were speaking to a stranger.

"Then why couldn't you have obtained the oxygen you claim you needed from one of those other satellites?"

"Because, oh fairest of the sadly mush-brained profession of hired truth-twisters, my poor battered little ship couldn't reach any of those other moons."

"Truly?"

Sam put his right hand over his heart. "Absolutely. *Joker* was like a dart thrown at a dartboard. I had aimed for a bull's-eye, but the aerobraking flight had jiggled my aim and now I was headed for Europa. Scout's honor. It wasn't my idea. Blame Isaac Newton, or maybe Einstein."

The Blonde said nothing more, but it was perfectly clear from the expression on her gorgeous face that she didn't believe a word Sam was saying. I looked up at the judges—it took an effort to turn my eyes away from the Blonde—and saw that none of the three of them believed Sam either. Mentally I added the possibility of perjury charges to the list Sam already faced.

It wasn't my idea to hit Europa—Sam insisted—but there wasn't much else I could do. Sure, I had my tanks full of propellant for the fusion torch, but I was gonna need that hydrogen and helium for the high-gee burn back to Vesta and the Twins. I couldn't afford to spend any of it juking around the Jupiter system. I was pointed at Europa when I came out of Jupiter's atmosphere. Act of God, you could call it.

(I couldn't fail to notice the grin that crept across Sam's face as he spoke. Neither could the judges. Either he was not telling it exactly the way it had happened or he was downright pleased that this "act of God" had pointed him squarely at Europa.)

I called the DULLards on Europa again and gave them a complete rundown of the situation. Recorded my message and had the comm system keep replaying it to 'em. They didn't respond. Not a peep.

I had nothing to do for several hours except feel good that I didn't have all those damned tubes poking into me. But even though I could get up and walk around my luxuriously appointed bridge and take solid food from my highly automated and well-stocked galley, my brain kept nibbling at a question that'd been nagging at me since before I hit Jupiter.

Why did DULL insist on keeping the whole Jupiter system off-limits to outside developers?

And why did the IAA agree to let them do that?

All of a sudden my comm system erupted with noise from Europa. They started screaming at me that I wasn't allowed in the Jupiter system, I can't land on Europa, I'd better haul ass out of there, yaddida, yaddida, and so on. Threatened me with lawsuits and public flogging and whatnot.

I told them I was on a mission of mercy and two human lives depended on my grabbing some of their ice. Three lives, come to think of it. My butt was on the line, too.

But even if they heard me, they didn't listen. They just kept screaming that I wasn't allowed to land on Europa or be anywhere in the Jupiter system. Different faces appeared on my comm screen every fifteen seconds, seemed like, all of them getting more and more frantic as I came hurtling closer to Europa's ice-covered surface.

"I hear what you're saying," I told them. "I'm not going to disturb your little green lichenoids. I just need to grab some ice and, believe me, I'll be out of your way as fast as a jackrabbit in mating season."

I might as well have been talking to myself. In fact, I think I was. They paid no attention to what I was saying.

A really nasty-looking lug come on my comm screen. "This is Captain Majerkurth. I'm in charge of security here on Europa. If you try to land here, I will personally break your balls."

"Security?" I blurted. "What do you need security for? And what army are you a captain in?"

"I am a captain in the security department of Wankle Enterprises, on loan to Diversified Universities and Laboratories, Limited," he replied evenly—an even snarl, that is.

"Well, if I were you, *mon capitain*," I said, "I'd start getting my people under shelter. My spacecraft is accompanied by about a hundred or so rocks that're going to hit Europa like a meteor shower."

That was the remains of my heat shield, of course. Most of the rocks had ablated down to pebble size, but at the velocity we were traveling they could still do some damage. Europa's icy surface was going to get peppered, and there wasn't anything I could do about it except warn them to get under shelter.

Well, to make a long story short (the judges all sighed at that) I landed on Europa nice and smooth, a real gentle touchdown. With *Clementine* still dragging along beside me, of course. The meteor shower I promised Captain Majerkurth didn't harm anything, near as I can tell: just a few hundred new little craterlets in Europa's surface of ice.

So I've got *Clementine* chewing up ice and storing it in her holds. Bypassed her dumb-ass mass spectrometer; otherwise, her computer would've stopped everything because it couldn't figure out what elements were going into which bins. Didn't matter. It was all ice, which added up to hydrogen for *Joker*'s fusion torch and oxygen for the Twins.

I expected Majerkurth to show up, and, sure enough, I hadn't been sitting on Europa for more than an hour before this flimsy little hopper pops up over my horizon, heading my way on a ballistic trajectory. For half a second I thought the hard-ass had fired a missile at me, but my computer analyzed the radar data in picoseconds and announced that it was a personnel hopper, not a missile, and it was gonna land beside *Joker*.

I buttoned up *Joker* good and tight. I had no intention of letting Majerkurth come aboard. But the space-suited figure that climbed down from the hopper wasn't the security captain.

"Mr. Gunn, this is Anitra O'Toole. Permission to come aboard?"

I stared at the image in my display screen. You can't tell much about a person when she's zipped into a space suit, but Anitra O'Toole looked small—maybe my own height or even a little less—and her voice was kind of . . . well, she sounded almost scared.

"Are you one of Majerkurth's security people?" I asked.

"Security? Goodness no! If Captain Majerkurth knew I was here, he'd . . ." She hesitated, then pleaded, "Please let me come aboard, Mr. Gunn. Please!"

What could I do? I could never refuse a woman asking for help, and she seemed to need my help pretty desperately. It was like the time I—

("Please stick to the facts of this case!" the chief judge demanded.)

Yeah, okay. So I let her in. Anitra O'Toole turned out to be young, kinda pretty in a cheerleader way, and very worried. Oh, and she was one of the three biologists among the DULL team on Europa.

And she was scared, too. She wouldn't say why, at first, or why she wanted to come aboard *Joker*. She just fidgeted and blathered about her husband waiting for her back on Earth and how she was afraid that her marriage was coming apart because they'd been separated so long and her career might be going down the tubes as well.

I only had a few hours to be on Europa, but while my brain-dead *Clementine* was ingesting ice I tried to be as hospitable as possible. I sat Anitra down in my quarters, just off the bridge, and programmed the galley to produce a gourmet dinner of roast squab, sweet potatoes, string beans—

("Mr. Gunn!" growled the Toad.)

All right, all right. I popped a bottle of champagne for her. *Joker* has the best wine cellar in space, bar none.

Now, don't get me wrong. I don't try to seduce married women, even when they tell me their marriage is in trouble. Especially then, as a matter of fact. Too complicated; too many chances for lawsuits or grievous bodily harm.

I was more interested in her saying that her career might be going down the tubes. One of three biologists on Europa, working on a newly discovered form of extraterrestrial life, and her career was in trouble?

"Why?" I asked her.

Anitra had these big violet eyes and the kind of golden blond hair that most women get out of a bottle. Sitting there beside me in a one-piece zipsuit, she looked young and unhappy and vulnerable, like a runaway waif. I stayed an arm's length away; it wasn't easy, but I kept thinking about the Twins as much as I could.

"The adaptation isn't working," Anitra said, miserable. "All this planning and genetic engineering and they still won't reproduce."

"What won't reproduce?" I asked.

She sipped at the champagne. I refilled her glass.

"Could you take me back to Earth?" she blurted.

I started to say no, which was the truth. But long, long ago I had learned that the truth doesn't always get the job done.

"I'm heading back to the belt. My company headquarters is in Ceres," I said. "I could arrange transportation from there."

She clutched at my wrist, nearly spilling my champagne. "Would you?"

"Why do you want to leave Europa so badly?"

Those violet eyes looked away from me. "My husband," she said vaguely.

"Won't DULL set you up with transportation? They have regular resupply flights, don't they? You could hook a ride back Earthside with them."

"No," she said, barely a whisper. "I've got to go now, while I've got the chance. And the nerve."

"But your work here on the lichenoids . . ."

"That's the whole point!" she burst. "It isn't working and everybody's going to find out and I'm going to be ruined professionally and nobody will want me, not even Brandon."

I figured Brandon was her husband.

("Is there a point to all this?" asked the chief judge, frowning.)

The point is this. Anitra O'Toole told me that the lichenoids DULL was studying are not native to Europa. They were engineered in a biology lab in Zurich and planted on Europa by the DULL team.

The courtroom erupted. As if a bomb had gone off. Half the spectators jumped to their feet, shouting. The Beryllium Blonde and her four cohorts were screaming objections. The chief judge was banging the stump of her gavel on the banc, demanding order.

But what caught my eye was the look on the splotchy face of the Toad. Weatherwax was staring at Sam as if he would have gladly strangled him, if he'd had the chance.

It took a while and a lot of whacking of the stump of her gavel, but once order was restored to the courtroom, the chief judge fixed Sam with a beady eye, and asked, "Are you maintaining, Mr. Gunn, that there never were indigenous life-forms on Europa?"

Sitting in the witness chair with his hands folded childlike on his lap, Sam replied courteously, "Yes, ma'am, that's exactly what I'm saying. The whole story was a subterfuge, engineered by the people who run DULL."

"This is outrageous!" Weatherwax roared. Everyone in the courtroom realized that he was *the* man who ran DULL.

The chief judge was a little more professional. She turned to the prosecution's lawyers, who were still standing and fuming.

"Cross-examination?"

The Beryllium Blonde stalked out from behind the table like a battle cruiser maneuvering into range for a lethal broadside.

She stood before Sam for a long, silent moment while the entire court held its breath. He stared up at her; maybe he was trying to look defiant. To me, he looked like a kid facing the school principal.

"Mr. Gunn," she started, utterly serious, no smile, her

eyes cold and calculating, "the allegation you have just made is extremely serious. What evidence do you have to support it?"

"The testimony of Dr. Anitra O'Toole, of Johns Hopkins University's biology department."

"And where is Dr. O'Toole? Why isn't she here at this trial?"

Sam took a breath. "As far as I know, she is still on Europa. They won't let her leave."

"Won't let her leave?" the Blonde registered disbelief raised to the $n$th power.

"She's being held prisoner, more or less," Sam said. "That's why Wankle put a security team on Europa: to see that the scientists don't talk and can't get away."

"Really, Mr. Gunn! And why isn't her husband demanding her return to Earth?"

"Because, as far as he knows, she's on Europa voluntarily, placing her career before their marriage. Besides, my sources tell me the guy's shacked up with a certain blond lawyer."

Her eyes went wide, and she smacked Sam right in the mouth. Hauled off and whacked him with the flat of her hand. The crack echoed off the courtroom's stone walls.

A couple of spectators cheered. The judges were so stunned none of them moved.

Sam ran a thumb across his jaw. I could see the white imprint of her fingers on his skin.

With a crooked grin, Sam went on, "He's here in Selene City. I could have him subpoenaed to appear here, if you like."

The Blonde visibly pulled herself together, regained her self-control by sheer force of will. She put on a contrite expression and looked up at the judges.

"I apologize for my behavior, Your Honors," she said, in a hushed little-girl voice. "It was inexcusable of me to allow the witness's slanderous statement to affect me so violently."

"Apology accepted," said the Toad. The chief judge's brows knit, but she said nothing.

So the Blonde got away with slugging Sam and even

made it look as if it was his own fault. Neat work, I thought.

She turned back to Sam. "Do you have any *evidence* of your allegation about the lichenoids, Mr. Gunn?"

"I have Dr. O'Toole's statement on video. I activated *Joker*'s internal camera system once I allowed her on board my ship."

"Video evidence can be edited, doctored, manufactured out of computer graphics—"

"Like the slides of the Europa lichenoids we saw earlier," Sam countered.

"You are defaming scientists whose reputations are beyond reproach!" the Blonde exclaimed.

"Nobody's reputation is beyond reproach," Sam said hotly. "You oughtta know that."

Turning to the judges, he went on without taking a breath, "Your Honors, none of these scientists were trying to hoodwink the public. They were drawn into a plot by the people who run Wankle Enterprises, a plot to stake out a monopoly on the resources of the whole Jupiter system!"

The chief judge answered sternly, "How can you make such an allegation, Mr. Gunn, without proof?" But I noticed she was eyeing the Toad as she spoke.

"Look, this is the way it worked," Sam said, ignoring her question. "DULL's operation on Europa is funded by Wankle Enterprises, right? Wankle's people went to DULL more than five years ago and suggested an experiment: they wanted DULL's scientists to engineer terrestrial lichen to survive in the conditions of Europa, living in the watery slush at the bottom of Europa's mantle of ice. The idea was to see how life-forms would behave under extraterrestrial conditions."

"Which is a valid scientific project," the Blonde said.

"Yeah, that's what they told the scientists. So the biologists engineer the critters and they send a team out to Europa to see if they can actually survive there."

The chief judge interrupted. "You are contending, Mr. Gunn, that there were no native life-forms on Europa?"

"No native life-forms on or in or anyway connected

with Europa. If they'd found native life-forms, they wouldn't have had to engineer this experiment, would they?''

"But DULL announced the discovery of native life-forms.''

"Right!" Sam exulted. "That's when our slimy friend here sprang his trap. They announced that the scientists had discovered native life-forms on Europa, instead of telling the media that the lichenoids had been engineered in a bio lab in Zurich.''

"That is utterly ridiculous,'' said the Blonde. I noticed that the Toad was slumping more than usual in his chair.

"The hell it is,'' Sam snapped. "The poor suckers on Europa were caught in a mousetrap. They were stuck on Europa, dependent on DULL and Wankle for transportation home. Dependent on them for air to breathe! They couldn't get to the media; they were surrounded by three dozen DULL public-relations flacks and a Wankle security team. Even if they could blow the whistle, it'd look as if they were in on the fraud from the beginning. One way or another their careers would be finished. DULL would never let them sweep the floor of a laboratory again, let alone practice scientific research.''

"Monstrous,'' muttered the chief judge. Whether she meant Sam's allegations were monstrous or DULL's actions, I couldn't figure out.

"Meanwhile, DULL's communications experts are putting the pressure on the scientists to go along with the deception. After all, once the lichenoids adapt to the conditions under the ice on Europa they'll really be extraterrestrial organisms, right? The scientists could announce their true origins in the scientific journals in a year or two or three. Who's going to notice, by then, except other scientists?''

The Blonde stamped her lovely foot for attention. "But why go through this subterfuge? It's all so pointless and ridiculous. Why would reputable scientists, why would the directors and governors of DULL, go through such an elaborate and foolish subterfuge? Mr. Gunn's wild theory falls apart on the question of motivation, Your Honors."

"Not so, oh temptress of the heavenly spheres," Sam replied. "Motivation is exactly where my theory is strongest."

He paused dramatically. Two of the judges leaned forward to hear his next words. Weatherwax looked as if he wanted to be someplace else. Anyplace else.

"Once DULL's public-relations program announced that native organisms had been found on Europa, what did the IAA do?" Before anyone could reply, Sam went on, "They roped off the whole Jupiter system—the whole damned system! Jupiter itself and all its moons, sealed off, embargoed. No commercial development allowed. Forbidden territory. No go there, *bwana*, IAA make big taboo."

"Mr. Gunn, please!" said the third judge.

"No commercial development allowed in the entire Jupiter system," Sam repeated. "Except for the company that was funding the Europa research station. They were allowed 'limited resource extraction' to repay for their funding the Europa team. Right?"

The chief judge murmured, "Right."

"Who was funding the Europa station? Wankle Enterprises. Who was allowed to develop 'limited resource extraction'—which means scooping Jupiter's clouds and mining its moons? Wankle Enterprises. Who has a monopoly on the thousands of trillions of dollars worth of resources in the Jupiter system? Wankle Enterprises. Surprise!"

"Limited resource extraction," snapped the Blonde, "means just that. Limited."

"Yeah, sure. What does 'limited' mean? How much? There's no definition. A billion dollars? A trillion? And what happens if the environmentalists or some other corporation or the Dalai Lama complains that Wankle's taking too much out of the Jupiter system? Wankle simply announces that the lichenoids on Europa weren't native life-forms after all. Ta-daaa! The scientists get a black eye, and Wankle has established operations running all over the Jupiter system. That gives them the edge on any competition, thanks to the monopoly the IAA mistakenly granted them.''

Weatherwax stirred himself. ''We've listened long enough to these paranoid ramblings,'' he rumbled. ''I haven't heard a single iota of evidence to support Mr. Gunn's ravings.''

''Call Dr. O'Toole back from Europa,'' Sam said. ''Or watch the video I made of her in my quarters aboard *Joker*. Call Professor Fossbinder in from Zurich. Call Brandon O'Toole, for Pete's sake; he's right here in Selene City. He knows that his wife was engineering lichen before she shipped out to Europa. He'll tell you all about it, if he isn't besotted by our Beryllium Blonde here.''

And he quickly raised his fists into a boxer's defensive posture.

The Blonde just stood there, her lovely mouth hanging open, her eyes wide and darting from Sam to the Toad and back again.

Weatherwax heaved an enormous sigh, then croaked, ''I move that we adjourn this hearing for half an hour while we discuss this new . . . allegation, in chambers.''

The chief judge nodded, tight-lipped. We all rose, and the judges swept out; the courtroom was so quiet I could hear their black robes rustling. The audience filed out, muttering, whispering, but Sam and I sat tensely at the defendants' table, he drumming his fingers on the tabletop incessantly, his head turned toward the prosecution's table and the Blonde. She was staring straight ahead, sitting rigid as an I-beam—a gorgeously curved I-beam. Her four cohorts sat flanking her, whispering among themselves.

After about ten minutes, a clerk came out and told us that we were wanted in the judges' chambers. I felt surprised, but Sam grinned as if he had expected it. The clerk went over and conferred briefly with the prosecution lawyers. They all got up and filed out of the courtroom, looking defeated. Even the Blonde seemed down, tired, lost. I felt an urge to go over and try to comfort her, but Sam grabbed me by the collar of my tunic and pointed me toward the slightly open door to the judges' chambers.

Weatherwax was sitting alone on an imitation-leather couch big enough for four; the other two judges were nowhere in sight. He had taken off his judicial robe, revealing a rumpled pale green business suit that made him look more amphibious than ever.

"What do you want, Gunn?" he growled as we sat on upholstered armchairs, facing him.

"I want my ships released and my business reopened," Sam said immediately.

Weatherwax slowly blinked his bulging eyes. "Once this case is dismissed, that will be automatic."

Dismissed? I was startled. Was it all over?

"And," Sam went on, "I want full disclosure about the lichenoids. I want the scientists cleared of any attempt to hoodwink the public."

Again the Toad blinked. "We can always blame the PR people; say they got the story slightly askew."

Sam gave a short, barking laugh. "Blame the media, right."

"Is that all?" Weatherwax asked, his brows rising.

Sam shrugged. "I'm not out to punish anybody. Live and let live has always been my motto."

"I see."

"Of course," Sam went on, grinning impishly, "once you admit publicly that the lichenoids on Europa are a genetic experiment and not native life-forms, then the embargo on commercial development in the Jupiter system ends. Right?"

This time Weatherwax kept his froggy eyes closed for several moments before he conceded, "Right."

Sam jumped to his feet. "Good! That oughtta do it."

The Toad remained seated. There was no attempt on the part of either of them to shake hands. Sam scuttled toward the door, and I got up and went after him.

But Sam stopped at the door and turned back to the Toad. "Oh, yeah, one other thing. Now that we've come to this agreement, there's no further need for you to keep the scientists bottled up on Europa. Let Dr. O'Toole come back here."

Weatherwax tried to glare at Sam, but it was pathetically weak.

"And tell your sexy lawyer underling to take her claws off O'Toole's husband," Sam added, with real iron in his voice. "Give those two kids a chance to patch up their marriage."

Without even waiting for a response from the Toad, he yanked the door open and stepped outside. With me right behind him.

By dinnertime that evening the media were running stories about how Wankle's chief public-relations consultant, Dr. Clyde Erskine of the University of Texas at Austin, had made a slight misinterpretation about the lichenoids on Europa. Sam whooped gleefully as we watched the report in our hotel suite.

He switched to the business news, which was also about the Europa "misinterpretation," but which included the fact that the IAA had decided to lift the embargo on commercial development of the Jupiter system.

Sam howled and yelped and danced across our dinner table.

"Weatherwax moved fast," I said, still sitting on the hard-backed chair while Sam did a soft-shoe around our dinner plates.

We had already been notified by the IAA that Sam's ore carriers were no longer embargoed, and Asteroidal Resources, Inc. was back in business.

Sam deftly jumped down to the floor and sat on the edge of the table, facing me.

"He's got the power to move fast, Orville. The Toad has a reputation for good-deed-doing, but he's really a power-clutching sonofabitch who's spent the past ninety years or so worming his way into the top levels of a dozen of the solar system's biggest corporations."

"And the IAA," I added.

"And he founded DULL to serve as a cloak for his plan to grab the whole Jupiter system for himself," Sam went on, a little more soberly. "This plot of his has been years in the making. Decades."

"And now it's unraveled, thanks to you."

Sam pretended to blush. "I am quietly proud," he said softly.

I leaned back in my chair. "To think that none of this would have happened if it hadn't been for the Porno Twins . . ."

Sam's face went quizzical. "Oh, it would have happened, one way or the other," he said, with a Puckish grin. "The Twins just provided the opportunity."

I gaped at him. "You mean you were after Weatherwax all along? From before . . ." His grin told me more than any words. "Then your testimony was a fabrication?"

"No, no, no," Sam insisted, jumping to his feet so he could loom over me. That's hard to do, at his height, so I stayed seated and let him loom. "The Twins' emergency was real, and the only way I could save them was to make that dash out to Jupiter, just like I testified."

"Really?"

He shrugged. "More or less."

"You had this all scoped out from the beginning, didn't you? You *knew* the whole business and . . ." I stopped talking, lost in stunned admiration for Sam's long-range planning. And guts.

He was making like a jack-o'-lantern again. "Why do you think Weatherwax got himself appointed a judge?"

"So he could make sure you were found guilty," I said.

"Yeah, maybe, if things worked out the way he wanted them to. But he also wanted to be on the judges' panel so that if things didn't work out his way, he could stop the trial and cut a deal with me."

"Which is what he did."

"You betcha!"

"But why didn't you take Dr. O'Toole back with you? You left her on Europa."

"Had to," Sam said. "Majerkurth showed up with his team and threatened to blow holes in *Joker* if I didn't let her go. I tried to drop an empty oxygen bottle on him, but it missed him and hit one of the PR flacks he had brought along with him.''

I laughed. "So that was the basis of the assault charge.''

"And the attempted murder, too. I would've offed Majerkurth if I'd thought it would've helped Anitra. As it was, I was outgunned. So I had to let her go—after promising her that I'd fix everything toot sweet.''

"Well, you did that, all right. I'll bet she's on her way home to her husband right now.''

"I hope so.''

I reached for my glass of celebratory champagne and took a sip. Then I remembered:

"The Twins! What happened to them?''

That was kinda sad—Sam told me.

I zoomed back to Vesta at three-plus gees with *Clementine* full of Europan ice that *Joker*'s electrolysis system was converting into oxygen for them and hydrogen for her own fusion torch.

(I noticed that Sam didn't slip in a sales pitch for *Joker*. He was feeling much better now.)

Once I got there, I could've patched their leaky air tank and booted up their recycling system and even fixed their stupid maintenance robot—all from the comfort of my bridge in *Joker*. But I wanted to see them! In the flesh! I was so doggone close to them that I fibbed a little and told them I had to come aboard to make the necessary repairs.

Mindy and Cindy stared at me from my display screen for a long time, not moving, not even blinking. All I could see of them was their beautiful identical faces with their cascading red hair and their bare suggestive shoulders. It was enough to start me perspiring.

"We never let *anyone* come aboard our ship, Mr. Gunn,'' said the one on the left. The one on the right shook her head, as if to reinforce her twin's statement.

"Call me Sam,'' I said. "And if I can't come aboard, I can't fix your life-support system.''

Well, we yakked back and forth for hours. They really

wanted to stick to their guns, but we all knew that the clock was ticking, and they were going to run out of air. Of course, I wouldn't have let them die. I would've done the repairs remotely, from *Joker*'s bridge, if I had to.

But I didn't let them know that.

"All right," Mindy said at long last. Maybe it was Cindy. Who could tell. "You can come aboard, Mr.—"

"Sam," breathed Cindy. I think.

"You can come aboard, but only if you agree to certain conditions."

The deal was, I could come aboard their ship, but I couldn't have any contact with them. They were going to lock themselves in their compartments, and I was forbidden even to tap at their doors.

I was disappointed, but hoped that they'd relent once I'd finished repairing their ship. They offered me virtual-reality sex, of course, but I was looking forward to the real thing. The only man in the solar system to make it with the Porno Twins in person! That was a goal worthy of Sam Gunn.

So even though I was bone-weary from being squashed by three-plus gees for several days, and still sore from the tubes that I had to insert into various parts of my anatomy, I was as eager and energetic as a teenager when I finally docked *Joker* to *SEX069*. Great stuff, testosterone.

I went straight to their bridge like a good little boy and got their maintenance robot working again. Just a little glitch in its programming; I fixed that and within minutes the dim-witted collection of junk was welding a patch onto the puncture hole in the air tank that the meteoroid had made. There really wasn't anything much wrong with the ship's air-recycling system, but I took my time starting it up again, thinking all the while about getting together with Cindy and Mindy for a bit of horizontal celebration.

Once I started pumping oxygen from *Clementine* into their air tanks, I began wondering how I could coax the Twins out of their boudoirs. I checked out their internal communications setup and—*voilà!*—there were the controls for the security cameras that looked into every compartment in the ship.

The first step toward getting them to come out and meet me, I thought, would be to peek into their chambers and see what they were up to.

Wrong! Bad mistake.

They were both in one little compartment, huddled together on the bed, clutching each other like a pair of frightened little kids. And they were *old!* Must've been in their second century, at least: white hair, pale skin that looked like parchment, skinny and bony and—well, old.

The teeth nearly fell out of my mouth, that's how far my jaw dropped. Yet, as I stared at them hugging each other like Hansel and Gretel lost in the forest, I began to see how beautiful they really were. Not sexy beautiful, not anymore, but the bone structure of their faces, the straight backs, the long legs. The irresistible Cindy and Mindy that we'd all seen on our comm screens were what they had really looked like a century ago.

I should have felt disappointed, but I just felt kind of sad. And yet, even that passed pretty quickly. Here were two former knockouts who were still really quite beautiful in an elderly way. I know a sculptress who would've made a wonderful statue portrait of the two of them.

They were living by themselves, doing their own thing in their own way, bringing joy and comfort to a lot of guys who might have gone berserk without them and their services. And now they were huddled together, terrified that I was gonna break in on them and find out who and what they really were.

So I swallowed hard and tapped the intercom key, and said, "I'm finished. Your ship is in fine shape now, although you ought to buy some nitrogen to mix with the oxygen I've left for you."

"Thank you, Sam," they said in unison. Now that I could see them, I heard the quaver in their voices.

"I'm leaving now. It's been a pleasure to be able to help you."

They were enormously grateful. Grateful not only that I had saved their lives, but that I hadn't intruded on their privacy. Grateful that they could keep up the fantasy of Mindy and Cindy, the sexy Porno Twins.

"Wow," I said, once Sam finished. "You were down-right noble, Sam."

"Yeah," he answered softly. "I was, wasn't I?"

"And that was the last you saw of the Twins?"

"Not exactly."

I felt my brows rise.

With a self-deprecating shrug, Sam admitted, "They were so super-duper grateful that they insisted on giving me a blank check: I can have a virtual-reality session with the two of 'em whenever I want to."

"So?"

Sam's grin went from ear to ear. "So I gave in and tried it. I've never been a fan of VR sex; I prefer the real thing."

"So?" I repeated.

His grin got even wider. "So I'm heading back to Ceres tomorrow. I mean, a blank check is just too good to ignore!"

And that's how Sam Gunn beat the rap on the charge of genocide and opened the Jupiter system for development. He went out to Ganymede and set up a new corporation to scoop helium-three from the clouds of Jupiter and sell it for fuel to fusion power plants all over the solar system.

Then he dumped every penny he had, and a lot he didn't legally have, into zipping out past Pluto to find Planet X. You know the rest: he found a mini–black hole out there and fell into it and found aliens and all that.

Now he's on his way back. You know, despite everything, it's going to be great to see him again. Life was pretty dull without Sam around! Productive, of course, and safe and comfortable. But dull.

Me, I never left Selene City. I'm still running Sam's old company, Asteroidal Resources, Inc., from our new corporate headquarters here on the Moon.

Of course, Sam wanted me to return to Ceres after the trial, but I happened to run into the Beryllium Blonde in Selene City, and she seemed so dejected and lonely—but that's another story.

**ABOARD TORCH SHIP *HERMES***

I REALIZE THAT THE INTERVIEWS I HAVE BEEN ABLE TO RECORD are somewhat fragmented and even contradictory, yet they represent the honest recollections of five people who were very close to Sam Gunn on five different occasions in his frenetic life. I attempted to interview a sixth person, Ms. Jennifer Marlowe, Esq., the lawyer that Sam Gunn refers to as the Beryllium Blonde. However, Ms. Marlowe declined to speak with me.

She is presently ensconced in the loftiest tower in Sydney, Australia, in the offices of Raippe, Pillage, and Burns, Attorneys at Law, where she is preparing to present her case against Sam Gunn to the Interplanetary Tribunal. Her contention that the statutes of limitations of the various suits filed against Sam Gunn should be extended by the same length of time that Mr. Gunn was allegedly in the space-time warp will, if successful, make a stunning precedent in interplanetary law.

How Sam Gunn will react to that precedent is anyone's guess. Based on his previous life history, however, it appears certain that Sam Gunn will not allow this challenge to go unanswered.